Enough Isn

K. L. Shandwick

To Jenette

love

K L Shandwick

EVERYTHING TRILOGY

Series Reading Order:

Enough Isn't Everything

Everything She Needs

Everything I Want

DEDICATION

Believe it or not, I talk…a lot, but I am not that great at expressing my gratitude to those who are important to me in words, but I hope my actions show this to them every day.

I would thank my husband, Peter for his patience and support in my crazy new venture. He has indulged me to take time out of my hectic life to keep going with my journey into creative writing. Thank you Pete, for picking up the slack at home, for your patience, allowing me to torture you by listening to the many 'sound bites' during the writing of this. I don't think you need many words to tell you how I feel about you. I think you know already.

I would also like to thank Russ Cleary for his support and encouragement to keep going with my ideas, for being a sounding board, and for allowing me to torture him with the raw content of the book before it was completed. It was his idea that I share Alfie and Lily's story with other readers.

Also, I would like to dedicate this to any one of the readers of this book, who wishes they had the confidence to put themselves out there, no matter what others think.

If you think that you can, you will, if you think that you can't… it will never happen. This book came to fruition on one of my 'I think I can days'.

It is never too late to be what you might have become. - George Eliot

Thank you to the readers of kindle for taking time to read my first attempt at story telling.

ACKNOWLEDGEMENTS

Russ Cleary Thank you for the great ebook Cover Design

Thank you to Kris Julie, Russ, Tracy, Vicky, Carole and Amy my Beta readers and for giving me their support by encouraging me to keep going.

CHAPTER 1

NEW LIFE

Nerves twisted my stomach in knots, and my mouth felt completely dry. A rush of adrenaline coursed through me while punching in the number I had rang hundreds of times before, but never with as much excitement as I felt right at that point. My body had let me down and began to perspire. The searing heat from the sun contributed to that too; it was damned hot in Miami.

I held my breath as I tried to control my racing heartbeat that was making my blood swish in my ear so that I could concentrate on listening to my call. I heard a click, and the unfamiliar tone that let me know I was connected to the cell number I had just dialed.

The ringing tone wasn't what I normally expected to hear, because everything was different across the pond. Even although we speak the same language, there are subtle differences. One of those differences was the connecting ringing tone, which sounds different in the United States than the one in the UK.

"Woo hoo! Lily,you're here!" Saffy and Holly were yelling and hollering down the line at me, I could hear the noisy roar of the traffic around them, and I deduced that they had the soft top down. I had finally landed in Miami, and my roommates were only three hours away from joining me. When they eventually arrived, I knew we'd finally be able to start the next chapter of our lives without the Atlantic between us.

"I can't wait for you to get here. It feels amazing to be at South Beach." Holly whooped a bit more, and Saffy called out, "Get some sleep you're going to need it. We're going out tonight." She started to say something else, but instead began shouting profanities to another car driver that almost drove into her. We concluded the call so that they could concentrate on getting to me in one piece.

I turned to face the Atlantic Ocean on the beachfront. I glanced up at the cloudless blue blanket of sky and couldn't help but notice how stark the contrast was to the dark gray, rainy sky I'd left behind in London yesterday. As I hit the end button on my cell, I hugged it to my chest, leaned my elbows on the barrier of the boardwalk, and stared straight ahead.

My eyes panned over the uninterrupted view of the ocean and soft, white sand. I became aware I was bouncing on my toes with nervous energy, so put my heels and soles down to still my restless legs.

Obviously, I wasn't acclimatized yet, and my t-shirt had started sticking to the hollow of my back.

Moist sweat erupted in beads down my back with the humid air around me.

Pulling the hem of my t-shirt free from my jeans, I began to waft it trying to catch some air underneath, but it did nothing to cool me down. Actually, I think it made me even hotter.

It was still early in the morning, but there was a swimmer out there in the ocean already. I pushed my oversized brown Gucci shades further up my nose, and scooped back my long, carefully straightened, dark brown hair, which had now kinked and stuck to the back of my neck. I twirled my hair up, and tucked it under my wide sun hat to help me keep cool.

Glancing over my glasses to test their effectiveness against the sun's rays, I almost blinded myself. The glare from the sun caught the ripples on the water, making me close my eyes and wince. The white light was still visible behind my eyelids when I closed them and I conceded my shades were pretty effective.

Turning, I tilted my head backwards holding my sun hat in place. I surveyed the building that was going to be my home. A wide smile played on my lips. I pushed the door open, and a waft of cool air hit me as I headed for the large cherry wood reception desk across from the entrance.

A middle aged, well-groomed, official looking man in a grey uniform looked up at me and smiled. "Hello, Miss Parnell. Good journey?" Tom, the doorman, greeted me, and I was flattered that he had remembered me from four months ago, when my friends and I came to view the apartment we were renting together.

He was very patient and took his time explaining everything I needed to learn to access the services the landlord offered. Smiling genuinely, I thanked him, as I headed for the elevator. The ride up to our apartment only increased the butterflies in my stomach, as the anticipation of finally beginning the next chapter of my life's journey got underway.

I drove in my little rental car from the airport through Miami, and my nerves were in tatters by the time I crawled off the highway as the satellite navigation brought me to my new home. I felt quite impressed with myself for having the guts to do the journey under my own steam, rather than grab a cab.

I had made myself a promise that from the moment I left home, I was not going to cut corners and revert to being the 'tourist' that I had been previously on visits here. This time was different. I was going to be living in Miami.

The planning to get to that day had been done with military precision. My parents freaked out when I chose my University. I had chosen Miami, because my friend Saffy studied there and maybe because the American music scene in Miami seemed a little more laid-back than that in London. Although, no less talented.

I wasn't interested in becoming famous or living the highlife. My parents had money, and I was wealthy in my own right, from a large inheritance left by my grandparents. I just wanted to learn my craft, and meet some like-minded people who had no pretenses or to feel pressured to do things with music, which conformed to whatever happened to be the trend at the time. Above all I wanted to learn about myself and become a more confident and self-assured person.

Eventually, I had managed to wear my parents down by making some decisions that they were even more scared about. I challenged their middle-class values by travelling to the Punjab to work in a children's orphanage for the summer.

My mother had been beside herself with stories of how basic the facilities were. As if that would be the most testing aspect of working with parentless children in a third world country.

Before I went to India my mother had arranged all kinds of immunisations with our physician and had him provide me with a medical kit that included needles, antibiotics, and an assortment of sterile bandages and dressings. She also had leaflets, tons of them, containing information on every disease she could think of. My mother didn't trust the internet to inform me about things.

Although I was there to study, I had also hoped to wipe out the memory of my one disastrous night with my BFF Elle's brother Sam; that happened after a stupid lapse in judgement on my part.

Feeling myself blushing, I remembered how awkward it had been. I blushed a lot actually, one of my many flaws. Poor Sam had always crushed on me, but never acted on it until the night of my leaving party. Alcohol was to blame; tequila shooters to be precise.

I don't particularly like alcohol, but everyone around me was in drunken-student- party-mode and were wearing 'Beer Goggles' by the end of the night. These usually made even the most attractively challenged people appear easier on the eye.

The shooters started out with the usual salt, tequila, and lime, but by the end of the night had advanced to a weird and sadistic variation. It went something like snorting the salt and squeezing the lime juice in their eyes or something. I had just come back from the bathroom, so wasn't exactly involved in that form of self-harm, thankfully.

Everything after that was a bit hazy. We danced a lot that night too. We all did this crazy group dance, jumping together like it was a really cool thing to do; when in reality, we must have looked pretty stupid.

In truth, we were probably just doing this because it seemed the most effective when we were drunk. It reduced any need to try to coordinate ourselves.

That evening worsened further when my best friend Elle, who was especially drunk and emotional, tried to give a speech. She looked dreadful with tears streaming down her face, her nose all red, and her face motled and blotchy. She dabbed the mascara around her eyes with a tissue, which really did nothing, as there were black lines all the way down to her chin, some of which had dried from an crying earlier in the evening.

As the club closed and my friends began to dwindle, there were more tears, hugs, and kisses between us. All of us promising to keep in touch with one another. Even as I was saying that, I knew I would be saying goodbye to most of them forever. Wringing at my cuff sleeve, I twisted it and I remember thinking it was a bit symbolic to me. It was like I was wringing out my heart to make way for the new people I'd meet, and who would eventually make their way into it.

I thought about how sad I'd felt about Jack, my closest friend, not being there that night. People found it strange that we were so tight together. Maybe because he was a man. He worked as a music reporter and was on assignment, covering a band at a gig launch in Paris, so he didn't make it back before I left.

Jack and I had seen each other through every chapter of our lives so far. We had been friends since we were four-year-old kids. He was the brother, and the boyfriend, I never had.

It was a weird relationship to the outsiders observing us. We knew everything about each other, and he was the only person in the world that I had no inhibitions with. He was like a second skin, and brought out my daring side and warped sense of humor.

Jack was such a liberating influence on me, and we pushed the boundaries of flirting. It was harmless fun to us, but our behavior confused the hell out of others as to what we were to each other. Jack always told people that think we have a weird relationship that they were just jealous because they could never have a relationship like we had.

By the time we arrived at Elle's place, there were eight of us left. These people had helped shape me, not that I was much… yet! I was hoping a few years in Florida would change me for the better. David never knew when to stop partying, and shouted, "Spin the Bottle," which made me groan loudly. The prospect of doing something daringly embarrassing filled me with dread.

Maddie was the first victim of the bottle and refused the dare, which was to pick a guy and demonstrate to us what was meant by 'dry humping'. She looked mortified. Her punishment was to drink a murky looking mixture of alcohols that Elle had 'found' in her kitchen cupboard.

No one even wondered how long it had been there. Maddie heaved and then wretched, but managed to keep it down, while we all cheered at her grimacing face. I rubbed her back even as I doubled over, giggling, when I saw the state she got into and knowing deep down she would have accepted the dare if her on-off boyfriend hadn't left already.

Sam was dared to pick a female to demonstrate a sensual massage on, but whilst the girl was fully clothed. He chose me. Feeling a hot tinge stain my cheeks, I still blush, when I think about how nervous both he and I were, at our public display, even though it didn't count, because he didn't actually touch my flesh in front of all those voyeurs.

At twenty-one, I was a deliberately slow starter in the carnal knowledge arena. Hell, I was a late starter period. Beginning college almost three years after my peers. I had only ever been to second base with a guy, having never found anyone attractive enough, for me to think of actually "doing it" with.

Eventually the game stopped, and I sat on the floor contented, albeit a little tipsy. Things were a little hazy, and my eyes drooped closed. A voice interrupted my thoughts and I heard a whispering, "I so want to do that to you for real."

Murmuring, "Hmm… huh?" I turned my head

slightly.

There was more ragged breathed in my ear while Sam said, "The massage, slow and sensual, my hands rubbing all over you."

Suddenly, my eyes snapped open. Okay, I was a little drunk, but a lot curious to know what that would feel like. "Yeah?" Sam's breathing became even more ragged, and he nodded eagerly at me. Pale blue eyes twinkled at me as they glazed with desire; at least that's what I think his eyes were doing.

Regarding Sam fondly, I knew I liked him, *Hell, he'd been my best friend's brother since he was born*…it had tickled my drunken mind that I'd thought that, and I had laughed out loud at the time.

He looked as if he had been mortally wounded when I laughed. Apologizing profusely, I told him that what I had been thinking had nothing to do with his proposition. He tilted the upper half of his body towards me and leaned in saying, "Lily, don't fuck with my feelings. What I just said took a lot of guts on my part." *Aww.*

Wanting to sooth him, I found myself cupping his face in my hands in drunken- affectionate reassurance.

"Hey, no… I'm flattered." *Damn, I was drunk.* Then I leaned in and sloppily kissed his nose in a sign of affection. Sam took this opportunity to grab my jaw, turned my face, and landed a soft, slow kiss on my lips. It was a gentle, tender kiss.

Pleading looks of desire flashed through his expressions as he stood and pulled me to my feet. Without talking he led me stumbling over the drunken bodies on the floor and out of the sitting room.

Sam took me into Elle's guest bedroom, where he was currently staying. Facing me, he closed the door quietly with his arms behind him and his palms flush with the door. Hearing the door click shut was like a starter pistol to Sam, and this was where his tenderness ended, the massage forgotten, and his drunken teenage testosterone surge took over.

Let's just say sex was *not* what I was lead to believe, and I was left thinking that there had to be more to it than that. I mean, if people kept on doing it repeatedly.

Smirking, thoughts reminding me of the private message he sent me on Facebook afterwards, telling me, "how great our first time was together," and that he hoped to repeat it again with me some day. Personally, my thoughts at the time were that Sam's experience with me would be his first, and his last. Those thoughts never changed on that particular episode.

Inhaling deeply, my thoughts turned to getting inside my apartment for the first time. Trembling fingers shook slightly as the key found the lock, and the pleasure I felt inside fizzed through me. When I heard the lock click, I swung the heavy wooden apartment door open. Eager, excited eyes scanned around the sitting room, taking in the sight.

The family room was huge and bright, with large stretched windows on one side, and a huge balcony patio window at the front. Oak hardwood floors gave a warm, rich appearance to the room in the sunlight. I walked in the direction of the balcony, passing the massive cream leather sofas and deep pile rug, which set the room off perfectly.

Black, wrought iron, clad around the span of the balcony, which was much bigger than I remembered and wrapped around the condo on two sides. Our apartment was situated on the corner, giving us a view to the west and south. Looking out on the balcony, I could see the quality extended out there as well, with an intimate patio breakfast table and two chairs.

Two distinct sections of seating were out there. A formal seating area, again with big cream rattan chairs, covered with deep plum cushions and a leisure area with a fantastic rounded daybed. Looking out at the undisturbed view of the ocean, and realized what a great location this was and how lucky I was to be here.

Although, I was fortunate to have lived and grown up in one of the most exclusive areas of London, everything here was a world away from what I was used to at home; in terms of having access to sea, sunshine, and sand. When I left yesterday the weather was cold, wet, and windy.

Here, I had bright sunshine on tap and just having that, made me feel much more optimistic about everything in general. I wandered through to my bedroom. The girls had already allocated the master suite to me because of my distance from home.

Kicking off my shoes the relief I felt in my feet was immence. I decided to use the time I had until my roommates arrived by having a leisurely shower and grabbing a nap. Feeling confident about the future, mainly because of my choice of roommates whom I already knew well.

Besides, I wouldn't have made the choice of college I had if I had to share a dorm with eighteen-year-olds fresh out of high school. Apart from my music, I came here to spend time with my friend, Saffy.

Saffy and I had been friends since we were spotty fourteen-year-olds. We met when my parents took me on vacation one summer to Colorado. My dad was a big hunting fan, and he rented a camper van during his getting-back-to-nature phase, my mother preferred to refer to it as his midlife crisis.

Saffy's dad was having the same midlife issues and had dragged his family to do the same. Her family was in the next pitch from us on the campsite for three weeks. Both families gelled immediately. Us girls both loved our guitars and wrote romantic love songs. Two of our songs, as far as we were both concerned, still stacked up with the best today.

Through the years, Saffy's love of science outweighed her love of music though. Her twin brother Max leaned toward being a penniless musician, so her parents more than encouraged her ideas of becoming a marine biologist instead of chasing rainbows with a guitar for a career.

At the end of our holiday that summer, we wept so hard when it was time to move on and vowed to keep in touch, and we did. During the last seven years there were times when our respective lives made our contact wane, but we still managed to rekindle our friendship and share the trials and tribulations during our teenage years.

Max realized his dream to be a musician, like I aspired to be, and now lives in Nashville, writing lyrics for a famous country artist, after leaving home as soon as he finished high school. I can still picture his handsome face in my mind's eye, but I hadn't seen him since I was seventeen.

CHAPTER 2

FIRST IMPRESSIONS

My amazing friends arrived in the early afternoon after their long road trip from Oklahoma, and they went straight to the coffee house near the condo. Partly because they were starving, but the deciding factor was that Holly desperately needed to pee and she just knew she wouldn't make it to the apartment.

My cell buzzed and vibrated on the nightstand. Answering, Saffy squealed excitedly for about thirty seconds, before telling me where they were and asking me to join them at the coffee shop.

Dressing quickly, I pulled on a cream maxi dress with a smattering of gold, and some cream flat shoes. Wrapping my long dark hair in my hands, I put it in a bun and tucked it under my large sun hat. Grabbing my keys, phone, purse, and shades, I headed out to meet them.

Holly waved at me excitedly from the window of

the coffee shop, before both she and Saffy ran along inside, waving at each window as they passed. They disappeared from my view for a second before bursting out of the door.

Excited screams pierced my ears, and the both of them hugged me in a group hug kind of way. "*Wow.* You look fabulous honey," Holly said in her slow Texas drawl.

We hugged tightly again. She looked great, and smelled of vanilla and peppermint chewing gum. Pushing me away from her and leaning back, but still holding my hands, as she took in my appearance. "Well look at you, pretty as a picture, and cute as a button, but we'll have to help you get a tan, honey, you're too pale." Giggling, she flashed her perfect white teeth at me.

Holly's pretty sun-bronzed face smiled sweetly, as her almond shaped brown eyes gave me the once over. Stunningly beautiful– a classic model shape – tall, leggy and lean, with natural platinum blond hair. No effort to look good was needed, she just did.

Saffy pushed Holly out of the way. "Hey, stop monopolizing Lily, she was my friend first." Saffy snickered at Holly, and Holly gave her a look of mock anger. Saffy always looked like a rock chick. She looked a bit like Avril Lavigne but with a bohemian, chic twist.

Petite and pretty, her hair was a sun kissed golden color; it cascaded thickly down to just above her waistline and she had stunningly vivid blue eyes. Her dad called her a 'pocket rocket' because she was small, but with a sassy nature and a fiery temper.

Wearing the cutest burnt orange dress, with

chiffon that hung on her curves and ended mid-thigh, few women could carry a look like that off. Gorgeous tanned legs with little ankle boots that were incongruent to the outfit, but on her, were perfect for finishing her ensemble. She'd accessorized perfectly with just the right jumbled assortment of beads and bangles.

Holly ordered some bagels and more coffee, and we all sat down to chat. Everyone began to chat at the same time. Trying several times to restart, we all began to talk together again. Once we settled down, though, and were chatting like old times. I felt ecstatic to be able to spend time with them, without worrying about how soon we'd be leaving as was often the case in the past.

Holly had been Saffy's friend since the age of five. Saffy's dad was an engineer, working at Holly's dad's oil company, but there was much more than an employer and employee connection. Their dads also spent time together outside of work, because they shared a common interest, a love of classic cars. The girls also spent a lot of time together growing up in their dad's garages with them.

Time flew, and we sat in the coffee shop until almost 3pm, making plans and talking about the past week. Saffy told us about the night before last very candidly, when she, "fucked a guy in the back of his truck," after spending an evening in a bar with friends.

Apparently, this really hot looking guy slipped his hand up her skirt when she stood at the bar, tugged the leg of her panties back and began fingering her. My mouth dropped open in shock and she threw her head back, her hair fanning through the air, as she laughed at my reaction.

Saffy was a free spirit usually and she was forward, but still, hearing her saying stuff like that, just like she'd just gone and picked up some milk or something, was too much. "*Saffy.*" I blinked hard at her, I couldn't believe my ears. The wicked grin on her angelic face was too much as she looked mischievously at me, and she shook her head giggling. She made me feel like my reaction was the one that was off.

"What?"

Blushing, I dropped my eye contact with her. She responded by giving me a loud belly laugh. "Oh. Sweet, innocent, Lily! You haven't lived until you've had some rough sex in the back of a truck. It was fucking hot. He was fucking hot, all horny and a really dirty boy!" She wiggled her brows at me wickedly.

Shifting uncomfortably in my seat, I looked around the coffee shop to see if anyone else was looking at us. Mortified by her behavior, I thought that only boys spoke about sex like that. Holly scolded Saffy for making me feel uncomfortable, as I tried to recover from what she had just said.

Saffy waved the back of her hand in my direction as if brushing me off and continued, "Talk about being uncomfortable, he fucked me so hard I could hardly walk yesterday." Holly and Saffy giggled again. Forcing a smile, I pretended to enjoy what she was saying, not wanting them to think I was a prude, but I had no real understanding of what she was talking about.

We made our way to the apartment, and I left the girls there. After I made a quick change to my attire again, I went to make myself look casual, in a jade green t-shirt that hung off one of my shoulders, with a black bra strap showing, and some three-quarter length white pants.

Jade was my favorite color and suited my dark hair, which I'd left long and curly, having given up on the straighteners for the day. Plus, the humidity was wreaking havoc with it. My hair was still kinking, even when I had put product on it.

Knowing I would just be wasting my time trying to straighten it at all, I'd resolved only to do it in the future for special occasions where I'm not outside. It wasn't that much of a problem really since my long dark brown curly hair didn't need much management when it was curly. They're nice curls, not the kind that were all over the place.

Friends always went on about how lucky I was, to have the choice of curly or straight hair, but I was not too enamored with the curls, as I thought they made me look younger and unsophisticated.

Even although I had only spent a short time in the sun this morning, my skin had a slight golden glow to it. Granted, it wasn't a tan by Holly's standards, but I could definitely see a difference in color. I was already feeling better; my eyes looked brighter, and I didn't feel as self-conscious about how pale I was.

Climbing into the little Chrysler PT Cruiser rental car, I headed out to the college. I knew I needed to organize a proper car, but for the next couple of weeks I just wanted to concentrate on getting settled in at college. Another bout of nerves hit me as I arrived at the college. Butterflies had taken up residence in my stomach and my palms were sweaty and this time I didn't think it was from the heat.

Following the signs to the registration office, I waited in line for my turn to speak to the gray haired woman with the soft, friendly tone. She was really helpful, and she seemed to take extra time to help me understand things.

Pointing out the 'meet and greet' sign, a place for new students to meet with existing ones, she suggested it would be a good idea for me to connect with people, prior to my courses starting.

Deciding to go with her suggestion, I began to make my way there, eager to network and cultivate new friends, especially with people who were like-minded and musically talented.

Nerves jangling with the anticipation of having to put myself out there with new people, I bravely forged on, determined to lose some of the shyness and immaturity that everyone else told me was holding me back.

There were no worries about my musical ability. I mean, I knew I wasn't exceptional, but I also knew that I could make people happy listening to me. I'd been playing guitar and piano since the age of six, and even I knew I had presence with that.

My dad once said I had the ability to capture the room in my hands when I played, but then again, he was my dad, and tended to be somewhat biased where I was concerned. My music tutors had no need to rave about me, even though they had for some reason.

Everyone also wanted me to sing. I knew my voice had an unusual tone and a wide range, but I didn't have the confidence to put it out there. There were no issues at all with people watching me play, but as far as singing was concerned, I thought I'd be less self-conscious if I were to model naked in a life art class, than I was singing with all of my clothes on.

Something about singing in front of people made me become incapacitated and tongue-tied when the focus was on me doing that. I knew it sounded crazy, but it seemed more intimate somehow. I had hoped that being in Miami might change that for me, and I'd be able to at least challenge myself to sing one day.

At that point, I needed to be very drunk to be okay with singing in public. No one knew me there, though, and I thought maybe I could reinvent myself. I've been told many times never to say never to anything. So the jury was still out on whether I could achieve singing in public or not in the future.

The campus was massive, and I got lost several times during my orientation, but I was able to collect some pre reading material as well as my study timetable. I turned and headed toward the sign pointing to the canteen, where the 'meet and greet' for the new students was taking place. On the way, I thumbed through the literature to check that everything was in order.

Choosing to study commercial music, gave me classes in music theory, ear training, music history, and also private instruction on my instrument. I'd added courses in; audio recording and production, and obviously, performance as a combination, focusing on voice and my guitar.

Writing lyrics and composing myself since I was thirteen, I hadn't wanted to take a formal lyrics writing classes, as I written over one hundred songs and felt my formulae was doing okay. I just didn't want anything to put that into a funk. Music was my first and only passion.

Proud of my song bank, twenty of these in particular, I was interested to hear what the expert critiques would say about some of them. Until that point, I'd never shared them with anyone apart from my cat, Saffy, and my parents. On the rare occasion I did sing in London, it tended to be in very dark places at the end of the night, and it had mainly been covers of other artists.

The managers of the clubs I sang at didn't want me experimenting with my own stuff, especially when I was being paid to entertain. They seemed to want popular tunes, from the sixties to date, to entertain their clientele.

Rounding the corner, I stayed on the path sign posted for the canteen. I stopped when I saw some musicians jamming on the lawn in a shaded area. Wandering around listening to some of them playing, there seemed to be a lot of talent on campus, but I was drawn to one sound in particular. Dulcet, low, velvety-rich tones from a male voice sitting some way back from the rest drew my attention, so I went looking for the guitar player with the great voice.

When my eyes caught up with the singer, I was captivated. Stunningly good looking, his appearance more than matched his amazing voice. Looking every bit the rock star sitting there, but with his strikingly unique draw he could easily have earned a living modelling as well.

I could only see a hint of his beautiful face. Head bent forward, he was looking down at the neck of his guitar. From where I stood, his face had perfectly symmetrical features, and his eyelashes were to die for.

Focusing on his mouth, it looked perfect, with luscious, plump, extremely kissable lips. He had a slightly chiseled look to his face, which complemented his amazing sultry look. The faintest stubble on his strong perfect jawline was just scruffy enough to be sexy without looking to make him look disheveled.

Frowning down at his notebook, he strummed quietly to himself, deep in contemplation of what he was trying to achieve. Transfixed, it was impossible for me not to stare at him.

Golden skin that looked amazing, flawless. His sandy blond hair, with little sun kissed flecks of lighter blond near the edges looked so clean, soft, and shiny.

If that wasn't enough, he had a little strand of hair in the front that kept falling forward. It was as if God gave it to him, for the purpose of attracting someone to sweep it back into place. I checked myself when I imagined how it would feel to run my fingers through it, or pull it into the palm of my hand at the nape of his neck.

Unsure of the effect he was having on me and whether it was his tone, or how, like the taste of melted chocolate his voice was when he sang, or how incredibly sensual he looked, that gave me goose bumps. Hairs on the back of my neck stood on end as the skin on my scalp retracted making my scalp tingle as the full effect of this man and his voice hit me.

Suddenly, I found myself trying to imagine how he would look naked. The mental image in my mind's eye was sensational, and an involuntary smile crept over my face, but I also felt my cheeks burn as I blushed and felt perverted to be thinking such a thing.

Oblivious to me; he was absorbed in his work, composing his music, and trying to lay the melody over this. His head was still bent forward, eyes closed, strumming away on his guitar with his strong, smooth, veiny hands and long fingers.

His guitar looked like an extension of him, just like my mine does with me, so I figured he'd been playing it since he was little as well.

Sitting down on the grass, I leaned back on my oversized bag, and continued to watch him intently. I had never spent this much time just staring at a man before, but he was irresistible to look at, so I allowed my eyes to soak up every delicious inch of him.

Still struggling with some lyrics, he played the melody over and over, trying to make it fit with the words of his song. Listening patiently, I observed him with interest as he tried to find the right line. It really wasn't a chore doing that I could have happily sat watching him all day long.

Lyrically, the song content was about making love, but the lyrics weren't crude, they were clever words, but the inferences were there all the same. Or maybe it was just my mind that was interpreting his words that way, since my knowledge had been broadened with my new sexual experience with Sam.

Inspiration struck and I had an idea for the

perfect line for his song. I didn't want to interrupt his artistic flow, but I felt compelled that the line needed to be in his song.

Stopping he banged the side of his guitar hard, his jaw flexed tensely, and then he lifted his head and stared straight at me. Our eyes connected briefly and a shocking pang of desire surged through me when his sparkling hazel eyes met mine. Feeling like I'd been hit by a lightning bolt; my heart raced, and I felt as if he could see deep into my soul.

Even more attractive when he looked like he was going to burst with frustration as each line he tried, didn't quite gel with the song, and he looked seriously agitated about that.

Thinking he was going to speak to me, I drew in a deep breath, but he shook his head and broke our gaze. Looking back down at his journal, he scratched out the words he had written.

CHAPTER 3

SEXUAL TENSION

Anger only made him more attractive. He looked so damned sexy and hypnotic to watch. I couldn't tear my eyes away from him. In fact, at that point, I would have rather had my eyes gouged out with a screwdriver than look anywhere else voluntarily.

Clearing my throat, for no other reason than the sight of him had given me a lump in my there, made him look up again. He seemed to stare directly into my eyes. I felt my cheeks flush as I saw the full effect of just how seriously hot he was.

My reaction to him was like nothing I'd ever experienced, and he hadn't even spoken to me. He oozed sex appeal in a rock star kind of way. I'd seen guys like him before, full of charm and seriously hot, and could only imagine his lap getting plenty of bottoms volunteering to sit on it.

Handsome in the extreme, the guy in front of me was the kind of man that women lost all self-control over. Previously, I would have given a guy like him a wide berth, but in this case, I could definitely re-evaluate my boundaries.

Dropping backwards, he lay flat on his back on the grass. He stretched out, splaying his hands high above his head on the grass, and I fought the urge to get up from where I was sitting to cover his body with mine.

He still didn't engage with me, and I began to feel uncomfortable sitting there watching him, especially when he'd stopped playing.

I was almost tempted to move away, but the sight of him lying there in his faded jeans that were hugging the contours of his muscular legs made it impossible for me to drag myself away. So I sat in silence instead, taking in the sight of him.

He was wearing a black Fender t-shirt which clung to his chest. It had risen up as he stretched out, exposing his abdomen. It showed just enough flesh for me to see the bottom contours of his abs and a lean muscular body.

There was also a hard ridge of V shaped muscles disappearing into the hips of his low-rise waistband. As his arms rose up, he laced his fingers and flexed his palms outwards. His movement flexed his hips upward as well. I could almost feel what he felt in his bones.

That stretch was one I did regularly, when I've played a long set and my fingers were cramped after working over the neck of my guitar.

Movement of his hips flexing caught my eye and drew my attention down his front to his groin. The tiny upward thrust he made was so sexy, and I felt a moist spot between my legs. My eyes flicked up as he brought his arms forward and down the front of his body, and I followed them again until I realized I was now staring at the bulge in his pants where they had landed. This was my second glance there, and I couldn't miss the bulge at the fly of his jeans.

Staring, I wondered if his cock was comfortable in the ridiculously tight jeans. I was curious then, how the hell he'd tucked his package in there in the first place. Blushed like crazy again when I realized what I was thinking and hoped he had no idea what was making my cheeks stain red.

He rose up onto his elbow on one side, and he seemed to have caught me watching him. *Fuck!* I smiled and realized that this could be mistaken for me smiling at what I'd been looking at. The situation was getting worse by the minute.

I looked up and shuddered at my thought processes about him, and his eyes met mine. He was looking at me as if he'd only just registered my presence, and it was as if he was checking me out.

His eyes raked up slowly from my feet to my face. When he was done, he raised an eyebrow at me, and gave me a lopsided grin. I thought then he knew what I'd been thinking, and I felt myself flush again.

"Hey," he cooed, his voice was like soft velvet, chocolate, and fluffy clouds all rolling off of his tongue. A low, mellow tone, tinted with a little humour and it definitely turned me on.

Gorgeous lips curved slowly to reveal a wide, lazy, sensual smile and his amazing hazel eyes, which were currently more green in color than brown and sparkling mischievously at me.

I knew I was damned when I saw a faint little dimple in his left cheek. "Alfie!" he said, and swept his index finger up and down the length of him.

"Are you majoring in music?" I nodded and blushed again.

"Lily," I replied and boldly pointed my finger at myself, but I didn't feel it had the same effect on him as he had on me with that.

Eyes squinting against the sun, Alfie looked at me and grinned. He kissed his fingers and threw them out there like he approved of me. "Well, hi, Lily, what a beautiful lady, would you like to come over and sit by me?" He threw his hand out and moved it in front of him.

I knew I should've said no and made an excuse to move on, but instead, I smiled bashfully and moved closer, doing what he asked me.

"That sounded interesting, how's it coming along?" I said as I plopped myself down opposite him. He gestured for me to move alongside him, so I did.

My skin tingled and my breathing became rapid and shallow as I struggled to keep calm. I was aware that the pulse in my neck was throbbing faster than ever. Moving myself around, I leaned back against a tree.

His arm brushed mine unintentionally as he moved closer, and I felt my skin react with a rash of goose bumps. He looked at his arm where it touched mine, then back to my face. "You're not from these parts?" he asked, turning to face me.

"No, London," I replied.

Smiling, he groaned softly, placing his hand over

his chest and stroked it down to his belly. "Oh, your accent turns me on. You are going to have to be careful around me, Lily," he teased, winking unashamedly at me.

My mouth dropped open, and I blushed scarlet again. I wished he hadn't said that because I knew how much he was affecting me already. "Are all the men this forward here?"

He grinned deviously at me, his one dimple showing. "Only when hot little chicks speak in an English accent to us." I giggled and found myself flirting back.

"Well, you know, the hot American male voice has its moments for us too." I blushed again, belying my confidence.

"Good to know." He grinned, wiggling his brows at me. "You want to cut to the chase and go fuck me then?" His words shocked me, I was stunned, freaking out inside by his boldness, but I giggled and pretended it didn't shock me. He was too forward and too easy to flirt with.

Desperate to change the subject; as I was feeling pretty uncomfortable, and knew I was out of my depth. "Okay, enough of the chitchat, back to business." I pointed at his notebook and tried to divert his attention. Alfie grinned again.

"Kinky business?" he teased and dug his elbow gently into my ribs. I rolled my eyes and laughed, but blushed again.

I knew instantly, Alfie could cause me a *lot* of trouble. He was so charming and sexy. I resisted the impulse I had to lean in and kiss him. "Are you open to suggestions?" I said, trying hard to take his mind anywhere but on me.

"Always, are you?" he asked playfully, his twinkling eyes holding my gaze, as he grinned wickedly at me again in a challenge.

"I'm thinking about your song." I pretended to be curt with him. "I have a line that I think could be a good fit with what you are singing about." There was hesitancy in my voice as I said it.

"Oh? Great. Well, give it up, then we can go somewhere quiet, and I can have some great sex with your perfect little body."

Fighting my embarrassment, I was determined to hold his gaze as he continued, "I have a good few fantasies already forming. I might need to act those out with you!"

Blushing yet again, I struggled to appear nonchalant.

"What makes you think I'd sleep with you?" I asked him playfully.

"Sweetheart, you definitely wouldn't sleep with me!" he stated. "Exhausted yes, sleep… nope, I'd keep you awake fucking you senseless." He smirked and winked at me.

My heart stopped and stuttered, before it kicked back in, much faster than it was beating before. I was taken aback by his statement. It made me feel like jumping his bones to see if his actions were as true as his words made him sound. For all his corny lines, I had never been as turned on as I was in that moment.

"Music is the sound of feelings, and she listened to what he felt." He looked confused. I thought his mind had shifted as he looked kind of distracted at me.

"Huh?" he murmured, staring into space. He shook his head to look at me again.

"The song," I stated, smiling.

Alfie continued to stare blankly at me. "The song?"

Refocusing, I felt as if I was being stripped bare by his eyes, and I was suddenly self-conscious of the attention he was giving me. I covered my body awkwardly with my arm.

"It's my suggestion for your song lyric. Music is the sound of feelings, and she listened to what he felt," I repeated.

Alfie broke his gaze from me and looked around him. "Well, shit! Where did that come from?" He looked surprised.

"Anon," I replied.

"A music quotation?" He seemed to be singing it to himself in his head and then his face broke into a wide grin. "Smart *and* sexy, *very* nice!" he flirted.

"Well the first part, 'music is the sound of feelings,' I added the rest, but yup, a quotation." I nodded and made a mock curtsey with my pants.

"How did you come up with that?" He looked at me with surprise and seemed impressed. I smiled slowly and bit my bottom lip.

What he didn't know was that I had a tattoo that circled my upper thigh, in small script writing, that said just that. What I said aloud was, "Well, maybe if you're persistent with your flirting you'll find out one day."

Alfie clapped his hands together in front of him. "Good enough for me." He laughed, then rubbed them together. "Now you have me intrigued." He scratched the slight stubble on his chin.

His eyes raked sensually over me again, and he drew in a sharp breath. "Okay, Lily, now about that sex you promised me…" He poked me in my belly and pulled me up onto my feet.

Before I knew it, he'd picked up both of our guitar cases, grabbed me by my wrist and dragged me down a grassy hill behind the campus buildings to some long grass. "Don't worry I'm not going to seduce you or anything crazy… yet." He cocked his head and smiled, making me shiver.

Shouted breathlessly for him to stop or at least slow down, my voice sounded shaky, and my feet were hitting the uneven ground hard. He pulled me along faster than my legs wanted to go.

"So what are you doing then?"

He shrugged, twisted his lips at me, and said, "I just wanted somewhere I could have you to myself to talk. I don't want to be interrupted."

When we stopped, he flopped down on the ground, flat on his back again, but this time bent his knees so that they were raised in the air with his black cowboy boots flat on the ground.

Labored breathing caused his chest to rise and fall rapidly from the exertion of running. I was excited at his impulsiveness, but kind of disappointed he had made no move on me. He just gave me this adorable lop- sided smiled, and panted breathlessly up at me from his position on the grass.

Playfully, I teased him, and raised my brow. "No long grass lovemaking then?" Instantly, he lifted his hand to block the sun from his eyes and looked at me.

Pursing his lips in thought, he nodded. "Some

men do that I've heard, but I won't make love to you Lily. I *will* thoroughly fuck you though. With your permission, of course, and maybe we'll get a little kinky." He wiggled his brows at me and gave me that panty-melting smile again.

"I don't do that slow, tender shit, Lily. It's overrated. Besides, I have other charms that will make sure you are well taken care of and sexually satisfied. By the way, has anyone ever told you how fucking gorgeous you are? I'm fighting a losing battle here, but I'll try hard to keep my hands to myself...for now." He smirked.

Never known anyone to speak to me that way before, I fought hard not to allow any outward reaction from me that would let him see the effect he was able to have on me.

Ignoring the last comment, I preferred to continue to flirt with him. "Damn, Alfie, you really know how to make a girl feel special don't you?" Giggling at him light-heartedly, I hoped I sounded convincing.

Alfie stopped smiling and gave me an intense stare, before he sucked in a deep breath again, then said animatedly, "You want to feel special? Then I guess I'm not your man... but, if you want to have special feelings, then I can most certainly do this for you. 'Friends with benefits,' if you will."

I was mortified at his suggestion and fought to hide my true feelings again. Keeping my face controlled and my breathing calm as my out- of- control heart thumped faster wasn't easy.

Unsure if that was because the idea excited me or horrified me. Locked eyes into a stare with his with his, I asked directly, "Are you interviewing me for the position of 'Fuck buddy'?"

Alfie's face broke into the most heartbreakingly handsome smile. "Ah, you are so smart, I love it. Intelligence, as well as beauty, the only thing left now is for me to be inside you to determine whether I've hit the fucking jackpot." Grinning, he raised his eyebrow at me.

My jaw wanted to drop, but I didn't let it out of principle. My first thought was that I should turn and run right back up the hill and never look back. I couldn't though. I wasn't ready to walk away. I was too intrigued by him.

The silence between us was deafening. He sighed, stood up, and stroked my hair. "I'm twenty-four years old Lily, music is the only love I have room for.

"I don't do romance, and I'm not a hearts-and-flowers kind of guy. I'm a highly sexed young man, and I do just fine for offers." He shrugged. "I'm not saying this because I'm an arrogant bastard, and I don't usually proposition women; they come on to me."

Alfie sighed again, and shrugged more slowly. "It's just how it is." I didn't doubt what he had said for a minute.

"Well, I have to admire your honesty, it is refreshing." I heard myself tell him, and tried to hide the shock from my face. *WTF, Lily?*

Swallowing audibly he said in a low, husky voice, "I just feel a connection between us." He motioned his finger between us. "An acute sexual tension if you will. It could make for some pretty amazing sex between us. I think we have great chemistry. I felt it even before I looked at you."

Wanting to call bull shit on that. "Wow, I've heard some chat up lines in my time Alfie. You know just how to seduce a woman, huh?" Smiling grimly at him, I sounded sarcastic, and hoped to goodness he hadn't seen just how naïve I was.

CHAPTER 4

FIFTY FIFTY

Alfie gave me a lopsided half smile again, flashing his dimple at me; too cute really, and leaned in toward me. He hooked his finger on the V of my t-shirt and tugged me closer to him.

My mouth went dry, and my gaze fell on his lips. He looked so sexually charged. He smelled slightly musky, masculine but clean, with a faint hint of the scent of a body wash I couldn't place.

When I made eye contact, his hazel eyes were flecked green and sparkled as he gazed intensely back at me. His head dipped as his face drew near to mine. His lips stopped only inches from my face. His other hand held my throat loosely, before he ran this up toward my jawline, and around to the nape of my neck, *wow!*

His touch sent a charge of electricity along the line his hand travelled. The electrical current trailed his touch and made my core drip juices onto my thigh. His other hand slid up to cup my chin.

I noticed his eyes drop to my lips, and he dragged his thumb lightly across them. He licked his lips and closed the space between us, pressing his lips lightly on to mine.

The kiss was feather-light, but the act was like a defibrillator jolting high-voltage electricity into my body at the same time. The pleasure I felt was so arousing, like no other kiss had ever affected me before.

That moist, hot tongue of his teased and traced my lips, then it parted them as it breached into my mouth. The hot, wet taste of him made me moan softly. He chuckled softly into my mouth, and it was as sexy as hell.

It was only a kiss yet, I was so slick between my thighs, my folds swollen and aching. The only places he touched me were above my shoulders. He was kissing me slowly, and I'd never felt anything like it before.

His hand moved up from my neck and sifted through my long hair. His palm wound around it as he gently tugged it back then applied pressure to the back of my head, deepening the kiss. He growled, and it made the whole act so erotic.

There was so much chemistry running through my body. I moaned loudly, and almost went over the edge with the sensation of his mouth on mine. Suddenly he growled again and dragged his lips away from me. "Holy, shit! I love the noises you make when I kiss you," he breathed.

I was almost senseless, my body felt bereaved at the loss of his touch, and I realized that this was the first time in my life I've really been kissed. I stood panting, breathless. Nothing else before that kiss ever compared to what I had just experienced with him.

Dragging his lips away from my mouth and down my neck, his head rose to hold my gaze. He nodded at me breathlessly, his eyes were wide. "Uh huh!" he said gruffly, clearing his throat and touching his lips with his calloused fingertips.

He looked dazed. After a few seconds his voice was still low and husky and he muttered, "Fuck!" His eyes widened further, and a smile slowly stretched over his face. "Damn it. I've never felt like that before." He shook his head, and smirked.

"Way more than I even suspected. You felt it too, right?" He wagged his finger between us. "This kind of connection doesn't happen every day. I just knew it. Oh, well shit, I'm even more than intrigued by you now," he said grinning again.

I lowered my head again because I was sure he would see the lust in my eyes. "Well Alfie, casual sex isn't something I'm comfortable doing, but I'll give it some thought."

He dipped his knees and bent his head to get eye contact again. When he locked his gaze on mine he smirked wickedly. "Uh huh…you too? Huh?"

"Damn I have the biggest boner now, look." He thrust his groin forward and pointed at the straining bulge in his jeans and was still smirking. "How can you say no to me now?"

I blushed, shocked at his reaction, but worse still, I was really turned on by him. The look on his face was…downright dirty. My panties were drenched. I couldn't believe his blatant approach toward me. I tried to avoid too much eye contact with him for fear he'd see what I was thinking. *Calm down Lily!* I smiled slowly, trying to appear unaffected. "Well Alfie, it's not something I'm accustomed to doing, but like I said, I'll certainly give it some thought."

I tried to say it as if I could take it or leave it, and this kind of thing happened every day, but when I said it, I sounded breathless and my voice gave away some of my emotions. When I thought I'd pulled it off, my body let me down again, and I started to blush.

His wide smile flashed his dimple again, and he thrust his palm out to me. "Give me your cell." I reached into my purse and handed it to him. I watched as he punched his number in.

He labelled his contact name as 'SEXPERT'. His cell started ringing, and I realized he'd rung his phone from mine. "Okay, now I have yours too." He winked and handed my cell back to me, and I laughed at his corny moniker when he gave it back to me.

"Want to think about it?" He looked hopefully at me. I took his cell and labelled my contact name as 'Pink Lady' and boldly handed it back to him. He read it and scrunched his brows at me looking puzzled. 'Pink Lady?'

I smirked, feeling really bold that I had the nerve to do such a thing. "Well, if you're touting for a 'fuck buddy', then she should have a name that implies it." Alfie's eyes widened immediately at my reference to the slang reference of the sensitive flesh inside the entrance of a woman's vagina as 'pink.'

"Well, my beautiful Lily, if my proposal is something you want to pursue with me, I just want to say one more thing. There are no guarantees in this life. I can't say you won't get hurt. Primal sex is a need in all of us. I can't offer commitment, but I will respect you as a person and give you honesty and consideration."

He went on, "If you decide to have other partners I will respect your right to form emotional bonds. I don't want to own you honey; you would be free to break the arrangement at any time, as would I."

My immediate retort to the arrogance of him, implying that I would fall for him was to say, "And likewise, I wouldn't be able to guarantee that you wouldn't get hurt either." A fleeting look of consideration passed through his eyes and was gone in an instant.

"No worries here," he said deadpan.

I dipped down to the grass and picked up my guitar case, slinging it over my shoulder and tugged at the strap. "Lily?"

I wondered if he was being arrogant and expected me to agree immediately, but I looked at him as if I didn't have a care in the world, and kept my voice as even as possible. "I need to head out now, Alfie, I have plans for tonight, but I'll consider your interesting offer and get back to you."

He sat back down on the grass, and laid back, casual, one leg bent at the knee, facing me, perched up on one elbow. "Take your time, I know I can be full on, but I believe in shooting from the hip. I'm straight and uncomplicated."

I walked away trying not to look back, even though I wanted to more than anything. I was excited by his attention, but I didn't really believe that I could consider the prospect of doing something that reckless. I heard him chuckle to himself, so I turned my head and called over my shoulder, "I'm not fazed by your offer, Alfie."

I had a raw sexual need that I wanted to explore. I held up my open hand, giving a small wave to him behind me. Even though he didn't say it very loudly, Alfie commented in a normal speaking voice. "I hope you get the guts to call me Lily; we'd be fucking great together."

It was a daunting thought. *Was I mature enough to do something like that?* I was already sure that I definitely wanted something with this guy, even at the risk of being burned by him. The thought frightened the crap out of me. I needed to talk to Saffy and Holly about his proposition. I wondered if they would laugh or be shocked by it.

I didn't feel it was something that I wanted to keep secret from them. But I knew that if it was something that I was going to do, I definitely didn't want them to know exactly who the guy was.

What Alfie wanted from me was on equal terms – a no strings, no emotions, physical connection for sexual gratification. It seemed really sordid and belied all of my beliefs, but in terms of where my life was at, I felt it might just keep things in order for me.

I could explore my sexuality without any emotional involvement. I'd be free to concentrate on music, picking and choosing when to spend time with him when it suited us both.

I headed up to the apartment still contemplating my strange induction to campus and Alfie's proposition. I struggled to contain the feelings of excitement and shame that I'd actually consider doing what he suggested. Alfie aroused me in ways I'd never experienced before with just a kiss.

When I got home I was ravenous, realizing I'd missed lunch, spending my time with Alfie instead. I'd forgotten to eat, hell, I'd forgotten to breathe at some points. What he was able to do to me with one kiss was mind blowing. I found myself weighing things out.

I was in a new place where No one knew me, so there was no reputation to tarnish yet. It would be ridiculous not to find out what else he had to offer and equally ridiculous that I was talking myself into his insane proposition. But the more I thought about it, the more enticing it became.

Saffy was sitting on the balcony, her legs drawn up at the knees, nursing a strong black coffee in her hands, when I entered the apartment. "Hey, Saffy!" I went over and hugged her.

She put her hand up, stopping me and whispered, "Shush, I'm delicate this afternoon. I'm never doing shots again!" She groaned.

Her voice was croaky. She told me that she and Holly had gone to a bar and gotten into a shooters competition with a couple of tourists there.

Saffy had slept off the liquor, but had only woken up about fifteen minutes ago with a blinding headache. She commented that Holly had been sick, and was passed out on her bed too. I shook my head and smiled, thinking they were taking their vows to party during their newfound freedom seriously.

I hugged her again and walked over to the fridge. I reached in and began rummaging around for something to eat. "Have you eaten yet?" I asked, peering inside the fridge.

"Goodness, no thanks! I couldn't... I'd barf," she said quietly.

I turned to look at her, trying not to laugh, but fought a smirk that threatened my lips. "It's a pity you're hung over, because I wanted your take on something, but if you're feeling unwell it may cloud your judgement on this one," I said.

She bunched her brows. "What is it?" she called indignantly to me as I walked into my bedroom to change my top. I laughed as I quickly pulled on a white tank top, before walking back through the condo to her, knowing that I had piqued her interest.

"Nope, this one needs a clear head, and you are not in that place this afternoon yet." I made her a ham sandwich and placed it in front of her. She groaned hard when she looked at it, puffing her cheeks out, while a hand slid across her stomach.

It took until dinnertime for both Saffy and Holly to be back in the land of the living. Holly recovered better than Saffy, to be fair, and she said it was due to the fact that Saffy drank way more than her when she showed off, drinking two to her one for the last three shots.

We went to dinner, and I broached the subject of Alfie, to see their reactions and seek their advice. "Okay, girls, I was propositioned today." I giggled and couldn't believe I was actually saying it, "I am... considering it."

I told them about Alfie, although not by name, and they were both animated, questioning me about him. "First off, for safety, is the guy really a student?"

Holly asked. I hadn't thought about that, but decided that he couldn't be anything else after sitting song writing on the grass. He just fitted in perfectly.

Saffy was *more* basic in her line of questioning. "What does he look like? I mean is he all that great looking, that he thinks he can proposition someone like you? I mean fuck, Lily, your looks are shit hot, and you can probably have any man you want anyway."

I tried to find the words to sum him up, but instead decided a gesture was more appropriate. I put my hands over my heart and pump them in and out. "He's breathtaking… sexy!" I said, giggling, still struggling for words to do him justice.

"Kind of young rock god… talented, slim waist, broad shoulders, muscular, ripped, inked, and packing 'hidden talents' I think." I smirked and blushed at my own crude joke.

"OMG, Sex on a stick you mean?" Saffy helped me.

"That's it exactly," I said, pointing at her, nodding, and stuffing a large piece of chocolate cake in my mouth. I licked my lips and caught some of the chocolate that had escaped. My eyes widened when she stared at me, and we both burst out laughing.

"Well." Saffy sniffed, examining her nails before giving me the wisdom of her opinion. "Men have fuck buddies all the time, well actually so do women, or they wouldn't have anyone to fuck!" She giggled.

Holly agreed, "As long as you want to and you don't go getting hurt…" I was surprised by their reactions, but both confessed to having one-night stands just for the sex. It seemed like I had been left behind with all of this stuff. I knew little to nothing about sex and relationships.

They thought it was probably better to have a fuck buddy than just random guys for fun. Saffy said, "If he turns you on, and he's into you, and you're okay with each other not being exclusive, then why not?"

"I don't see a problem with that, providing you both practice safe sex, and make sure that you're both mature about it." Holly looks excited. "So are you going to call him?"

Maybe it was the courage of the mojito I'd just had or the fact that I was way past curious about sex and wanted to know more. Or maybe it was what I thought he could do for me that made up my mind. "You know what Holly? I think I'm curious enough to explore it."

"Promise me one thing though if I do this?" I said. They both look at me expectantly. "The pact is that we *never* discuss him with anyone. No matter what… got it?"

"*Agreed,*" they said in unison. We knocked our glasses together to seal the deal.

Saffy said, "Do it now, before you talk yourself out of it, Lily." I scrolled in my contacts list and found 'SEXPERT' and pressed the call button. He answered within one ring.

"Hey," he cooed, and my breath hitched at the sound of his voice. "Pink Lady, do you realize how happy you've just made me?" I was silent, his voice was so seductive. I almost forgot to speak. "May I take it this as a yes? Are you free later?"

My heart began to race, but I played it cool. "I

told you I have plans tonight, and I'm still out. I want to discuss some stuff with you though. I haven't decided on my answer, I'll call you when I'm alone," I told him.

"Hurry up. Go home, you're killing me, babe," he groaned into his cell. I didn't reply and pressed the end call button and tried to appear cool, but realized I was smirking.

I may be naïve, but I knew enough to know that there had to be some boundaries. I needed to be smart if this crazy arrangement was going to happen.

I was petrified and thrilled in equal parts; I should have been ashamed and disgusted, but instead I was full of lust, intrigue, and excitement.

My behavior was so out of character that I was scaring myself. I'd gone from the virgin that I was a little over a week ago to entering into a very detached sexual relationship. More than that, this would only be my second partner, and right now I didn't even care.

CHAPTER 5

STRETCHING LIMITS

When I arrived home, I rang Alfie from the safety of my apartment bedroom. "Hey," he cooed. Instantly, I was affected by his voice. "Hi, gorgeous, well, I'm glad you rang back." The tone of his voice sounded gravelly and seductive.

"Hey," I responded shyly, my voice getting stuck in my throat. I didn't know what else to say. I hadn't really thought this part through so I almost got cold feet and hung up, but I felt really excited by him, so I didn't. My heart was pounding wildly in my chest.

Alfie took the lead, "Give me your address, and I'll come over." My heartbeat kicked up yet another gear and it felt like it was bursting out of my chest. *Too soon!* I fought my nerves.

"Whoa," I said, stopping him before he started dictating terms. "I think we may have a few things to hash out before we get down to... Sheesh... anything." I didn't know what to call it and giggled. I heard him snicker sexily as I huffed. *Damn this isn't easy.*

"Is this an equal relationship or a dictatorship? What I mean is, do *we* call the shots or is it only you that does that?" I said playfully.

"Equal all the way, babe, tell me what you want," he said, and I sensed a smile in his voice. It made me tingle, the way he said it, and there was a sudden rush of moistness between my legs. Just talking about this was arousing me.

Finding my courage again, I said, "Okay, we need a few rules. I need to know what I'm getting into."

Alfie waited and when I didn't say anything else he prompted me. "Hmm, okay… shoot." His voice sounded relaxed and playful.

"First, we've established that it is equal, so that means it isn't only at your beck and call. My needs are to be considered as important as yours. I may want to call you for this too." I placed my hand over my mouth because I couldn't believe that I'd just said that.

"Dang, that's an excellent idea honey." Alfie said, excitedly. Of course he did, I had just confirmed that I wanted him.

He encouraged me to continue, and I thought most guys would have done the same with the prospect of getting into a woman's panties. "Go on," he cooed again.

Calmer, I said confidently, "Safer sex practices, and regular checks for both of us."

"Done!" he agreed. I told him I needed to think about the girls here too.

"One more thing, I share an apartment with two other girls. We need to think about where it will happen between us. You can't just turn up here. I don't want you here when they are home." I waited for his reply.

"Deal, I have my own place, and I don't share, so you might feel better here in that case."

There was an awkward silence as I thought about what to say next, as I had exhausted my list. I cringed as I said it, but sounded confident. "Okay, your address?"

I could hear the excitement in his voice at the prospect of me getting over there soon. "It's on its way." My cell beeped with a text alert. Sure enough his home address and zip code were on there. "You're coming over now? He sounded excited.

This wasn't my intention when I asked for it, but I really wanted to see him again. Shit, I should just go before I chicken out.

I heard myself say, "Make yourself pretty I'll be there in thirty minutes," and hung up.

I clutched my cell and sat trembling. My palms were sweating, and I was in denial that I had just agreed to it. I gave myself a pep talk; I was fed up being a good girl. Therefore, my mind was made up, I was doing this.

I convinced myself that this would be reckless, but fun. Alfie was a hot guy who turned me on and if it felt horrible afterwards, the arrangement could be scrapped. I wanted to find out if I could really go through with this.

I took the fastest shower on record, pleased with myself that I had shaved this morning. All the while still muttering, that I couldn't believe I was going through with it.

I quickly picked out a blue satin and lace underwear set, the cut of them was square like boy-short briefs, but they showed a little of my ass cheeks, and the bra held my breast cleavage to perfection.

I stared at myself in the mirror. *Dear God, what have I just signed up for?* I pulled on a little purple dress that hugged my figure beautifully. Accentuating my curves, it looked tailored and the hem ended mid-thigh.

Brushing my hair, I pulled it to the side in a low ponytail halfway down its length, and made a mental note to free it when I got there.

I had left details of where I was going in my drawer in case for some reason the girls couldn't find me, or he kidnapped me. I knew this was crazy, but I wasn't thinking that straight. A flood of doubt began to creep over me. Yet still, I felt compelled to go through with it.

Driving to his address, the neighborhood he lived in wasn't what I expected at all. It was a family subdivision, with a gazebo and a fountain near the entrance.

There were some yellow colored lights in the tropical plants around a beautiful lake. It gave the place a welcoming feel to it. The houses were all single family residences, and it looked very well kept by the residents.

Pulling up outside his house, I was confused. The area screamed middle-class, American suburbia, not at all in keeping with his image. I was surprised to find him living in a house and not an apartment like most guys his age.

It seemed strange that he lived somewhere like this alone. I checked again that the satellite navigation had brought me to the right address. My fingers trembled as I reached for the key to kill the ignition after I confirmed that this was the correct place.

Looking out from the darkness of my car, I could see warm lights glowing in his sitting room window. He stood up and walked across the room inside, playing his guitar, and now that I was here, I felt scared.

My heart thumped in my chest, and my mouth went so, so dry, as the adrenaline rush came at me like a tidal wave. I could hear blood swishing in my ears. It was kind of flowing in time to my rapid heartbeat.

Pushing myself out of the car, I Hesitated and I almost wigged out, and was about to climb back in. Just at that moment, he looked up and noticed me through the window.

He headed to the door and when I saw him looking at me, I knew it was too late to back out now. He swung the door open. "Fantastic, you found me."

As soon as I laid eyes on him again, there was no question in my mind about backing out. I pasted on a smile to hide the half frightened, half thrilled feelings I fought with.

Alfie looked even more beautiful than he had that morning. He was casually dressed in a navy blue t-shirt that hugged the contours of his torso with promises of a hard, toned body underneath.

Faded jeans that were looser, than the tight skinny ones he was wearing that morning, were hanging low on his hips with a button fly, and his feet were bare. Damp hair from the shower he'd obviously just taken. I could smell his bodywash, and his stunningly handsome face seemed clean shaven.

Smelling so clean and fresh, Alfie's scent was almost overwhelmingly seductive. The urge to grab his t-shirt, pull it to my face and inhale him was almost too tempting.

Slowly he gave me a panty melting smile, his dimple showing, and although panties didn't exactly melt, the material between my legs became saturated. I had the most amazing attack of butterflies, and Alfie hadn't even touched me yet.

Closed the door, Alfie placed his palms on my upper arms and stilled me. The rush of chemistry from that little action between us at that moment was undeniable.

Hazel eyes turning green as they roamed up and down the length of me as Alfie checked me out, twinkled in the low light of the room; his pupils were dilated, and his eyes were darker, the green hue in them brighter now.

"Damn, Lily, you are even more beautiful than you were this morning. I can't believe you're here," he told me smiling widely, his husky voice slightly cracked.

Smiling shyly, I said, "You're not too shabby yourself." Curving his lips into a smile he began to grin playfully.

"Oh, you like what you see?" He was nodding playfully again, the tone of his voice seducing me all over again.

Moving closer, his face stopped only an inch

from mine. Turning his face from side to side, Alfie brushed his nose over mine. Adjusting his head, his lips brushed lightly against my mouth. The way he was handling me felt intimate and sexy.

He stepped back locking his arms straight and tilted his head back to look at me again. "God, I'm…" he whispered shakily, his words trailing off, the sentence unfinished. His eyes narrowed, showing the slightest concern. "You're sure you're okay with this?" I nodded slowly.

"Yeah, I think so…I'm here aren't I?" I swallowed hard and he watched me. "I need to warn you, I have limited sexual experiences, so I probably don't have much in the way of technique." I laughed nervously, slightly embarrassed to be telling him that I was basically a novice, but not a virgin.

Alfie smiled slowly, drawing me into his side and hugged me with one arm. "Leave the imagination up to me. You are all that I need to work with," he said playfully.

Bending his knees slightly, he swept his arm under my legs just above my knees. He picked me up, as he swept me off my feet and into his chest, holding me tightly in his arms.

The incredible smell of his skin on his neck was close to my cheek, so I boldly brushed my nose against his smooth, silky skin there because it was too irresistible not to. Alfie's arms tensed when I did it and he inhaled sharply in reaction to what I had done.

"I thought you didn't do romance," I teased.

"I don't," he said in a low growl. "This… isn't romance, this is lust…and the quickest way to my bed," he said seriously, and chuckled.

Pushing the door of his bedroom open wide with his hip, Alfie he set me down on my feet, still holding my hips. He gazed into my eyes and smiled slowly as he walked me backwards, until the back of my legs hit the bed.

He guided me down slowly, laying me gently on the bed. Alfie stood motionless and silent as his eyes raked over me. He was thoroughly checking me out again.

He sucked in a breath, and let the air escape his lungs so slowly then, shaking his head in disbelief, he whispered, "You are so fucking beautiful... no... you're perfect." He confirmed to himself, nodding.

"Thank you for coming to me. I have to admit, I'm a little nervous with you and I've *never* got nervous about getting off before." He smirked, as he crawled over me and began placing slow, sensual kisses up my neck, spiking a rash of goose bumps over my body.

Stopping briefly, Alfie nibbled my left ear, and stared intensely into my eyes, as he smoothed my hair down. Fixing his gaze on me for what seemed like ages, he simultaneously ran his fingers through my hair, spreading it out above my head.

Alfie's actions felt tender and intimate. His touch was causing insane sensations which were shocking every time his fingertips made contact with my scalp. It made me shiver and it and aroused me even more. "Fuck, you look like an angel," he murmured against the side of my mouth, as he finally dropped his eyes and placed his lips on mine.

His first kiss was gentle, and held a little more passion. The next one had more force to it. There was the same urgency that was present when he'd kissed me on campus.

His tongue explored my mouth, while mine explored his back. He stole my breath away and groaned into my mouth. "God." The vibrations hit directly at my core. I softly moaned and Alfie broke the kiss to murmur at the side of my mouth. "Fuck, I love those sounds you make, they're so fucking sexy."

Between my legs there was no mistaking my need for him. I was overflowing with moist slick juices, as he hit more and more of my zones with what he was doing. His fingertips trailed down the length of my dress, skimmed over my breasts, and down past my hips.

My body hummed as his fingers touched the bare skin of my legs. They skirted around the edge of my dress, and I shivered with shock, the sensation making me jump.

Alfie pulled away to look at me, Alfie widened his eyes and cocked his head at me. He growled and muttered, "Oh God," as his mouth moved down and he nuzzled his face into my neck.

Gasping at the sudden thrill this gave me. "Ah."

He dropped his eyes and followed the movements of his own hands as he traced upwards over my breasts again. It felt incredible. He took my breasts in his hands, kneading and teasing my nipples softly through the material of my bra and dress.

Alfie's hand slid down to my hemline again, and he raised himself to standing. Sitting me up, he pulled my dress up and over my body in one swift movement, I was so aroused and in need of much more from him than what he was doing to me right then.

So I reached out and pushed his t-shirt up weaving my hand up inside it. Alfie inhaled harshly in reaction. "Fuck." His body felt warm, hard, and satiny smooth. Sweeping my hand over his hard abdominal muscles his breath hitched again, and he shuddered slightly at my touch.

Alfie sat back on his heels and pulled his t-shirt over his head, tossing it to the floor. Alfie leaned forward so that he was hovering over me, and relaxed his arms, letting his skin contact mine.

He felt warm and hard as he dragged his strong taut body down the length of mine, still taking some of his weight on his arms.

As I looked at him, he inhaled sharply. "Fucking incredible," he murmured in a hiss, as he exhaled. I now knew what lust looked like in a man's eye. I could see he really wanted me, but I felt he was holding back.

He pulled himself up and sat back on his heels, tracing his hands up to my ribcage and down my sides with the pads of his fingertips. I shivered and smiled softly, but winced at the same time, trying to squirm away from the pangs of pleasure and the ticklish sensation he was awakening in me. "I enjoy touching you, Lily." He smiled.

He was watching my reactions, smiling seductively at the effect he was having on me. The more aroused I became, the less inhibited I felt. My passion was building for him, and I wanted more than this.

My hands explored his beautiful, strong, hard

body, and he shivered when I hit an erogenous zone just under his ribs on the side.

When I did this, a loud groan escaped. "Fuck, you're driving me crazy. I want you, so much." His voice was shaky and he threw his head back when I kept stroking his body. I traced his tattoos with my finger.

On his left arm there was a tattoo of a man from behind, his lover's head resting on his shoulder, her legs wrapped around his waist. Script font is scrolled in a swirl around his feet and legs 'All You Need is Love.' It was fitting, Alfie is a fellow Beatles fan, and I smiled at that.

Unexpectedly, Alfie began tugging at my bra with his teeth, and placed his mouth fully over one of my nipples through the material. He blew his hot breath on it, and sucked my nipple through the material. It pebbled, and I moaned, "Oh. Hmm."

His thumb skimmed the edge of the bra. "Pretty underwear honey, but I always find it looks better on the floor. Don't waste it on me next time," he muttered looking deadpan. My jaw dropped, and I giggled at his cheesy comment.

Raising his head to look up at me, he fixed his eyes on mine. He was watching my reaction with his sparkling lusty eyes. "Mmm…" he said, licking his lips as he unfastened my bra, freeing and cupping my breasts. "Perfect," he growled again.

Alfie's tongue flicked over my nipples, one after the other, his eyes never losing contact with mine. He took his time fluttering his tongue back and forth lightly, giving both breasts his attention before sucking them harder.

The erotic sensation as he sucked strongly hit me all the way down to my clitoris. I mussed his hair, and he slid up to my face, taking over my mouth again as he kissed me deeply. I moaned again at the side of his mouth. "Oh, God." My mind was numb, apart from the fabulous sensitive pulses that blocked me from forming thoughts when he was doing this.

Trailing his hot, wet tongue up my neck, he suddenly stuck his tongue into my ear, giving me a shock and creating a massive goose bump reaction that made me shudder. It also gave me pangs of pleasure deep in my core.

I found it so hot, and moaned again, "Oh, God, no!" I could feel my moist wet arousal seeping down the crease of my ass and leaking onto the bed.

Alfie started to tease his hands between my legs. His breathing was ragged and uneven as his fingers slid underneath my panties grazing my moist, sensitive flesh.

The sensation of his touch there was almost too much for me, and I jumped. He smiled and massaged around the entrance of my sex. "Oh, Fuck, Lily, you are so wet and slippery down here." The look in his eyes told me that what he was feeling gave him pleasure as well. "Goddammit."

Instinctively my hips arched under his touch wanting more, as I stifled a moan. Alfie looked up at me and gave me a half smile. "You like that, huh?" he said, nodding, and started placing little kisses all around my panty line at my belly.

Alfie held me in place by my hips when I tried to wriggle free of him and when the sensation became too much. Looking up, he grinned wolfishly at me.

He took my belly piercing, rolling his tongue around it. "Shit! Lily, so full of surprises, you have a piercing?"

I murmured, "Oh…yeah." Half aware of the conversation, half enjoying his touch on my skin as his tongue licked over my flesh, teasing me.

There was a mischievous, yet seductively small smile on his lips as he whispered, "We are not going to be disappointed sweetheart."

CHAPTER 6

HEAVY METAL

Alfie placed his thumbs on one side of my panties, tore the lace apart, reached over and repeated this on the other side. It shocked me. Pulling the ripped garment out from between my legs, he discarded it on top of the growing pile of clothes on the floor.

"That's much better." He chuckled, but stopped laughing when his eyes took in my fully naked body. "Damn… fuck!" he hissed slowly, as he saw my fully naked form for the first time.

Kissing my feet, he began to move slowly up my legs, his head travelling up the inside of my thighs, as he spread them wider with the palms of his hands.

"Oh Fuck, Lily! You have a tattoo?" His sparkling, green tinted eyes widened in surprise. I giggled. Feeling very embarrassed that he'd lifted my leg and exposed my most private area to read what it said. "Music is the sound of feelings." He began to chuckle.

Smiling, and felt a little smug at how surprised he was to find it. "I did say that if you were persistent you might find out how I managed to remember the quotation I gave you."

Alfie ran his thumb over the words, accidentally brushing the outer folds of my labia with the rest of his hand as he did this. My breath hitched, and he grinned instantly, like a child in a candy store.

Stopping, Alfie stared into my eyes again, then began to gently stroke my hair away from my face. The effect of his touch and his gaze did crazy things to me inside, and I couldn't wait for him to kiss me again.

"Dammit, you're so fucking sexy. I'm kind of scared that I'm never going to get enough of you," he murmured again, his face completely serious.

Sliding his hands under my ass from between my legs, his arms spread my legs wider, as he dragged me gently down to the end bed. "Sweet little Lily, you are just full of surprises," he muttered, smirking almost to himself as he settled his head between my legs.

His face dropped, inhaling the scent of me, and he looked up. "Look at me, Lily," he commanded. My eyes held his as I watched his tongue poke out through his luscious lips and tentatively glide over my sweet spot.

Alfie's first taste was with the slightest touch of his tongue, like I was a delicacy. It felt exquisite when his hot, moist mouth connected with my most sensitive flesh, and I shuddered.

"Oh Fuck." He lifted his head, smiled seductively, adjusted my legs, and licked his lips. "So sweet, your taste is amazing– it's like nectar... like... the sweetest honey." He shook slightly. "Damn, you're so fucking incredible. You're actually making me buzz inside."

Alfie turned his attention back to my nub, and fluttered his tongue around my sensitive flesh. He spread my outer folds with two fingers and licked up and over my clitoris. It felt sensational.

What he was doing was driving me insane, lapping and licking up and down my entrance. His teasing moved from rapid, greedy licks to more slow and leisurely flutters. He spread my legs wider still, placing one of my legs over his shoulder.

I had no idea a man could make a woman want him so badly. Grinding my sex in his face, I tried to get closer, frustrated that I couldn't get him near enough. I was so near the edge sometimes, but it was like he was anticipating my orgasm and would stop just as I was about to come.

My sensitive flesh ached for him, and I started whimpering. "Please, Alfie...more, don't stop. God... I need more." He looked up with a slow smile spreading on his lips, and he replaced his mouth with his hand. He rubbed and fondled me as he held my gaze.

"Not yet, babe, I want to take my time with you," he cooed. His eyes reflected the need he had for me. His finger drew down the slit of my sex and slipped slowly inside me. Alfie wiped his face and chin with his other hand.

He ran his fingers along his lips, before he slipped them into his mouth and sucked leisurely on them. "Mmm." He smiled behind his fingers. This kind of freaked me out and turned me on at the same time. He pulled his finger out of me and sat back on his heels.

"Oh, Lily, what I am going to do to you," he whispered, his voice sounded full of intent and his gaze was transfixed on mine. Two fingers slipped back in, and I felt desperate for more.

I began to beg him, "Please, oh God. Please Alfie…more." He stood up, unbuttoned his jeans slowly, and shook them to the ground. Damn, he was hung.

I swallowed hard, suddenly a bit scared. I didn't think that was going to fit inside me. I tensed, and he sensed it, asking, "What's wrong?"

"That's not going to fit," I said quietly nodding in the direction of his cock.

Alfie chuckled and bent to kiss my knee. "Trust me, it'll fit," he cooed.

I reached out my hand nervously and wrapped my fingers around his heavy cock. I wondered again if I could really take it. At my touch Alfie hitched his breath and groaned loudly, "Oh sweet… fuck." He shuddered as he struggled for words, and his lower belly trembled a little.

I stroked him from the base along his shaft to the tip. I stopped suddenly, when I saw a glint of metal embedded in the thick, purple, shiny gland at the head of his cock. I knew what it was. I'd seen one of these before when I watched a late night television documentary on body piercing last winter.

"You have an apa?" My mouth gaped, and I swallowed hard. I was just getting used to the idea of him putting this inside me, but then I had to contend with his size *and* a foreign body attached. I had to fight to stop myself wigging out. I reached out and took him in both hands, stroking his veiny, velvety, hard shaft up to his purple shiny glans and ran my thumb over him and his apa.

Alfie hissed and his cock twitched as a moist bead of pre cum leaked out. "You like her don't you." He gestured his head playfully toward me as he pretended to talk to his cock. It twitched again and he smiled. "Yeah, dude, me too." It was too cute and funny, and it lightened the tense moment for me.

Stroking over his glans again, cause him to suck air in sharply. He muttered, "Shit," and threw his head back as his eyes fluttered closed.

"Does it hurt?" I asked concerned, but I was still stroking it gently. Biting his bottom lip, his eyes widened, then closed again before he answered.

"No… it did when I had it done, but not having sex for six weeks hurt more. I had the most severe case of blue balls imaginable. It was worth it for the sensation I have now, though." Alfie smiled seductively at me. "You can give me your verdict on it later." He said, winking.

"Lily, can we stop talking now…just get down to what we're here for?" he murmured into my neck and pushed himself back, giving me a pleading look. "I just need to fuck you so badly Lily, I want to be inside you and make you come."

Alfie's statement was raw and honest. If anyone had spoken to me like this before I'd have hated it, but right now, it was crazy hot.

Tightening my hand around the girth of his cock, I had an overwhelming urge to taste him. I didn't really know how to do it, but took him in my mouth.

Alfie let out a low guttural sound and moaned, "Oh. Christ!" He hissed in a rushed tone and pulled himself away from me. Pushing my head away, he pulled me up, and I thought I'd done something wrong, but he was smiling.

Turning me around onto my knees, he pulled me over to straddle him with my ass up in his face. I felt really vulnerable in this position and embarrassed, I couldn't see him because I was looking down at his lower body. My ass in the air and my knees near his head.

This all felt completely alien to me. Alfie was lying underneath me and he pulled my hips back so that my sensitive folds met his lips. When he started licking my sex, I reached out and wrapped my hand around his cock again. He moaned into my core, "Mmm."

Taking the tip of his cock in my mouth again, I didn't really know what I was doing, so I just tried to do what I thought might make him feel good.

Fluttering my tongue around his apa made him groan again. "Ah fuck," he gasped, arching away into the mattress then thrust himself further into my mouth.

Alfie was sucking my clitoris in small pulses at almost the same pace as I stroked him and took himself in and out of my mouth. What he was doing to me was an incredible feeling, and I moaned around his cock. He gasped at the sensation the vibrations made as my moaned resonated up his shaft. "Oh. My. God. Fucking. Amazing," he whispered.

Sucking him tightly, I hollowed my cheeks in

long fast sucks as my head bobbed up and down. I fisted the length that I couldn't fit in my mouth and kind of twisted it as I pushed and pulled. I didn't know if I was doing this right at all.

I'd seen it done once in a porn film when I'd found a DVD in the player of someone I had babysat for. I remember feeling grossed out, but hypnotized by it at the same time. I was glad I found it because Alfie seemed to enjoy what I was doing.

The effect he was having on me was almost too much, as his tongue delved deeper into my entrance. An exquisite feeling of pleasure, but it was almost overpowering. I tried to move away when it got to be too much, but Alfie's arms gripped around my thighs and kept me in place, heightening the impact of what he was doing to me.

Pressure built like a small thrill inside me, and I could feel I was on the edge of climaxing. Alfie seemed to sense this and the more I squirmed, the tighter he held me in place, and the faster he licked.

Aching with pleasure, I could feel his apa each time I pulled him in and out of my mouth. When I held my tongue flat against his glans, he let out a strangled whimper, I tasted some pre cum that escaped and coated this around his shaft with my swirling tongue.

Alfie's breathing was fast and ragged. He pushed me off of him and rolled me onto my back. Dragging my ass off of the end of the bed, he knelt as I balanced on my elbows to look at him between my legs.

His fingers were inside moving back and forth, his thumb circling my clitoris. "You do it. Play with your clit for me, I want to watch," he said stroking his cock slowly. I was totally exposed and hesitant. "Do it!" he commanded.

Placing my middle finger over my clitoris, I did, because I was so far gone I couldn't leave it like that any longer. I began to stroke myself for him. Feeling partly mortified and self-conscious but seeing the effect it had on him helped me past these thoughts.

Inhibitions were laid aside as I began to enjoy it, besides I was close again. Alfie took a condom from under his pillow, ripped the foil, and carefully rolled the latex down the thickness of his stiff cock.

Alfie's hooded eyes stared at my sex watching me pleasure myself, before taking over with his thumb, as his palm stretched over my belly. Rubbing the tip of his cock at my entrance at the same time, he stroked my clitoris and all the way down my slit smearing my juices around.

Lust filled eyes were shining with passion, as he drew my legs up bending them at the knees and he lifted me up onto his hips, pulling my legs wider apart.

He positioned himself at my folds and began to rock into me. It was a little painful at first, but he very slowly inched inside of me, stretching me to fit.

My entrance felt burning hot and tight as he thrust his cock inside me. "Oh. My. God. Oh. Shit. You're so fucking tiny honey…so fucking tight," Alfie growled as he penetrated me inch by inch.

Pushing his way in deeper, he suddenly stilled. "You okay?" I nodded, but it burned; he was much bigger than Sam. With a small thrust it was getting a little less uncomfortable though.

"Relax, you need to relax Lily, you're killing me in there," Alfie hissed and stilled again. I adjusted my hips. "Please stay still or I'll come," he groaned.

Holding me still, he waited for both of us to adjust, before he grunted and thrust deeper inside me again. "Oh. My. God," he hissed. I don't know what happened, but my body just seemed to relax and after another small thrust he was able to give a longer glide and was inside me to his root.

Moaning loudly as he filled me, I flexed my vaginal muscles, squeezing him a little then relaxing, his response was a low guttural sound.

Alfie's breath was ragged with pure lust. The coolness of his breath mingled with the beads of sweat on my body as he pulled all the way back then thrust long and slow back into me to the hilt. I cried out, "Oh fuck," inhaling sharply, and he gave me a low growl, "Fuck."

Stopping for a moment, he smiled, gazing intensely at me again and bringing his forehead to touch mine. His intimate movement turned me on even more. "Are you okay?" he whispered. I nodded, speechless.

"More than okay," I said softly back at him, smiling.

Smiling back wider, he kissed me as he thrust forward again. His movements were slow at first, but he began to alternate between thrusting into me rapidly before slowing to a more sensual languished pace. Each time I felt I was near the edge, he changed it up again, making me work for my release.

I held my breath as he took me close, building the pressure in me. I clung to his ass, trying to get him to continue this rhythm to get me off. "Yeah, just like that… just…please keep going!" Each time I felt I was progressing and only one or two thrusts from an explosive climax, he would stop, robbing me of reaching my peak.

The sensation he created in me sent tingles rippling through my body. My leg muscles fizzed and quivered as I sat on the brink of my orgasm.

He stirred me up like nothing I'd ever felt before. I whimpered, "Please. God. Alfie. Please. Don't. Stop." I pulled at his hips, and ground myself on him, chasing my orgasm. He chuckled, and I knew he was teasing me, pushing me to my limits.

Alfie whispered sexily in my ear, "You're so fucking hot, this is incredible. I don't want this to end." I didn't speak, just lay there staring into his eyes, dazzled, as he pounded into me.

I was so aroused and found him so sexy, I almost lost my mind. Scratching his back, I gripped his ass, and continued to grind myself on him. The sensation of his apa on my sweet spot inside was tantalizing me.

Begging him, I screamed out loud, "Please Alfie, I need you to let me… I need to come." He took me so near, so many times, my scalp crept with the almost orgasms. His stamina and sheer willpower to hold back was incredible.

Pulling himself free of me, he flipped me over, penetrating me from behind, pulling my hair back, and scooping it into a ponytail. Alfie tugged my head back so that my neck extended and my face reached back before he leaned over and crushed his mouth on mine.

"Please keep going… don't stop, please," I moaned into his mouth. I began to whimper, feeling beyond desperate.

Alfie curled over me. He moaned into my neck, whispering, "Shush, I'll take care of you. Keep looking at me, I want to see you when you come." Pulling back onto his knees, he started stroking his fingers down my back. Fingers curled and gripped my hips again, as he began thrusting into me again. His pace was steady this time.

Without warning he pulled me back onto him harder, grabbing my shoulders, pulling my whole body back, as he pounded his cock into me relentlessly, over and over.

I heard myself chanting, "I'm coming! I'm coming! Don't stop, don't fucking stop!" It was shameless of me to cry out, "Oh Fuck, Yes! Yes!" My insides tightened, squeezing his cock as I came around it. I shuddered as my stomach muscles contracted in waves. My orgasm washed over me. My knees gave way beneath me on the bed as I jerked and shook over and over and screamed his name.

Alfie was still riding me hard and grunted as he cried out, "Oh! Fuck… Fuck…" for what seemed like an age, until I thought I was going to pass out with the pleasure.

Then I felt him seize up and freeze. Feeling his length pulsate inside of me, his body jerked and he growled while he thrusted a few more times before stopping. My whole body was limp, and I was drenched in sweat. Rolling me sideways, we collapse onto the bed.

We lay there for a few minutes, both of us

panting until our breathing steadied, and he pulled himself out. Alfie rolled onto his back. "Fu…fuck. Wow." Bright, clear eyes were shining as he stared at me, and his hair was soaking wet and his hard, muscular body glistened with sweat.

Grinning widely, Alfie commented, "Shit, I'm in trouble! What a fucking rush!" Pulling off the condom, he tied a knot in it and aimed it at a small waste bin across the room near the dresser. He aced the shot.

CHAPTER 7

SECOND HELPINGS

Lying in silence, I panted breathlessly, licking my dry lips. I tried to get my head around what had just happened between us. Alfie didn't know just *how* inexperienced I was. "Your body is so fucking responsive, I *knew* it. It was as if your body was made for me. I just knew that sex between us would be so fan… fucking… tastic. "

Still breathless, he turned his head to face me. "I love making you scream, Lily! You're so fucking hot, honey." Glancing down, I noticed he was still semi hard and talking about what we had just done was making his cock twitch. When our breathing was normal and we'd recovered a little he lifted me up, carefully turning me around to straddle him.

Shuffling us to the edge of the bed, he pulled up a nearby chair. Throwing a pillow on it, Alfie lowered my head and shoulders to rest on this. Placing a hand under the crest of my ass cheeks, he supported my weight.

Alfie snapped on another condom, rolling it expertly with one hand and positioned his now erect cock at my entrance again, putting both hands under my ass cheeks and squeezed them gently.

Tilting me, he bent his head forward between my legs and began licking my clit and entrance again. "Damn, you're still soaking wet, and ready for me." He came up to kiss my mouth hard and leaned back to take position with his cock and began to enter me again.

His apa rubbed the sweet spot on my anterior wall inside. I felt a bit raw and sore inside from our previous time, but watching him, watching me, turned me on so much I didn't care.

I began to move my hips in time with him, and he squeezed my ass cheeks rhythmically, the look he was giving me intense. I was trying to keep him deep inside. He was teasing me; pulling all the way back, almost coming out of me each time.

His little finger stroked up and down my anus sensually, and I froze and shook my head. I didn't feel comfortable with that. "Trust me," he whispered. He didn't do anything else with it, so I learned to trust him with it being there.

Alfie pulled out and looked at me, before he dipped his fingers into my entrance and made them moist, before he continued to let his finger slide smoothly over it. Teasing me with this, he increased the sensation of his thrusts at the same time.

Actually, it felt incredible and his cock moved more freely inside me in this position. Alfie pulled my ass cheeks slightly apart and it felt more open for him giving him more room to plunge deeper.

Alfie felt me when I began to clench down on him as I neared my climax. "Don't come yet! *Don't come*," he ordered me. My legs were trembling and I bit my lip and tried to do as he asked, but my eyes were silently pleading with him.

I tried to concentrate on his abdominal muscles flexing on his belly as he rocked deep inside me. Using that as a distraction was futile, it just increased my arousal.

"I can't…" I whimpered.

Alfie stared into my eyes. "Hold it, Lily. I want to come with you."

The concentration pulled his face into an agonizing expression and my head was swimming as I tried to hold the flood of ecstasy back. He pounded into me so ferociously again and again, and I tried desperately to hold on. My fingers were digging into the chair fabric. "I can't…"

My legs began to quiver with my impending climax that I was losing control over, when I heard Alfie say, "Let it go Lily."

I didn't need him to repeat what he said. Suddenly I was screaming his name again. We were both shuddering and bucking at the same time, pure bliss in his eyes that didn't close. His abs contracted and relaxed as his orgasm tore through him.

His smile was so beautiful with his amazing dimple. It made me feel weak watching him as he gazed back at me with his sexy just fucked hair. He looked perfect.

I kept trying to rock on him, and he bit his bottom lip as I milked the last drop of come from him. Falling backwards, he pulled out of me in one fell sweep, and I fell on my ass.

"Ouch!"

Alfie raised his head, one eye peering over at me, the other closed, and he chuckled sheepishly, before collapsing back on the bed. "Sorry…did the earth move for you too, honey?" he said playfully. Stretching his arms lazily above his head, he let out a deep sigh that sounded like contentment as I pulled myself up off the floor.

Smacking his thigh for letting me fall, his eyes widened playfully. "Oh kinky! I love it! But I'm a little tired right now honey, can we do that another time?" Grinning wickedly at me, Alfie closed his eyes again. I loved his funny, playful side; it only made him even more appealing.

Standing up a little shakily, I padded over to his bathroom. My hips, legs, and lady parts ached. Alfie was lying there, his cock all shrunken, and his condom still in place. It looked like an old sock hanging off him.

I smirked at how this hot guy could make himself look so ridiculous in a split second and I was tempted to get my camera out, but I'd have hated if he'd done that to me.

As I closed the bathroom door, I heard him say, "Damn it! I'm in trouble." In a softer tone he said, "Shit… pity I can't love you, Lily."

Fixing myself up quickly, I snagged a quick shower and leaned against the tile as the water sprayed down on me. I was feeling the unfamiliar pang of hurt, unsure what he meant by his last comment, and I tried not to overthink things.

Wrapping myself with a small towel, I cracked open the bathroom door to see Alfie sound asleep. He had passed out. His breathing was slow, and he lay flat out in the same position I had left him in, minus the condom.

I didn't disturb him, but leaned over and switched the nightstand lamp off, before letting myself out.

By the time I arrived home, I was too tired to think about what I had done and fell into bed. When I woke up it was still dark. Turning on the nightstand light, I went to pee and caught sight of my naked form in front of the floor length mirror. I didn't look any different considering what I'd done earlier.

My inexperience in the bedroom had me doubting whether Alfie would want to do that with me again. He may not want to continue with our arrangement. From my perspective, he did all the work while I just kind of lay there.

Clearly, he'd had a lot of sex in the past from the way he teased my body. Even with my novice status, I could appreciate how much control it took for him to hold back with me like that.

Maybe I wouldn't be enough for him, and he'd move on to someone with more experience before giving me the chance to learn how to please him properly. From my perspective, he more than lived up to my expectations. The sexual chemistry and tension between us was almost tangible.

Alfie's strong, sexy body, talented mouth and magical hands had pleasured me in places I had never imagined as erogenous zones before. I really wanted to repeat the experience with him and hoped he felt the same way.

Turning away from the mirror and turned the bath faucet on filling my bath tub. The sensitive flesh between my legs ached, and I wanted to soothe it. I sat nursing the ache, and it worked. After a while I didn't notice it anymore, until I rose to get out of the bath again.

It was a pleasant soreness though, it reminded me of the fabulous feelings Alfie had stirred in me. Pouring some rose scented body wash onto a sponge, I enjoyed the silky feeling on my skin as I washed myself.

It was so comforting and pleasant, the smell reminded me of home, and I made a mental note to call my parents this afternoon.

As I lathered myself, I was thinking back to the things we had done the night before. Rinsing out the sponge, the water seep back into it again when I re-submerged it then squeezing it out over my breasts. I watched as the water cascaded over the foam, washing it down and off my body.

Definite feelings stirred in me about wanting to see Alfie again. I wasn't that confident he would want to see me though. I didn't feel I knew enough to keep his attention. I wasn't sure if his comment about not being able to love me was meant for my ears or something he had said to himself, and I had no idea what he had meant.

Stepping out of the tub, I enveloped myself in a huge, fluffy white towel, as I made my way back to my bedroom. I grabbed my cell from my purse and remembered I needed to charge it for the next day. As I plugged the cell into the charger I noticed there was a text from Alfie. My mouth was dry, and I was kind of reluctant to open it, afraid of being rejected by him.

> **SEXPERT: Pink Lady, I am writing to confirm that your recent application for the position of fuck buddy has been successful. Terms and conditions as negotiated prior to start date. I look forward to having you... and your assets on board.**

My mouth stretched into a slow smile as I read it and started to text a reply.

> **Pink Lady: I am writing to confirm my acceptance of said post, to which you refer. I am happy to bring my assets to support your more... hidden talents. Together I am confident that we will utilize these to their full potential. I look forward meeting the challenge of a demanding work schedule and hope to fulfill your requirements leading to many satisfactory outcomes in the future.**

I hit the send button and held the phone to my chest, closing my eyes. Within a few seconds I heard another text arrive.

> **SEXPERT: Are you awake?**

Pink Lady: No multi-talented, I always text in my sleep!

SEXPERT: LMAO, want to play? Can I come over?

Pink Lady: Nope, my roommates are sleeping. *wagging finger and shaking head*

SEXPERT: Sad face.

Pink Lady: Really? You were smiling, when I left.

SEXPERT: but you left! I might not have been done.

Pink Lady: Oh, believe me, from what I saw:snoring face, you were most definitely done :smug face

SEXPERT: I'm a quick recoverer! :raised eyebrow

Pink Lady: I don't believe 'recoverer' is even a word, besides short of CPR you weren't recoverable from the angle I was observing you from :angel face.

SEXPERT: Oh, you like to watch?: smug face, :ninja face. *Checks out Alfie junior, looks back up and smiles* but I have

**now and would like a rematch
:flirty face.**

**Pink Lady: So this is a
competition now? :confused face.**

**SEXPERT: If that's what it takes
to get you back in my bed…hell,
yes.**

I was chuckling when I hit the call button. "Ah, I won", he gloated when he answered. "You called me. You have to come back here now." I thought he was kidding me.

"I'm not ringing because I want to come back." Blushing crimson, I was glad he couldn't see me.

Alfie screamed, and pretended to cough. "That arrow just went right through my heart! You slay me, girl." He chuckled. "Would now be the right time to tell you I don't handle rejection well?"

I giggled again at his fun side. *Damn, he's too cute!* "It's six in the morning, Alfie," I said finding it incredulous that he was serious.

"Your point being what? You know how to tell the time? You're not a morning person?" he teased with a smile in his voice. "But you're up anyway, so… you might as well… you know…" He chuckled again then sounded pathetic. "Pleeeease?"

Sighing heavily I said, "I have to start college today Alfie."

Alfie gave me an exaggerated sigh back, mocking me. "Well, what better way to start than being mellow after some good sex? You won't be nervous and everyone will remember you as the cool

English girl on the first day." Hearing the smile in his voice, I imagined a grin teasing his lips.

"Are you always this good at arguing your point?" I smiled.

"Only if it leads to orgasms and primal sex," he answered in a mock seductive voice. He was too sexy to resist.

"Will you make me breakfast if I come?" I asked innocently.

"No, honey, I'll make you breakfast because you're here. There's no pressure to come, but I'll make you come anyway, several times if you're a good girl. See you in thirty." Alfie ended the call before I could reply.

Leaving the condo a little after six, I drove back to his place. It wasn't far from the college, and I told myself we wouldn't be having sex again. Besides, I thought I might be able to get to know him a little better.

Alfie was beyond hot and I wanted to spent time with him. His voice melted me, and his body rocked me. Even when he stroked my cheek the last time, I had feelings no one has ever given me in my life before.

Rumors I'd heard about certain people having 'the touch,' a connection between two people, seemed like a myth until it happened to me with him.

I suspected it must have been the same for him, not because he was telling me, but because I didn't mistake his reactions to me, from that first time when we were behind the college buildings to when his belly quivered when I touched him.

Before he'd even kissed me I was covered in

goose bumps, and I was hooked. I knew I needed more of that touch, but at the same time, I repeatedly told myself, this won't last forever. Guys like him like to share themselves too much.

CHAPTER 8

BREAKFAST

When I arrived at Alfie's, his front door was already open for me. "Through here, Lily." I walked through the formal lounge with the vaulted ceiling and into the kitchen. I stopped in my tracks as soon as I saw him.

Looking absolutely amazing, I felt breathless at the sight of him and thought that I couldn't believe that this man; who could probably have anyone, actually wanted me… for now.

Smirking at me, he stood in a relaxed stance with his fuck-me hair, fresh from the shower. He was wearing his low slung jeans from earlier that were hanging low on his hips, bare torso exposed and his ink made him look like a sexy, bad-ass boy.

Leaning back casually against the countertop, his hips were resting along the edge, and he had a glass of orange juice in one hand. His other palm was resting flat on the granite countertop.

Shiny, clean, smooth skin tantalized me and I had to fight the urge to stroke my hands over his body. I imagined it would feel cool and smooth to the touch, after his shower.

Alfie passed me the glass of orange juice. "Breakfast!" he announced as his face broke into a seductive, slow, lop sided smile. Blushing when I took the glass, his fingers brushed against mine.

My skin reacted violently and goose bumps radiated to all areas of my body. His eyes widened when he noticed, and he smiled. I blushed again. "Damn, so responsive to me," he said, curling my t-shirt in his fist to pull me closer to his face.

Alfie held my gaze for what seemed like an age, and I watched his eyes darken with passion. Starting to feel too self-conscious, I was about to look away when he dipped his head and let his lips brush mine briefly, before letting me go. "Hey," he cooed.

I tried to act like he'd had little effect on me, focusing on, and gesturing at, the orange juice. "Breakfast, that's it? Hmm... it's definitely not good enough, Alfie," I mock sneered and shook my head at him, crossing my arms.

Alfie pushed himself off the counter by his backside, and his hips jutted toward me before he righted himself as he found his balance, obviously the guy had no idea how even a subtle movement could have sex appeal if observed by the right person.

Saddling over to me, he placed his hand at the base of my back. The thumb of his other hand grazed my lips and he pulled me in close to him, rubbing his hard-on across my pubic bone creating friction, as his hips connected with mine.

One hand went to my neck and drew a line down my spine, finally settling on my ass. Alfie cupped it possessively, pulling me even closer. His mouth crushed onto mine; his hot, wet tongue teasing me.

I felt him grow in his pants even more as he leaned in flush against my whole body. He held me by the nape of my neck and whispered, "Am I doing better?" as he stepped back with a lopsided smile.

Intensely staring at me, Alfie stole my breath, and I panted airily, "Much, breakfast was wonderful!" I smiled up at him, before resting my head on his chest.

I smelled his fresh body wash… and as I suspected his body was cool and satiny from his shower. I inhaled his scent deeply. "You smell amazing."

Alfie chuckled and looked at me mischievously. "Good enough to eat?" he teased.

I blushed and moved away, swatting his arm with the back of my hand. Alfie caught it, and quickly pulled me back into his chest. I looked up, and he held my gaze as he shook his head at me.

His other hand slipped around my back and pulled me tight against him again. He walked me backwards, his legs outside of mine, into the sitting room still locked in our stare. I was mesmerized by his perfection.

Pushing me back on the couch, Alfie's hand skimmed over my skin, gliding up between my thighs under my skirt, his nimble fingers pulled my thong to the side. "Damn, you're wet for me already," he murmured as my breath hitched at his sudden movement.

Peppering kisses along the length of my neck and up to my ear, at the same time, Alfie was massaging my swollen, wet, folds. Expertly strumming my sensitive area it with his fingertips, and making me shuddered with pleasure.

I wondered if my goose bumps had their own goose bumps; his touch had such an amazing effect on me. Teasing me with his hot, tongue, Alfie traced my lips, and my body almost hummed such was the tension between us. "C'mere." He cooed as he swept me up into his arms, before half running up the stairs to his bedroom.

"Everything off!" he commanded as he set me down on my feet in his bedroom. The intense lusty gaze adding weight to is command. Without hesitation, I pulled my t-shirt over my head and dropped it on the floor.

Inhaling deeply, Alfie took in the sight of my naked breasts. My bra was in my purse, having already decided that I would put this on after my visit with Alfie.

Bending down with my legs straight, I began peeling off my thong, before I kicked it free, making a pile with my t-shirt. He walked around behind me and sat on the bed. "Stay bent over, Lily." His voice was barely a husky whisper now. An audible swallow from Alfie let me know it was affecting him.

Feeling self-conscious again, and stood up straight, asking myself why did I place my trust in him so much? *Alfie* stroked my ass, kissing my neck from behind and encouraged me again to bend down. "Keep your legs straight for me, honey." Breath sounding raspy and uneven, "Open your legs wider for me," he ordered and I did, then cringed and turned my head to the side, peering up at him. "What are you doing?"

"Just looking," he mused, a penetrating stare in his eyes. "I just want to see you from here." He gave me a lopsided half smile, which was so sexy, I couldn't refuse.

Bending over with my head down between my legs, I could see him as he watched me. It was very arousing watching his reactions to having access to my secret areas.

Alfie placed his thumbs into my folds gently and parted my lips. "God, you are so very lovely, honey." His eyes changed in color and a lusting appearance crept over his face, the green of his hazel eyes became darker and bolder. They also had a hooded, heavy appearance, and his jaw was clenched in concentration. As his fingers moved to spread my folds he licked his lips and scraped his teeth along his bottom one.

Initially, I felt embarrassed at allowing him such an uncomfortable request, but as soon as I saw him reacting, becoming engrossed in me and seeing that effect, I never doubted that I would do it again.

I wondered what he was thinking, and would have given anything at that point to know.

He drew his fingers down my slit, and when a finger slipped inside me, my breath hitched. Alfie's eyes closed for a second, and he swallowed hard then pinched his lips together.

He started making circular movements inside me. I moaned, "God." It came out a breathy whisper, and he bit his lip again, still looking at me and shaking his head. He shifted his other hand to cup my ass in response to my moan, his fingers squeezing a little.

The atmosphere between us was intense, but unhurried. This seemed much more intimate than anything we had done already. I wanted to straighten up, but he slid his other hand from my ass, to rub my clitoris, before he drew his one finger back outside of me and replaced it with two.

I felt tight, and he gently stretched me little by little until it became more pleasurable. I moaned loudly, "Oh, fuck, yeah." He smiled and bit his lip again as he concentrated on what he was doing.

My legs were weak, the passion and sensation of his expert hands started to make me feel insane with lust. My legs started shaking, from my thighs to my toes, like an electrical current was passing through.

I struggled not to fall over the edge with pleasure. Taking his fingers out, but still rubbing my clitoris, Alfie maneuvered me over to the bed and lay me down on my side.

Lifting my leg over his shoulder; making me more open to him, Alfie then bent his head and sucked hard on my clitoris. Drawing his head back, he stretched the sensitive skin between his lips making me moan, "Oh, yes... please... don't stop." I lay completely shameless before him. I could feel myself tightening, needing to come, and arched myself at his mouth.

His tongue slipped inside me, then he flicked my clitoris faster. Without lifting his head, he mumbled around it, "Come, Lily, let it go, come around my tongue." As soon as his tongue entered me again, I screamed, my high pitched staccato noises bounced around the room as my body shuddered, and my legs shook uncontrollably.

I tried to close my legs and block him. The pleasure was so intense. His arms clamped around my thighs, and held me down as I came so hard.

He was relentless, making me ride it out, punishing me with pleasure. As my climax ebbed away and then rose into another. "Fuck me, no… please… I'm going to die… stop… stop!" I tried to get away from him, begging him to stop.

"Please… no more," I whined and pleaded. He chuckled softly, sitting back on his heels on the floor, wiping his mouth, as I stared at him breathlessly.

My mouth was dry, and I glistened with sweat. Leaning over, he kissed me roughly. "That was for last night. I owed you one, since I let you fall on your ass, then I passed out." He smiled and winked.

Groaning with exhaustion, I rolled over, and closed my legs. It felt so good to close them tight, with my knees together. My hips were aching. I closed my eyes.

Alfie propped himself up on his elbow, beside my head and pursed his lips, shaking his head at me. "Oh, no! You don't get to do that." He slapped me on my ass playfully. "Come on honey, time is marching on, my turn!"

Peering through one eye, he said in all seriousness, "Are you fucking kidding me, really? I don't think I can move, let alone to do whatever else you have up your sleeve."

Smirking wickedly at me, he said, "Here, read this." He shoved his tattooed wrist up at my face. "Don't limit your challenges, challenge your limits."

"Trust me Alfie. My limits have been well and truly challenged," I mumbled.

"Nonsense!" He smirked again. "Think of me as a challenge." He winked, and jumped up, and began shucking off his jeans.

Adding them to the top of the pile on the floor, he smiled; his erection pointing directly at me. Grasping his cock with his fist, he stroked it gently and noticed me watching. Grazing his thumb over his apa, he flashed me a sinfully, sexy smile.

I groaned with tiredness, but knew it wouldn't be fair to leave him in that state. "You'll need to come here," I murmured.

Alfie laughed, his eyes had that mischievous glint in them. "Exactly my intention, lady, right here." He pointed downwards, and I knew what he meant.

Alfie crawled up beside me, moving past my body, lining his cock with my mouth. I licked out at his glans, teasing the apa with my tongue. "Christ!" he moaned and hissed before sucking his breath in hard.

"Stroke it," he encouraged as I placed my lips over the head, kissing it, lightly fluttering my tongue over it before I placed my tongue flat and licking it roughly with my taste buds.

He gasped and shuddered a little, his body trembled. I smiled up at him. "Fuck," he growled. I took him in my mouth halfway, and then even more with each bob of my head.

I pumped his thick cock slowly with my fist down at his base, and pulled it up the shaft to where it met my mouth. I sucked in my cheeks forming a vacuum around him, gripping him gently at first with one, then two, hands increasing the pace.

He groaned loudly, "Sweet Jesus, you are so fucking good, I can't believe I found you, I don't know that I'll ever get enough of you." He placed his hand lightly on my head to keep it there, adding a little pressure by gently rocking his hips.

Alfie's length was so hard and smooth, I made a popping noise when he slipped out from my mouth and giggled, Alfie shouted, "Fuck!" thrilled from the vibration. "God, I love when you do that," he husked. He became more vocal, moaning and grunting, biting his lip and hissing, especially when I rolled my tongue around his glans and apa.

A low growl came from his throat and he arched his back, pushing himself deeper into my mouth, I gagged the first time but learned to adjust to it. I cupped and sucked his balls, rubbed and gently scratched his perineum with my fingernails. This made his legs spread wider. "Sweet Jesus, this is too fucking amazing," he hissed in almost a whisper.

Feeling the skin around his balls tighten, I began to suck harder, pulling his cock in the opposite direction. Alfie held my head in both of his hands, fucking my mouth gently, but quickening the pace. Voice shaky, he said, "This is insane…I'm coming Lily, take me out of your mouth." Ignoring him, I kept sucking, wanting to know what his seed tasted like, and almost choked with the force of the hot spurt of his cum hitting the back of my throat.

Swallowing greedily and tasting salty, I sucked a few times to milk him. The taste wasn't that bad. My face was sticky as some had escaped, and I wiped my mouth with the back of my hand.

Alfie stood there looking down at me with a just fucked smirk on his lips and he was playing with my hair, he commented, "Where did you learn that? You blew me away honey, literally!"

Falling back on the bed with his eyes closed, he looked sated. I could see a pattern forming already, and smiled. Everything reeked of sex, myself, the bed, Alfie and the air the room in general and I needed to brush my teeth.

Untangling myself from his limbs, I smarted from the pain between my swollen folds. Going into the downstairs shower room, I stepped under the shower. The water wasn't hot, and I was feeling a bit raw. Taking some warm water on the washcloth, I held it between my legs; it was bliss.

Alfie was still lying passed out on the bed. *Sex on a stick... now I know what that means.*

I looked at the time. It read 7:40am. Glancing in the mirror, my eyes sparkled brighter than I'd ever seen them, and I looked great, even if I didn't feel it. I left him sleeping and headed to college.

He was definitely fun to be with, but I worried that I would become attached to Alfie. Even though it was in its early days, I knew I would have to find the strength to pull back, or even end it if I began to become emotionally dependent.

Alfie had already made it clear that this was only going to be a physical relationship . Already, I was kind of worried that I might struggle to keep it that way.

By the time I'd sifted through stuff in my mind, I had arrived on campus and sat through countless induction and orientation sessions. It was a morning of learning how to go to college, and how things worked, like the library, music rooms, recording studio.

There was a lot of other stuff that seemed to be beyond boring, such as fire procedures, evacuation routes, and all the usual rules and regulations that go with entering a large institution.

By lunchtime I felt drained from my hectic sessions with Alfie, and from trying to pay attention to everything that the administration thought we needed, for our time at school. My stomach growled and I remembered my breakfast of a kiss and a sip orange juice. It wasn't substantial enough to get me through the rest of the day.

CHAPTER 9

NIGHT OUT

Wandering over to the canteen, I grabbed a sandwich, before finding a spot on the campus lawn to enjoy the sunshine.

Small groups of students milled around, others were sitting alone reading, texting or listening to music through ear buds. It was a beautiful cloudless day, but then, nearly every day is sunny in Miami.

I turned to the sound of laughter. There was a group of students nearby. One of the guys in the group was teasing a pretty dark haired girl as she was rolling around laughing on the grass; he was tickling her.

The girl was helpless from laughing and her giggle was so infectious that I found myself grinning at the sound of her. She looked relaxed and was obviously very familiar with the guys she was with.

Feeling more than a little envious of her relaxing with her friends, right then, while I was missing mine.

The small group continued to joke around and were all teasing each other. Swatting 'tickling guy' the girl shouted, "I did not, that's not what I meant, and you know it." They all started laughing again.

Catching me watching them, the girl tried to compose herself. Leaning back on her hands, still chuckling a little, she flicked her bobbed head back in acknowledgment of me, "Hi."

Smiling, I tried to look confident. "Hey, are they giving you a tough time there?" I lifted my hand and gestured toward the guys she was with.

Snorting at them she replied, "What these two reprobates, nah, they're harmless really." Pointing, she introduced them to me. "This is Neil and his partner in crime, Will. I'm Mandy. I saw you around earlier are you majoring in music too?"

Nodding, in affirmation, "Yeah, I am, I'm ready for the courses to start, now that all that boring stuff is out of the way." I stuffed the rest of my sandwich in my mouth and mentally chastised myself, because this was the best small talk I could think of.

"Oh, you're English?" She smiled again, and looked interested.

"Yeah, long story, but very glad to be here, though." I smiled warmly at her. Mandy put her hand up inside Neil's t-shirt and rubbed his back.

"Neil and I have a gig at Bailey's bar tonight. Would you like to come with us? Will could use the company. His cousin has a date tonight, and she's left him high and dry." She quickly added, "That is, if there isn't anywhere you need to be."

Mandy's fingers plucked at the lawn. "Sure, it would be cool to hang out with you, if your friends don't mind." I was just pleased to be included in someone's plans.

Will seemed fine with Mandy's suggestion. "Great, the more the merrier, I only get to do one song with them, and she's right, I could use the company." He said and smiled warmly.

Mandy waved her hand in Neil's direction and said, "He doesn't get a say, he's my boyfriend!" She leaned in and kissed him on the cheek.

That much was already apparent from the way her hand was roaming absentmindedly around his body. I swapped cell numbers with her to get the details later, and we started to head back to class, falling into easy conversation. We all shared a lot of the same classes together, so it would be good to get to know them.

Mandy's petite frame, with short bobbed black hair, made her look sophisticated without having to try. Her haircut was super sexy, with a side part and razor cut edges. She seemed completely comfortable and confident with the guys, and I kind of envied her apparent sense of identity and confidence. Maybe one day I'd be confident like that.

Turning the corner, my step faltered when I saw Alfie right in front of me. He was sitting on a bench by the pathway, guitar in his lap, surrounded by a group of girls. I smiled when I saw him and wondered whether to go and say "hi."

Deciding against that, I and stood watching him instead. He was deep in conversation with the girls and had a captive audience. They appeared to be hanging on his every word.

From what I could tell he'd affected them the

same way he affected me yesterday. His easy conversation was keeping them interested, something that had attracted me as well.

Alfie was a feast to look at, with his stunning rock star appearance, great personality, and bad-boy charm. Sex appeal oozed out of him, and the girls were drawn to him like moths to a flame. As if he had sensed I was watching him, his head snapped up as he flicked his loose strand of hair out of his eyes, and he stared directly at me, holding my gaze.

When I began to smile at him, he turned away, completely ignoring me. Alfie turned his attention back to the girls and didn't look back in my direction again. Alfie leaned forward and brushed his hand over the cheek of one of the girls who sat Indian style on the grass in front of him.

After our earlier intimacy, I really didn't expect that at all. I was mortified and needed a way out of this situation. I rummaged in my backpack as if I'd forgotten something and spotted my cell phone.

Taking it out, I pretended to take a call, saying loudly, "Sorry, I didn't hear you, it was on vibrate." I turned away from him, throwing my head back, before I walked past him nodding as if someone was talking to me on the other end.

I didn't know what else to do except get away from him. Horrified at how he'd treated me, it put me in a funk for the rest of the afternoon, until I could get out of there.

When I was safe in the privacy of my car after class, I couldn't help but think about his behavior toward me today. What a contrast to the needy, funny guy I'd been with this morning.

It was like I never even fucking existed. He did say no strings, but he never said anything about not acknowledging me in public. *So what happened to the consideration he promised me?*

Switching on the radio; as if on cue, Adam Levine was singing *Lucky Strike* loudly and I felt he was singing it about me. The words were resonating in my ears.

The song sounded too familiar to the situation I had put myself in last night and this morning. I was disgusted with myself and what I had accepted as 'normal' just so that I could do that with him.

Feeling like I needed to rethink the arrangement, I wondered whether it would be enough to have sex with him with absolutely no connection outside of the bedroom. *What the hell happened to friends with benefits?* I was furious with his attitude. *What happened to Alfie's speech about respecting me?*

I called Mandy, and Will offered to pick me up early and grab something to eat before the gig. He seemed like a lovely genuine guy, but after the way Alfie had dismissed me, I would prefer to rely on myself for a while.

Not wishing Will to get the wrong idea, I told him that I may bring a friend with me, so I made my excuses around Saffy and told Will we'd meet him there. He sounded a little disappointed, but I reassured him that I was looking forward to getting to know everyone better and was looking forward to going to the bar.

Saffy was excited about going out with me. She had resigned herself to a night watching Matt Bomer in an episode of *White Collar*.

I teased that she was blowing him off to go out to have drinks, listen to music, and if she got lucky, a potential orgasm. She looked at me with a wry grin, telling me that my idea was a much better prospect, and was happy to swap her television boyfriend for a flesh-and-blood one. She set off to pamper herself, and I headed for the shower.

Applying a liberal amount of cleansing lotion on the cotton ball, I rubbed it over my face. I blew my long dark brown hair dry, and straightened it.

Even I had to admit I liked how I looked with my tanned skin, light blue eyes, and long dark hair. I looked different from the girl that arrived in Florida a few days ago. Then again, I was much less innocent now as well. My lips twisted wryly at myself in the mirror.

My attire was some black skinny jeans and a chic little raspberry red silk top, which hung off one shoulder with a black bra underneath. I slipped into some black patent stiletto ankle boots that gave me height and made my legs look longer.

When I walked into the sitting room, Saffy gave me a low whistle. "Sexy girl!! Who's the lucky guy?" She clapped then frowned. "This effort isn't for your new fuck buddy is it?" she said, wagging her finger at my outfit.

"Nope, he won't be there, I just feel like I need some attention tonight." I shrugged and smiled.

"Damn girl, you better pack a fly swatter dressed like that, especially with no man in tow," she teased.

Saffy flicked her hair back behind her shoulders. She looked adorably cute. Hell, she only had to look in the direction of a group of guys to have them all following her around, so my chances were increased for having her with me, not the other way around.

We left home twenty minutes after we intended to and were soon headed up the highway with the music blaring. "*Smoke on the Water*" by Deep Purple played, and we sang along very loudly, but Saffy was so out of tune that we giggled and gave up.

We didn't get far into the ride when she turned her attention to me, sitting sideways in the front passenger seat facing me.

"So?" she asks. I bunched my brow and darted my head to her before looking back at the road. I knew instinctively what she was asking. I also knew she was expecting me to dish the dirt, and I tried to play dumb.

"So… what?" I said, trying to sound innocent.

"Lily Parnell, come on, dish… and don't leave anything out!" I tried so hard to look casual. My heart sped up at having to say out loud what had happened.

"My 'fuck buddy', you mean?" I was still stalling from telling her.

Saffy snorted at me, "You mean there are others, girl?" She raised her eyebrow, pretending to be shocked.

"What do you want to know?" I tried to sound like there was nothing much to tell.

Saffy gave me an incredulous look, and huffed. "Lily! Are you going to hold out on me? I'm your best friend for fuck's sake," she explained, like this gave her rights to my every movement.

I rolled my eyes and took a deep breath exhaling slowly. "Well… he blew my mind and then some. It was great sex, some of it a little rough, some not so rough, and I had some orgasms. He wasn't selfish and took his time. Oh and did I mention I had some orgasms? Well, four orgasms to be precise, since last night. He also has a little surprise in his repertoire." I sounded like I knew what I was talking about. I'd heard loads of girls talk like this before. Saffy looked at me puzzled.

"What's the surprise?" She stared me down. Raising her eyebrow as she leaned forward listening intently.

"He's pierced," I stated. "He has an apadravya piercing, which feels incredible. It added a little... spice. It was different, you know?" I tried to sound like I had experience.

"Damn, I'm so jealous. That's fucking kinky. I've never had anyone with an apa before." She looked wistfully at me. "I hope I get some orgasms soon, I'm getting a tad frustrated. It's been nearly a week since my truck fuck," she mused, and we both laughed.

Alfie definitely wanted to give me pleasure, but I think he got off on that as much as having actual intercourse. I was never in doubt that I was there because of his needs, though.

I had felt fine about what happened at the time. I hadn't really thought too deeply about what I was doing, just that I was doing it... with him. Maybe I had experienced the female equivalent of men thinking with their dicks.

Alfie had made it clear that this wasn't ever going to be a hearts-and-flowers relationship. It was just primal lust and a physical attraction. He had been honest with me going into it, but I was still angry about being ignored by a man who I had been so intimate with just a few hours earlier.

Realizing that Saffy was still looking at me, I shrugged, "I don't know what to tell you, Saffy, he's definitely very experienced."

"Is that enough for you? We hooked up, had great sex, I came home." Saffy didn't argue with me, she seemed contented with my answer.

The bar wasn't difficult to find, and it was already packed out. Will waved at us from the bar, and Saffy clocked him. "Fuck me. That's the guy?" She was already staring at Will. I nodded as he wove his way through the tables to meet us. Saffy pulled me back whispering, "I'm calling first dibs." My lips stretched to smile at her when Will grabbed my arm.

He gently guided me back through the crowd to a table that was near the little stage area. Will put his hand on my shoulder and squeezed it a little. "Glad you could make it," he said as he pulled a chair out for me, and then Saffy.

Will told us that this place was one of the main venues for statewide live rock artists and that Mandy and Neil were well on their way to being famous. There was a band named Bad Buzz already rocking out what seemed to be original material.

Will shouted over the music, but I mainly read his lips because the lead guitarist's solo was reverberating through the bar, stopping all conversation. I cupped my hand round his ear and shouted loudly, "Saffy, my roommate," gesturing at her with my thumb to the side, by way of an introduction. Saffy already had designs on Will, and was peering seductively at him through lowered eyelashes.

Will's glance told me he wasn't immune to her come-on either. With her track record, I wondered if I would be driving back alone, or waiting for her to crawl out the back of his car with just- fucked hair and a satisfied look on her face.

The bar had a warehouse feel and was jam-packed with students. It felt great to be at a live music event.

Mandy and Neil went on stage to do their set. They really sounded fantastic together. At the end, I was in awe; Mandy's range was amazing, and her identity was most definitely that of a rock chick.

She aced everything that came out of her mouth and the crowd went nuts, hollering and cheering after each song. The girl could have made *Happy Birthday* sound amazing.

CHAPTER 10

I'M STALKING YOU

Singing my heart out, I was pleased that no one had a clue how much of a challenge it usually was for me to sing spontaneously. I was lost in the music, feeling a freedom here that I struggled with back home.

No one knew me there, or what my hang-ups were. I was practicing my new approach to life. Determined to be what I wanted to be, which included being comfortable singing.

When their set finished Mandy came over, and I jumped up hugging her. "Mandy, wow! I want to be just like you when I grow up!" Mandy giggled. She looked amused by my comment and slightly embarrassed at the attention.

"You and I are going to be great friends," she said hugging me again. I hugged Neil and congratulated him, then excused myself to go to the restroom before the next set started.

As I made my way back from the bathroom, I was looking around, taking in the venue, when I froze. Alfie was sitting near the back of the bar at a raised table area. He was with a beautiful, expensively dressed woman. She looked very sophisticated and maybe ten years older than him.

From his body language I could see he obviously liked her a lot. I felt sick watching the level of attention he was paying her, given what he'd done with me this morning.

Staring silently, I watched as he ran the back of his hand down her cheek, smiling at her. It made for quite an intimate scene. *Shit!* I pretended not to have noticed him.

The lady seemed to be doing all the talking and he sat, smiling, and began flipping a white napkin over and over absentmindedly while he listened intently to what she was saying.

Forcing myself to go forward, I began to walk back toward our table, glancing back at him from a distance. I could see that although he was still dressed casually, his appearance was much more polished than I'd seen before.

Alfie was wearing a crisp, white button-down shirt, his ink hidden by long sleeves, and a red suit vest. He looked effortlessly handsome and very sexy.

Wishing he would stand, so that I could assess the complete effect of his attire on him. I was more than curious as to whom the woman was. *More than that, if he was with her, why he had made a play for me, when he obviously has no shortage of female company?*

As I turned away, Alfie leaned forward to talk in

her ear. His female companion threw her head back, smiled, and clasped her hand over his.

Devastated and hurt, I also felt very ashamed that I hadn't thought of any other dynamics around our relationship. And I wondered how many others he might have the same arrangement with. My face must have been registering how I was feeling, because Saffy picked up on my mood immediately.

"What's the matter?" I shook my head.

"Nothing, why?" I asked hoping I sounded convincing.

"You look hurt. What's wrong, Lily?"

Laughing, I was hoping I'd pulled it off. "No, I'm not hurt, you're crazy." My voice came across as quite carefree. "I'm just a little tired." Saffy's furrowed brows told me she wasn't convinced, her eyes searched mine until she was satisfied, and I saw her face relax.

"I'm not tired at all, I have loads of pent up energy," she said, pushing herself back in her seat and staring at Will again. "In fact, I feel as if I could go on all night." Saffy's last comment wasn't lost on him. He smiled and bit his bottom lip and widened his eyes at her.

Looking between them, I giggled when she pretended to look embarrassed at this. Will and I both knew that Saffy's comment wasn't a Freudian slip.

She knew exactly what she had said and what she was doing. By the time the gig finished, Saffy was draped all over Will, his focus completely on her, and it was clear that I was going home alone.

Everyone had packed up and began to leave, so I made my way outside to my car after saying my goodbyes. Stepping into the warm air Alfie was right in front of me with the same woman he'd been with in the bar.

His car was parked about ten feet from the door. They were standing talking; Alfie had his back against his red Mustang. He'd already seen me step out, so I had no choice but to walk past him to get to my car.

Ignoring Alfie was easy because he didn't acknowledge me. The woman with him looked even more attractive close-up, and although she was older than him, I could see why Alfie would be drawn to someone like her.

I watched as he played the perfect gentleman for her. Settling her in his car first, he quietly closed the passenger door behind him. He walked around the hood. His eyes looked up briefly and darted in my direction. Then he slipped himself into the driver's side.

Dirty and disgusted with my-self, that was how his little show had left me. Another bout of shame hitting me, that I'd stooped so low as to sleep with him, and seeing how he was there in front of me, with her, I felt I really did need to revise my thoughts about him.

Especially with the negative feelings he was evoking in me. I was invisible when I walked past him, and I felt less than nothing to him.

During the drive back, I was ashamed at how far my moral compass had fallen in such a short amount of time. *What the hell is wrong with me?* I had guarded my V card vigorously until a week ago. Since then, I'd slept with not one but two guys.

Worse than that, I wasn't in a relationship with either of them, and I'd had sex with someone I'd only just met. I knew nothing about him at all, yet I'd put myself at risk with him. Even more shockingly, I was thrilled with the whole dangerous situation.

Alfie drove off first, and I sat in my car for a few minutes collecting my thoughts. I pushed the key into the ignition and fired up the engine.

Driving home gave me the creeps because I was the only person on the road. After a few miles I saw another car up ahead at the intersection. It made me feel less edgy to know someone else was still on the road.

Changing my mind as I drove past the intersection and recognized the familiar model was actually Alfie's car. The sight of him made me furious. I must have seemed so naïve to him when he singled me out at the college.

The way he did that, and how he'd behaved since this morning, had made him seem predatory. Especially when I realized that there was actually someone else in his life.

Alfie pulled out behind me and at first I thought he was just going the same way, until I turned into my condo building car lot. He had followed me home. My blood was boiling now.

As soon as he got out of his car, his stride was aggressive in his approach toward me. "Are you fucking following me, Lily?" His face was twisted in anger, and he spoke to me through gritted teeth.

My jaw dropped at his audacity, so I pointed at him animatedly, completely pissed at his attitude and tone toward me. "Don't flatter yourself. Who the fuck do you think you are, talking to me like this? You were behind me, remember?" I couldn't hide my rage as it laced my voice. "Technically, you were following me." I stared puzzled, and I was sure my anger was apparent by this point.

"What do you want?" I sounded worn out.

Strutting around me, he stopped and grabbed my arm, handling me a little roughly. Alfie's brows were furrowed in a frown. "I thought you were cool with how this works." I pulled my arm away in a violent movement and exhaled slowly, my hands went out in front of me pushing palms down in an effort to calm him.

"Okay, you've lost me. I'm not sure what you're talking about, but you're scaring me." He pushed his hair back.

"You followed me tonight, didn't you?"

Sneering, laughing at him. My temper was getting right up there now at his cheek. *Did he really think I'd follow him?* "I did? I followed *you* to *my* friends' gig you mean?" I snickered. "Damn, you're an asshole Alfie. You're so fucking self-absorbed, aren't you?"

I ranted on, "What time did you get there? Are you sure you didn't follow me? Oh, no. Wait…you wouldn't have done that with a woman in tow would you?" He looked sheepishly at me, his head briefly dropped, but he tilted it to make eye contact with me again.

"You were really there by chance?" he asks quietly.

Lustful eyes raked me over, his anger diminishing and being replaced with desire as he took in my appearance. The hint of a smirk reappeared. Immediately, I mentally kicked myself for wearing my boots with the fuck-me heels and my tight jeans with my favorite off the shoulder top.

I had known it was a sexy outfit when I wore it, but I didn't want to tease him with what I was wearing, especially when he was checking me out. I wondered if he thought I was stupid or just weak.

"Lily, what the fuck are you doing to me? I can't think straight around you. Do you realize how fucking turned on I am right now? You're so fucking sexy when you're mad." He tried to saddle up to me. I couldn't believe his complete shift of mood or his confidence.

"You're a shit, you know that?" I had to do something to put this Neanderthal in his place. "You're a good lay, but you're not *that* good." He seemed to wince at my lie. "Did she blow you out Alfie... your date? Is that why you're really here? Am I a bootie call?"

I began to pace. "What? She wouldn't put out like I did?" I strode inside my building and pushed the button for the elevator before folding my arms and willing it to hurry up. He followed me to the elevator before it arrived.

When the car arrived, the doors opened, and he pulled me inside. I stared him down and pushed the button for my floor, leaning against the wall of the elevator. His hands landed on either side of my head as he turned, pinning me against the wall.

"What you saw was a business meeting," he started, staring straight at me. I laughed.

"In a bar with live music and all that touchy-feely

stuff going on between you Alfie? More like the 'kinky business' you kept going on about earlier." He bent his elbows bringing his face nearer, so that his lips were just a fraction from mine.

He stared into my eyes, and I could feel his hot breath on my skin. The smell of his scent and his nearness stole my breath away. His stare was intimidating until his hair fell in front of his eyes, breaking the connection. He moved a hand to smooth it back.

When he did, I could see him trying to control his feelings. His frustration was beating right there, in his temple vein that was visibly pulsating.

Crossing my arms, I stepped to the side of him. "So… obviously you owe me an explanation, for the crazy stalking and the bi-polar behavior." I waved my hand in his direction, and he stood there silently until I spoke again. When he said nothing, I sighed. "I thought as much, you're full of shit Alfie. Go home."

The elevator door bell dinged its arrival on my floor, and I pushed myself off the wall making for the door. Alfie grabbed a hold of my wrist, pulling me back into him. No one had ever handled me that way before. "We're not done yet."

His jaw tightened and twitched again. "The hell we're not," I retorted, my voice louder as I tried to pull away from him. His grip tightened, and he swung me around, looking intently at me,

"Jesus, girl. Stop. Take a breath." I was speechless.

"M…me? You…" His face relaxed and there was a hint of a smile on his lips again.

I took advantage of his momentary lapse and

used my free hand to swipe his from my wrist. I placed both my hands on his chest and shoved him out of my way walking quickly to my door. He began to apologize. "Aw, come on, honey…" I turned on my heels to face him.

"I am *not* your honey. Go home, we're done for today." I opened my door and banged it shut with him on the other side.

Alfie knocked softly on the door. "Don't do this, Lily." His voice was soft through the door. The guy was infuriating. He'd started all of this with his paranoia.

"Go home. I'm not going to change my mind. If you don't leave I'm going to call the door guy to remove you." He didn't knock again, but I could hear him sigh and what I imagined was his head knocking softly against the door, then nothing. I heard the elevator arrive, and when I looked out of the peephole, he was gone.

Holding my wrist in my hand where he'd gripped me, his touch, even in anger, sent those familiar goose pimples coursing over my skin. My heart was still pounding rapidly in my chest.

Holly was working tonight, and I knew that Saffy wouldn't be home any time soon. Tears pricked my eyes and one escaped, streaking down my cheek. I sniffed and blinked, trying not to let the night end with me sobbing into my pillow.

What happened between Alfie and I made me feel desperately homesick, and I was about to ring Jack, until I remembered it was only 4am in the UK. I turned on my laptop and wrote a long, rambling email to him and copied it to Elle. I had just finished pouring my heart out to them when my cell beeped with a text alert.

SEXPERT: Sad face

I didn't reply. Alfie had made me so confused about myself. I had loved spending time with him last night and this morning, but hated what had come next.

Maybe I already saw things a lot differently from him, because all the fucked up stuff that's followed since made me wish I'd never met him. I pushed myself off the couch and went to my room.

Standing in the dark with just the glow of my laptop for light, I began to get ready for bed. I tugged at the hem of my top and pulled it off, the static electricity crackling loudly, making small bursts of light in the semi darkness.

Feeling sweltering hot, I thought living in Miami made everyone get clean, whether they wanted to or not. The shower was a godsend. I don't think I've managed more than about seven hours without one since I arrived. As I stepped under the shower my cell beeped again, so I quickly showered and rinsed off. Grabbing a towel, I sat on the bed to read the text.

CHAPTER 11

SPOONING

SEXPERT: Don't stay mad at me, Lily. Make-up sex is the best.

SEXPERT: What are you doing? Are you awake? Please don't stay mad, talk to me. :sad face.

I was confused; *what did he want from me?* It didn't seem like the carefree arrangement he'd proposed when we were at the college.

Pink Lady: I'm taking a shower and going to bed.

SEXPERT: Oh, sounds good to me… can I shower and have make- up sex?

**Pink Lady: Definitely not. I'm
pissed off, and I have a headache.**

**SEXPERT: #1 headache remedy
:smiley face**

**SEXPERT: Please, I don't want
to leave things like this.**

**Pink Lady: I'm so angry with
you, you need to redeem yourself.**

There was no denying his ability to get around
me, even if he was the cause of my low feelings. *How
could he be the cause and the cure?* I was already
mad at myself because I knew I was going to cave in
eventually.

I'd never felt more alone in my life, and I didn't
want to stay on my own tonight, but I most definitely
didn't intend on having sex with him.

**SEXPERT: How can I redeem
myself with a door between us?
I'd like to do my redeeming now.**

Pink Lady: Where are you?

SEXPERT: PEEPHOLE?

My jaw dropped, *he was outside my door?* I
wrapped myself in a towel, and pulled on some boy
short panties before going to check. As I looked
through the peephole, my cell buzzed again making
me jump.

SEXPERT: Are you objectifying me through the peephole? :ninja face.

Although I fought it, a smile played on my lips. Even though I tried to stay mad, he was too cute for his own good. I was also aware that I was vulnerable to his charms. Sighing, I opened the door.

Rushing to me, swung me around behind the door, and pressed his body flush to mine. Alfie's hand was instantly sifting my wet hair, while his mouth came toward mine.

Placing my hand between my face and his to stop him, Alfie kissed my fingers. His lips brushed against my hand, and I pushed him back. "No Alfie, this isn't a game; this isn't one of your sessions. If you want to speak to me, stay. If you want more than that, then you need to go elsewhere. I'm truly not interested."

"Thank you," he husked.

"For… allowing you to apologize? For, forgiving you for being a pig?" I sounded annoyed and exhaled loudly.

Alfie nodded and smirked. "Okay, I deserved that." His lips twisted to the side, then pursed before morphing into a half smile.

Turning to walk away, his glib attitude was making my temper rise again. I was too close to him and wanted some space between us so that I could think, but he caught the end of my towel, and I walked straight out of it. "Now, that's better." He grinned appreciatively. "But you need to lose the underwear, it's obstructing my view." He snickered.

Grabbing at my breasts to hide them, "You're fucking unbelievable, Alfie." I curled forward in an attempt to hide myself. He tried to reach out, but I smacked his hand and took the towel back.

"Stay there I'm getting dressed. I'll be back. Come near me and you're back on the other side of the door, you get me?" His smile was fixed, but then he realized I wasn't playing and it slowly deflated until his lips were settled back into position.

"Okay, I'll behave," he said, shaking his head low as if he knew he'd been defeated.

I quickly pulled on some sport shorts and a functional white cotton bra and finally a pink tank top then went back to the sitting room. "You want something to drink?" I asked walking around the edge of the counter and opening the fridge.

Reaching into the fridge, I grabbed myself a soda. "Water?" he asked. I pulled one from the door shelf and tossed it at him. He caught it in both hands and broke the seal, inhaling half of the bottle in no time.

I was careful not to sit near him, choosing to face him at one end of the couch. I curled up, hugged my knees, and he smiled.

Waggling my finger between us, I asked, "What is this, Alfie? What are we doing?" His eyes searched up into his brow, as if he was looking for the answer up there.

"Our arrangement?" he asked gnawing his bottom lip at the side.

"What are you doing with me, why are you doing this?" I said bluntly and took a sip of my soda.

"I don't understand why you hit me up for our little arrangement when you're dating already." He shifted himself on the couch and looked uncomfortable.

"I'm not dating her, and I never promised you anything, Lily." This was true, he hadn't.

"Yeah, but Alfie, you did all that intimate stuff with me, and you are with another woman the same night? That's just downright dog-like behavior." I sighed. "Why are you still here? Why didn't you go home? We owe each other nothing."

Nervous eyes flicked up to mine, and he moved toward me. "I didn't fuck her, only you, and it wasn't intimacy between us, it was sex."

Snickering at him, I said, "That makes all of it okay? You didn't fuck her? No? Why not Alfie… she wouldn't let you? I bet that pissed you off. You bought her dinner and she didn't put out for you. Makes me damn cheap, I only cost you an OJ." He started to move along the couch, and I held my finger up to stop him. "Tsk, do you want to leave? Don't come near me, I don't want you to touch me."

Alfie sighed. "It was business, and she paid for dinner." I glanced at his body language.

"Huh…so she paid, and you never got laid." I giggled. "You don't have the right idea about being a playboy do you?"

Stretching out the tension in his neck, he moved his head from one side to the other. I could see he was struggling with what to say. His hand began rubbing one side of it to get the kinks out of his muscles. "Can we just drop this, please?" He looked a little tired, and his eyes were pleading with me. I sensed that I wasn't going to get any answers tonight.

"Fine, it's late, I need my bed. You can stay, but I want you gone first thing." He smiled and nodded.

"Oh, and you're definitely not having sex with me, do you understand?" The smile died on his lips for the second time. "You try it, and I never come near you again."

"Can I lie beside you? I haven't slept with a woman in a long time." I think back to his comment about him doubting that we'd sleep together, and smiled.

"Yeah, sure, it'll be a novel experience for you, I'm sure."

I brushed my teeth and changed from my shorts to some short PJs, climbing onto the bed. It was too hot for sheets or the comforter. I curled up with my back to the bathroom door, where he was getting ready for bed. He seemed to be in there for a long time, and my eyes began to droop.

Bright light streaked across the room as the bathroom door opened, Alfie's silhouette briefly moved across the drapes. Turning to look, he was walked toward me wearing a towel low on his waist, before the timer light behind him went off.

Rolling my head back in the direction I was facing as the sight and scent of him was too alluring, I felt a deep dip in the mattress near me as he crawled into bed.

Alfie smelled incredible, and the cold, satiny skin on the back of his upper arm brushed mine as he settled himself down beside me. "Are you awake?"

His voice softly echoed out in the darkness. I didn't answer and tried to keep my breathing slow and steady so that he'd think I was asleep.

"Shit, I'm sorry Lily, I truly am. I don't ever want to hurt you," he whispered softly. I lay pretending to be asleep until I heard his breathing becoming deep and even. Then, I was exhausted and sleep eventually washed over me.

I could hear music when I woke up in the dull light of the room. The heavy blackout drapes kept most of the light out. Alfie's arm was tight around my waist. He was spooning with me, and his erection was digging into my back.

At first I just lay there, feeling his warmth around me, but I soon realized our thighs were actually stuck together with sweat.

Trying to move, felt like I was ripping a band aid off, slowly. Alfie shifted and moved his arm, and I quickly rolled away from him. Softly bouncing off the bed, I stood and scooted into the bathroom, locking the door.

The force of the water in the shower struck my hand as I turned on the faucet. I stuck my hand in to test the temperature and stepped in. Alfie was tempting, lying in my bed, but I was determined to fight my feelings on this.

Alfie's looks, charm, and magnetism were a lethal combination with my inexperience. I had no defenses against him. Alfie was capable of making me do stuff I would have disowned friends for doing.

I could've reasoned with myself why a guy like him wasn't taken. Alfie isn't boyfriend material. He did warn me that he didn't do emotional relationships, and from what I saw last night, he was definitely a player.

It's a pity, because the guy was a sexy, gorgeous mess for all his fucked-up-ness. But I was afraid he was getting under my skin. I opened the bathroom door and could hear music coming from the sitting room. Someone was home. I groaned inwardly as I watched Alfie lying on my bed, still sleeping

Sneaking out of the bedroom, I went to find Holly who was sitting on the couch looking washed-out after her night shift, and crunching on some toast. It smelled heavenly. "Sorry Lily, I didn't think anyone was home. Saffy isn't here, and I figured you had both gone somewhere last night after the gig."

Quickly glancing at the bedroom door, I spoke softly, hoping I didn't wake Alfie. I didn't want Holly to know he was there. "I know she hooked up with some new people I met at college yesterday."

"Yeah? Tell me more, I'm missing out on all this sex, working night shifts." She smiled tiredly.

"Well, really, it's Saffy's story to tell, but she's with a guy called Will." I told her about meeting Mandy, Neil, and Will yesterday and Mandy's invite to the bar.

"And?"

I laughed softly. "Saffy was horny!" Holly didn't need to be told anything else.

Holly got up from the table and walked away muttering, "All these fucking orgasms." She put on her thickest Texas accent and drawled, "I'm like Arizona here, hot and dry." I couldn't help giggling at her. "I'm off to bed. Maybe I'll get lucky in my dreams."

Disappearing through her bedroom door, I saw her kick it closed with her heel. It made a loud bang, and my eyes darted back to my bedroom door again. A sudden need to get Alfie out before she woke and before Saffy came home hit me.

Making some coffee and went to wake him. He was already in the shower. "Alfie, we need to move, I have to be on campus in less than an hour." I pulled on a green skater dress over some functional underwear and matching pumps and was ready to leave when he came back into the room.

"You look beautiful. Can I see you later?" he asked.

"Let me think about that. I'm not sure what is happening today." I was expecting some resistance, but I think that Alfie knew he was on thin ice after last night, and he let it go.

On the way to college, I was alone. He'd driven his own car. Something he said as we were walking to our cars made me think he wasn't in the same year as me though. I had already thought he was a few years older, and maybe a mature student.

I was going to ask him about it, and about ignoring me when we got to college, but a lawn truck shed a load of cuttings in front of me, and I got a fright. I was just glad to get to college in one piece.

When I arrived there at the same time and parked next to him in the campus car lot, he got out, slammed his door, and locked his car. Without looking at me he said, "I'll text you later," and he was gone.

Taking a hold of my guitar and rucksack from the trunk, I headed off to find Mandy, who was sitting in the canteen nursing a coffee and a sore head.

"You were fantastic last night Mandy, you are very talented!" Mandy's face immediately brightened. "Thank you honey, I'm always pleased to get feedback from fellow musicians."

"Do you sing?" She looked at me in anticipation.

Nodding hesitantly, I said, "Yeah, but I'm a bit worried about performing here, everyone I've heard so far are on a different plain from back home."

"Nonsense." She smiled warmly at me. "Listen, how about we do some jamming at lunchtime?"

"Writing and rhetoric is first up this morning, so I'll be ready for some escapism," I said, rolling my eyes and Mandy smiled, nodding her head in agreement.

"It isn't my one of my strengths," she admitted.

"I don't think there is anything stronger than your voice Mandy." I could see what I told her had meant a lot to her, and it was dawning on me that Mandy wasn't as confident as she first appeared.

"You've got yourself a date for lunch." I smiled, squeezing her hand before I dropped it and hitched my guitar over my shoulder. We turned and headed in the direction of our first class of the day.

The morning passed quickly and by lunch break, I felt that although there was a lot to take on technically, I was able to apply what I was learning to things I had written previously.

My appetite had left me, so I just pulled an apple from my backpack, and I sat on the lawn flicking through my notation pad for a score that I had been working on in the UK. I was deep in thought about how to improve this when I heard Mandy call out to me.

"Lily honey, we're just going to get started, are you coming?" I gathered my things and went over to join them. There were a couple of other people from Will's class that had also joined us.

Will looked a little coy. I smiled at him, and he took my hand kissing my cheek. I squeezed his hand to let him know that I was cool with him hooking up with my friend.

I stupidly inquired, "Good night?"

Coughing at my question, Will blushed and sputtered, clearing his throat, "Eh, yeah, it was, um, very cool."

Blushing but feeling bold, I leaned forward and whispered, "Don't worry your secrets are safe with me." Will dug me in the ribs, and grinned wickedly at me. I blushed again, and he pulled me in for a hug.

CHAPTER 12

WHAT GOES AROUND

When it came down to all of us jamming, we meshed really well together. Will played the saxophone, amongst other instruments, and he was incredibly talented. We played a few well-known tunes together as a group first to learn the group's strengths.

There was a guy, Landon, who did beat boxing and produced the most ridiculously complicated bass beat percussions, adding a totally different dimension to our instruments.

When we were done, Will asked me if I could play Oasis *Wonderwall* so he could accompany me on sax, just as a duet.

I felt a little nervous as we were under the scrutiny of our peers, and we had never played together before. I needn't have worried though, because just a few bars into the piece, and I was lost in the music.

Will's playing was like a knife gliding through butter, and his arrangement was amazing. His intuition for playing at certain points during the piece gave it a unique sound.

Everyone sat around in silence apart from the beat boxer. The guy couldn't contain himself a few times, but again, his timing was impeccable. Cheering, loud clapping, and a few piercing whistles came from the people watching, which told us that they had enjoyed it as much as we had.

Looking beyond the people sitting with us, I noticed that a lot of the other students had stopped to listen.

My cheeks stained red when I noticed Alfie, nervous about what he was thinking. Standing with his arms folded, he grinned and winked at me when our eyes met. I looked away and hugged Will.

When I looked back, Alfie's eyes had darkened and his brow formed a crease in the middle of his eyes, a fleeting look of worry in them, before he smirked and his face brightened. Striding over, he chatted to the group, congratulating Will on his performance and inviting him and indeed, everyone sitting there, to a beach party performance later that evening.

Informing us there was going to be a stage and that some artists were going to be welcomed to showcase before the main artist's performance. The band that was scheduled to perform was quite well-known in the state.

Will, Mandy, and Neil really wanted to go so we arranged that we'd be there. I noticed that Alfie still didn't acknowledge me personally during this.

No one seemed to notice that he didn't speak to me or comment about me. Will turned and looked tentatively at me. "Do you want to come and do that again tonight?"

I was about to refuse when he added, "It's not every day I get an opportunity to perform in public with my saxophone. People either want a guy with a guitar, or if I do get to play, it's usually a one minute instrumental for someone else's showcase." *When he put it like that, how could I say no to him?*

"Sure," I agreed. "We'll need another rehearsal before we play to an audience tonight though." I frowned.

"Why? You were fucking perfect! You play beautifully, there's so much passion in your performance. Don't underestimate your talent, it's amazing, honey. I can't believe my luck, playing with you."

Mandy nodded as well. "Do you really have no idea how great you are, Lily? We really need to do something together. I so want to perform with you, it'll be a blast." She looked at me genuinely, but I thought that she was just being kind.

Arriving home a little after five, I'd found it difficult to concentrate after lunch. My mind kept wandering, thinking of Alfie, and how he'd been watching us play. I wondered if I'd misread his fleeting reaction to Will hugging me. I couldn't understand it, when he's already told me that he has no issues with me forming emotional attachments elsewhere.

Holly was just arriving back from the beach when I arrived at the entrance of the apartment block.

"Thank goodness I finally have a few days off," she said. "Where are we headed tonight, I need a night out." I told her about my day and the beach party. "Well hell, Saffy and I need to come and support our little British contingency." She smiled.

"Oh great, so now I'm even more nervous," I mock groaned, but was pleased that I was going to have familiar faces there who loved me. Saffy came breezing in, with a new pencil skirt and blue satin blouse on. She was glowing.

The outfit was great and she seemed more than happy with her date last night. "Well, howdy girlfriends," she gushed humorously. Holly groaned, "Oh great, she's got the fucked-senseless-and-now-gloating face on. We're in trouble Lily." Saffy pretended to look hurt, but her face slowly stretched into a big grin.

Slapping her hand over her heart, she squealed, "Oh. My. God! He. Is. A. Fucking. Stud. Girls! That man had me coming every which way, until I didn't know what day it was. He must be related to James Deen. Talk about keeping me up all night. He actually growled and ripped my fucking panties off."

"Who's James Deen?" I asked innocently. Holly and Saffy's heads snapped round to stare at me.

Holly cocked her brow at me. "Seriously, Lily?" Dismissing my question completely and turning her attention back to Saffy. Holly threw her hands up covering her ears and shaking her head vigorously. "I don't want to hear any more, you're taking liberties now. Everyone's having orgasms but me."

Saffy chuckled wickedly and then tried to comfort her. "Okay, honey, we'll make it our mission to get you laid tonight, won't we Lily?"

I raised an eyebrow, giggling now too. "Well, we'll try to find you a man to give you some attention, but as for getting you laid, I think he'd have to take over from us."

Picking up some laundry I'd folded earlier, I began to make my way to my bedroom, still laughing. Saffy called out to me, "Lily… if you don't know who James Dean is… you seriously need to google him."

Pampering ourselves meant the apartment smelled of perfume, various bath foams, body sprays, and hair products. I was nervous as hell about performing. When I felt nervous I always power dressed using my sexuality to help me feel less self-conscious and more confident.

Both girls gave me a gasp of approval when they saw me. "Wow. Wow. Wow," said Holly. They both looked great, but they had dressed in shorts and blouses, some lovely accessories. They were so effortlessly pretty anyway.

They could have worn old overalls and still looked sexy. I had purposely dressed to impress though. If I was going to make an ass of myself up on some stage, I would at least look hot doing it.

My attire for the evening was a tight bronze and black sequined vest top with shorts that made my ass look a little bigger than it actually was.

I knew my legs looked good, but they looked much longer in my little shorts and my black Christian Louboutin heels, with their signature red soles. Saffy looked puzzled and stared at my feet. "Fuck-me shoes to the beach?"

129

Giggling at her description, I nodded, "We're eating first, right? I have some strappy roman sandals for the beach, but I wanted to wear these to perform in, then if I bomb they won't remember the guitar playing."

They both giggled at me. "You are not going to bomb, honey. You are shit hot on that thing." Saffy motioned her head toward my guitar, which was leaning on the wall near the window. "Stop worrying."

Holly continued, "Besides, men will be stunned into silence just by the sight of you, Lily. Most won't hear you play a note, they'll be too busy fantasizing." I blushed and she threw her head back chuckling. "You are way too innocent for your own good," she teased.

I hadn't really noticed men looking at me at home. Sure, guys hit on me, and Jack told me I was hot, but I seemed to be getting more attention here than I had in London.

This was especially true when I went out with my girlfriends. Saffy and Holly had teased me about being a man-magnet the few times we'd been out together. I couldn't see it myself, thinking that they were the ones that were attracting the attention.

We walked into the Italian restaurant, and the smell of garlic and parmesan hit me immediately, making my stomach growl. I inhaled deeply, and my stomach suddenly ached for food. Holly groaned, "I'm starving." She lifted a menu from the menu holder at the front desk and flicked through it.

There were a few guys sitting at the bar near the reservation desk and a fabulously hot looking guy with blond hair and tanned and toned muscles swivelled around on his bar stool to look at us.

Appreciative eyes scanned over all of us before settling on Holly. His mouth spread into a wide smile. "At last! There you are honey. I've been waiting for you forever. " Holly turned and looked behind her expecting someone to be there.

Saffy and I noticed her and giggled loudly. Holly realized he was talking to her and smiled broadly at his forwardness. Saffy dug me in the ribs and nodded for me to look at Holly's wide mouth. The guy gave her a broad smile and winked at her.

Holly was, naturally, a very forward girl, and walked over to him, gently squeezing his knee. "Don't get me wrong, I like what I see, but I'm starving for food right at the moment. My energy levels need recharging an' all, but if the entrée doesn't satisfy me, I may need dessert."

Drawing in a sharp breath as she raked him over with her eyes, she leaned into him with her cleavage almost in line with his mouth.

Glancing at it and smirking, he looked back up at her as she murmured in a seductive low voice. "So… don't go running off anywhere just yet, I might get back to you, honey!" She winked.

Stepping back, she blew him a kiss, and turned back to us as we were about to be seated. "Just as well I hadn't planned to leave just yet, the night is still young," he called after her chuckling.

Holly sat down and stared at us both, picked her napkin up and flicked it across her lap saying, "That my girls, is how you pick up a guy."

We ordered the delicious lasagna, garlic bread,

and red wine, and it tasted amazing. Holly wouldn't eat the garlic bread for the obvious reason sitting at the bar. I prompted the girls after checking the time. I didn't want to be late meeting Will.

I needed another quick rehearsal with him before we took our spot on stage. "Okay girls we need to head out, I don't want to be late for my first proper gig here."

Saffy caught our waiter Ben's attention, and we settled the bill, getting up to leave. We passed the hot guys again. "You're leaving us?" Holly's suitor said.

Holly eyed him up and down. "We're going to a gig on the beach, Lily's playing. I didn't get time for dessert, and I'm still hungry, you want to come?"

The guy jumped down from his bar stool and grinned at his friends. "I always want to come, honey, but if I have to sit through some music to make it happen, I'm game."

Holly nodded, her eyes widening and she licked her lips and smirked. "Honey, you're just my kind of guy." She put her hand out and he put his in hers, but yanked her to him.

Her hand went close to his chest, and he placed his arm around her shoulder.

"Brett," he cooed.

We squeezed into my little car after I changed into my sandals and drove to the beach park. Will was waiting in front of the venue for us. I smiled, and he looked awkward again when he saw that Saffy and Holly were with me.

He walked over and hugged me. I whispered, "Don't worry about me Will. Saffy likes you. Don't feel awkward about it around me." He smiled and squeezed my hand appreciatively, then smiled and winked at Saffy.

"Are you nervous?" He smiled, but was concerned for me.

"Nervous? Nope. Petrified, maybe, " I said, pulling my lips into a twist. He chuckled putting his hand around my shoulder, and hugged me to him again.

Saffy moved in, wrapping her arms around his waist, and pulled him closer to her. His arm dropped from me, and she moved forward and began kissing him.

Poor Will looked disheveled when she was done with him, and Holly and I giggled. I think his pants suddenly shrunk, and he adjusted himself by stretching his leg out.

This didn't go unnoticed by Holly, who said, "Wow, Saffy that's a long tongue you have there. You've managed to fiddle all the way down to Will's pants, honey!" Will cleared his throat, stifled a smirk, and turned away awkwardly.

He excused us, grabbing me, and told the girls that we needed to find Alfie. We still had to tune up and grab a quick rehearsal. Alfie was backstage with an entourage following him around. "Hey man!" he said to Will. "All set?" Will gave him the thumbs- up. "Yeah, we're good. This is Lily, who's playing acoustic guitar with me."

Alfie ignored me completely, and began telling Will where he needed to be and what time we'd be up, before someone called him and Alfie moved away to deal with them.

Will looked straight at me, his brows bunched

together. "I don't know the guy, but he needs to get some fucking manners. Sorry about that, honey."

Shrugging, I tried to look as though it hadn't affected me. "Let it go, Will, don't let it spoil things for you," I cooed but he was still scowling.

"You're just too nice!" he commented. "If he ignored me, I'd put him on his ass," he said.

The talent on show during the party was of a high standard, they all seemed to be quite accomplished musicians and serious about their craft. I felt a little out of my league and insecure about my ability as a performer.

By the time we were up, I had changed my shoes again and amazingly, they gave me the confidence boost to push myself out there on stage. Will took my hand, kissed my temple, and whispered, "You look beautiful and you're going to be amazing enjoy it, Lily." He made sure I was comfortably seated before we began.

I could see he didn't want to screw this up by rushing things. Will played the intro for the song alone and the crowd cheered. I came in with my guitar.

We sounded great without words, just the music and the arrangement that Will had cleverly put together.

Will did his instrumental pieces, then I joined back in as agreed and the piece ended. The crowd was cheering for more, and Alfie called out to Will, "They're going to let you run, you need something else." *Shit!*

"Okay, Clapton, *Wonderful Tonight*?" Will asked. It was a good choice. I've never met anyone that didn't like Eric Clapton's music.

"Okay, but tell them we haven't rehearsed it, and I'm not singing."

Will shushed the crowd. "Lily and I only met yesterday, so we're still learning about each other through our music here. We'll play this one and you'll forgive us if it doesn't pan out okay... and you can sing along if you want." The crowd gave another ripple of applause.

Will played the intro, and the crowd erupted in applause at recognition of the song. Will grinned between breaths, and I picked up the chords. I had to admit we sounded amazing. The crowd was all singing loudly, and I didn't really want it to end. Afterwards, the party-goers were really appreciative, clapping loudly.

CHAPTER 13

PLAYING GAMES

We rushed off stage, out of the bright lights and into the darkness. Will grabbed me, lifting me up and swung me around. He bent down and planted a kiss square on my lips. I was laughing, still on a high from the crowd, until I saw Saffy scowling at me. "Wow, Will," I teased, "got caught up in the moment. You have the wrong woman."

Will smirked. "Sorry Lily, I'm just stoked." He looked sheepishly at Saffy. "Hey there!" he husked, stretching his hand out to her, smiling. She took it and he pulled her in close and kissed her softly.

Clearing my throat as a warning, when I saw a few people waiting to speak with us, Will joined me and spoke to the small group that had formed. A couple of club and bar owners wanted to hire us and left business cards. Will was very adept at handling this.

Mandy, Neil, Holly, and Brett were at the beach

bar. "You were both brilliant, I can't wait to work with you on something," Mandy said keenly. Neil fist bumped his friend and hugged me to one side of him, lifting me off the floor.

"Great gig honey, you're sneaky, packing all that talent into a cute little package… oh and… even greater shoes." He winked. Mandy swatted him on the arm.

Saffy said, "Yeah, they're Lily's fuck-me shoes, aren't they just fantastic?"

Embarrassed by Saffy, I briefly wished the floor could have opened and swallowed me. I grabbed my purse. "Let me get the drinks please," I pleaded. I rummaged in my purse and saw there was a text message on my cell.

SEXPERT: FUCKING ACE! WOW I Love the fuck-me killer heels.

Annoyed that he'd ignored me again, I texted him back.

Pink Lady: The fuck-me heels are reserved for emotional fucking with attention to detail by the 'fuckee'.

SEXPERT: You're a very sexy lady, when I saw you today on campus playing I wanted to scoop you up, take you home and fuck you senseless. When I heard you play, you were inspiring and

altogether too fucking hot.

Pink Lady: Why do you ignore me?

SEXPERT: Ignore you? What am I doing now?

Pink Lady: Sitting naked holding your dick?

SEXPERT: LMAO, I meant I'm not ignoring you.

Pink Lady: You have a tongue in your head, use it.

SEXPERT: I used my tongue very well yesterday don't you think? As for ignoring you…do you want people to know I'm your fuck buddy?

Pink Lady: Hmm, and that's why you ignore me?

SEXPERT: hence the distant stance. Who would ever think my tongue had been where others can only dream of?

Pink Lady: Hmm…good point. Let me think about that, maybe I'll get back to you.

SEXPERT: Can you do that quickly or I am in danger of creaming my pants at the sight of you.

Pink Lady: Easy remedy, take your pants off.

SEXPERT: I'd much rather you took them off.

Pink Lady: Take my pants off? I am not wearing pants in case you hadn't noticed.

SEXPERT: Oh, I noticed all right, no panties either. I saw the slightest hint of pink when you bent to put your guitar in its case with your legs open

Pink Lady: Pervert! You shouldn't have been looking.

SEXPERT: You shouldn't wear clothes that get you noticed then! Let's get the fuck out of here

Pink Lady: I came in a cab with the others.

SEXPERT: I don't want to know what you did in the cab or who with. Meet me at mine.

I laughed at the last comment. I was buzzing after all the attention. Alfie's playful mood was also turning me on. He was right, if we were going to do this, then we didn't need anyone judging us for it. I felt better now that I knew he was protecting our relationship by not drawing attention to us.

> **Pink Lady: I'll come to your place.**

> **SEXPERT: Grammatical error there my dear, you mean you'll come *at* my place, but you'll beg first. See you at mine in 30.**

Making my excuses, I told Saffy, Holly, and the others, that I needed to be elsewhere. I whispered to Holly, "Don't wait up." Saffy winked, and I called a cab to take me to Alfie's house.

When I pulled up, he was already home. He opened the door, and his eyes had a naughty glint that told me that he was fired up and ready to go.

I had just about got through the door when his arm slid around my waist, twisting me in a half turn. He caught the door with his heel, and it closed with a bang behind me. He dipped slightly and caught my legs in his arm just above my knees, lifting me up to cradle me in his arms.

Alfie's mouth came crashing down on mine as he walked upstairs with me to his bedroom. I was in heaven. The room was softly lit, and he placed me down gently on his bed. Sliding his knee between my legs, he pushed them apart before leaning in on me.

Crawling over me, Alfie took most of his weight

on his elbows. Our pelvises were mostly aligned so that his erection rubbed hard against me, through the fabric of our clothing and against my clitoris. I gasped at the feel of him doing amazing things to my body while I was still fully dressed.

Grinning at my reaction, he began to pepper kisses around my neck and collarbone, leaning in to kiss my mouth hungrily.

Alfie's tongue lashed inside my mouth, duelling with mine, until he seemed to give up and caught my bottom lip in his mouth, sucking it. This sent jolts of electrical pulses running through my veins.

Drawing his head back and balancing on one elbow, he shifted his weight a little to see me. "Jesus, baby, you made me so fucking horny tonight in your fuck-me heels." I laughed and arched my head back on the bed.

Alfie quickly took advantage of this and licked up my neck to my earlobe, then nuzzled my neck. The effect this had on me was electrifying, and goose bumps crept over my skin, my moist sex throbbed, and I groaned loudly. "Oh your sounds turn me on so much," he murmured huskily to me.

Jumping off of the bed, he ran downstairs, leaving me wondering *WTF?* He returned a few minutes later with a white carrier bag full of stuff. "What do you have there?" I asked puzzled. "Supplies!" he said, grinning wickedly. "Take all your clothes off… leave the heels on. I want to fuck you in those…please, please," he said making a praying motion with his hands.

I laughed hard at his request. "Well, there was emotion in your voice when you pleaded with me there," I replied playfully.

"Pinch me, am I alive or did I died and I'm in heaven, cuz I swear you've been killing me since I met you," he mused. I giggled at him, it may not have been emotional, but he was funny and sexy.

Raising my eyebrow at him, I asked, "Do you always say what other people think? Don't you have a 'thinking' voice Alfie?" He winked grinning again.

"Well… If my 'thinking' voice were to become my out- loud voice, then you really would have to worry." He wiggled his brows and began tickling me by drawing his fingers down my ribs.

Placing his mouth over mine in a sensual kiss this time, suddenly we were serious again. I felt the chemistry build between us, not to mention his restrained cock that appeared to be straining in his pants.

Moving position to adjust himself, he groaned, and I couldn't decide if the experience was more painful for him feeling it, or me watching him suffering. "Stand up," I commanded boldly. Alfie stood, and I caught his zipper and ticked it down slowly. He gasped when my hand brushed over his erect cock just a few threads away behind his boxer shorts.

Pulling his jeans down below his knees, I told him to take them off, freeing his straining bulge. His boxers tented, and I giggled at how ridiculous his size was. Hooking my fingers inside the waistband of his jeans, I unveiled his cock, as I drew his boxers down his legs.

Alfie's thick, veiny, wide cock sprung forcefully toward me at its release. He shucked his boxers off and threw them onto the pile of clothes on the floor then grabbed his bag of "supplies." He delved into it and produced a bottle of champagne and a tub of ice cream. He paused to smirk at me, before setting them on the nightstand.

Sitting on the edge of the bed, Alfie was standing in front of me. Cupping his balls in my hand, the skin was smooth. Gasping, he closed his eyes.

I began to massage his scrotum and stroked a finger delicately up the shaft of his cock and very lightly tapped my finger on his apa and glans. He gave me that sexy guttural sound he did in approval.

Alfie's breath hitched, and he seemed to hold it for a second before letting out a low moan. I felt my slick juices leak onto my thigh when he did this. I rubbed his glans with my thumb and saw a little pre cum escape from the slit. I massaged this around him and continued to twirl around his apa.

He rolled his head back, his eyes closed, and I moved my palms on either side of his cock, sandwiching it and rubbing it gently up and down. I saw more pre cum escape, and pressed my lips to his glans, taking just the mushroom shape into my mouth and supped it lightly, before sucking a little harder. "Damn," he growled.

I allowed my lips to linger, kissing his head, and rubbed my tongue flatly over it. He sucked in a breath of air hard. Gathering my hair into a ponytail, he held it and thrust himself deeper into my mouth, groaning loudly, "Jesus, ohhh, yeah! Just like that. There you go." He stared down at me gripping my hair from behind tugging it lightly. "Look at me, Lily."

Staring up into his eyes, as he said this, and I

143

sucked harder. "You like that, huh?" I moaned long and loud into him, sending vibrations through his sensitive flesh, and his legs began shaking. I took all of his cock in my mouth, and he growled again.

Alfie pulled away. "Enough, sweetheart. I don't want to come yet, I want to come inside you." He held my gaze and smiled slowly at me, seducing me all over again. He pulled me level with him and started undressing me. His hands were slightly trembling.

"You're so fucking lovely," he purred into my neck before pulling my short pants off, and gasping at my waxed mound.

The color of his hazel eyes changed instantly, taking on a greener look, as he studied my sex. He stroked me gently with all of his fingers, his hand side on, across the slit of my folds, and sucked his fingers, licking them one by one.

He was grinning and moaning as he did this. My juices seeped from my seam. I wanted him so badly I was whimpering and squirming with every touch.

He turned me inside out with his charm, looks, touch, smell, taste. No one has ever made me feel like this, and I lost myself to him when we were together. Alfie increased the pressure of his hand after the first few strokes, increasing the sensitivity in my clitoris.

The buzz lasted longer with all four fingers being drawn lightly down my folds from my clitoris to my puckered anus, with the slightest touch.

He rubbed on both sides of the hood of my clit, then bent down and blew a BRRRRRRRR on it, making me laugh and instantly producing more juices as the vibrations tickled me in the most pleasurable way. I giggled and squirmed again. "It's too tickly." Snickering, I tried to push his head away from me.

Alfie sat up and knelt back, grinning, his eyes widening playfully at me. "Yum!" His fingers wrapped around the hem of my top and he scooped it over my head,

"I fucking love this top!" he said, "It makes your tits so pert."

Swatting his arm, I said, "Hey, they are pert!"

Contemplated what I had just told him, Alfie threw the top to the floor then nodded, "Point taken."

Leaning forward, he turned his attention back to my breasts, teasing a nipple between his lips, and stretching before letting go and blowing lightly on it.

Feeling no shame whatsoever, I was lying with my body on display for him, my arms relaxed above my head. Alfie was watching me, his eyes sparking with want as he stroked me, taking me in.

Tracing my tattoo again. "This is so fucking sexy, Lily, It's so fucking unexpected, you don't seem like the kind of girl to have a tattoo," he said as his fingers traced around my thigh.

I shivered as he ran his finger over it. He moved his head over my belly and nibbled at my piercing. He stared up at me watching him, a crooked smile passed over his lips.

When I asked about the tiny intricate tattoo he had on the back of his hand under his thumb, I actually saw emotion.

Alfie had tears in his eyes when he told me about it. The script writing around it could only be read by people who were intimate with him. It said, "We look down on each other Mom."

He explained that he put the angel on the muscle under his thumb, so that when he strummed his guitar, he would always be reminded of his mom, who taught him to play, and who died when he was eighteen.

The last thing she had said to him was, "Always remember I'm looking down on you honey, and you will never feel alone."

I felt that this creative gesture was an amazing memorial to his mother. It definitely didn't lend itself to him not doing the emotional thing he kept banging on about. When he spoke his eyes clearly displayed his changing emotions, and it was the only serious feeling I've seen from him.

I was fascinated by his eyes and how they displayed his changing moods. I'd never known that before with anyone else. They shined when he was being playful, had a definite glint when he was being cheeky and flirty, and were more hooded and darker in his seductive phase with a much more vibrant green and serious look, depicting his raw lust.

Watching him lust after me turned me on so much. I was watching him watch me and seeing the effect my body had on him when I was just lying there. He seemed so into me when he was with me, and I wished that we could have this relationship all the time instead of hiding away.

I was having the time of my life when I was with him, yet I wasn't allowed to feel anything emotionally. I knew that I would have to play it cool for Alfie to continue to want me.

There were no illusions that if I was to suddenly express anything other than a physical attraction for

him that Alfie would be gone, and I wasn't ready to
let him go just yet.

CHAPTER 14

DESSERT

Alfie sat up, and rested back on his heels. "Hey, I nearly forgot… you want some ice cream?"

My eyebrows furrowed and looked at him skeptically. "Now?"

Grinning widely, he nodded, "Oh, yeah, especially now!" He looked animatedly, right before he grabbed the bag of supplies.

Taking a tub of vanilla ice cream in his hand, he scooped some out with his fingers. "Here," he said. Alfie pushed some of it into my mouth with his fingers before I could protest.

It was runny and had begun to melt. Some ran down his arm almost to his elbow. He quickly tried to lick it, but I grabbed his arm and licked and sucked his arm clean. He shuddered at my touch, "Stop. This is my trick," he scowled at me.

- Taking some more ice cream in his fingers and fed it to me again. The coldness was stark contrast to the hot, sensual feelings of arousal running inside of me.

Alfie's mouth was on mine as soon as he'd scooped ice cream in it, licking and sucking my tongue and lips with his hot mouth. It was so hot. I moaned long and loudly, "Ohhh." He drove me insane with the feelings of lust he was triggering deep inside me.

Shivering, he gave me chills, and my folds were swollen as my sensitive flesh ached for him. The whole thing was so erotic. His hand fell between my thighs. "Aha. That turned you on a little, hmm?" My lust filled eyes locked into his, and I was pleading with him to take me.

I was so wet and aching to have him inside me now, and I couldn't stop squirming. He took some more ice cream and smeared it on my breasts, it was freezing. "Argh, oh, God, don't…" I squirmed again trying to crawl and get away.

Pinning me down by my hips, he chuckled, and licked off the cold, melting ice cream. He sucked my nipples hard, and the sensation was incredible. "Christ." Alfie licked around my areola and sucked hard, sometimes chuckling at me when I squirmed, sending pangs of ecstasy to my loins.

He scooped more onto my stomach and used his tongue to lick it into my belly button, then his mouth formed a vacuum over it as he sucked it out again. His cold hands gripped either side of me. "Don't worry," he whispered playfully. "I'll be sure to lick you clean girl."

I shivered and shook, my blood was on fire. "Please Alfie. Please I need you inside me," I pleaded as I squirmed and writhed around. He continued to hold me in place as he enjoyed my body.

Suddenly he sat up, offering me a reprieve, and opened the champagne. "Want some?" He waved the bottle from side to side. He popped the cork, and it banged loudly.

Alfie didn't blink when it fizzed and overflowed onto the bed. The cork disappeared toward the oak dresser in the corner of the room. He quickly put his mouth around the neck to try to catch it, but it was too fizzy and the gas forced some out of his mouth as he chuckled.

He took some champagne in his mouth and spurted it into mine. I swallowed a huge mouthful, a trickle escaping from my mouth. The alcohol burned my throat a bit on the way down.

"That's better!" he said, pouring more into my belly button and licking and supping at the little puddle he'd made. "You taste so sweet honey! You're ruining me, you know that?" His voice was serious and ragged when he said it.

Pushing his head away, I tried to protest. "That's not fair, you are driving me insane here with all of this, and I don't get to do anything." Alfie pulled himself away and flopped on the bed, lying semi recumbent, with the champagne bottle in his hand. "Oh, so you *do* want to play now, eh?"

Pouring a little of the champagne down his chest, Alfie gestured playfully at his belly. "Go on then, give it your best shot!" I sat up and put my hand in the tub.

The ice cream was really runny now, and I scooped some out dripping it into spots on his belly to mingle with the champagne already there. He screamed, and bent double.

"Ah, not so bold now are you?" I teased pushing him back. It was good to be in charge of him for a few minutes.

Smearing it up over his chest and stomach, I watched his reaction. "Jesus Christ, that's freezing…oh…fuck." His mouth made a silent scream of shock. I giggled as I licked and sucked my way down his body as he replicated the effect it had on me, intermittently shivering and moaning.

Alfie's eyes met mine. "Oh fuck, honey, you are so fucking incredible. How did I live without you?" I hesitated when he said this. Swallowing audibly, I shook his remark off as heat-of-the-moment and dragged my tongued all the way down his happy trail, stopping short of his cock, which twitched.

Ignoring his length, I smeared the ice cream all around his groin and inside his thighs, each time stopping short of actually touching his cock.

He began stroking my shoulders and hair, and he kept trying to pull me up to him. I resisted, and pushed him back down, driving him crazy with want for me.

"I need to have you now." I smiled, giving him a taste of his own medicine.

"Soon…" I took the champagne and swigged some, keeping it in my mouth.

I kissed him and allowed him to drink from me. He took some more, but before my mouth was empty, I took his cock in my mouth. "Shit! Fucking…" he muttered loudly. The alcohol burned in my mouth, but instead of swallowing it, I swished it, making the liquid froth around his glans.

He got up and pushed me back on the bed again, scooping the last of the ice cream and smearing my labia, he pushed some inside me with his fingers. The freezing sensation shocked me, and it started to have a numbing effect.

Screaming with shock, I shivered as he teased me with agonizing delight. His mouth was immediately on my entrance, sucking and licking, his tongue delving deep into me. He took his cold tongue up to my hard clitoris and drew it all the way down my seam to my anus.

I screamed again and arched and begged, "No more, I can't take it, please fuck me." He began lapping harder and faster at my clitoris, inserting two fingers inside me.

"Are you ready for me, Lily?" he teased and I whimpered, "Please, please, I can't…"

He whispered into my throat, "Go for it girl." He sucked hard on my clit, while moving his fingers inside me rapidly.

I felt lightheaded and held my breath as my orgasm tore through me. I came so hard, bucking and thrashing, my head thrust forward, and I screamed his name, "Alfie!"

He watched me, and smiled, as I continued to ride out my climax, almost forcing Alfie's fingers out of me. He sat up, wiped his mouth, and smirked at me, then announced loudly, "Vanilla sex, my version anyway."

Alfie rolled over onto his back and pulled me to him; still erect, but in no hurry to finish off. He peered over at me, "You okay?" I nodded and gave him a weak smile.

He rubbed my arm and drew small circles on it with his thumb, as I lay my head over his chest. I heard his heart beating strong and steady.

We lay in silence for a few minutes until I spoke. "What are you thinking?" I felt an immediate pang of regret after I asked him because I suddenly wasn't sure I wanted to know the answer. I was beginning to think he didn't want to continue, as he hadn't completed what he'd wanted me here for.

"You want to know…seriously? Lily, I don't know what you're doing here with me." I was stunned.

"What do you mean?" He turned his head to look at me.

"You…you are so fucking incredible. You don't need to be with me. You can have any guy you want out there. Trust me… I've seen how men look at you." I wasn't expecting that at all. I pulled back and perched myself on one elbow to look at him.

"I thought we had an understanding. I don't want any other guys, I'm happy as things are, now that you've explained why ignoring tactics. You're exaggerating how attractive I am."

Staring intensely me, Alfie very slowly moved a strand of hair off my forehead, and sighed heavily. "I can't love you, Lily. You should be with someone that can give you everything." I worked a swallow and felt hurt. It was so difficult to hear him say that to me, especially when I was forming an attachment to him.

"I won't love you Alfie; isn't this why we are doing this?" I held his gaze and his eyes narrowed a little, then he moved and kissed my neck. I wondered if he was hiding any real feelings he had. *Maybe he was trying to let me down gently?*

"Alfie, if you don't want to do this just say and I'll leave." As soon as I said it, I was afraid of his response. *Would I be able to just up and leave without another word?*

"Can I have a minute?" he said, lying back and pinching the bridge of his nose with his thumb and forefinger. His breathing was a little deeper as he seemed to struggle with his feelings.

Debating whether to get dressed or not, thinking I didn't want to be naked when he blew me out, but I didn't get time to think about it when Alfie rolled toward me. Tracing his index finger down my belly slowly, I could see him thinking before he spoke in a gentle tone. "Lily, sweetheart…"

I swallowed hard as tears were beginning to form in my eyes and I blinked hard, while trying to fighting them back.

Sighing deeply, Alfie's face was serious. "Lily, you are the whole package, the whole fucking package." He trembled a little. "You're beautiful, intelligent, funny, playful, a fucking goddess in the bedroom and too fucking sweet and innocent to do this."

Annoyed that he was judging me, I wanted to bite back. "Is that so? Why did you ask me then? You know nothing about me Alfie. I don't want to be in a long-term relationship right now. Your offer wouldn't have appealed to me if I did."

Alfie lay on his back again, and stared at the ceiling. Then turned and met my gaze again and held it. "Tonight… you were so fucking hot tonight! I almost came just watching you in those heels, playing that fucking guitar. You play amazingly. I want to play with you, by the way." He added incidentally, and smiled shaking his head in disbelief.

Not knowing how to respond, I stayed silent but blushed that he was paying me compliments about my music, and how I looked. Having heard comments about how I looked all my life it was just a normal thing people said, but the comments suddenly had meaning when they came from Alfie. It was like I craved his approval. "You can do so much better than me, Lily. Don't waste your time with me, honey."

I felt panicked. I really didn't want this to end this with him. "If you want out, just say." I threw back at him. When his eyes darted at me, I knew he didn't feel that way because of the way his eyes snapped to mine when I said it.

"I'm in. Only if you insist you're sure," he said quickly. There was another silence.

Alfie's next question was totally unexpected. "So what's the deal with Will, are you fucking him as well?" I sat up and gave him an incredulous look, hurt that he could think that of me.

"Where has that come from? I'm not a slut, Alfie." I wasn't prepared for that at all. "Anyway, isn't the deal we can fuck whoever we want with no strings?" I felt so hurt that he could think that, but I wasn't going to show it.

Alfie perched himself up on one elbow saying, "Oh, honey, I didn't mean to make you feel you were under the microscope. I was curious, that's all. I want someone on my level, and I believe now that you are.

I'm more than happy with things."

Immediately changing the subject and lightened the mood, Alfie said, "Come on." Pulling me up off of the bed, he led me into the bathroom.

It didn't escape me that he'd diverted the conversation, but I was curious as to why he thought that about Will and me. After him saying that, I wasn't sure we'd be doing this for much longer.

"It's time to get clean," he stated, darting back to his bedroom and returning with the champagne bottle and a couple of condoms from his pants.

Turning on the shower faucet, Alfie pulled me into the shower with him. "Come on, you need a scrub, you're a very dirty girl," he teased playfully, swatting my ass. I wasn't turned on at all, but as soon as he started peppering my neck with kisses again under the shower, I was a panting mess again in no time. The guy turned me on at his will.

Lathering a face cloth with bodywash, Alfie began to wash me. He turned me away from him and began washing my back. It felt amazing as the soft, satiny bubbles cascaded down my body. The cloth soon dipped under my arms and over my breasts as he held me to him with one hand in front of my belly.

I could feel his hard cock grow and press into my lower back. This only increased my arousal, along with the fact that the cloth was now dipping between my legs, as he washed the most sensitive areas of my body.

Strangely, I found the act of him washing me more intimate than anything else we had done already. It was odd, given that he didn't do emotions. He certainly made me feel quite emotional when he took take care of me like this.

Taking the cloth from him, I repeated his actions, washing the sticky ice cream away. I smoothed his long cock, which felt so silky soft but so ridged at the same time, as I stroked the soap bubbles over it.

As I was doing this, I saw some feeling in him that he would never admit to. There were fleeting torturous looks, longing and affection in his eyes. He kept leaning into me, burying his face in my neck, breaking eye contact before I could fully recognize what he was feeling.

Cupping water in my hands, I washed the soap away and crouched down, taking his cock in my mouth and sucking him gently. Alfie threw his head back against the tiles with a dull thud, his face skyward. His lips parted in his own moment, and he moaned softly, "Oh honey, damn... I... God," then hitched his breath letting it go in a slow hiss.

Tugging at my arms, he pulling me up and shook himself dry with the towel before reaching over, and tearing a foil packet with his teeth.

He rolled the condom down his shaft with care. Alfie's breathing was ragged as he looked into my eyes. "Sexy girl," he cooed and dipping head to rest his forehead on mine and closed his eyes for a few seconds.

CHAPTER 15

MY TWO MEN

Alfie dipped down and picked me up, pushing me against the cold tile wall of the shower. He held my ass cheeks, then lowered me on to him. I glided slowly down the length of him as he sank himself deep inside of me. "Oh, God… your little pussy is so tight," he growled.

"Fuck," I gasped as he filled me to my core.

He leaned back, holding my gaze as he thrust at a leisurely pace in and out of me. "You don't have to stroke my ego by calling me your god," he teased jokingly.

My eyes widened and he smiled. I smiled back and dropped my head to his shoulder. Alfie held me while I made soft, barely there sounds, moaning with pleasure.

His movements inside me were slow and unhurried. He kissed my neck and mouth, then after a while he began to increase his speed. I was bobbing up and down, his strong arms holding me in place.

Chuckling softly at the noises I was making; some from the ecstasy I was feeling, some from giggling as it tickled. Alfie scolded me, "Stop it, Lily, I'm getting tickly."

Thrusting faster and harder, then slowing up a little to make it last, Alfie's face was twisted in concentration. As my muscles began to clench around his thick cock, he began fucking me as hard as the shower and his strength of holding me up would allow.

Grunting loudly, I urged him, "Don't stop, Alfie, yeah, just like that, just like that…" When we both came we were breathlessly clinging to each other.

"Lily, fuck." His head crumpled into my neck and he growled, "Goddammit."

Leaned into me, and still supporting me against the tile wall with just his body, his hands splayed against the wall, Alfie exhaled sharply. We stayed there for a minute, still breathless and panting hard.

Slowly he slid out and carefully placed me down, before sliding us to sit on the shower floor. He turned and kissed my head and pulled me close for a hug.

Alfie recovered quicker than the previous times, and he stood up and stepped out of the shower. He dried himself off, wrapped the towel around his waist, and left the bathroom without speaking to me.

When I came out of the bathroom to look for my clothes, he had flipped the mattress over and was making the bed with fresh sheets.

I began picking up my clothing and he turned to look at me. "You don't have to go home, it's really late." I didn't know what to say, so continued to pick my things up off of the floor. "Stay, I'd like you to stay," he sighed.

"Why?" I think I meant to think this, but it came out anyway.

Alfie ran his hand through his hair. "We both know what this is, Lily. It's just that I don't want to think of you running around at all hours because of me." I stood and watched him make the bed, not sure of what to do.

When he finished what he was doing, he slipped between the sheets and patted the bed. "Come on Lily, it's really late, and we don't have to get up early in the morning. Wouldn't you prefer to snuggle than having that ride back?"

I was tired and curious to know him better. *If I stayed would I learn more about why he was like he was?* I nodded. "No sex though," I warned as I crawled into bed and hugged myself. Alfie made no attempt to touch me, despite his enticement of snuggling to get me to stay.

He turned his back to me, and I felt disappointed. The mixed messages he sent me were messing with my head. Within a few minutes I could hear his slow, even breaths. Alfie had already fallen asleep.

I sighed, thinking I should have gone home. Instead, I was lying next to this stunningly handsome complex man who took my breath away, and I know I'm in denial now, because it would be really easy to want more with him.

Alfie was this amazing guy, who connected with me physically like no one else ever had. Made me want to do things I never would have dreamed I would have, and I could have him in my bed whenever I wanted him to be.

The snag was with no strings attached. My heart cracked a little when I admitted this to myself, because I knew that ultimately I wanted the whole hearts-and-flowers romance.

Definitely world away from that with him, and I found myself getting upset when I realized I'd never have that with him. Alfie's attitude toward sex slightly perturbed me, with his lack of emotion and his charm that switched on in private and off in public.

In my mind I was wondering if something had happened to him, for him to be so adamant about not getting into a relationship. He may just be detached and disassociated from his feelings. I nestled down in the bed, pulling the comforter up under my chin.

Obviously, I knew before we started this, that it wouldn't last, but I'd been foolish to think I could handle something like this.

Turning to face him because this was the side I usually fell asleep on. When I did this I could feel his body heat radiate toward me. The smell of his fresh bodywash on his just showered body drew me to him, and it took everything I had not to slip my arms around him and nuzzle close.

A tear rolled down my face as I thought about the fact that we could enjoy each other's bodies in the ways that we did, but a caress without sex was unacceptable as it intimated affection.

"You've ruined me." The words of a barely there whisper from a dream I didn't recall having woke me up. I had a headache; my throat and mouth felt dry from the champagne.

Remembering where I was; and it was so hot, Alfie's legs and arms were tangled around me. He was cuddling me, his arms wrapped firmly around me, one hand softly caressing my ass cheek.

My face was buried in his chest, my arm draped over his hip. I swallowed hard and lay there for a few minutes, listening to his steady heartbeat and smelling his scent.

Enjoying the feel of his soft skin, the comfort f his embrace, and his deep breaths wafting over my forehead, as he slept, I peered up trying not to disturb him. Alfie's stunningly beautiful features were relaxed, and he looked so peaceful.

Perfect lips looking so succulent that I wanted to press mine against them. When I tried to free myself and his eyes fluttered, and he tightened his grip on me; readjusting himself, to get me closer. Firmly, his hand slid up to cover my lower back, keeping me in place.

Opening his eyes slowly, Alfie confused me because he made no attempt to free me. "Hey," he cooed and smiled slowly as he looked down at me. Pulling me closer into him, his erection stirred on my belly.

It was too comfortable lying beside him though. It felt so right and wrong at the same time. I was in danger of tearing up so I pushed free of him. "I need to use the bathroom." I rolled over and pushed myself off of the mattress.

Sitting on the toilet with my head in my hands, I wished I hadn't stayed over. I was facing an awkward morning-after thing, and my clothes were still on his bedroom floor.

I considered asking him to pass them into me, but I knew that would just make a bigger deal of things. So I cracked the bathroom door open and stepped back into his room. I picked up my clothes and began to dress. "Hey… what's the hurry, honey?"

"I want to get home, Alfie. I have stuff to do today." He looked disappointed but didn't try to dissuade me from leaving. "Can you call me a cab?" I tried to make my mood sound light when I asked this.

"Okay, you're a cab… is this a new fetish?" he smirked.

When he saw that I wasn't laughing, he sighed. "I'll take you home, Lily."

I shook my head. "I'd rather go by cab." Again, he didn't push it.

Throwing back the sheets, he got off the bed, and began walking around naked, his morning wood standing proud. When he found his tablet, he looked up, found a number, then dialed it on his cell.

Taking some jeans out of the closet, he pulled them on, and disappeared downstairs, leaving me to finish putting my outfit on. When I went down, he was in the kitchen, the radio playing, and he was busy singing along and making himself an omelette.

He twisted his body around to see me, switched the stove off, and leaned against the counter. Following me, his eyes never left me as I came downstairs. "Thank you for last night. I had a great time with you." He folded his arms over his chest, rubbing his left pectoral muscle, and he smiled at me.

I don't know why, but I sounded cold. "No, problem Alfie, I had a good time too." His smile slipped for a moment, but was soon back in place as he moved toward me and put his arms around my waist.

"Why don't you spend the day here?" I felt it was a strange offer, especially with the no-strings aspect of us. I would have stayed in a heartbeat, if I thought that he felt anything toward me.

But he didn't. "Well, maybe this is all you can think of, but I have other stuff that holds my attention just as much," I teased, trying to sound lighthearted. "Besides, I'm meeting Will later. We have some stuff to discuss."

As I was saying this, the cab he'd called for me pulled up. Before he could come over in my direction again, I was out the door and seated in the cab.

He stood holding his front door. His head turned and followed the cab until I lost sight of him. I sat back in the seat and let out a huge sigh, closing my eyes. This didn't feel as uncomplicated as I had expected it to. I made a note not to stay over again.

Arriving back at the apartment shortly before Holly and was freshly showered, sitting in my bathrobe, when she opened the front door. She was sneaking in with her shoes under her arms and froze when she saw me.

I burst out laughing. "What are you like? Where have you been?" I asked, still giggling. Holly rolled her eyes.

"Oh, honey, I've been in heaven." Then she laughed so loudly, I had to shush her so we wouldn't get any complaints from the neighbors.

"Okay, come on, dish the dirt," I said.

"Well, honey, I'm not sure I want to share with y'all yet," she teased. I scowled and crossed my arms.

"Holly, you have been complaining like a drain that we've all been having orgasms and you were in Arizona, or somewhere, remember?"

Smirking, she raised her eyebrow. "I was?"

I started laughing and waved my hand away. "Okay, don't tell me, I don't want to know. Please keep your sordid details to yourself."

Holly grinned, and pretended to look dejected. "Oh, that's not fair, I do want to tell you!" I twisted my lips as if I was considering whether or not to allow her to do this.

"Okay, let's top up the orange juice, grab some toast, and I'll feel like I'm at the movies." She chuckled at me.

"Go do that honey, I need to pee, be right back." And she sashayed off to the bathroom.

We settled down to breakfast, and Holly gave her account of last night. "Well, Brett, as you know is gorgeous, six feet three inches, big dick, big hands, big…" I giggled.

"I get it Holly, Big Brett," I finished for her. We both laughed.

She bit into her toast and continued, "Okay, so he asked me to go for a late drink; his friend has a bar. We sat after hours, talking for a while and just connected. We have so much in common." She smiled.

"He's an oil man like my daddy, but he's taking some time off right now. Anyway, I ended up at his place, and he was the best lay I've ever had honey. I'll definitely be going back for seconds."

I blushed at her as she lay back on the chair fanning herself with her hand. Holly finished gushing about her night with Brett and yawned, then took herself off to bed. I went to dress and caught sight of my outfit.

Dressing like the girl I wanted to be today, I wanted to be taken seriously for my music, not for my looks. I had to find my confidence without power dressing, except for the occasions when I actually performed.

Pulling on a plain, baggy, blue top and jeans, my hair scooped back in a low ponytail, I dressed down. The only makeup was confined to a touch of mascara and lip gloss.

Picking up my guitar case, I slung it over my shoulder, stuffing a notation book and some music theory notes in my backpack. I bit an apple between my teeth and headed off to campus.

When I drove into the parking lot Will was sitting on a concrete bollard. He sprung up and headed for my car. "Hey. Lily! I was hoping you'd turn up today."

Smiling warmly at him, I said, "You read my mind I was hoping the same thing of you. I don't have your cell phone number yet."

We smiled at each other again and swapped cell numbers. Will began to discuss how well everything had gone for us the previous night, delighted with the feedback we got. Apart from the offers of bar work, a guy had approached him about playing an instrumental with full credits on a track he was recording.

I was so pleased for him. I hugged him spontaneously, and he hugged me back. As we were wrapped around each other Alfie's car swung round and parked in the lot, right beside us.

Hesitantly, I was about to pull away from Will, in case Alfie got the wrong idea. Will was still hugging me absentmindedly; rocking me back and forth, as he finished telling me his news.

We were both looking at each other and laughing when Alfie got out of the car. "Get a room Will, or go get some ice cream and cool off!" I blushed slightly and stood hanging on Will's waistline, his arm still around me.

"Vanilla's a good flavor for good girls I hear," he teased, but his jaw was tense. Seeing Will and I like this wasn't about to dissuade Alfie that we had nothing going on.

Alfie kept walking and shouted back at us without turning around, "Great gig last night. Y'all blew my mind." I knew there was another double entendre in his comment and felt a little bad that Will wasn't in on the private joke, but I still couldn't help smirking at that.

Letting go of Will, I stood back and he looked annoyed with Alfie. "Sorry, the guy's a moron." Shrugging helplessly at me with a small smile.

Smirking, I felt for Will didn't and commented, "Oh, he's insignificant, don't worry about me. I can more than handle him. You have no idea how good I am at handling guys like him."

As I said this, I remembered how silly he looked lying flat out on his bed, his condom still hanging from his dick and giggled out loud. Will looked concerned. "Are you sure?" I smiled at Will's concern.

"Of course, I've met asses like him a lot in my

line of work. I've been around bars since I started playing at sixteen." I winked. I knew Will was convinced when I saw him visibly relax.

CHAPTER 16

PARTNERSHIPS

Will's fingers tightened on my hand, and he looked at me a little concerned. "Lily, are you sure you want to duet with me? I know last night's response was brilliant, but you've only been here a day. I didn't really give you a chance to find out if there was anyone else you want to team up with."

"Will, working with you has given me so much already, and I think finding somewhere to perform together so early is amazing. I think you're very talented, and I'd love to work with you." He hugged me again and became quite animated in his conversation.

"Mandy wants to do some gigs with us. She didn't stop raving about you last night. Do you sing, Lily?" he asked.

"Sure, not like Mandy, though." He smiled.

"Mandy is… Mandy," he offered by way of an explanation. "I want us to develop, so we need to sing too. Will you do that?"

I swallowed, telling myself I could do this. "Sure," I gulped.

"If you are serious, could we jam together and rehearse some material over the next couple of weeks in the evenings and put a set together?" His eyes searched my face waiting for my response.

"Sure! I'd love that, I'm so excited about this." I fidgeted nervously with my guitar strap and hugged him yet again.

Will noticed my sudden shyness. "C'mere." He pulled me closer by my waist into another hug, and my hand came up to rest on his forearm. Alfie appeared when I was in Will's arms again. We moved apart just as Alfie strode passed us. Alfie looked annoyed, but didn't comment, just got in his car and drove off.

Part of me wanted to run to Alfie to explain, but he told me he didn't care about me seeing anyone else, even though, he looked irritated every time he saw us together. I began to wonder if he was really as unaffected by the thought of me being with someone else, which would mean that he was feeling something for me.

I decided to test this by creating some space between us. Maybe it would give me some perspective on all of this too. *If I stayed away from him, would he start to miss me?* So there and then, I decided that sex was off the menu right now.

Meanwhile, I wanted to concentrate all my efforts on getting to know Will and putting the best set together we could.

Saffy was a little miffed at me taking up so much

of Will's time and snapped at me a few times. I asked her to meet me for coffee so that I could mend some bridges with her. I hadn't spent a lot of time with her and was feeling kind of like a bad friend, but to be fair, she was always with Will when I wasn't.

This made it difficult for both of us to see each other. I could feel the strain in our friendship because I was spending so much time with Will, and I felt she blamed me for the times Will didn't see her.

We entered the coffee shop, and I ordered two skinny lattes and some coffee cake from the barista before sitting down at the far end of the coffee shop. Choosing a seat away from the other customers ensured we weren't disturbed. Saffy stared out the window, but there was a car directly in front of the window and she couldn't see much, so I knew she was doing it because she was angry.

"I'm glad we could get together Saffy. I really wanted to spend some time with you."

She snorted at me. "You did? I'm surprised." She looked hostile and flicked her hair behind her shoulder. I'd already felt the tension from her on the short drive here.

"You have been going on about what you've both been doing all the time. Do you have a crush on Will, Lily?"

My jaw dropped, I was stunned at how off the mark she was. "Men make women irrational, huh? Saffy, what Will and I are doing is just like any other people that are teamed up to work closely together." Smiling, I reached out to place my hand over her forearm as she held her coffee.

"If Will was a police officer and I was his female

partner, you wouldn't be able to do anything about that? Would you be upset if he spent ten hours working with me then?" I asked. "There's no comparison is there?"

Saffy sniffed, and I continued to help put this in context for her. "How different is it? They would be partnered together for a reason, because it made sense to put them together, or because of their skill mix. Can't you see this is the same with us? Will benefits from me and my instrument. I can play with most students here, but Will can't. He is an exceptional player Saffy, but his saxophone is a little more of a niche instrument."

Sighing, I felt sorry for her. "Your man has a lot of talent, Saffy. Playing his instrument alone doesn't get him a huge amount of attention. There isn't as much work unless he does jazz music. He might get the occasional piece, but he doesn't want to be pigeon-holed into one genre of music. He needs my help to show people how versatile he can be. It's easier to do a set with a guitarist, or in a band. There are very few saxophonists who do more than play jazz."

Smiling warmly at her, I said gently, "Will doesn't want to be restricted in that way. He needs someone like me, and possibly Mandy, who are willing to help him get the break he deserves. Don't think I'm doing this selflessly either, he brings out a side to my performance that's been lacking, and I'm learning heaps of new stuff from him every day, so the deal is both ways." I sat back and waited for her to digest what I'd just said.

Saffy looked close to tears. I felt for her, she

really didn't get it. "Look, Saffy, I can see that Will is special to you, but he's special to me too, but not for any other reason than a bond through our music. Will's music and friendship will continue with me no matter how you play this. He already knows we're good together musically, and if I don't work with him someone else will. We're students, honey, this is part of our study. I'm sorry if that makes you feel jealous, you are my best friend for goodness sake. No man will ever change that. The last thing I want to do is hurt you, but if you persist with your possessiveness, he is the kind of guy to walk away."

A tear fell from Saffy's face onto her hand, and I passed her my napkin. She blew her nose and looked sadly at me.

"Will's music needs to come first right now, Saffy, he's on the verge of doing something with it for life, and you need to understand this. He'd be doing it with or without me. Besides, would you really prefer him with another person, maybe another girl? He could be with someone that you had no clue about? At least you know where he is, and what he's doing, because I tell you."

She put her head down, and I bent my head to look under her bangs to make eye contact. "He's working with me when we're together. We're not just hanging out."

Saffy gave me a watery smile, her eyes welling up, and smiled wryly at me. "I'm just so into him, you know?"

Rubbing her back, I tried to sooth her, "Damn, Saffy, you've got it bad girl," I teased. She agreed with me that she needed to tone her control down or risk losing Will though.

"Thanks for making me see straight." She gave me a small smile.

The next four weeks were hectic for both Will and me. We all but moved in together to work, spending every waking moment trying to put a set together. We worked seven days a week rehearsing and getting ready to raise our profile as artists.

The money was important to Will as well. I had found the courage to sing three numbers, and I surprised myself by feeling okay about that. Will, Mandy, and Saffy all told me that my voice was fabulous. Personally, I'm obviously not hearing what they are.

Spending most of our time at Will's place was great, because he had no roommates to interrupt us. Will rang Saffy each day when we were winding up, and she came around as I was leaving. In the morning we'd swap places again.

Sometimes, though, I was exhausted and napped in a chair while Will made us sandwiches or had a shower. I didn't know how he kept going sometimes. "How do you find the stamina to keep up at this pace?" I groaned stretching out one afternoon when he was spreading mayo on some bread, and I was half-lying on the kitchen counter.

Will smirked. "Workouts, they energize me." My jaw dropped, when did he find time to do that?

"You've been going to the gym too?"

Grinning wickedly, Will suddenly looked smug. "Nah, I'm doing the Saffy workout." He grinned wider and wiggled his brows playfully at me.

Feeling mortified at how open he was about his

sex life with Saffy, but giggled, and blushed. Will pulled my head under his arm and ruffled my hair. "You're so adorable when you blush." He chuckled.

Accepting his comments, I wouldn't have been as comfortable with another guy apart from Jack or Alfie talking about their sex lives with me, but Will was different. I poked his belly. "You had better take care of her Will," I said, threatening to him. He pretended to bite his fingernails and look scared of me.

When I got into bed that night I was going over what had happened in the past few weeks. I felt like I'd grown up a lot in the past month, in terms of my music and my relationships. For the first time since I arrived here I seemed to be coming to grips with myself. I had been with Alfie, three times in total, but had kept my distance since the night I stayed over.

Actually, it seemed mutual. I hadn't seen him, and he hadn't called. I almost caved one night when a song came on that reminded me of him. It had been playing in the background the first night I'd gone to see him.

Since then, though, I have enjoyed my new life, doing well, feeling great, and I'd begun to network with the other students too. I was sleeping better as well.

I was often woken by my cell buzzing, and today was no exception. I was clammy from the humidity in my room as I reached over and grabbed my cell. Will was meeting me on campus and wanted to remind me to bring something we'd burned to CD.

Quickly showering, I dressed in some black, gray, and white plaid shorts, a black tank top and some flip-flops. I had really toned down my attire. Florida was definitely the place where lazy people could still look cool.

Other people were commenting on how my appearance had changed since I'd arrived as well. Will said my tan made me even more beautiful, and he wasn't the only male giving me attention. There were a couple of guys from my course that had asked me out, but because of our commitment to work I had declined.

They were nice guys, though, and I asked for a rain-check not wanting to offend either of them. But I wasn't really interested in getting into something after Alfie.

Part of me was more cautious after what happened with him. He had obviously found our last encounter as awkward as I had. So it seemed natural that we were no longer in contact.

So I was surprised when I walked into the canteen with Will, only to see him there larger than life after all that time.

As soon as I set eyes on him again, I realized that I had feelings for him that I had been trying to suppress. Almost five weeks had passed since our last night together, but just catching sight of him gave me a buzz like nothing else ever had.

The change in atmosphere in the canteen, was what alerted me something was going on, and I could see some girls focusing on something behind me. They were giggling and nudging each other. One of the girls was lusting after someone and blew a kiss. Before I even saw him, I felt his presence. I just knew in my heart, it was him…Alfie.

As I turned and saw him, he blew a kiss. Smiling playfully, but not at me, he was looking at the girl that had just made the gesture toward him. She swiped the air, catching the imaginary kiss and closed her palm. She brought her closed fist to her mouth before touching her it with her fingers and smiled. Her hand then fell over her heart.

The group of girls she was with giggled shyly beside her, and she rolled her eyes skywards. When I looked at Will, he was smiling, still watching the exchange. His eyes then seemed to move slowly downwards, and I realized whoever he was looking at was coming closer.

Will's head began turning slightly and his body tensed, as the person came along beside me. Recognizing his scent immediately before he brushed his hand lightly against my arm, Alfie stopped in front of me.

When he had made contact with my skin, the air was suddenly sucked out of my lungs and my heart fluttered wildly inside my ribcage. His touch floored me, his tiny contact with me, caused such a violent reaction in my mind and body. Closing my eyes, I hated and loved the way his touch made me feel. His presence beside me made my body hum.

I had forgotten just how stunning he was and the effect he had on me. When I heard him talk, I melted. "Hey," he cooed. The contours of his muscles flexed as he leaned across the table to fist bump Will, before he began chatting with him about some tour he'd been on.

The effect of his rich, deep, voice made me weak in the knees, but I was screaming inside because I hadn't seen him in all this time, and he was completely ignoring me again.

Rage built in me, angry that he couldn't even offer a smile. I didn't really hear their conversation because my heart was thumping so fast and hard. My mouth was dry, and the shock I felt was making me tremble inside.

When Alfie left, Will noticed that he'd spoken with him as if I hadn't been there at all. "The guy is an ass at times," Will said angrily once we were alone. He went on looking infuriated. "And what the fuck is with that tattoo he has?"

I looked puzzled. "The one of the couple making love?" I asked.

His face contorted into a sneer. "Jeez, no, the script on his left wrist and that stuff on his right hand," Will said.

"Oh, I'll look next time," I said not wanting him to know that I'd already read it.

Alfie's left wrist, like his right, had a motivating scroll it read, "*The question isn't who's going to let me. It's who's going to stop me?*" I sometimes wondered if that was in relation to his attitude to sex. Also, the other wrist read, "*Don't limit your challenges, challenge your limits.*"

He had obviously been around judging by the things he'd done to me sexually. Until now, I had pushed the thought to the back of my mind, but I suspected that there could be more. I kind of expected that if he had done this with me, he could be doing it with someone else.

Maybe he'd already moved on, and he was really trying to let me down gently that night.

Will's voice broke into my thoughts as he pulled me in for a cuddle. "Come on girl we have work to do." And pushed me in the direction of the class.

CHAPTER 17

COMPLICATIONS

After college, Will drove me back to his place to run through one of the pieces and for me to collect my car. I had slept on his couch last night. Actually, I didn't sleep on his couch. Instead, I lay trying to block out the noisy lovemaking going on in Will's bedroom.

Coming out of his room in boxers to get some OJ, Will looked all cute with his bed hair, and with a shiny 'I've-fucked-her-senseless' look in his eyes. Seeing I was awake, he gave me a sheepish grin of embarrassment. I blushed at the sight of him.

Looking over in my direction, he smiled and I covered my face with my hands, signaling that I had seen and heard too much already. He made a wicked 'muwahaha' noise at me, ran over, and planted a kiss on my forehead. Grinning, I swatted him away, before he disappeared back into the bedroom again.

I was mortified, and it was really awkward

getting ready for college together, blushing each time we made eye contact. We didn't mention it all day during our rehearsal time, but as we were driving back, he obviously got a pang of guilt about it.

Traveling along in silence, he suddenly mumbled, "Sorry about last night." I decided to tease him to get my own back, like I would have done with my best friend Jack.

"Huh? Oh… you mean the loud grunting and fucking, or not including me in it?"

Will's mouth dropped open, his jaw hanging. I wanted to squeal at his reaction, it was so funny. His head snapped around to look at me. "Wh… what?"

Deadpan, I fought to keep my face straight, determined not to laugh. "Well, I heard everything, but it was like being invited to a party and being told not to eat, drink, or dance." Will was dumbstruck, and I could see that he was freaking out, but trying to act cool at the same time.

It was too funny, but I struggled and kept my face passive, and Will cleared his throat. "Um Lily, Saffy's your best friend," he said awkwardly and almost inaudibly. I pinched myself to stop from bursting out laughing, it was hysterical.

"Yeah, and your point being?"

Will was really struggling by then, and I looked intensely, but still deadpan at him, saying, "You know Will, we do usually share everything."

His head swung around again. "You do?" His eyes went wide, and he was openly freaking out now.

Shocked eyes ticked over my face. "Watch the road Will," I prompted, and his head snapped back to face the front.

"You know Lily, I've never had a, a… ménage a trois. I don't think…" I burst out laughing. Will's jaw dropped. "You were shitting me? Lily! Oh, thank God!" His hand shot up to his chest and slapped his sternum. "I hate you… so fucking mean, girl." He chuckled.

Slapping his hand against his chest again, he said, "God, you were so serious." I giggled hysterically at how gullible he'd been. "I truly shit myself there about how to deal with you."

Will swiped his hand at me, but I think he could have backhanded me hard, and it wouldn't have registered. I was too busy curling up on the seat, screaming with laughter.

"I get it Lily. I'll get you back one day. Just because you don't get involved with anyone, doesn't mean I can't get my own back one day." *If only he knew.* We were both still chuckling as we passed a poster advertising our gig.

A bald guy in flip-flops and baggy shorts was wearing a sandwich board, which said, 'Live Music' at the corner of an intersection. It had the bar we were going to play at and our names on it.

I noticed another hobo-type guy on another corner of the same intersection with a billboard advertising the name of the bar with a gigantic yellow arrow pointing in the direction of the venue.

We both looked at each other and screamed, "That's us!" We screamed, and I stamped my feet on the car floor with excitement.

By the time we arrived at Will's we were both feeling relaxed after laughing so much. We spent an hour together on the arrangement for one of the pieces we were doing tonight. Afterwards I went home to get ready for the performance.

As soon as I got home, I filled the bathtub with bubbles and laid back. I pulled the bubbles through my fingers, watching them disperse with the movements.

My mind drifted again to how much better things were going for me and hoped that wouldn't change now that Alfie had reappeared on the scene.

Seeing him today unnerved me. I didn't outwardly react to him at all in front of Will, but the feelings I thought I had dealt with involving him still came rushing back.

The sight of him had taken my breath, and I had wanted nothing more than to wrap my arms around his neck, and pull his mouth down to mine. Saffy interrupted my thoughts by knocking on my bathroom door, asking softly. "Hey Lily, are you decent?"

"I'm in the bath come in."

Saffy hesitated, "Um… do you have bubbles in there?"

I giggled. "Why? You're not thinking of joining me are you?" She chuckled at the other side of the door.

"Well, what I want to know is… are your naked bits on show? I mean you're not going to show anything you wouldn't want your dad to see are you?" I was laughing heartily now.

"He's not outside the door is he?"

"Just answer me!" she snapped.

Gasping for breath, and still laughing, "Okay, I'll bite… my boobs are covered in bubbles is that good enough for you?" The door cracked open and her head popped around before she pushed the door wide and Max, Saffy's twin brother, was standing in the doorway.

"Surprise. Hey baby girl, pity about the bubbles, they ought to be illegal." He grinned.

The sight of Max, my crush for about three years when I was a teenager, shocked the hell out of me, and I dove under the bubbles. He closed the door again, and I re-emerged, with a silent scream on my face, and my mind running at ninety miles per hour.

I had butterflies and felt an excitement that equaled first dates and lots of other firsts. I quickly finished my bath and began to get dressed, suddenly desperate to check that he was really here.

Dressing in a purple mid-thigh length tube dress, I inspected myself in the mirror. It clung to my slender frame, accentuating my curves. The low cut scoop of the neckline made my breasts seem fuller and gave me the perfect cleavage.

I liked the way that particular dress seemed to make me curvier all over. Accessorizing to complete the outfit, with few long beaded necklaces as well as the platinum and diamond tennis bangle my parents had given me when I turned twenty-one.

Reaching up into my closet, I pulled down a black box. I smiled when I saw my favorite red stilettos and matching purse. My hair hung in long unruly curls down my back, I had preferred a wilder look for my public appearance tonight.

Checking my final appearance in the mirror, the girl I was the last time Max saw me, and the woman I had become were very different. I wondered what he would think looking at me now.

Spraying on some Coco Chanel as I straightened my dress, I headed for the sitting room.

Max's reaction took me back a little. His jaw dropped, and he was speechless. Shaking his head, he seemed to recover from the initial impact I appeared to have had on him. "Wow," he whispered, staring at me in disbelief. "Oh. My. God, Angel you look perfect."

He closed the distance between us and took hold of my hand, stepping back. His eyes trailed from my head to my toes. "Look at you," he cooed. His eyes darkened with each second that passed. I felt very self-conscious as he scrutinized me.

His head dipped toward my face, as his lips brushed feather-light against my cheek. His hot lips softly paused on my skin. He inhaled deeply before he pulled my body flush with the side of his hip.

Saffy wasn't paying attention when he did this, as she was running around, getting her stuff ready to go out. His lips brushed my ear, and he whispered gruffly, "You are the most beautiful girl I have ever seen, Lily." Saffy was sitting on the far side of the room and had turned just in time to see me blush with the effect he was having on me.

"What did he say to you Lily? Don't be mean, Max," she scolded.

"I wasn't mean, and if I'd wanted you to hear what I said, I would have said it out loud," he told her as he led me over to a chair. I sat down and he stood in front of me, still looking at me. He began shaking his head.

"What?" Saffy asked. "You haven't seen a hot woman before Max?"

Max's mouth slowly curled into a smile. "Y'all know that I've watched my lil' Lily grow over the years, and dang if she hasn't gone and blossomed on me." Saffy laughed and Max chuckled at his own comment. I blushed again as my heart fluttered with his appreciation.

Luckily for me, Holly arrived home and the attention steered toward her while I gathered my thoughts. Max's gaze kept landing on me until he was outright staring at me.

His stare was full of intent, his pupils dilated. I've seen that look in Alfie's eyes, and Max kept me close from the moment we left the apartment until we arrived at the venue where we were playing.

Will was already there, setting up. When he saw us he grabbed me excitedly, hugging me tightly to him. I noticed Max puffed out his chest and smirked. Turning to Will, I pointed at Max. "This is Saffy's twin brother, Max

"Max… this is Will, the other half of my duo," Saffy chipped in. "I'm seeing Will, Max." He puffed his chest out again, as if to say, "don't-you-dare-fuck-my-sister."

Will looked uncomfortable, but tried to act naturally, offering his hand for Max to shake. He did this reluctantly with a primal stare that spoke volumes in terms of treating Saffy right.

Max seemed fine with Will touching me from that point onward, knowing that he had no designs on me. Will, on the other hand, had been watching Max.

He was still staring at me, and Will picked up on it. "Oh, maybe I'll come and sleep on your couch tonight. Looks like you'll be having noisy, monkey sex if Max has his way. The poor guy's been eye fucking you since you arrived." My jaw dropped open at Will's comment.

Everyone settled in the seats, and when we started to play people were chatting as if we didn't exist. We were only a few bars into the song when people seemed to stop and listen. The first song we played was *Walk on the Wild Side* by Lou Reed, and the arrangement for it was a little different.

We were nervous to switch it up, because it was a classic, but it went down well, and we held the audience's attention after that. Will smirked and winked at me, and we started to relax after that. I was more than happy, because I had sung, and it sounded okay.

The rest of the set went down just as well. I performed and sang one piece of my own, an acoustic version of *Heaven* by Eric Clapton. Will performed Gerry Rafferty's *Baker Street*, and all I could hear in the room was the haunting sound of his beautiful saxophone tones in the air.

We finished the set with some duets again. The reaction from people in the bar was excellent. We were on a high. A few people wanted to chat with us, and there were more contacts asking for our diary dates.

Saffy told me that Max was sleeping in her bed tonight, and she was going to Will's with Mandy and Neil. I was a bit fed-up that she couldn't take the time to see her brother. Holly had disappeared halfway thought the set, and I wondered if she'd taken Brett to our place as well.

When I asked Saffy if she knew where Holly was

she just shrugged. I checked my cell to see if she had left a message for me. I had three texts that had come in when I'd been performing.

SEXPERT: Missed you baby.
Oh! That dress, those legs! I need
to stroke them desperately.

I looked around. I didn't know Alfie was here tonight. He had a cheek really, I hadn't heard from him for five weeks.

Then again, I supposed that he didn't need me when he was off touring as there would be plenty of groupies. I was definitely struggling with the concept of the no-strings thing we had going on.

Pink Lady: Swat! Need you to
keep your hands to yourself I'm
working.

SEXPERT: Can't you're too
irresistible and it's been weeks.

Pink Lady: So... you should be
over your withdrawal by now.

SEXPERT: Meet me at mine?

Pink Lady: Nope, I have
company tonight.

SEXPERT: Bring your company
she can have a spare room. Need
to see you.

Pink Lady: Sorry, HE wouldn't go for that.

SEXPERT: HE???

Pink Lady: Yeah, it's a boy, and we're almost ready to leave for my place.

SEXPERT: PITY: I guess I'll just have to entertain myself some other way.

Pink Lady: You've managed this long without me, I'm sure you're resourceful.

Alfie didn't reply after that and I checked the other two texts.

Holly: gone to Brett's, mwah!

Unknown: This is Max. Saffy punched your number in my phone in case we all got lost. Do you want to get a late dinner? Max.

I smiled and text back.

Pink Lady: Please, I'm starving, give me ten minutes.

I packed up and said my goodbyes. Max and I took a cab back to the condo. "I'm starving, do you know somewhere to eat or do you want to order in?"

I nodded. "There's a place near here that's open late. We can walk to it," I said while searching in my purse for the keys to my apartment to make sure I had them.

Max and I chatted about old times and our years apart melted away. He stared at me a few times, and there were a couple of intense moments where I was the one to look away, but after a while we were completely comfortable with each other.

When Max was talking about our past, a stray lock of hair fell across his forehead. I instantly leaned over and brushed it away. Max caught my hand, drew a breath, and smiled. He held my gaze with his, let my hand go, and looked away.

CHAPTER 18

OLD FLAMES

As we sat drinking wine, feeling mellow, Max's questions became more personal. "Are you seeing anyone Lily?" *Alfie doesn't count.*

"No."

Smirking, he raised an eyebrow. "Are you kidding me, why not?" he asked surprised

There was no way I could tell him about Alfie so I said, "There was someone briefly, but it didn't come to anything." I wanted to shift the spotlight from me. "What about you Max, I bet the ladies are falling over you."

"Well! Yeah they are." He chuckled truthfully. "But I'm too picky, I guess, and I got bored of one-night stands."

Max was completely comfortable talking about this. "Tell me about your, didn't-come-to-anything-guy." He smiled.

"There's nothing to tell really, other than he

doesn't do serious relationships.

Max bunched his brows. "Is the guy nuts?"

I shrugged not wanting to get into that again. "Anyway, he moved on, and I got my shit together with Will. We've had no real time for socializing since, until tonight."

We started talking about our common love of music, and it was like the last four years melded away. We had a long history as friends. While he was talking I drew my fingers up my wine glass. Dipping my middle finger briefly in my wine, I circled it around the rim of the glass, making a tune.

Max reached over and took my hand in his, lacing his fingers through mine. "Sorry honey, you can't do that with your finger, it's turning me on." I giggled at him, thinking that he was just being funny. When I met his gaze, his eyes were darker in color, and his sensual stare made me see he was completely serious.

Gesturing at our hands by holding them up, he said, "Remember when we used to do this when we talked at night in the camper van?"

Smiling, I had. "Yeah, I do, Max."

He smiled and continued, "I can tell you now, I thought I'd never felt hands so soft and delicate, and that you were my little angel."

Smiling wrinkling my nose at him. "Aww."

He lifted my hand and kissed it gently. I felt a small thrill ran throughout my body. I looked at Max and sighed. "We should head home. I need my bed."

Max muttered what I thought was, "Me too."

However, when I looked at him, he smiled like he hadn't said anything out of place, and I thought I'd misheard him. Max looked gorgeous in his red shirt and easy fit jeans. The red color suited his skin tone, his dark tan and blond hair made him look striking.

Catching me looking at him, he smiled slowly, signaling to our waiter for the check. He glanced at it, and threw some folded bills into the wallet. Walking along the dark road on the way home; toward the lights of the condo building, Max leaned in and automatically threw his arm around me. Tensing initially because it felt weird, Max smiled and started rubbing my arm as he chatted and I felt myself relax. Lifting my hand to meet his, we clasped our fingers together again. "We used to do this too." He grinned gesturing at our hands again. Still smiling, he tilted his head toward the sky and inhaled deeply.

Neither Max, nor I, changed our position as we entered the building and walked over to the elevator. I definitely felt safe with Max, but I had butterflies at the same time because this was very different. This was everything I'd ever dreamed of as a young teenager with him. When the elevator car arrived I was nervous of what might happen between us.

On the way up, I began to talk about the beach, but Max had put a finger up to my mouth. "Shush." I stared at him. "I want to kiss you." He smiled affectionately, bringing his hand up, he took my chin between his index finger and thumb, tilting my face up to him. Our eyes met and I smiled back.

"You used to kiss me all the time, Max."

Gazing into my eyes, his voice became huskier. "Hell, I used to kiss you like a brother. This kiss will definitely not be like that." I swallowed audibly, and wet my lips subconsciously, but became conscious I was doing it, and felt myself blush.

At that point I wanted that too. I had always wanted Max to kiss me properly not just a peck on the cheek. My mind was in conflict, though, because of my slutty behavior with Sam and Alfie. The timing sucked, but I knew I may never get the chance to experience a kiss with Max again if I rejected him.

My eyes searched his. "Okay, if it feels weird we could stop… no awkwardness… deal?" I wrinkled my nose, and he smiled broadly.

Licking his lips, he motioned towards me. He moved his closed lips back and forth on mine before pressing them to my mouth with more pressure.

Max's hands slid around the small of my back, and moved up to my ribs, before he stroked downwards, toward my belly, then he suddenly pushed me against the elevator wall. I kissed him back, and he murmured, "Oh God." An intense heat grew between us, and I was moist between my legs.

His hands traveled up to the sides of my face, caressing my chin on both sides. He put his hand on the back of my head, pulling me into him as his tongue probed deeper into my mouth. Our breathing was ragged and hurried now. It left me breathless.

The elevator dinged its arrival at my floor, and he rushed me out backwards, pinning me against the wall in the hallway. He pushed one leg between my thighs, his body flush with mine, and I felt his hard cock straining against his pants.

Feeling the friction between his pant leg and my bare skin was sensational. I felt so guilty doing this, but I felt helpless to stop it, because I wanted this to happen at the same time.

I slipped my hands up inside his t-shirt and felt a wall of solid muscle. As I slid my hands around his back, he shuddered and jerked, before moving his mouth to my neck.

This was going way too fast for me. I needed time to think. I pushed him away and tried to collect my feelings, taking my time finding my keys in my purse. I glanced up, and Max was looking at me like he was going to rip my clothes off.

Breaking contact I tried to slow things down a little. "Hey, well, I think we can say no worries to the awkward kissing thing. You can check that off the list." I sounded casual, but my heart was racing.

Max grinned and nodded, and I thought I had taken the heat out of the moment. I figured once we'd thought about it, we'd tell each other that it wouldn't be a good idea.

Fishing my keys out of my bag, I started to open the door. As soon as he heard the latch click Max pushed me through the door, banged it behind him, and pushed me gently back toward the couch.

Max's hands skimmed up my thighs and under my dress before I could stop him, and he stalled in surprise. His face was registering shock. "No fucking panties, Lily?" I blushed, more than a little embarrassed.

"They were visible under this dress." I shrugged, and he raised an eyebrow.

Max began slipping my dress up, and I grabbed his wrist. "Stop!"

"I can't," he murmured near my mouth. He lifted it over my head, then free of my arms.

I still couldn't believe we were actually going

beyond our friendship.

"Love the delicate lace on your bra," he murmured as his thumbs ran briefly over my breasts before he reached around and unclipped it.

My breath hitched. He stroked around my belly and breasts, curled my nipples between his fingers and thumbs, kissed them, sucked them, and pulled them together, wobbling them. I laughed.

Seeing his appreciation turned me on, and his touch was making me want more than just messing with him like this. I didn't really believe that we'd actually have sex though.

Pulling Max's t-shirt off was the start of everything. He then drew himself down the length of my front, skin to skin. I shivered with delight, and I raked my fingernails lightly down his back. "I can't believe I'm making out with you," Max cooed.

Smiling warmly, Max leaned in and kissed me from my neck all the way down to my mound. I tensed and moved away a tad. This was going beyond making out. He frowned, but slid his hands up the back of my legs before they moved to my inner thighs and pushed my legs apart. I didn't stop him.

Blowing lightly on my sensitive flesh, Max then licked and flicked lightly on my clitoris with his tongue. Max had a lighter touch than I'd experienced before. The sensation he was giving me was so erotic and sensual.

My juices were flowing, running down the crease of sex. My skin flushed from the heat he was generating in me as my body hummed. I knew this wasn't going to stop short of us having sex.

Max spread my legs wider, resting his head on

one thigh and explored my sex, "You're really very pink and swollen down here, honey, does this mean you want me?" He smirked and I blushed, which turned into me laughing with embarrassment, as I tried to squeeze my legs closed.

Holding me in position, he smiled. "Not funny Lily, I want to see you." His finger skimmed the length of my slit. "Damn, so slick, so ready," he growled as he hugged me again.

Covering my face with my hand, I was really embarrassed by his comment. Max slipped a finger inside me gently. I moaned and he pulled it back out to look at it. "Fuck. Look," he hissed, showing me his finger glistening.

Running his finger it along his lips, he then slipped it back inside my core and curved it, pulled it out again and then sucked it again. It was very erotic to watch. "Damn, you smell sexy." His voice sounded as if he was fighting to control himself.

I was in denial that this was actually happening because of our innocent history. That 'my Max' was talking to me this way.

Kissing my mouth again, he thrusting his tongue deep, making me moan, "Oh God."

Trailing down my belly, he made little gentle kisses, talking in a whisper. I had to concentrate to hear what he was telling me.
"I…want…you…so…fucking…badly."

Max buried his tongue deep inside me letting out a low moan into my wet heat, which reverberated through my body. "Shit." It tickled.

"I want you inside me Max."

His head whipped up. "Did you say that or was

that my fantasy thinking out loud?" I smirked.

"You didn't imagine it." I giggled and shook my head, shyly. He spread my folds and drew his tongue from my clit down until he stuck his tongue in me and sucked hard on my clit again. The sensation was incredible.

Max replaced his mouth with two fingers inside as he gazed up at me. "Say it again. I want to see you say it."

I worked a swallow and it was hard. I had no reservations by then. "Fuck me, Max."

Grinned wickedly, he smirked, "Fucking Hot Lily, but…nope." Chuckling, he began flicking my clitoris, first with his thumb, then with his tongue again.

"Fuck me, Max." I was beginning to get frustrated with him.

He pulled his head back to look at me again, smirking wickedly. "Actually Lily, I know you were brought up better than that. Where are your manners?"

"Please fuck me Max!" I whimpered.

Max stood suddenly. "Yes, ma'am!" Smiling, he saluted, pulling his pants off. "Oh shit! I don't have any condoms. I didn't expect to get laid on this trip!" Max looked worried.

"There are some in the left nightstand drawer," I said hurriedly. Max ran off to get them and was already sheathing himself as he walked back.

"Wait… You have condoms in your bedside drawer?" Then added quickly, "Don't answer that, we'll deal with that later."

Reaching out, I wanted to touch his cock. "Nah,

you can't touch it at the moment, if you do, I'll blow before we get down to it. See what you do to me girl," he growled.

Max lifted me up and sat on the couch, pulling me over to straddle him. He stroked my back, staring at my body, cupped my breasts, and weighed them again between his hands. His beautiful brown eyes searched my face. There was no mistaking how he was feeling.

Stroking my hair gently, he studied me, and wriggled down the sofa. He lifted me above his straining cock, slowly lowering me on to him. His eyes closed and he groaned, "So fucking tight."

He held my ass in the palms of his hands and bounced me gently at first as his thrusts became deeper. He opened his eyes and smiled slowly. "You always used to rib me for being bossy Lily, go on you take charge. I'll let you ride me, then, and if you're good, I'll return the favor."

Lowering me, Max sat me across his lap, and I rocked myself back and forth, rolling my hips on him. Max had one hand on my hips supporting me, the other trailing between my breasts, his chin tilting up now and again when he sought eye contact.

Changing the rhythm, I started to gyrating in a circular pattern on him, then lifted my legs into a kneeling position feeling the length of him leave me and taking him back inside.

Rocking back and forth again, the friction from his pubic bone rubbed my clitoris. I moaned loudly. "Fucking incredible. Damn, Lily," growled Max, his face twisted with the pleasure he was feeling. He moved his palms to cradle my ass cheeks again, and started bouncing me on him and thrusting upwards. His tempo increased as he thrust into me.

Tingling feelings told me I was getting there and I gripped him inside me as Max held me against him. He lifted us off the couch and flipped me onto the floor. My legs were high on his waist as he thrust in and out of me, so deep, as he placed his thumb over my clitoris.

He pumped slowly inside me, then quickened the pace and kept it steady. He drove me crazy, I was so near the edge. My fists tightened as his speed increased, and he kept it going.

I felt myself begin to clench tighter around his cock. "Go Lily, do it," Max whispered into my ear. I rode my climax, shuddering and shaking.

I screamed out, "Max," as I buckled under him.

Max chuckled softly at me, but continued to ride me until I came again before he suddenly jerked and his eyes closed as he pulsated inside me. His mouth went wide, and he rolled his head back then he curved forward to bury his face in my neck.

CHAPTER 19

SUNRISE

My mouth was dry. I was exhausted and glistening with sweat. The room was too hot. Max had gone to the bathroom and came back rolling on another condom. He wasn't even soft. "Come on lazy enough lying around. Let's get to it, the night's getting short."

He turned me over and lifted my ass in the air, smacking it gently. He blew gently on my sex and stroked lightly with his fingers. Briefly, he licked my sex and dragged his finger into my folds checking that I was wet before he entered me.

Dragging the condom covered head of his erection down the crack of my ass, over my anus, and down into my folds. He didn't enter me, just kept repeating this, before putting his hand between my legs to rub my clitoris. He went down on me again, his hot mouth sucking, his tongue probing inside me.

I gasped, "Sweet…Jesus." What he was doing

sent strong shivers of delight through me as he teased me until two fingers sunk deep inside me again. Rocking my hips against his hand, I was trying to get more contact from his fingers. I was fully aroused again.

"You like that? You want me inside you again?" he whispered.

I moaned in ecstasy. "Please," I whimpered back.

"Sorry?" Max chuckled wickedly against my back. "I can't hear you."

I muttered loudly, "Fuck me Max, do it now! Please fuck me!" I didn't even recognize myself.

Max turned me to face him and he held his cock against my entrance, suddenly thrusting deep into me in one glide. He stilled and inhaling deeply. "You are so fucking tiny inside," he hissed, before he pulled back and sunk himself deeper with a long groan then growled, "Amazing."

Each thrust rubbed at a spot inside of me over and over and I moved wildly, chanting, "Oh, yeah, like that," rocking backwards and trying to get him deeper. The noise of his balls slapping against my ass as his skin connected with mine only heightened our arousal.

Max held me tightly, his hands almost grazing my hips, making gruff noises and soft moans. He began to growl and grunt louder. I reached behind, cupping his balls as I felt myself begin to come and tried not to. "Let. It. Go. Come, Fuck."

"Oh, sh… shit, I'm coming." He grunted with each thrust. The pressure built up, and I came squeezing his cock hard. His pace picked up, and he growled when my vagina walls clenched down on him.

Max went stiff and began to jerk, his come filling the condom inside of me. He rolled me over with him into a spooning position, still inside of me. He growled his appreciation and started laughing. "Fuck."

I must have fallen asleep and woke with Max scooping me up. "Shush, I'm taking you to bed." I moaned sleepily and melded into his chest. Pulling back the covers, he placed me down gently on my pillow. I felt him kiss me softly on the forehead before pulling the sheet halfway over me.

"Do you want me to stay with you, or go to Saffy's bed?" He sounded unsure.

"Huh?" I said drowsily.

"What do you want, Lily? I don't want to spoil the night, tell me what to do." I was exhausted.

"Stay." I husked. "We're adults Max, are you ashamed? Are you worried about Saffy? What she'll think?" I sat up, more awake now. "Do you want to stay?"

Max stroked my hair back and locked eyes with me. Bending, he put his forehead on mine. Inhaling sharply he smiled, "Absolutely!" He scrambled in and crawled up to spoon with me.

His right hand cupped my left breast as he tugged me closer. It felt so different to have someone care for me after what we had just done. Max lay nuzzling my neck, playing with my hair, stroking it, then smelling it.

"Is that roses I smell? Your hair smells awesome," he murmured. His breathing and wriggling slowed until his deep, even breaths told me that he'd fallen asleep, right before I did.

When I woke Max's strong arms were wrapped around me; he'd nestled me to his chest. It was hot, and we were sticky. I hated waking up sweaty.

I felt him slowly peel himself away trying not to disturb me, and I fell asleep again as soon as I heard my bedroom door close.

The next time I woke, it was to the sound of water running, and I deduced that he'd gone to shower in Saffy's bathroom. He was in the shower when I padded through. "Are you leaving?" I asked, feeling slightly apprehensive about what he thought about last night.

"Hell no! Why would I do that, when I have a hot chick right here?" Winking at me. I felt relieved. "It was too hot, and you looked so cute asleep. I woke up with your legs stuck to me. I just thought I'd cool down, that's all."

Wrapping a towel around his hips, as I scooted in the shower after him, Max looked at me seriously, "Regrets?" I stopped shampooing my hair and turned to look at him pursing my lips.

"You mean last night?"

Max held out his hand to me. I rinsed the soap from one of mine, put it in his, and gave it a squeeze. "Max, I had a crush on you for years, I don't regret finding out if my crush was worth it." I smirked.

"You did?" Nodding slowly, I smiled at him, conscious I was biting my lip. "Well fuck, I've been hot for you since I was fifteen. I remember wanting to kiss you so badly." He stood holding his bottom lip. His mouth broke into a wide grin. "Glad I waited though, because I got to kiss *all* of your lips!" he said chuckling and wiggling his brows at me.

My jaw dropped at his crude comment. Turned back into the water and rinsed my hair. When I was finished, he wrapped me in a fluffy white towel and leaned back on the counter. I began rubbing myself dry, and Max stood watching me with fascination.

I became embarrassed at him staring and stopped. He sighed. "Amazing."

Blushing, I asked, "Breakfast?"

Max shook his head, as if to clear his mind and smiled. "I thought you'd never ask I'm starving." He chuckled.

We crept through to the kitchen wondering who else was here, and grabbed some ham, Cokes, and a tub of humus from the fridge before heading back to the bedroom. We closed the door and sat on the bed with our feast.

"Oh, we forgot to get any breadsticks," I said. "No worries, it tastes better this way anyway." Max scooped some onto his fingers and placed it in front of my mouth, for me to suck his finger. A pang of sadness hit me when I remembered how Alfie had fed me. With Max it felt a lot less sensual.

I enjoyed being with Max though. For the first time, sex didn't seem complicated and secretive. Saffy is going to freak.

Max's face became serious. "What? What's wrong?"

Twisting my mouth inquisitively, I asked, "What?" mirroring his question.

Max rubbed my arm. "You look worried, what's wrong?"

I sighed and put my head down. "Saffy. She is

going to go berserk that I screwed her brother."

Max chuckled. "Firstly, can you not talk about me like I'm not here?" He smiled crookedly at me. "Secondly, I am not about to let my sister dictate terms for us. You said it yourself, we're both adults. Did you enjoy what we did Lily?" I felt oddly shy when he asked, which was ridiculous considering what we'd done together.

I met his gaze and could see he looked a bit worried waiting for me to answer. "Max, of course I did, but it was a bit unexpected," I whispered. "Did you?"

Max sat in contemplation for a moment before his fingers curled around mine, as a slow smile curled his lips, and his eyes closed as if in relief. "Lily." He swallowed, and I watched his Adam's apple bob up and down in his neck.

Standing up, he walked around the bed, still only wearing his towel. He clasped his hands behind his head, stretched, then brought them down again. Max sat on the bed facing me and held my hands. I swear I could almost hear him thinking as he did this.

"Lily…sweet, little Lily." He sighed stroking my cheek. "Last night-" He cleared his throat again. "When I saw you in the bath, your pretty little head poking out of the water, you made my heart leap."

Moistening his lips when his gaze fell onto mine, he continued, "You looked so fucking cute. However, when you came out of your bedroom... looking..."He swept his arm down the length of me, lost for words.

Max's eyes scrutinized me again while he thought about what to say. "You looked so delicate, beautiful, and a sexy as hell little vixen, I ached for you. I had the biggest case of blue balls in the car on the way to your gig." I giggled and he grinned.

"Your performance gave me a hard on all over again, you made my head swim, your voice gave me goose bumps. The only part I didn't like was when Will cuddled you. I wanted to beat the shit out of him."

Max snickered. "I must be one pretty fucked-up brother to be relieved that a guy is fucking my sister instead of her friend." Chuckling, he looked embarrassed by that. I realized right then, just how much risk had been involved in our actions last night. We may never have spoken again if this had gone badly.

Lying back on the bed, I closed my eyes digesting what he said, but thought about Saffy and what she would say when she found out. Max traced his finger over my knee, and lay down beside me, clasping his hands behind his head.

Max propped himself up on one elbow and faced me. "Can I kiss you Lily?"

I smiled. "This is your usual pick up line, right? Isn't that how it started last night?" I rolled my eyes at him and smiled.

"I believe my question was first," he chided.

"Well, it's actually, "May I kiss you." But of course," I said correcting his grammar.

He leaned in and kissed me gently, then began to touch me, stroking my arms and across my belly. "Wait! You did all that before, you have the advantage," I said, pushing him back on the bed. Max looked puzzled "My turn." I smiled sweetly.

Stroking his forehead, I ran my fingers through

his hair, Max tried to kiss my arm, and I scolded him with a finger signaling that he had to lie still.

Trailing my hands over his chest and belly, I ran my hands down his sides and over his hips, then traced his V muscles trailing my finger down. I could hear that Max was turned on by the way he moaned.

Bending forward, I trailed my tongue over his lips, pushing them apart, kissing him softly, then with more urgency. My tongue tangled with his, making him moan again. It gave me a buzz, his little sound, and turned me on. I moved from his mouth down his abs to his erect cock.

Watching his reaction to my touch, while stroking down his groin on both sides was amazing. I teased him without touching his genitals. Max gasped when I blew lightly on his glans. He growled, "Tease." He said, smiling, and I leaned over to kiss his cock softly. Max groaned loudly, "Oh God," his legs reacted by opening wider.

Stroking his shaft was beautiful, it felt the silky, his taut skin stretched over his hardness, and I kissed it again. My mouth closed over his glans, and I sucked him hard, the suddenness obviously giving him a thrill.

Max gasped, "Fuck." He brought his head to stare at me. "Oh…fuck! I want to watch you," he said, pulling a pillow to support his head.

Licking the length of his shaft, before taking him in my mouth again, "Look at me," he commanded. Using my flattened tongue around the glans, he watched me lick his sticky pre cum, before I crawled up and kissed his mouth again.

"Can you taste yourself?" I asked.

"You're so fucking hot!" he murmured into my mouth. Max pulled me away. "No more, I'll come. I don't want to waste it. I want to keep it for you." He positioned us facing each other. Max's hands were now grasping my ass, our hips tight together. "We're going to do this slowly now okay?" I just smiled and nodded.

CHAPTER 20

SNEAKY

Max got up, turned the light out, and opened the curtains. The dawn was breaking, but the light was barely there yet. He put a condom on from the drawer, bent and licked the crease of my sensitive flesh, making slurping noises.

"Damn." He smiled into my thigh, then inserted his tongue and moved it around. I was dripping and wriggling to be taken by him.

I wanted him inside me as much as he needed to be inside me. He turned me to face the window and spooned behind me, slowly entering me until he was halfway, then pulled back, almost out, then he moved deeper inside, slowly, relishing the feeling.

After a few minutes he lifted my leg to give him more freedom to penetrate me deeper. We watched the sunrise as Max rocked in and out of me gently. He was unhurried, kissing my neck and back as he moved slowly against me. After what seemed an age, the pressure started to build between us, and our need for each other became less passive.

Max rubbed my clitoris slowly, and I turned on my back. He crawled over me, kissing me deeply, his tongue mimicking his cock as he slid back inside me, spreading my tight space. He stilled for a moment, before thrusting with more pressure.

It felt tender, but my hips picked up his rhythm, and I began to arch up to meet him. He slowed me down again, but our speed increased together after a short time again, and I wrapped my legs around his waist.

He felt me clench around him and tighten. "Come with me Lily, look at me." He began to thrust harder, and I came apart, writhing under him, squirming and shaking.

"Open your eyes," he commanded, and as I did, he stiffened, his jaw dropped and his eyes closed as his head rolled back. "Amazing, fucking… amazing," he rasped.

We lay together for a minute, until Max left me to discard the condom. I must have passed out and when I woke, I was alone in the bed again. Max hadn't come back. I got in the shower again, and quickly pulled on some gray sweat shorts and a white vest, before heading to the fridge for some OJ.

He was sitting on the balcony. He turned when he heard me and walked over beside me. His mouth kissed my shoulder, as his arms snaked around my waist. "Did you sleep okay?" He smiled down at me. I nodded, rubbing his bare abs.

Taking my hand, "I've ordered in, and it should be here soon, there wasn't much in the fridge. I was going to wake you when it arrived." I smiled up at him and went to sit on the balcony. The sun felt hot on my skin and the view of the ocean was breathtaking. Pulling my legs up on the chair, I hugged my knees.

Tom buzzed the apartment letting us know the food had arrived, and the delivery girl was on her way. There were no awkward silences between us during breakfast, but I did try to tackle how we were going to deal with Saffy about us.

"She'll be due back around noon," I said. "What do you want to tell her?" I asked.

"Let's be honest with ourselves first, Lily." He gave me a half smile. "I would love to stay here, but you know I can't." Max looked a little sad. "I can come and see you maybe once a month. I have a contract commitment and you have college. You can maybe come and see me sometimes if you get some slack time. It sucks, but that's our reality." He frowned.

Sighing and staring grimly at me, he shook his head. "I don't want to tie you down, and I don't want to let you go. You are fabulous and I love you, you know that. The danger for me is that I could fall *in* love with you. That wouldn't help your situation here or mine. So, how about, we try to spend some time together, if it's meant to be, it will be." He told me with a small smile on his lips.

"I know if we tried to be together, you would start to resent me. I know what music is to you, it's the same for me. We live a long way apart, I'm here now, but I need to go back Sunday night, so that gives us three days." Max was being practical. I smiled at his honest assessment of the situation.

"If we tell Saffy anything, it's that we're interested in each other, and we care about each other. I don't want you to be a secret Lily. I have loved you for the longest time, but I was a kid. I was worried about going to second base with you, never mind a home run. Now, I feel like fucking Babe Ruth. I could do it again and again! I never want to leave, but I will. It's your call. We can spend time while I'm here if that's what you want, and we'll take it from there. What do you say?"

Everything he was saying was true. "Damn Max, you're letting me speak now?" We chuckled. "I hear what you're saying and I agree." I felt a little sad, because if the timing was different I was almost certain that Max would have been a serious contender for a long term relationship.

We were laughing when Saffy walked in. She looked worn out, but with big sparkly eyes. There was obviously a twin thing going on between them because Max's face looked blank to me, but Saffy got really angry with him.

"Don't look at me like that Max. I'm an adult for fuck's sake."

Max twisted his mouth. "Yeah? Well, so are we, but we came home last night, can you say the same?" He winked at me then turned his serious face back at Saffy.

"Just because you didn't get any, doesn't mean I have to go without." She jutted her jaw out indignantly at him.

Max stood up crossing his arms saying, "Who said we didn't get any?" Wiggling his eyebrows and teasing her. I blushed, mortified at his blatant behavior, we'd talked, but I didn't expect him to actively seek out telling her what happened between us.

Saffy's jaw dropped. "Are you telling me you got laid here, Max?"

Max smirked, nodding at her. "Absolutely!"

Her mouth dropped open in disbelief. "Liar!" He raised one eyebrow as if to goad her. Saffy continued, "Really, so where *is* this mystery woman, or are you fantasizing again Max?" She folded her arms, mirroring his stance, waiting for him to reply.

Looked at me, I knew what Max was doing and I gulped hard. "Well sis, I thought I was for a bit, but… yup, I had the sweetest, dirtiest, tightest fucking sex of my life, honey." I was stunned into silence, so embarrassed by his description of our night together.

Saffy was also shocked, but not enough to render her speechless. She turned to look at me, gesturing her head toward him and pointing, "You see what an ass he's turned out to be? Don't listen to him, Lily, he'll only corrupt you."

Walking toward her room, she turned. "Max all I can say is, in your dreams bro', you're full of it." She disappeared from our view and banged her bedroom door.

Throwing his head back, Max started laughing at her reaction. He turned to me, pretending to look wounded, hands over his heart. "Well, I tried." And we both snickered.

When Saffy went to her room, Max and I sat around the apartment watching television, and Max fell asleep. I always thought that he looked older than his years, but seeing him sleeping, he looked boyish laying across from me on the couch. Everything from his cowboy style clothing to his tall, muscular frame and golden blond hair fitted Max's personality to a tee.

He was rugged, but strikingly handsome at the same time, another charmer. No doubt about it, Max was extremely attractive, and he had probably had many women already.

He wasn't at all nervous about having sex, and he didn't appear to have any inhibitions. I began to think this might just be a 'male thing,' and that men viewed sex differently than women.

I was still staring at him when my cell buzzed again. I gingerly walked to the balcony. I didn't want to disturb Max and glanced down at the screen. Alfie was texting me, and I suddenly felt guilty about what Max and I had done.

There were a few times last night when Alfie crept into my mind, but I had pushed those thoughts aside because I told myself that unlike him, Max was emotionally connected to me. Being with Max taught me that I didn't want to have a meaningless relationship with someone, no matter how good the sex was.

**SEXPERT: Still missing you.
Your company gone yet?**

I felt like one of those slutty girls I'd known in school, sleeping with one guy and texting another. It was like all the movies I'd ever seen about a love triangle, minus the love part. The good guy was asleep on the couch and the bad-ass guy was still managing to command my attention.

Pink Lady: No he's very much still here.

SEXPERT: Very much? … Come see me.

Pink Lady: Sorry I can't. I need to spend time with him here.

SEXPERT: When does he leave?

Pink Lady: Sunday.

SEXPERT: Sunday?? Hope the dude keeps his dick in his pants and his hands to himself.

I thought his comment was strange, given the arrangement we had. From the behavior he displayed around me with other women he was the last person that got to make comments like that.

Pink Lady: Umm…that's not your business

SEXPERT: You fucked him?

Pink Lady: Hmm…I'm supposed to disclose my life outside of our arrangement? What happened to no-strings?

SEXPERT: Ominous answer

**Pink Lady: Fair point I'm
making, I think**

**SEXPERT: He must be good if
you're turning me down, cuz I
know that I am.**

**Pink Lady: I've neither
confirmed nor denied anything,
nor do I intend on doing so.**

**SEXPERT: Huh. So…you did
fuck him, otherwise that would
have been a straight no.**

Pink Lady: No comment.

**SEXPERT: So…are we doing
this?**

Pink Lady: The arrangement?

**SEXPERT: Is our arrangement
threatened?**

Fair question Alfie; is it? I really liked spending
time with him, but my feelings were growing, and I
knew I was going to get badly burned. Just seeing
him again the other day after all those weeks
confirmed I had feelings for him, and it sent my mind
into chaos.

Falling hard for Alfie was something I could do
very easily, and that would be a terrible idea. Maybe
being with Max helped me realize that I wasn't able

to settle for sex without an emotional connection.

Thinking I could handle Alfie, and the excitement of doing something so reckless, probably made me feel truly free for the first time in my life.

The idea of doing something that wrong had excited me; he excited me, but I was stupid to think that I could fall into something as casual as what he offered me. Especially, with someone as addictive as I had found Alfie was to me. The guy was right, he had given me some special feelings, but it left me feeling like I was just an object of his desire.

The guy wasn't going to let our arrangement go anywhere. The reality wasn't a healthy situation for me. As much as I liked him, I knew then that I needed to get out before it was too late. It would only end in disaster.

Alfie always left me feeling elated and miserable at the same time. I had known from the beginning that he was not a long-term prospect for me, and he had been straightforward about what I was to him. When I finally admitted that to myself, hard as it was, I knew what I needed to do.

> **Pink Lady: About our arrangement. Been thinking about that... thank you for picking me as your favorite... you were also my favorite fuck buddy. Great sex... excellent reference supplied if needed... contract terminated: hugs: kiss face.**
>
> **SEXPERT: Seriously... we're done?**

Pink Lady: no regrets… thank you for the time we had together x

SEXPERT: Sad Face resignation not accepted without an exit interview… can we at least talk about it?

Pink Lady: Sorry it won't change my decision. We both knew what this was. Take care.

I heard the sound of feet shifting over tile, and I looked up. Max appeared in the doorway, leaning against the door frame. "What's so important on that cell, that I wake up alone and cold?" His voice sounded husky from being asleep. He looked handsome with his sleepy eyes and dishevelled hair. His hand was rubbing over his left pectoral absentmindedly.

Gesturing with my phone in my hand, "I was only making space for new contacts." My answer came out more wistfully than I'd wanted to sound.

"Contact… Sounds like a great idea, come back to bed with me." I shook my head and rolled my eyes.

"Do guys only ever think about sex?" It's nearly two o'clock in the afternoon, I need to go shopping. I need proper food, Max." He gave me a sad, pouty face, and I swatted him as I passed him laughing.

"I'm going to shower, I'm sticky again."

Grinning wickedly, he started moving toward me. "Oh! I *love* when you're sticky." Shaking my head, I took his face in my hands, kissed him softly.

After a quick shower we went shopping. Max sat on my bed Indian style playing my guitar while I got dressed. Saffy was still asleep when we left the apartment for the store.

When we arrived and entered the store, Max smiled down at me. "Would it be okay for me to cook dinner instead of going out tonight?" He slid his arm around my waist and waited for my reply.

"Sure, I would prefer it actually. I like cooking as well."

Max smirked. "Did I mention that I cook naked? I'm a messy chef." He winked and pulled me in for a hug.

CHAPTER 21

SEX, LIES, AND DISCLOSURES

Max wanted Italian food for dinner, pasta specifically. "You're not one of those girls that doesn't eat carbs are you?" I shook my head, and he piled Italian sauce, and the ingredients for a meatball dish into the cart.

He wasn't a very controlled shopper. We had more in the shopping cart than we could possibly eat and would have bought more if I hadn't called a halt and headed for the checkout.

Stacking our food on the checkout conveyer belt, we then waited in line. Max was behind me, so when I was finished, he wrapped his arms around me pulling me back into him. I felt him stir at the small of my back, and the bulge in his pants grew to full arousal as he wiggled himself into place.

It turned me on; the effect I was having on him. I turned my head back to look up at him, raised my eyebrow, and gave him a half smile. Grinning mischievously, his eyes filled with lust. Max placed a hand flat across my belly, and pulled me closer to him.

Lips curled into a smile as he dipped his head toward me. "You see what you do to me?" he whispered seductively into my ear, as he continued making small movements to create friction between the bulge in his jeans and my butt. I could have moved away if I'd wanted to, wild horses wouldn't have made me though.

As we stood waiting patiently, he bent to kiss my neck before he kissed the top of my head and left his mouth there to linger. I was pleased that I could have this effect on him fully clothed.

Melding into his firm body, I felt good having his strong arms envelope me that way. I kept reminding myself I was in a grocery store and fought the urge to turn and kiss him deeply.

Glancing back toward the checkout operator, and my heart flopped inside, and inhaled sharply as the smile on my face froze. Alfie was walking toward us, groceries under his arm. From the moment we saw each other, his eyes locked onto mine.

Suddenly, I felt as if I had betrayed Alfie, being there with Max. I thought that's what it must feel like to have been caught cheating. It was a weird reaction to have, considering what we had been to each other.

Max felt me tense and held me tighter, whispering in my ear. "What's wrong babe?" Briefly, I was reassured by the fact that Alfie always ignored me in public. At most Alfie may nod as he walked past. Glancing around and up at Max, I managed a small smile.

"Sorry almost lost my balance." I was glad I was facing away from Max and could turn my head before I let slip that I wasn't being honest.

When my eyes reconnected with Alfie's I could tell that this wasn't the usual cool guy that would ignore me in public. He was staring directly at me and headed toward us, a slight sneer on his face and his jaw twitching.

My heart was pumping so fast, and my mouth was dry. I started to panic. Max must have sensed something because his arms held me tighter.

"Hey," Alfie cooed. "Lily honey, how're you doing?" Alfie leaned in and placed a small kiss on my cheek. His touch was electric. Max's arms tightened their grip again as I struggled to control my breathing and sound calm.

"Hi Alfie," I said as calmly as I could, but swallowed hard.

He wasn't perturbed at all by the fact I was in Max's arms. Leaned in, Alfie had the audacity to brush my hair away from my face. I almost screamed out loud, because I knew my body would react. Alfie's touch buzzed through me, the sensation pooling at my core.

Fighting my body's natural instinct to stiffen; when Alfie's lips touched my cheek was pointless. I hadn't wanted it to betray me while I was in Max's arms. "Alfie's studying music as well, he's partly the reason Will and I perform together," I explained to Max.

I closed my eyes and swallowed for a brief second, and as they opened Alfie's eyes penetrated mine again. I searched Alfie's face, wanting to know why he would do this. I felt Max's arms relax a little. He hadn't noticed any reaction, and I was relieved.

"Is everyone in England this rude?" Alfie asked, deadpan. "I'm Alfie, a good… buddy of Lily's," he said unsmilingly but putting a hand out to Max. "And you are?" His eyes flicked between Max and I.

"Max," he said, curtly. "I'm a very close friend of Lily's," Max declared it like he was staking a bigger claim to me.

Max reached out to shake Alfie's extended hand, but held me in place with his other arm. The tension between the two men made me feel uneasy. Fortunately, at that moment, it was our turn at the checkout. I was relieved to focus on something other than this awkward situation.

Moving toward the checkout, Max relaxed his grip on me, which allowed me to place the shopping on the belt. I was praying that Alfie would just leave, scared that he may say something to humiliate me. Instead of leaving he became more vocal.

"I'm glad I ran into you actually, there's an event that I wanted to talk to you about. I wanted to know if you'd be interested in performing a couple of numbers with my band next month." My jaw dropped, and he gave me his seductively sexy-dimple smile.

Alfie's focus was completely on me now. Max was forgotten in the exchange between us. His sensual stare was so irresistible. "Some of *our* other friends are coming over for drinks tonight. Do you guys want to come, and we'll talk about it then?"

Still stuck on his use of the term '*our friends*,' when Max looked at me before mumbling, "Sorry buddy, thanks for the offer, but we're going to have a more intimate party of our own tonight."

Firstly, I was annoyed with Max almost staking a claim to me in front of Alfie in that way. Secondly, I was also confused to see a fleeting look of anger and something – I couldn't place – in Alfie's eyes. I saw his jaw twitch, so I knew what Max had said had gotten to him.

Max seemed to have missed this as he had turned to pick up the bags. Alfie reached out and his fingers brushed up my thigh, stealing my breath briefly. He grinned wickedly, his eyes widening, as he ran his tongue over his bottom lip and bit it slowly, his eyes now raking over my body.

Alfie had the same look in his eyes that he had whenever he had been undressing me. Excitement coursed through my body at seeing him act this way, and I struggled to keep my breath even. He could feel my heat, and I blushed. Alfie's face was instantly passive as Max turned around to face us again.

Fighting hard with the feelings that were coursing through my veins, as my thigh tingled and burned from where Alfie's fingers had traced moments before.

My panties were moist, and I ached for him to touch me again. My thinking voice was screaming for him, but my face was a blank canvas. No way could I show him that I still wanted him. Besides, it was crazy, I was here with Max.

Max took the bags in one arm and pulled me close to him with the other. "Okay, honey, we're done, we got to get going." He excused us and led me toward the exit. I couldn't help thinking that Max kissing the top of my head, then nuzzling my neck on the way out was his way of marking his territory a little for Alfie's benefit.

Alfie didn't follow us, rooted to the spot as he continued to watch us make our way out. Walking to the car, I was engrossed in what was in the trolley, but thinking of Alfie, and when I looked up, Alfie was leaning against his car door parked in the opposite row to ours, his gaze fixed on me as he spoke on the phone. I noticed his fists were clenched as I got into the car.

Max stared him out and looked pissed when he got into the car, banging the door. His weight made the car seat huff as he landed heavily on it. His head whipped around to face me. "You need to watch that guy, babe." He looked cross.

Sliding into the car, I didn't comment. "Christ!" He spat out, "Does he always look at you like that?"

Pretending not to know what he meant. "Like what? I don't know what you mean?" I lied.

Max growled, his voice cracking, "Like he wants to fuck you hard Lily, like that look!

Shaking my head in denial, "That's garbage!" I said trying to sound casual about him.

"Seriously, you don't see that, Lily?" Max's voice was so low with emotion he was almost growling at me. It was strange watching his reaction, and I tried to make light of it.

"He's just an intense guy," I quipped trying to laugh it off.

Max became really angry at my reaction. "It's not fucking funny Lily. You are going to have to tread carefully around that guy. He'll fuck you senseless if you look at him the wrong way." He shifted in his seat and hit over at the wheel. "Damn!"

Max's words put me off balance. Alfie was only after sex, as I had been. The thing that was different about this was that he had engaged with me outside of the bedroom, and Max had seen his lust.

I thought Alfie's reaction was due to not taking rejection well. I imagined his looks, bad-boy image, and charm made him irresistible to most women, and I had just dented that image. Watching Max's reaction, though, helped me understand why Alfie had ignored me in public.

Strange that Max reacted like that, and I wondered if his reaction was just that he'd recognized Alfie's behavior, because he had been thinking the same thing about me. They both wanted to have sex with me.

Reaching over, I touched Max's arm in reassurance, I said, "Don't worry about me Max, I'm a big girl, and right now, I want to spend time with you. Please let's not argue about anything, least of all Alfie, he doesn't figure. The guy barely knows me. Let it go Max, especially today."

Max came closer and kissed me softly, before cupping his hand behind my head, pulling me in to deepen the kiss. I smiled at him when we broke free, but I hated knowing that Alfie was watching while Max had been kissing me.

Trying to avoid Alfie's stare, I focused ahead as I started the engine. It made me feel sick to do this in front of him.

As I drove past him, Max's blood boiled again. "He so wants to fuck you, though. Look at the way he's watching you," he threw out there. I looked over at Alfie trying to figure out what his game was, and why he was doing this.

Max turned to face me. "Are you truly not aware how that man feels about you, Lily?" I was stunned by the intensity of Max's reaction to Alfie.

"Max, all the guys I've met that have wanted me have only wanted my body."

My mother used to tell me that she saw beauty as a curse sometimes. I often wondered what she meant by that, but I think I was beginning to better understand her now. I couldn't help how I looked, but I could help how I felt. "Trust me, Max, Alfie isn't interested in me."

We sat in silence during the drive back. I think that I gave him something to think about with my self-righteous speech about men. I also noticed that Max never contradicted me on my point about men in relation to himself either.

As we neared the condo, Max reached over and took my hand, sprinkling small kisses over my knuckles. His hand then slid along the back of my seat and into my hair. He massaged circles into my neck as I drove.

Peering at him over my sunglasses, I said, "Is this the female equivalent of a blow job at the wheel?" I teased trying to divert his thoughts. Max threw his head back with a loud chuckle, and his mood was instantly calmer.

Saffy was up and about when we burst through the door, weighed down from our shopping trip. "Where have you been? I've asked Will over and thought we could all go out on a boat this afternoon."

Coming from the Midwest, Max and Saffy didn't get much of a chance to see the ocean. Neither did I, come to think of it, until I arrived here. Max disappeared into Saffy's room, and I went to change for the trip.

I pulled on a red bikini and black shorts and packed some soda and water in a cooler for us. As we headed downstairs to meet Will, Saffy linked arms with me. "Thank you so much for taking care of Max last night, honey. I owe you," she said quietly to me.

Max heard her and snickered. "Yeah, it must have been a real chore for her." He gave me a sly smile, and I blushed crimson.

Saffy caught it. "What was that look?" She pointed between Max and me, and he threw his hands open.

"What…what look?"

"The look you just gave her, like some secret smile or something. You're sick Max."

Chewing the inside of his mouth, Max tried not to smile. "Saffy, I've come a long way to see you!" He snorted. "You skipped out on me, leaving poor Lily to keep me company."

Looking at my feet, I pinched the underside of my thigh where my hands were, to stop myself laughing at the guilt trip he was putting on his sister.

Relentlessly, Max continued to make Saffy and I feel uncomfortable. "Then, when I was honest with you this morning, you freaked out, calling me a liar, and now this? Makes me wonder why I bothered to come. My trip would have been awful, except little Lily took me under her wing."

"See!" Saffy spat at him, "You just contradicted

yourself!"

Looking confused, Max raised his eyebrow questioning her, "I did?"

Saffy nodded, pointing at me. "Yup, one minute you were off getting laid, and the next, Lily was keeping you company."

Max's eyes were pleading with me, and I wanted to support him, so I gave him a slow nod and blushed. I scrunched my eyes up and pulled my shoulders to my ears as I waited for the onslaught when Saffy found out.

Chuckling as he looked back at me, it was clear he was making Will look uncomfortable. Will rubbed the back of his neck looking awkward at being there. Max turned to Saffy. "Listen to me Saffy, I'm only going to say this once, so you need to listen carefully. I *did* get laid last night, *fact*."

He struggled to keep himself from laughing. "Lily *did* keep me company. The two events don't have to be mutually exclusive you know." My heart stuttered as I waited for the onslaught of Saffy's response when it sunk in.

Swallowed hard as my adrenaline kicked in, making my heart pounding in my chest. Saffy's head snapped round and she stared at me silently for what seemed like a *really* long time. Her facial expressions changing from disbelief, shock, horror, disgust, then settled on anger.

Will shuffled his feet, his eyes flicking between us, and he looked like he wished he was anywhere else, except here. He seemed thoroughly embarrassed, his eyes darting between Saffy and me several times. I could see him cringe like he was hearing something he'd never recover from.

He was also staring at me as if he couldn't believe I'd have intercourse with *anyone*. Of everything that was going on, his face was the one thing I found the most amusing during this whole obtuse situation.

Saffy stood digesting Max's disclosure. I was blushing, mortified that anyone was discussing me having sex. Her head swung round to Max. "Max Barclay. You fucking man whore. You fucked my friend, you piece of shit? You fucked my best fucking friend?" Her head snapped back in my direction.

"Lily? *Lily!* You let my brother fuck you?" She pulled her hands up and gripped her hair.

I knew she'd be disappointed with me, but I never dreamed she'd react this badly. I thought she was going to hit me she was so crazy.

Clearing my throat as if to speak, I thought better of doing so. Instead, I stood with my arm across my body holding my other forearm.

Will, who seemed to have recovered from the shock that I'd actually let a man do things to me, looked bemused and kind of smirked at me.

At one point I thought he was going to laugh, but he started stroking down both cheeks to his chin with his thumb and forefinger to hide this. Will's eyes were darting between all of us now, taking in everyone's reaction. I was betting that he would think of this as payback for what I did to him yesterday on the way home in the car.

CHAPTER 22

BEING A FRIEND

Max pleaded, "Come on Saffy, Lily and I are consenting adults. I mean it's not as if I tied her down or anything, although…"He smirked, then continued, "anyway, I don't think I took advantage of her, do you think I did, Lily?"

I found my voice and said, "Not at all. I am more than happy with what happened."

Will's, "I bet," fell out before he was conscious of it; his thinking voice falling out of his mouth.

Saffy turned and batted him on the chest, then snapped at him. "Shut the fuck up, Will." Will shuffled his feet, biting his lip, and it was my turn to smirk.

Will cleared his throat, and seemed to want us to see him sticking up for himself after she chastised him. "I think you just need to calm down Saffy, it's not like it's the end of the world or anything."

She snapped her head back in his direction now,

giving him a scowling look, but Will became braver. "The thing is, honey, I think you've got no right to get on your high horse, we were at it all night. What's good for the goose …" Max growled at Will, who had just admitted having sex with his sister.

Giggling at Will's attempt to make it better, I had made it worse by putting himself further in the firing line. It was becoming so ridiculous. What we had done was a natural adult activity by consenting adults. The way Saffy was behaving was like someone had committed a major crime.

Holding my hands up, I couldn't keep my face straight because the situation was becoming so absurd. "Will you all stop this?" I giggled again, and tried to compose myself. Turning this back on Saffy, "If you hadn't gone with Will, would Max and I have happened last night? Highly unlikely, I think."

I rolled my eyes and glanced at Max's smirking face. "Do I think we would have had sex some other time? I think so if the circumstances arose. Max and I have always had a kind of 'thing' about each other. We're just old enough to see where it takes us now. We enjoyed spending time with each other and know that if it doesn't go anywhere, we'll still love each other because of our history."

Max rubbed Saffy's back and pulled her in for a bear hug, kissing her forehead. "You'll get used to it Saffy. We won't be in your face with this, but we don't want to stop." Saffy struggled to hold her gaze to me.

"Please Saffy, be okay about it." She sighed.

"I don't ever want to lose you because of a bad relationship with my brother, and I don't want you not to have a relationship with Max if it makes you both happy either." She sniffed.

"Saffy, we are very cool with what happened, we're just going to see where it takes us. Nothing's changed." I hugged her affectionately.

Max said, "True Lily, nothing has changed, except we had some incredible orgasms."

I threw Max a, you're-dead-when-I-get-you-on-your-own glare, and Saffy slapped Max hard on the arm. "That's way too much information Max! TMI."

Will raised an eyebrow at me, and I couldn't help but think that someday this conversation would be used to get his own back for the prank I pulled on him about his sex life. He winked and grinned at me.

"What's the female version of a stud?" he asked, teasing me before chuckling again. I had been doing really well, but now that the focus was more about the sex, I blushed again.

Max and I continued to have a great time together in the following few days. When Sunday arrived, it came too quickly for the both of us. We lay tangled in each other, him holding me tightly, stroking my arm, after a tender lovemaking session.

We had stayed awake all night talking, not wanting to waste time sleeping when we could share it with each other, enjoying the darkness, and watching the daylight creep in.

~ * ~

When I drove him to the airport, we stood holding each other and stared ahead at the security desk that would take him airside. My stomach sank when his flight was called.

We had a torturous parting, with Max coming back to kiss me deeply twice, pained about leaving me, while I was trying to be strong and not cry.

Biting my lip, I stood watching him until Max told me to stop or he'd drag me to a bathroom for another farewell session. Looking up at him, with tears welling in my eyes, I stretched up on tiptoe to peck his cheek.

Max kissed my nose one last time, and I watched him looking back at me. He looked as torn as I felt. He cleared security and disappeared out of sight. I sighed and a single tear ran down my face. My heart squeezed when I could no longer see him.

Driving back, the radio was full of music that did nothing to lighten my mood. It was dark by the time I arrived home, and the apartment was empty.

I was thankful for that at least, I didn't feel like talking and went for a hot bath, filling the tub with bubbles. The smell of the bath oil was intoxicating but it didn't make me feel any better.

Saffy was staying with Will again, and Holly was working. I hadn't seen her in days. I crawled into bed and tried to do some homework for college, but my mind was still with Max. My cell buzzed in my purse, and I leaned out of bed to reach for it, almost toppling out of it.

Max: Lying here, remembering your sweet face.

Lily: Me too, not that your face is sweet…it's handsome.

Max: You like what you see, huh?

Lily: Nah, honestly…you're a troll.

Max: LMAO My time with you was wonderful, Lily, thank you.

Lily: I had a great time…it sucks we didn't have more of it.

Max: True, but I will try to repeat, I don't want you to sit waiting for me though.

Lily: You mean I should see other people? Not sure we're on the same page with that.

Max: If we don't put boundaries in place, then we're less likely to get hurt if one of us isn't strong.

Lily: Hmm… I guess…Night Max x

Max: Sweet dreams honey, mwahx

Max's text made me feel uneasy. It was almost like been there done that, but you don't have enough to hold my attention. It was a complete contrast to what he was saying when he was here.

He told me he really wanted to try to have something between us, that it was only the distance that made him hesitant. His texts didn't read that way at all. I made a note that the next time we spoke, I would need to clear this up with him.

Exhausted by the time I finished texting, I realized I hadn't had much sleep this weekend. Clutching my cell phone in my hand and turning it over and over, I then placed it under my pillow and snuggled down to sleep. When I woke it was buzzing against my cheek. It was 7am.

> **Will: Meet me at 8:15 I've snagged a recording booth for two hours.**

> **Lily: Sleepy, can we do 8:30am?**

> **Will: Nope, see you at 8:15am. Aren't you energized from your 'fitness regimen' this weekend?**

Rolling my eyes, I stretched out, groaning. It was easy to see that Will was going to milk my situation for his own amusement. He was going to give me as much shit as possible over his observations of what went down with Saffy, Max, and I.

I stepped into the shower, and the temperature was only tepid, so I didn't linger. Once I'd had a quick scrub in all the important places, I threw on some cropped jeans and a crisp white Ralph Lauren crew neck t-shirt.

Placing a small red wooden beaded necklace around my neck, I let it hang down in front; breaking the plain effect, and began to gather my stuff to leave for campus. Holly was arriving home from her night shift and looked gray with tiredness. I felt so bad for her doing night work.

Hugging her, I picked up my guitar and rucksack, and shoved some toast in my mouth as I ran out of the door. Will squeezed me tight when I arrived at the car lot at college.

We settled in the recording booth and got straight to work on an arrangement he had put together the night before. He asked about yesterday with Max, and I mentioned his strange comment in the text he sent me.

Will sighed. "Sorry, honey." He looked awkward.

"For what?" I asked confused.

Will exhaled. "Max." I sighed sadly thinking he meant about Max having to go.

"Well, we like each other Will, but the distance and where we are in our lives right now…" I hesitated, "we'll see how it goes."

By the look on Will's face I realized that wasn't what he meant. Will was moving the gravel around under his foot. His eyes flicked to mine, and he exhaled heavily again before he spoke.

"So you're still going to do the long distance relationship thing with him? Try to keep your relationship going?" I nodded and gave him a weak smile, because after Max's text I wasn't confident it would work.

"Well, yeah, that's the idea… that's what he said. He's going to try to be here once a month." Will's brows bunched together, and he shifted uncomfortably on his feet.

"What's the matter with you, Will?" He pursed his lips into his mouth and shook his head but didn't give me eye contact.

He rubbed his eyes with one hand. "Nothing." The defeated way he said it told me it definitely wasn't.

Searching his face, I knew there was more to this than he was telling me. "Will, I think I know you better than this by now, come on out with it."

Will exhaled loudly. "Aw, well, shit! Lily."

I waited, but when he didn't say anything I asked quietly, "Did you and Saffy break up?"

Taking my hand in his, Will said, "No!" He inhaled sharply, shook his head vigorously, before his voice took on a much softer tone. "No, honey it's nothing like that." He let out a shaky breath attempting to control it.

Will chewed his lip and huffed, still struggling to look at me. Eventually, his eyes met mine and held my gaze. I'll never forget the look of pain in them.

"Well, what is it? You're scaring me Will." He stroked my hand, then my cheek.

"Lily… in the time I've known you…" He took a deep breath.

"Okay, out with it, just say it," I snipped. "My nerves can't take any more of this shit, Will." His eyes fell to the floor.

"If I tell you Lily, I don't want it to affect our relationship or yours with Saffy." His eyes looked dull and concerned. I knew whatever he had to say wasn't good. I watched his body language prepare to tell me something that he knew I didn't want to hear.

"Will, whatever it is, you can't keep it to yourself now. I promise to try to keep our relationship as it is, you and Saffy are like family to me now, so I figure that whatever it is, we'll weather it."

Breathing deeply, Will's face looked grim and I could feel his angst. The atmosphere between us was very tense. "You sure you want to hear this?" he asked giving me a sideways glance.

"Just tell me." I was getting really annoyed now.

"Okay, here goes nothing." He sighed. "On Saturday night, when we were at dinner, and I went to the bathroom, do you remember that?" I nodded. Will struggled with his thoughts, then continued, "Okay, well, Max… he was on his cell…In the hallway I mean."

Waiting for him to reply, holding my breath. "He was talking to a female saying, something like, 'it's been a pain to be away from you, I won't be long until I'm home now, Kelly. I can't wait to see you tomorrow.' I thought I'd heard him wrong, then he said, 'I've missed you too, babe.' I was going to confront him, but then he said, 'Okay, we'll get some time and meet with them, talk soon' and hung up." I had felt there was something that Max avoided, nothing I could put my finger on, but it made perfect sense when Will told me what he knew.

Max was reluctant for me to visit him in Nashville when I tried to pin him down with a date during one of our conversations at the airport. *How stupid am I?* Of course Max would have a girl, and he cheated on her with me. I felt devastated that he could betray me like that.

Will enveloped me in his strong arms and squeezed me, resting his head on mine for a moment, before letting me go. "Lily, I know I'm not wrong. I'm a guy, from how he was speaking to her. I don't think it was just a friend. Kelly's his girl." Will looked terrible at having to tell me this, and I could see he cared about me. I felt that the last thing he wanted was to hurt me.

"There was something else. He was texting a few times on Friday to someone when we were on the boat, and he was smiling kind of wistfully when he was reading the replies. You were looking at your phone were you texting with him?" I shook my head. "I thought he was texting with you, but when you stopped, and he kept going, I kind of realized he wasn't texting with you at all."

Twisting his lips, Will worked a swallow. "When my hat blew off on the boat and landed on his lap, I leaned in to take it back, and I think he thought I'd seen one of the texts. He winked at me and switched his phone off, before I could ask him what's up, and shoved it in his pocket. He looked guilty about something."

When Max gave me an awkward smile, "I thought, why the fuck are you winking at me, dude. It felt strange at the time, but after overhearing his call I sort of put two and two together." Will looked uneasy and gave me a half smile.

"He's good though. I'll give him that, how he was all attentive and shit toward you. That was the only thing that made me decide not to tell you sooner." I quickly wiped a tear that was rolling down my face. How could he do that to me, we had been friends.

Will saw how the news was affecting me and pulled me back into his chest in a bear hug. He rubbed my back, and I sobbed into him. Will stood silently holding me, he'd said enough. I pushed away from him, but he pulled me back and held me tightly. Will's soft voice vibrated in his chest, "Sorry honey, it really is better you find out now than later, huh?" Then he kissed my head again.

I straightened up, and stepped away from him. "I need to go home Will, I can't do today now." I stared up at him. Tears streamed down my face. I felt stupid, ridiculous, and ashamed that I had let someone else take advantage of me.

"You look so fragile honey, I'm coming with you." He gave me a half smile. "There's no way I'm letting you get behind the wheel of a car in this state." As we walked to his car, he pulled me into him again. Every once in a while, he looked at me and wiped his thumb over my cheeks in an effort to stop my tears.

I felt I just wanted to go home to the UK. I had got everything wrong here. I'd made so many mistakes and now seeing Saffy or bumping into Alfie would leave me with constant reminders of what a stupid fuck-up of a girl I was.

CHAPTER 23

I'VE GOT TO BE ME

Sighing heavily, and breaking the silence between us. "I'm fine Will, I'm partly to blame too. I allowed it to happen. I got involved too quickly." He stopped walking and turned to face me, and brushed the last of my tears with his knuckles. His face was desolate, and I could see that it broke his heart to see me so unhappy.

"I knew it was a risk to get with Max. Here's the thing, I had no experience of sexual relationships until the week before I came to live here, but ever since I've made some pretty epic mistakes." I knew I needed to learn from them and learn fast.

I sniffed and stared at Will. "I'm only sorry that you have had to be involved in this at all, Will. It isn't your place to support me when the simple truth of the matter is I've given myself too easily."

Will looked seriously at me and shook his head. "It's only one relationship Lily, don't let it affect you." He looked at me supportively. Only it wasn't one relationship with Sam and Alfie. *Sleeping with both my best girlfriends' brothers? Having a 'fuck buddy'?* My sex life so far… It sounded like a bad B movie in the making.

Will put his hand on my shoulder and squeezed it sympathetically, then cuddled me tightly and drew little circles my shoulders with his thumbs. He gave me a small smile again. "Hey, come on, we'll get you home," he said softly. Will started driving me home, and promised he'd pick me up in the morning to bring me back to college to collect my car.

When we arrived back, he came up to the apartment with me. "Let's go to the beach and jam together." I didn't really feel like it, but he was right, I needed to move on as quickly as possible or this could consume me. He began organizing me. "Okay girlie, get your sunscreen and hat, we can't allow your fair ass to fry out there! I'm gonna head to the surf store for some shorts; when I get back I expect you stripped and ready for the beach." He strode to the door and it banged closed as he left to buy something more fitting to wear for the beach.

What he bought transformed him from Will, the cool sax player, to Will, the hot surfer dude. Fabulous looking, in the red and white surfer shorts and the white sleeveless t-shirt he was already wearing, I was a little surprised by his great physique, I had never really noticed him in that way before.

Very handsome, actually, scratch that, he was a great looking guy, with his messy, chestnut brown hair, that looked so shiny he could model for a hair product company. Will was quite powerfully built, and I wondered again why I hadn't seen this before. I mean I'd seen him in his boxers that one time, but I was too mortified to take in what he looked like. Anyway, I'd never really noticed because he was with Saffy.

I whistled appreciatively, teasing him. "Damn! You're a hottie Will, a damn fine specimen." I wiggled my brows at him. Will grinned kind of embarrassed and chuffed at the same time.

"Yeah, I know," he said, nodding and checking himself out, behaving as if he were in love with himself.

Launching into an overacted scene, Will answered playfully, "Thank you, ma'am…" then commented, "Hey, I thought you were off men?" I paused, putting my fingers to my chin pretending that I was contemplating what he'd just said. I began tapping my lips, pretending to think.

Chuckling, I threw my head back. "Definitely! No guy is getting in my panties without being totally emotionally connected and hanging on my every word, and even then, he'll have to beg. I am going to concentrate on leaving the passion in the bedroom to others and put mine into my music from now on, at least it won't fuck me over," I said determinedly.

"Atta gurl!" he growled, grinning devilishly at me.

My mood was lifting and I pretended to give a Will my best seductive look. I leaned in and whispered, "As for you, looking great in those swimmers, who says I can't still window shop?"

Giving him a mock exaggerated look of appreciation, my eyes widened, like I was objectifying him. "I mean, I appreciate the finer things in store windows all the time… it doesn't mean I have to buy anything… does it?"

Will grinned, leaning back his hands stretched out to the sides pretending to give me a better view. "You like what you see huh?" he said in a slow southern drawl and turned nodding his head. He wiggled his eyebrows suggestively pretending to flirt with me.

Laughing loudly, it felt good to have someone I could just be me around, without any demands on our relationship. I was beginning to really value Will as a friend and his loyalty to me.

What made it even better was that he seemed to care about me. Will and I were honest with each other, and I hoped that it would always be like that between us.

"Lily girl, you are a wonderful, sweet, gorgeous girl, you're going to work this out. I know it hurts a lot right now. By next month, it will hurt a little less, a month after that? Max, who's Max?" He looked wistful for a split second then it was gone.

"Been here, huh?" I asked.

Tapping on his heart silently, he nodded, "It's getting there." I took that as a yes.

We headed for the beach, the feel of the sun, the smell of the sea and the warmth of our friendship enhanced our music and lifted my mood to no end.

Amazing scenery helped us to be productive, with ideas and new material flowing. It was a lot of fun with him and our easy conversation and similar thoughts about music helped bond us closer during the day.

I was messing around with some chords when something I played triggered the memory of a song for Will, and he started to sing it. "You know that song?" I looked incredulously at him, rising to my knees on the towel then sitting back on my heels. I didn't think that band had cracked it in the USA. Will said, "I don't know about that, but I heard the track when I was in London, so I downloaded it to my iPod. It brings back happy memories for me."

Grinning, I loved that song. "Will! It's one of my favorite songs, can we sing it together," I pleaded. My hands were praying at him.

I began to play the introduction to *Come Up and See me, (make me smile),* by Steve Harley and Cockney Rebel. We both started belting it out, not really caring that we were making noise around some sleepy sunbathers.

We weren't even sure that the words we were singing were the right ones, but they fit the music, and I felt some of the stress leave me. I felt like I was home for a few minutes.

It was ironic that this was the song that came to his mind. It's about band members quitting on Steve before he became famous. It fitted in with my mood, not that I was going to be famous, but maybe Max will feel sorry for his treatment toward me one day.

Some beachgoers sat up to listen to us, and applauded when we had finished our impromptu concert. Will and I were slightly embarrassed, but grinned and laughed about our spontaneous performance, which was anything but polished. "I feel much better after that."

He slung an arm around my shoulders and

squeezed me against him side on. "I'm glad you're feeling stronger honey, but now I had better make myself scarce before Saffy comes home, or she'll be mad that we spent the day together on the beach."

Will's eyes looked moody and troubled now. "She's possessive as hell, and as much as she loves you Lily, she has trust issues."

I looked wide-eyed and seriously at Will. "Agreed!" We packed up and headed back to the apartment, already aware that Saffy didn't like us spending time together as it was.

Stroking Will's arm as if to show him my sincerity. "Thank you so much for today Will, and for telling me. It means a lot to me that you have my back."

Will took my hand, squeezed it, and brought it to his lips. It was a tender thing to do. "Always." Leaning in, he kissed my forehead gently. Will's lips were soft and warm. It felt so comforting. Turning away, I walked inside, rummaging in my bag for my keys. There was a text message envelope waiting on my phone.

Max: Missed hugging you last night. Missing me?

I found my keys, dragged myself inside, and sat down heavily on the couch before replying.

Lily: Coping well, so much better than I thought I would.

Max: Cool, I'll try to come soon, won't be able to stay away long.

I took a deep breath, I didn't want to play games with people's lives, and I didn't want them to play them with mine.

Lily: would you tell Kelly it's me you're coming to see?

Waiting for a return text; and when it didn't arrive immediately, it confirmed what Will suspected. Well, at least Max didn't protest his innocence, or worse, say that she meant nothing to him. I knew him well enough. He knows I know him too, so he'll be trying to find a way around hurting me and saving face. I wasn't surprised when the next text did arrive after ten minutes.

Max: Ah, too complex to explain by text or phone we'll talk when I come to see you.

I knew I needed to be completely honest with him and that there would be no repeat of what we had in the future.

Lily: No explanation necessary Max, we're friends. I used you for sex, just like you used me. You've done all the 'coming' you're going to do with me, chapter closed. Don't hurry back, but we will get past this for Saffy's sake.

My phone rang immediately, caller ID showed Max. I let it ring out, switched it off, and threw it back in my bag. When I did this, I knew I'd be strong enough to get past this hump in my life.

I'm not happy with the person I'm turning into here. Everything I was doing was so out of character for me. Maybe I was giving out vibes I wasn't aware of, and I needed to be far less trusting of men.

The most honest thing that's happened to me was Alfie, which didn't say much for me as a person at all. *Why had I been willing to have sex with someone that didn't care how I felt?*

Worse still, I was still coming to terms with how much I missed him, even though I ended the arrangement. I was horrified with the thought I still missed him, even when I was wrapped in Max's arms.

Nothing about Alfie felt easy though, but his slightest touch made my body respond impulsively. When he touched me, my body hummed and buzzed, like an electrical charge had been applied.

Correction, he even makes me feel weak without touching me. I thought I understood Superman's Achilles Heel 'thing' much better now with the Kryptonite; Alfie was mine.

Why have all my relationships been so complicated lately. I had to admit it wasn't like that with Will, though, except that Saffy was an issue for us.

We had to come up with a white lie today to make it easier on her. Will and I agreed to tell her that I was brought home by him, but that was the extent of our contact outside of college today.

I felt bad that we weren't able to be truthful with her, but for all our sakes, it was better to play it off as if our time spent outside of college was minimal, and we didn't (?) just hang today, no matter how innocent it was.

Fraining sickness, I said that Will had driven me home. Saffy still probed me about it though. "Where did he go afterwards?"

I felt bad lying, "Not sure, I think he went home."

Well, it was a kind of honest… I mean… he did leave me and go home. Saffy seemed satisfied with this and went to change before dinner. I called home to the UK tonight. I felt I needed to hear my parents' voices and tried to draw strength from talking to them.

~ * ~

I did well to cover up how I was feeling, because I knew at the first hint of discord, my parents would have dramatically swooped in and brought me home. I was sounding so upbeat when I spoke to my parents. I almost convinced myself I was fine.

They had no idea what had been going on with me during the past six weeks in my new life, except that I had partnered up with Will.

"No Mom," I sighed in mock frustration. "No, mother, no romantic involvement with him, he's Saffy's boyfriend," I answered exacerbated by my mom's hope. I rolled my eyes, glad that she couldn't see me, as she lived in the hope of me giving her early grandbabies.

My mom wanted me to be a teenage mom, and my dad wanted me to be a nun. Looks like both my parents were jinxed with me. My mother told me about Elle's part in a West End Musical, and how excited they all were for her.

Missing my friend, I was feeling bad that I had abandoned Elle in London for America, and made a mental note to call her after arranging a time by email. It was our only means of contact, due to time changes, Elle's work, college, and her attending auditions. She was a dancer and worked odd hours.

I had known she was attending an audition on Friday, but Elle hadn't caught up with me yet, to tell me she'd actually got the part. I berated myself for not being a better friend to her.

Homesickness hit me, I missed everyone back home, but even more so today, because of how I was feeling. I knew that what was happening was my own fault and wanted to believe that everything would be all right in my world eventually.

CHAPTER 24

MISCONCEPTIONS

Saffy had made dinner by the time my call was done, and us girls ate dinner together for the first time in ages. I lay back, rubbing my stomach. I was feeling fit to burst, stuffed full of her fabulous enchiladas. We were listening to her crooning about Will and his sexual prowess.

I began to feel a bit uncomfortable with some of her comments. He felt like a brother, and I wouldn't want to hear about my brother's cock and sexual ability in bed. I also had to work with Will on a daily basis.

"Honestly, I had no idea that sex was so…so sexy," Saffy gushed, her face completely serious. Holly and I howled with laughter at her. Holly figured that Saffy was the epitome of a rock star, when it came to sex.

Holly's summation of Saffy was that she was usually "a use-'em-up-and-toss-'em-aside kind of a girl," as far as sex was concerned. Holly deduced that Will must definitely have something for Saffy to be harping on about him.

Our evening was fabulously indulgent. We talked about boys all evening, pampered each other, painted nails, conditioned hair, and did face masks; we all looked a mess, and the apartment stunk of chemical and organic products.

We had a great time catching up though. By the time I went to bed, I was feeling a lot better. That was until I was lying in the darkness of my room with my thoughts again.

My mind crept back to Alfie as it usually did when I had quiet time, especially in bed at night. *Did he ever lay in bed and think about me? If he did, what exactly did he think about?*

Tears gradually filled my eyes and silently streaked down the side of my temple soaking my pillow. I was so hurt, and it didn't help when I told myself it was my own fault. My heart had been shattered by a guy whose only interest in me was in my body. I wasn't crying for Max, I was crying for Alfie.

What made it worse for me was that when he had taken me to his bed, he'd had the knack of making me feel like I was the most special woman in his world. *How was he able to do that and feel nothing?* It was sick, I was sick... lovesick. Alfie had become my first conscious thought in the morning and my last at night.

Learning to deal with the Max and Alfie issues, I put them to one side and concentrated on college life. I had begun to make friends in some of my other classes, and there were a couple of interesting Indie-type performers that kept me entertained with their great lyric writing and cool music arrangements.

Neil and Mandy were doing great as well. They were getting a lot of gigs and invited Will and me to join them a few times. We didn't get paid. Well, we did – in beer – but we were at least showcasing ourselves. Neil was really encouraging us.

Apart from that, Will and I were getting a little following of our own, which was great. I used to feel that Mandy was just being kind to me, because I was helping Will, but as more and more people asked questions about my music background, I began to believe that maybe she really did see something in me.

Several of my tutors and students commented that they thought I had 'a recording voice'. Again, the first couple of times I heard this, I didn't believe it. However, with it being said in a few settings now, I was starting to feel more comfortable about singing. People liked my voice.

There were several venues we played at during that month where I crossed Alfie's path more than once, but we never spoke. He always seemed to have a glamorous woman hanging off of his arm, and I always felt hurt whenever I saw him.

Several times he stared intensely at me, and I stared back, not wanting to back down and show him any weakness. In those moments I felt our connection so strongly that the air seemed thicker in the room. A couple of times I thought he was going to come over and speak to me, but he never did.

Once, when I was grabbing some beers from the

bar during a break in our set, I turned to see him watching me. His date was doing something with her phone. As I turned my head, my eyes instantly fixed on to his. Alfie smiled a little at me, stroking his thumb over his lips. My heart raced at his action, and I instantly wanted to be his thumb.

Angry feelings took over, as I struggled with how his little blatantly sexy and flirty gestures could cause those brief, intense moments like that. I was frustrated that he didn't want what I wanted between us, yet couldn't leave me in peace.

Alfie's selfish behavior was exactly what I needed to help me move past him, and my rational side began to kick in. I'd seen him with eight different women, not including me, in the time I'd known him. Not that I was counting or anything.

His type… well they were all glamorous, older women. The only exceptions being me and the blond girl that sat with him that day on campus. No matter how many times I told myself I'd had a lucky escape with him, I still couldn't shake the damn guy out of my system.

Everything about him screamed that I shouldn't want anything to do with a guy like him. Deep down, I didn't want to want him. I just needed to learn *how* not to want him, and everything would be fine.

Tonight was different from all the other nights when we've been at the same gigs. He was alone, drinking his beer slowly. He was listening intently and appeared to be scrutinizing the acts. This gig was like a mini-festival. There was a lot of talent in the room. As well as Mandy and Neil and Will and I, there were four other bands performing.

Our group of friends were all buzzing after the gig, chatting excitedly about how we did and what we thought of the other acts. Holly did a hilarious impersonation of Mandy singing, which we were laughing about, when Alfie suddenly appeared beside us.

"Hey," he cooed, grinning at us just enough to show his cute dimple. My heart skipped a beat. I felt like he'd taken it in his palm and squeezed hard with that one word. I had a dull ache in the center of my chest and could feel my body instantly react to him.

I was shocked, my body going into flight mode, as the adrenaline rushed through my veins and the air seemed to get sucked out of my lungs. Eyes glanced fleetingly at me, expressionless, before he turned his attention and greeting everyone. I was frozen.

The pulse at the base of my neck ticked, as my body reacted to my proximity to him. He was standing so close to me that I could almost feel the electricity arc between us, the air in the space between us felt heavy with awareness, and it threatened to turn me into a jittery mess.

I couldn't help but inhale his scent, it tantalized me. It was the same familiar body wash and him – his unique body scent – with traces of tequila and beer. I always loved how he smelled. It was such a turn on and right then it was overwhelming me.

Alfie then smiled a half smile at me, and I knew I blushed as I struggled with how close he was to me, silently cursing my body for reacting to him like that.

A brief, sexy smirk teased at his lips, as his eyes narrowed at me. Alfie knew the effect he had on me, and I wondered if I had the same effect on his body as he did on mine.

Turning to Will, Alfie put his fist up, both men doing that stupid bump thing with them. Will's eyes darted to me, almost like he felt guilty for doing it, and he looked sheepish. I knew he felt disloyal because of Alfie's lack of attention to me.

Smiling, I reassured Will, I was okay with it. It wasn't Will's fault Alfie behaved shitty, and I didn't want me to be the cause of Will feeling that way. I stepped back, creating a little distance between us, and watched as he chatted easily with my friends.

After a few minutes I sneaked another peek at him, I couldn't fight the urge to look at him. As I watched his face I felt my heart expand and tear at my loss. Not being able to touch him was almost unbearable.

My mind wandered back to the times where he had cupped my face and pulled me in for a kiss, or when he had pressed into me so that I could feel the pleasure I gave him.

Alfie's voice drew me back into the present. "You were fabulous honey." He smiled at Mandy. He leaned forward and kissed her lightly on the cheek. He praised her voice and performance and invited her to sing with him on a bigger stage when they were supporting artists for some rock band in a few weeks. Alfie had said that to me once too though. Maybe it's a pickup line.

Mandy jumped up and down with excitement. She glowed at the prospect of working with him. I know it was irrational, because Mandy and Neil were solid, but I felt consumed with jealousy that he was paying so much attention to her.

I ached for him to turn to me, give me praise, and wrap his arms around me. I diverted my eyes away from them, and my heart fell further at the hole he left in my chest, now that we weren't anything to each other.

When I stole another look at his features, he was still the same handsome man who oozed sex appeal. His looks, personality, and talent were a lethal combination, at least to me. He stood there talking, so unaffected by what had happened between us, and I wanted to feel numb like that.

Not confident I was going to be acknowledged by him at all, other than that little smile, I stood awkwardly. All these weeks we'd passed each other and not a word since the day I'd seen him in the store with Max.

Humoring myself, I smirked when I had the outrageous thought, that maybe I would only be acknowledged in public, when someone else had their arms wrapped around me.

Lost in my daydream, my eyes must have wandered to look down absentmindedly. When I raised them again, I was still smirking. Alfie noticed this, and his sparkling hazel, green-flecked eyes locked into mine.

Lips curving upward at the edges, Alfie had the slightest hint of humor on his face. It was as if he was in on my secret. I think he thought I was looking at his bulging jeans. Truly, I wasn't.

My first thought was to just walk away. Don't give him the satisfaction of ignoring me in public again, and I was planning to do just that, but he turned to face Will, gesturing toward me by jutting his chin in my direction.

"Are you going to introduce me?" Will looked like he'd been asked to undress me, his mouth gaping, because he'd tried to do just that, on more than one occasion, but Alfie had shut him down.

Clearing his throat, Will stuttered awkwardly, "This is my… eh, mine…" He struggled for what to introduce me as. I thought it was funny and was going to wait it out and let him label me as his 'something', but he was my friend, and as a nice person, I wouldn't let him suffer like that.

"Hey," I said, putting my hand out. "Lily… I'm Will's colleague." I gestured with my index finger and pointed down the length of me, just as we had both done the first day we met.

Seeing Alfie's eyes reflect on that action, and for a moment he smiled. Will shot me a glance as if to say sorry. Smiling again, I wrinkled my nose at him as a sign of affection, and saw him relax again.

Alfie took my hand in his, and I melted. My legs trembled and my skin flushed. Smiling, his eyes widened as he watched the effect, his touch on my skin had on me. It was like an electric current passing through me, making my body buzz in anticipation.

No one else had this effect on me. Goose bumps sprung up all over me, and I shivered. He noted this by running his thumb over the goose bumps with a slow sensual smile. "Hi, Lily pleased to meet your acquaintance," he cooed in his sexy, low, velvety voice.

Lifting my hand to his mouth, Alfie's eyes continued to lock into my stare, and he grazed his lips sensually over my knuckles. His tongue made the slightest moist trail as he did this, which looked like nothing to an outsider.

Expert in seduction, Alfie's technique stole my breath briefly; it hitched in my lungs and his effect panged at my core. My eyes fluttered closed briefly.

Luckily, the room was noisy though, and there was a lot going on so no one appeared to notice what he was doing to me. No one apart from Alfie, that is. His eyes sparkled, the hue much more green, which told me he still wanted me.

Recognizing the look he gave me, it was the same one he always had, right before he entered me. He raised his eyebrow; almost as a question, before dropping my hand. At the same time, he drew his bottom lip in between his teeth, and let it spring free, moistening it with a flick of his tongue.

The sight was such a sensual experience on such a perfect mouth, and I was mesmerized. I wanted nothing more than to crush my mouth onto his and explore inside with my tongue as I had before.

Slick juices pooled even more at my core, and the small strip of material between my legs was drenched, I was so affected by his attention, I didn't trust myself to speak.

Mandy interjected again, asking for the dates of the gigs Alfie had mentioned to her. I broke his gaze and walked past him. Suddenly, before I was out of earshot, he was giving an open invite to his house for drinks.

Saffy and Holly were keen to go; Alfie was definitely a charmer. Will had some split loyalties and wondered how I felt about it, given Alfie's previous treatment of me.

Initially, I complained that I was tired and was going to head home, but from the response from our group, I didn't feel I could object anymore, so I went along with it.

Sitting quietly in Will's car on the way over, I was dreading having to spent time in the same space and not touch him. When we got to Alfie's place, Will found me and squeezed my hand in support, because he kind of knew I didn't want to be there. "Are you okay with this?" Nodding; abet too quickly, a reassurance to him, as I still tried to convince myself that I was. I had to keep reminding myself to act as if I hadn't been in his house before.

Strange, hurt feelings and a rush of memories hit me as I walked through the door that Alfie had pressed me into, so playfully. Glancing at the stairs, heat stirred in my core again and my folds pulsed, as I became overwhelmed by the memory of him carrying me up to his bedroom. Remembering all the things we did together in his room directly above this one, I longed to have that with him again.

Blushing, I was still affected by those memories, and caught him smirking into his beer bottle, when his eyes caught mine for a second. His eyes flicked to the stairs and rolled up toward the ceiling, as if he was reading my mind again.

Alfie didn't pay attention to me. Well, that's not entirely true, his attention was demanded by everyone else in the group, once everyone arrived. Especially, when they found out how popular his band was becoming, as they supported major artists in the states.

When I was listening to him, I was genuinely

pleased, because he was definitely talented from what I'd heard. Alfie was an exceptional singer, so I could only imagine how great he'd be with a band backing him.

Already a fan of his lyric writing, I'd since heard a few more of his songs, and they stacked up. As a fellow musician, I couldn't deny that he was truly gifted.

Will brought me a white wine spritzer, but my quirk had always been to have crushed ice in it.

"Sorry, is there any ice?" Alfie motioned toward the kitchen, still holding his beer bottle, and gesturing in the direction of the kitchen with his index finger.

"Sure, there's a dispenser in the fridge." I blushed again, because this was a pretense, and I knew that.

I wandered into the kitchen. It was beyond weird, being here, being familiar with all his things and pretending not to know anything. I just had to keep telling myself over and over that I could do this.

This was a normal gathering of a group of friends, nothing crazy about it. We would just drink, chat, and go home. What made it different was that I had been here before. No one else in the room was aware that we knew each other intimately or that we had a history of mind blowing sex together. Wild sex with that amazing looking guy who hosted that little get-together, and he was acting as if he didn't really know me.

My concentration was gone again; lost in reflections of those times, when the crushed ice spattered out of the dispenser, and spilled over my blouse at breast level missing my glass. *Shit!* The ice

263

immediately melted, leaving quite a see-though area in the front, my lacy bra showing through.

CHAPTER 25

MIND GAMES

Leaning over the counter to get some paper kitchen towel, I felt a his calloused fingertips slide around my waist. Strong hands pulled me back into an erect male body. His scent told me that it was Alfie.

My breath hitched, and I held it. Eyes fluttered closed as I endulged momentarily in his touch. My beating heart stuttered for a second and pounded rapidly in my chest, but I didn't move.

He swept my hair to the side, exposing the nape of my neck. His fingers left a tingling, burning sensation on my skin. Familiar bumps appeared in the wake of the trail like a rash. I could feel his hot breath on my neck as he moved his head forward, bending to kiss the soft spot behind my ear.

I felt his lips curl into a smile on my neck and that felt so right. His breath became hotter and more ragged as it dispersed on my skin in short pants.

White heat shot through my body, resulting in a flushed effect. Becoming so aroused, I had to I fight with everything I had, not to turn into him.

Feeling his hands on me was so amazingly perfect. His arms wrapped around my waist, and as fast as he held me, he was gone. I had never even caught sight of him during the whole interaction.

Alfie left me standing breathless and shaken. I tried to steady myself; legs weak, my heart beating so wildly, I could feel it in my mouth. White fingertips clung to the countertop, as I tried to gather my thoughts.

I heard him talking in the living room again as if nothing had happened, while I stood where he left me. My heartbeat continued to pound hard with the breathless effect he'd had on me.

I must have stayed there longer than I should have, because when I managed to go back to the group, Will mouthed, "Are you okay?"

Plastering on my best smile, I mouthed back, "Sure." I placed my glass to my lips and sipped the wine, minus the ice I'd gone to get, while trying to avoid eye contact with Alfie.

I think Will would have noticed more going on, if it hadn't been for Saffy. She was hanging on his neck, and I think he had his own distractions with her.

Stealing a glance, Alfie was looking directly at me. "Lily, what's been the hardest part of today for you?" I blushed at his double meaning, and as the focus was on me, I knew exactly what he was doing.

Trying to look confident and unaffected by what he'd just done to me, I replied, "Nothing really, I mean, there is nothing hard that I can't handle. If something is perceived to be hard, I usually deal with it by breaking it down into bite-sized chunks," I responded deadpan.

Grinning widely at my response, he held up his beer bottle saluting me, as if I'd won that round. I was instantly annoyed by how turned on I was, just by looking at his fucking adorable, smiling face.

About to place his beer on the counter, Alfie turned his head sideways to look at me. He lifted the bottle again in a second salute before flinging his head back to take a big swig of his beer.

Alfie smiled into his bottle again, holding it to his lips, while his eyes continued to bore into mine. I could hear his breath as air escaped his nose onto the bottle neck as he breathed raggedly.

Saffy decided she wanted to be under Will, literally. He must have been in agreement, because he suddenly wanted to leave too, and ushered us both in the direction of the front door.

He placed his hand on my back in guidance, but Alfie positioned himself in front of the door as I was walking out.

Everyone else was either in the process of leaving or standing on the sidewalk getting into cars when he placed his hand on the small of my back. He slipped it under my t-shirt and traced the waistline of my jeans. My breath hitched, and I tried to move away without being obvious. With his other hand slid down around to my crotch and between my legs, the seam digging into me. My sensitive flesh became swollen and ached for him to do more. I stifled a moan.

Pretending he was scratching his nose he inhaled

and leaned in. "You're arousal smells fucking awesome," he whispered in a low, sexy voice.

I managed to keep my face expressionless, shocked and stunned at the liberty he had taken with my body, but determined not to make a scene. I gripped his hand and pulled it away, pushing it down before anyone saw it.

Putting his mouth to my ear, Alfie's his breathing was a little ragged. To the others it may have looked like he was being friendly. "You still want me, don't you? Say it and I'm yours…anytime," he whispered seductively.

Smiling sweetly, and said firmly, "Thanks again, Alfie…Goodnight." I didn't remember much about getting to Will's car just that I flicked onto autopilot to get there. Once seated, I fought to keep my breath even. My senses had gone into overdrive.

Will glanced over at me. "You're quiet tonight Lily, everything okay?" I sighed. "Yeah, it's been a long day Will, I'm just tired." He nodded and let me continue in silence, while he and Saffy debated whether he'd stay at our place or go home. Once I was home, and closing my bedroom door, my cell buzzed.

SEXPERT: You felt so good in my hands tonight and you smelled so fucking amazing…I wanted nothing more than your legs wrapped around my waist.

Pink Lady: Exactly who do you think you are, don't you ever touch me again. I don't want you

to touch me… last thing I want is my legs wrapped around anything to do with you. If you do that again, I will scream sexual assault.

SEXPERT: Your head might not have wanted it, but your body most definitely wanted me badly… why didn't you call me on it? If we'd been alone, I would most definitely have taken you tonight, and you would have let me.

Pink Lady: What do you want from me?

SEXPERT: I want to ride you so hard until you scream my name… but I'm a realist, we're not F B anymore, so we'll be friends.

Pink Lady: Hmm, I don't think so.

SEXPERT: Sure we will. See you on campus tomorrow. BTW: Will= new FB? What does he have that I don't? I'm interested to know.

Did he really think I was that easy? I wasn't even

going to dignify that with an answer, that was the second time he'd implied something was going on between us. I was exhausted and mentally drained from his games. I slipped out of my clothes, too tired to do anything but brush my teeth.

I slid my legs between the cool sheets unable to comprehend fully what happened tonight. I felt numb, and I couldn't even cry. Alfie had frustrated me with his behavior.

Coping okay, I had been doing well to control my feelings for him, but Alfie had turned up the heat again with his games, and it was leaving me feeling scared that I'd cave in to his demands again.

I was determined not to allow him to pull me back into something I wasn't able to handle. So Turning over, curled myself up, I spent my night once again, lying thinking about the one thing that I'd never have with him.

Arriving on campus the next morning, I was still mulling over what had happened last night. As usual, Will was waiting for me. Serious expression on his face, Will was staring up at the stormy sky. I assumed he had another argument with Saffy.

Saffy wanted to have more control over their relationship, but Will was standing his ground. "Hey, Will." He gave me a small smile, but it didn't quite reach his eyes.

"I'm all the better for seeing your sweet face honey. I had to drag my ass away from Saffy's whining this morning. I'm into her, but not into her clingy ways." I leaned up and rubbed his shoulder. He bent forward, giving me an affectionate little head bump, and left it to rest there for a moment with his eyes closed.

As usual with Will's PDA, Alfie seemed to appear out of nowhere. I immediately felt guilty, although I didn't know why. I thought it might be because he saw me being affectionate with Will. Alfie obviously thought I had moved on with Will.

Alfie's texts last night hadn't helped these feelings I had about my relationship with Will. I settled for thinking that it was because I didn't want Will to become embroiled in Alfie's tangled mind. I wasn't sure of the real reason, but I just felt weird.

"Hey," he cooed. He looked up. "We're going to have a storm today." I was wondering what his game plan was this morning. Alfie's eyes flicked between us. He scowled, his eyes shifting between us darkly. "So Will what's the deal? You and Lily got it going on?" he said, pointing his index finger and moving it back and forth between us.

Will looked at me, then at Alfie. "Hell no, we're the best of friends." He looked awkwardly at me. "I'm with Saffy." Alfie's face showed sudden realization and smiled at him, looking more relaxed.

Mandy called out to Will from across the lawn. He turned and gave me a questioning look. "You want to see what she needs, Will?" I said, flicking my chin in her direction, encouraging him to go to her.

As soon as Will was out of earshot, Alfie rubbed his hands together, his head down looking at them, then tilted his head to look at me. "Do you remember me fucking you Lily?" His voice was low and seductive. To onlookers we would have been talking about any mundane thing.

Standing straighter, I was a little shocked at his

crude question. I shrugged, embarrassed, not wishing to rehash our encounters. Of course I remembered. Jeez, I never thought much about anything else when I saw him.

Fixing his gaze on me, Alfie sneered. "Well? What? You do… you don't… you're indifferent?" he hissed, his eyes darting to where Will was, and then back to me.

Swallowing hard, his nearness made me unable to think. "Yes," I said quietly.

"Which part?" His eyes searched mine with an unnerving intensity.

"Of course I remember. It isn't as if I'd done a lot of that before," I said in a small voice.

Alfie smiled. "I remember as well, Lily. Although, I had… done a lot… well, you know…" He straightened and stuffed his hands into his leather jacket pockets, smirking at me.

I didn't know where this was going until he exhaled hard. "You felt all those amazing feelings *with* me. I wasn't there on my own," he said, shaking his head at me.

Blushing at the memories of what we had done. "You're going to throw this back at me now, to try to have me again? You wanted no ties, Alfie… you've got them."

His voice was husky. "No ties, right. It doesn't mean I don't want those feelings… you want those feelings again, Lily, don't you?"

Shaking my head vigorously, I said, "I, one hundred percent, don't want that with you, like that, without feelings involved. I don't want to be 'mind fucked' by you either, Alfie." My voice was echoing the anger he was instilling in me.

I stared at him, fighting with everything I had in me, to keep myself strong. "I just want to be left alone to study and have a normal life. You're killing me with this." My voice was low and angry. I turned on my heels and walked in Will's direction, leaving him standing with his arms crossed, staring smugly at me.

My heart pounded as I was making my way to them, but the skies opened and the rain came down so hard. The ground became saturated, covering the lawn with a few inches of rain in seconds. Will and Mandy had turned and were disappearing into a building behind them, and I had to turn and make my way back to the one nearest the car park.

Clearing the first door, I began to make my way inside, when a hand grabbed my wet, slippery arm, and pulled me behind the heavy, wedged open door at the porch. Alfie swung me around, pinning me hard against the wall behind the door, by his hips. The cramped space meant I had nowhere to go.

Firm hands slapped noisily either side of my head, caging me in. Offering a slow, sexy, lop sided smile, his expression changed to that of intense, the longer we stood there. He didn't speak, just did that intense-stare-thing he does. "Stay here. The rain won't last long," he whispered huskily.

Feeing he was aroused when the bulge in his pants kept brushing against me, made me swallow noisily. The sensation was so tantalizing and sweet, yet it stung that this was all I was to him. I didn't move.

Breathless from running, the rain, and him, my

chest heaved, as I panted to compensate for the oxygen loss. My body hummed in anticipation and awareness of him, and I struggled to keep myself from shaking.

Alfie's closeness, his familiar smell, his beautiful face – it was too much. I closed my eyes briefly, because it hurt to look at how fucking intoxicating I found him. When I opened them and focused, it was on his hair.

I didn't want to look in his eyes and see the lust that he'd probably see reflected back at him in mine. So…avoiding his gaze, I stared at his soaking wet hair, and immediately wanted to run my fingers up the back of it.

Spots of rain dripped off the ends of some strands and ran down his neck. It teased me, and I wanted to lean in and press my mouth to his neck to catch them.

His t-shirt clung to his fabulous hard body, and his defined abs were visible. I stood frozen on the spot, mesmerized by him. He was so delicious.

Shaking my head, I tried to shake my feelings off, as well as the water from my hair. My blouse was transparent from the rain, and I noticed his eyes had dropped and were now feasting on my white lacy bra and cleavage. I tried to think of how I could get away, but he dipped his head forward, his face only an inch from mine.

The feel of his breath was cool when it landed on my lips. "Do you remember my kiss, that feeling when my tongue penetrates your lips into your hot mouth? Remember the feelings when I sucked on your tongue, Lily?"

My eyes dropped to his mouth, briefly flicked to

his eyes, before they once again focused on his mouth. I had remembered; and it aroused me, just hearing him talking to me about it. "You're so fucking beautiful, I can't stand it," he whispered in a sad tone.

There was friction again, as he grazed his denim clad erection over my mound. I almost groaned, but managed to catch it and turn it into a small cough, so turned on by him.

Alfie was such an expert in seduction and so damned alluring. It was taking everything I had to control the urge to give in to him. I had very little immunity to him. I began to think of how great his mouth had been on me, and I ached to have him give me those feelings.

He ran his tongue over his bottom lip quickly to wet it, and I shivered. He noticed and grinned, his eyes widening in recognition. "Look at you. You're so fucking turned on right now. Do you want me to kiss you?" He smirked.

"Do you want my mouth on yours exploring you? Allow yourself that one word, Lily, and I can make you feel so good." At that moment I wanted that more than anything. Everything he said sounded so sexy and tempting. I struggled to resist him, it would have been so easy to just move that fraction of an inch and make contact with him.

Licking his tongue over his bottom lip quickly to wet it again, I trembled in anticipation of what he would do next. He noticed and crouched slightly pressing his hips further into me, as he tried to make contact with mine.

When he did this, he chuckled softly, his eyes

widening in response to the lack of control I was having over my body's reaction to him. "Do you want me to kiss you? Do you want my mouth on yours exploring you?" he whispered in a sexy, seductive tone.

I was already resigning myself that he was probably going to kiss me, and was deciding whether or not I would kiss him back. It was like it was already a foregone conclusion.

CHAPTER 26

THIS HAS TO STOP

Holding my breath, I waited to see what his next move was going to be. I was scared to move, in case he thought I was making my mind up that he should just do it. Still pinning me by my hips and staring at me, made me swallow hard. My mouth felt parched and I licked my lips because they were so dry.

Alfie bit his bottom lip again in response. His arms were slightly trembling, and I was distracted by this and almost leaned into him, but I eventually managed to squeak out, "No." *Shit*, I was disappointed with how weak and pathetic my voice sounded. *I couldn't even convince myself, so how the hell was I going to convince him?*

Raising an eyebrow at me, and moved closer, until his lips almost touched mine, his forehead slightly brushing mine. He licked his lips slowly. *Kiss me,* I thought.

I couldn't move. Breathing unevenly, his breath

felt hot on my face. Closing my eyes, I prepared myself for the fabulous rush of sensation his kiss always gave me and… he pushed himself off of the door and moved away from me. Turning, he traced a fingertip down my cheek as he swept himself around the other side of the door and disappeared out of sight.

I stood breathless, exhaling through my nose, my legs shaking. My senses were battered from his touch, his smell, his smile, and all the familiar sensations he stirred in me.

Alfie had made me ache for him again. I was so turned on and full of want for him, engulfing anger, frustration, sadness and loss.

What the hell did he want from me? Was he punishing me because I didn't want to continue with our arrangement? I wished at that moment that I wasn't so attracted to him. But it was more than that, I felt a need for him that I hadn't felt for anyone before in my life.

Somewhere along the line, I'd developed strong feelings for Alfie, which made him a dangerous sexual magnet for me. In my stunned silence, I became aware my cell had beeped. I had a text message.

Will: where did you go honey?

Lily: I'm in the building next to the car lot.

Will: stay there I'll be right over.

Will ran toward me, his feet splashing on the

saturated lawn and his hair was still damp. He looked in a better mood than when I first saw him this morning.

Smiling warmly, he said breathlessly, "Mandy has invited us over this evening, you up for that?" I nodded, and wiped some water from his neck absentmindedly.

"Yeah, it'll be nice just to hang out."

Will looked a little embarrassed. "I don't want Saffy to come, Lily."

Looking concerned, I questioned him. "Will?" He shrugged, and sighed heavily, holding my gaze with a sad look. "I just want a little space Lily. It doesn't make me a bad person, does it? I just want to talk with people without accusations from her. I'm not looking to do anything wrong." I understood his frustration.

Sometimes it felt obtuse. We had found ourselves sneaking conversations with each other, on one occasion reverting to text messages to arrange a gig, because she was being ridiculous with her jealousy.

Squeezed his hand in support, I said, "You need to work it out though, Will. I don't want to be stuck in the middle of this. You're both my friends."

Giving me a small smile, he kissed my forehead with affection. "I knew you'd get me, Lily."

During the day, were very productive at college, working some great arrangements into our music. In the evening we went directly to Mandy's from campus. She had a very cute ground floor condo with a small private garden.

A garden was the one thing I missed about living in an apartment block. Mandy's parents had sold their family home, and bought this for Mandy, while her mother and father were working overseas.

She was a great little hostess and had made hotdogs, burgers, and salad. Will devoured as much as he could fit in his stomach. No doubt about it, the man enjoyed his food. I was in awe at where he put it all because there was not an ounce of fat on him.

Neil arrived, with a few other faces I vaguely knew, and we all sat on some stacking plastic patio chairs. The atmosphere was so relaxed, and conversations between us flowed easily. With all of us studying music, we had so much in common.

I felt happier than I had in weeks. When the doorbell chimed I wondered who else could be coming, because most of our group was already here.

Strange, but I think I felt his presence before I saw him, but I was still shocked when I looked up and he was leaning against the patio door frame.

The effect he had on me when I saw him was incredible. Alfie stood there looking very cool with a beer in his hand, and his eyes boring holes through me.

My heart beat was off the charts fast, and I was trembling as my body reacted to the mere sight of him. Trying to continue the conversation I was involved in, I struggled; conscious of him watching me. Will was sitting close to me, and as if on cue turned and gave me a slow smile. I returned this automatically.

He began teasing me about something that had happened during one of our sessions and grabbed me playfully by the neck, pulling my head down and into his chest.

Everyone laughed, and Will squeezed me in a hug, saying, "Only kidding, you know I love you, honey." Alfie's face darkened, his brows furrowing. He looked really unimpressed with both of us.

Alfie's beautiful plump lips were drawn into a thin line as he stared at me. Shrugging this off because I thought that he'd be thinking that Will was my new 'buddy' in his sense of the word, I tried to ignore him.

Mandy came through and turned her attention to Alfie, asking him something about the gig he had just performed at. He was forced to shift his focus, leaving me free to move around without him being able to follow me.

She then went around picking up paper plates and placing them in a garbage bag, still talking to him. Mandy asked about the band he was opening for in a few days. I didn't wait for his answer, pushing myself out of the chair, and using her distraction to make my way to the kitchen.

Will was right behind me, placing his hand on my shoulder. I tensed, but when I turned and realized it was him I smiled. "Sorry honey, I couldn't resist telling them about that, it was too cute when you did it at the time." He grinned, referring to the story he told.

His hand lingered on my shoulder, and Will began rubbing circles absentmindedly, while he was talking to me. I smiled widely at him and started giggling, because in hindsight, the story he was talking about was funny.

It was nice that he made sure I was okay with him sharing the story. "It's fine, it didn't bother me at all." He cuddled me close in a bear hug, rocking me from side to side.

"You know it's been lovely just to spend time with all of you without Saffy getting the wrong idea."

Agreeing it had been nice, but I still felt sad for Saffy. Pushing myself from Will's chest, I had just broke the hug and he was still smiling at me. As if on cue, Alfie appeared in the kitchen, waving his empty beer bottle between two fingers, and walking in our direction.

"You're very tactile for friends." He used quotation marks with his fingers on the word friends to accentuate his point. "Where do I find another one of these?" He asked, waved his empty beer bottle at us.

Will moved away from me, looking a little stressed by his comment, and ran his fingers through his hair. "There's plenty in the box over there."

Will motioned with his head and signaled by pointing at the patio door that he was going back to the garden. He walked away, leaving me alone in the kitchen with Alfie.

As I went to walk past him to follow Will, Alfie slammed the palm of his hand down on the counter. It made me jump and effectively blocked me from leaving. My heartbeat picked up pace, and my breathing was fast and shallow. I tried to control the feelings of both excitement and dread at being so near to him again.

"Excuse me, I want to pass please?" Alfie bent to make eye contact with me, and I inhaled his scent. I realized I had missed it.

"Is that what you *really* want?" He gave me a

seductive half smile. "You wouldn't rather come back to my place and let me make you feel good, Lily?" My jaw dropped, just being near him did crazy things to my heart, and he stole my breath away every goddamn time he was in the room.

Pressing my hand to his hard chest I pushed him back. In my heart, I wanted to grab his t-shirt and pull him closer, not push him away.

"Stop it. I've had enough of your games. I don't want you Alfie," I hissed, my eyes darting to the patio doors to make sure we weren't being watched.

He grabbed ahold of one of my hands and placed it over his heart. As he reached out, invading my body space again, he placed his other palm over mine. It wasn't a sexual touch. I voice may have been saying one thing, but my body couldn't lie to him. My heart was pounding in my chest, as was his.

"Forgive me, but I'm hardly convinced by that. We drive each other crazy with want." Giving me a smug smirk, he nodded his head toward his palm. He dipped his mouth to my ear and whispered to me. "I don't think you've had n early enough of me, sweetheart, and I know I'll never get enough of you." Alfie's soft breath fanned over my ear and my neck.

Smiling sexily at me, his eyes held that sensual gaze that usually melted me. He ran his small finger ever so lightly along my thumb, as he continued to hold my hand in his.

I flinched and tried to move it away, and he let his hands drop by his sides. He was right, of course. Alfie knew exactly what he did to me. Turning to walk away, I fought back tears, blinking rapidly.

Grabbing my arm and swinging me around, he

pushed me back into a corner of the kitchen with his body, out of sight of the window. He placed his palms on either side of me on the wall, again blocking my escape.

Alfie moved closer, slightly parting my knees, and leaned against me, hip to hip, his face bending toward my neck but not touching it. His breathing was ragged, and I could feel his arousal as he rubbed himself against my pubic bone.

Inhaling my hair, Alfie's mouth then found my neck. "I want you so fucking much." Swallowing hard as he stared into my eyes. His words and the sensation of his touch became too much for me. I was being overpowered, and I could feel myself letting go. Melting into his body, my eyes closed in surrender to him.

Distracting me, as his tongue traced up my neck, his mouth stopped near my ear, "Say it, tell me to take you." He rested his forehead on mine. I had stopped breathing, frozen.

Alfie pulled his head back and opened his eyes. We were looking intensely at each other. I could see the lust there in the hooded glint in his eyes, his breathing was ragged. Burying his face in my neck he groaned again and his tongue licked up to trace my jawline, while I fought to control the release, of the breath I had been holding.

Removing a hand from the wall, he traced it down the front of my body. I inhaled sharply, my body reacting to the heat of his touch. I bit my lip and he licked his. "Oh yeah, sweetheart, you most definitely want me," he murmured softly.

My defenses were gone, his for the taking. All he

had to do was kiss me. His fingers traced my lips with a feather-light touch. He leaned closer, and I closed my eyes expecting his kiss.

I waited…and nothing happened. I opened my eyes and saw Will. I was confused, Alfie was just here, and now he was nowhere in sight. Will was standing looking concerned at me.

"Are you okay? You didn't come back." He put out his hand to lead me back and I let him, trembling. "Are you cold?" he asked.

"No, just tired." I managed a weak smile. I didn't know how I faced being around everyone after that. We stayed another half hour, then I told everyone I was exhausted and needed to go home.

Will followed me out to my car. I didn't see Alfie again while we were there. We'd arrived in separate cars, and he walked me to mine when we left. We arranged to meet as usual in the morning, then he hugged me tightly rubbing my back.

"I've had a lot of fun this evening, thanks for understanding Lily." I smiled tiredly at him.

"No worries." My response was muted, but it was the best I could manage. He kissed my nose and sat me in my car.

"Remember, you haven't seen me this evening." He winked.

I felt bad because I knew that as soon as I saw Saffy, she was going to ask me about Will. It was a horrible situation and I was going to have to lie. *Why was everything so complicated here?*

Shifting my car into gear, I drove off feeling drained about Alfie. As I rounded the corner, he was leaning against his car, flagging me down. I was torn between running him over and stopping.

Stopping, I wound my window down partway. My heart was pounding at him being there again. "Truce?" he asked, tapping his fingernails on the side of my car, smiling sheepishly.

"What is this, Alfie? This has got to stop. I can't deal with this shit, you're scaring me." I swallowed hard. It was true his behavior was freaking me out now.

My voice sounded quiet and shaky when I was speaking, and he looked a little shaken by my statement. "Can we talk? Just talk, no mind games?"

Sighing in exasperation, I said, "I'm really tired Alfie, I just want to go home." In truth, his stalking had taken the last of my energy.

"Can I drive you home? We could talk like this." He wagged his finger between us. "I'll collect you in the morning to come get your car."

I shook my head. "No, I don't want that," I stated firmly. I really had feelings for Alfie. I was not going to be emotionally bullied because of my physical attraction to him though.

"Can I get in then? Would you drive me home, so that we can talk?" This was the last thing I wanted, but I figured that we needed to clear the air so that he would stop behaving like this toward me.

"Please Lily– I just want to talk to you." He gave me a half smile and looked sincere, but I knew that his smile had worked with many other women in the past. Even so, I was intrigued to find out what he had to say for himself.

Aware I was making a pretty stupid decision even before I agreed, I resigned myself to try to conserve some normality around him. And that meant I'd have to discuss it with him.

"Okay, I'll take you home, but cause me any problems, and you'll have to walk back to get your car." He grinned and jumped in the passenger side before I could change my mind, making the leather seat squeak.

Edging away from him, I faced the front, driving a little too carefully, waiting for him to speak. His hand slipped along the back of my seat. "Do you mind, I don't like distractions when I'm driving." He chuckled, and I turned to glare at him. He realized I wasn't joking with him and took his arm back.

"Why did you stop?" I shook my head incredulously at him.

"Why did I stop the car? You were in front of it," I huffed.

"No. Us." he husked, wagging his index finger between us again.

I swallowed hard, and stammered trying to speak before my thoughts had fully formed in my head. "It just wasn't for me… the whole 'fuck buddy' thing, and there was no 'us'," I stated flatly.

He snickered. "I was there Lily; I still feel you, and you still feel me, so that's bullshit. *And,* it was for you, you can't tell me you didn't like it," he bit back at me, his mouth curled in a sneer.

CHAPTER 27

FRIENDS

Sitting quietly, my breathing was a tad fast from his nearness, and from the exchange that had passed between us. "Okay, it wasn't what I wanted. I thought I could do the no-emotional-ties sex thing. It left me with a bad taste in my mouth Alfie." He narrowed his eyes in a hard stare for what seemed like ages, not speaking.

Sighing in exasperation, I said, "I warned you that I wouldn't get emotionally involved with you, Lily. I can't ever love you," he said, shaking his head. "I want you, but I can't ever make a commitment to you." My heart squeezed hard at his harsh words.

"Why is that?" I whispered sadly. "What's wrong with me?" Alfie squeezed my hand, his face looking sympathetic toward me. "God, there's nothing wrong with you. You're fucking perfect. Believe me, Lily, I just can't."

"You tell me you can't, but don't I deserve a

reason? I'm flesh and blood, a young woman, not a fucking toy or some whore off the street that you can pay for. I don't want to have any kind of relationship with someone who only wants my body and only speaks to me when no one else is around."

I was feeling incensed at his on-off way of dealing with me. "When we were alone, you treated me like I was special, and I don't mean your special feelings shit. You were so into me when I was with you. Yet, you emotionally wreck me in front of my friends by ignoring me, and play fucking games with my feelings so that you can get off on it?"

Both of his hands held the back of his neck, elbows out. Stretching backwards, he looked awkward and I could see that what I'd said had some effect on him. I just didn't know what though. Alfie asked me to stop the car. I refused, continuing to drive him home because I felt that all the time I was driving he was less likely to try something.

He sat in silence for some time. "I told you Lily, no hearts-and-flowers, you knew that when we agreed the arrangement." I bit my lip, looking at him. He bit his in return, and I wished for just a second he hadn't looked so sexy doing it.

"You told me that we could terminate the arrangement at any time. So what? We're both fucking liars?" I spat back. I thought about the girl I'd seen him around campus with and was about to ask him about her. "Interesting choice of words you keep giving me Alfie."

Frowning, he raised an eyebrow. "What words?"

I gave him a small smile. "I can't love you, *can't* ever give you a commitment. Can't love me? It sounds to me like there is something or someone stopping you. People don't sign up for commitment as soon as they start a relationship Alfie. So, it seems strange to me that you would put that out there before you even know someone, unless there's a reason not to get involved."

Feeling this was so draining, I said, "I'm tired of this drama. I think I get what you want. I tried it, but it just wasn't for me. I've seen you with all those other women Alfie, why would you wine and dine them without fucking them, then call me when you're done? Do you get off on secrets and lies?"

Alfie stared at me, not offering anything as a reply. "I've seen your other women Alfie, it isn't like I'm anything special anyway." His finger trailed over the back of my hand as I gripped the steering wheel.

"You're my favorite girl, Lily. You are so much more than them. They picked me, Lily, but I picked you." He ran his fingers through his hair and for the first time, I really thought that what he was saying affected him.

I knew that women probably threw themselves at him. Christ, he was irresistible to me even after he told me what he wanted from me that first time. "I don't want to be your favorite Alfie, I just want to have a normal relationship and be respected for who I am."

He clasped his hands and stretched his arms turning his palms out in front of him. "You want me to pretend that I'm your boyfriend, is that it?"

Our conversation was becoming more and more bazaar. "No Alfie. Listen, I enjoyed what we did, our connection was amazing. I don't want you to feel bad about any of it. I was as much invested as you were. However, I've moved on. I can't be with you… that way, any more."

Alfie placed his hand on the steering wheel. "Stop the fucking car."

I looked at him quickly, but continued to drive. "Stop the fucking car now, Lily." I became worried about his temper and pulled over, not entirely convinced this was the right decision.

"Look at me." He had swung sideways to face me. My face spun to look at him. "Can I try something?" He must have seen the fear on my face, because he tried to reassure me more softly. "Don't worry babe, I won't hurt you."

Biting my lip, I said quietly, "You do Alfie, every day you do this, you do hurt me."

His head moved back as if I had slapped him, his mouth dropped.

"That's not what I'm trying to achieve here, Lily, far from it." Shaking his head, he asked again, "Can I try something?" I looked apprehensively at him and he said, "Trust me." I looked away. I had trusted him, and this was where it had gotten me.

Yet, I was curious about what he wanted to try. "Okay." I sounded almost inaudible. Alfie leaned over and moved my seat back, giving me more leg room. "Face me Lily." I swung my legs around.

Alfie cupped my face with his hands; stroking my cheeks with his thumbs. A tear fell from my eye and streaked down my cheek. He caught it with his thumb, bringing it up to his mouth. His face closed in on mine, and I shut my eyes.

I didn't want to look at him, it hurt me too much.

His lips landed on my closed eye, kissing one then the other, as his hand stroked the back of my neck.

It wasn't a passionate embrace. It was a tender, comforting one; a side to Alfie I'd never seen previously. His face moved to my neck, and he whispered, "Lily, I really don't want to hurt you honey, all I want is to make you feel good." I pushed him back.

"I've told you it doesn't make me feel good. It's killing me, Alfie, please stop," I pleaded.

As I was talking to him, I couldn't stop my feelings. I was frightened because despite how he was making me feel, I had fallen in love with him. My heart sank to my stomach. This is not how it was supposed to be.

Alfie sat back and stopped touching me. He huffed out slowly, his breathing ragged. He gripped the sides of his seat as if he was restraining himself from touching me again.

We sat in silence, but grief washed over me. The reality of why I'd been so tormented by this was hitting me like a tsunami. Not only had I fallen deeply in love with Alfie, but I'd fallen in love with someone who could never love me back.

I heard myself say, "Don't do that again, don't touch me. I'm starting the car, and I'm going to take you home now." We sat in silence and by the time we arrived at his house, my face was streaming with tears.

Too distraught to fight him when he pulled me into him, I let him comfort me, "Shush," he whispered. "I really don't want to hurt you, honey. You need to stay here tonight. You can't drive home like this."

Tensing, Alfie tried to sooth me and rubbed my back. "I promise I won't come near you, I'll sleep on the couch." I started to protest, but realized that I was such a wreck it wouldn't be safe for me to drive home. I was too distraught to argue any more.

Alfie was true to his word, he walked in front of me, putting the nightstand light on and left the room. He reappeared a few minutes later with a bottle of water and some headache pills.

His face was full of concern, but I asked him to leave me alone and he did, closing the door behind him.

All I could think about was his touch and that he didn't want me. His bed smelled of him, and I inhaled his pillow, then cried so hard into it. My sobs racked through my body until my throat and my head ached.

Rolling onto my side, I pulled my knees up tightly. It was like I was trying to protect myself, but it was too late. My soul had been ripped from my body, and he was playing with it. I lay there rocking myself for the longest time until eventually I fell asleep, exhausted.

When I stirred, it was to a low grinding noise. Then realized it was coffee being ground in the kitchen. I could feel the warm sun on my face and before I opened my eyes, I felt calm. But then I remembered I had to face Alfie and panicked. I jumped to a sitting position, my eyes wide.

The sunlight streamed through the large window with the blinds that never got drawn down when I went to bed. Remembering I was in his bed, I scrambled out of it and into the bathroom, locking the door behind me. *Oh. My. God, I can't be here.*

I began to clean myself up, my eyelids were puffy, and I looked tired. My eyes were clear and shiny though, and I looked a little 'doe eyed' after my marathon sobbing session, but my skin glowed. I put my clothes on in a hurry, putting two legs down the one leg of my crop pants in my haste. My body just wouldn't cooperate.

Finger brushing my hair, I scrubbed my teeth with some paste and was tempted to use his toothbrush. I found some chewing gum in my purse, and popped it in my mouth to erase the final traces of bad breath.

Stand watching him from my vantage point at the top of the stairs, Alfie was singing along to the radio, wearing boxer shorts that hung low on his hips, and nothing else.

How was I supposed to deal with this? I couldn't stop myself from staring at his form. His appearance was mesmerizing to me, an incredible, beautiful man; the contours of his profile were perfect. As he moved around the kitchen, different muscle groups flexed and relaxed with his movements.

There he was going about his daily routine like nothing had happened; like he didn't have a care in the world. Again, he had managed to distract me without any effort.

Tilting his head in the direction of the stairs, his eyes fixed on me when he noticed me standing there. His lips curled and spread into a wide grin. As soon as he engaged with me, I hadn't been able to retrieve the practiced phrases I wanted to use on him, because they went clean out of my head when his eyes connected with mine.

My plan was going to be a quick thank-you for allowing me to stay, a request for him to leave me alone, and I was going to be on my way home. I never got to say any of it because he spoke while I was still collecting my thoughts.

"Feeling better?" *Nope*. I forced a smile.

"Yeah, yesterday kind of sucked," I croaked and smiled wryly. My body let me down again, when he raked me over with his eyes, by blushing.

I became a little awkward and hugged myself, and began to move toward the door. "Okay, well, thanks for the bed, but I need to run. All my stuff is back at my place. Do you need a ride to your car or can you get someone to help you?"

He raised his brow, and said, "I could come by and you could take me to get my car after college." I shrugged, but I knew I was going to ask Will to help me out there. Alfie pulled at his bottom lip with his index finger and thumb. "Lily, can I ask you something?" I really didn't want to get into another argument with him this morning.

I nodded, but didn't speak. "Is it better with Will? Is he a stronger lover?" Fuck, I felt so hurt. He really still thought I was sleeping with Will. I stood still, trying not to show the shock and rage I was feeling at his presumption.

"You both play together like you are lovers, when he's blowing his sax I wonder if he's imagining he's blowing you Lily." He smirked. I laughed almost hysterically at his comment.

"You're absurd! You do know that, right?"

Alfie poured himself a coffee, but didn't make

light of it, and I realized he really was serious about Will and I. "I'm sorry, my bad, it's none of my business?"

I sighed tiredly. "Damn right it isn't. What Will and I have… is much stronger than anything physical." Alfie looked like he didn't get that. "Will doesn't get my body, Alfie. What he does do is he fucks my heart and soul, emotional stuff, that's where our connection comes from."

Alfie had a strange look on his face. "I don't like to think of him with you, Lily."

Raising an eyebrow, "You're jealous? That's an emotion, Alfie."

"It isn't jealousy, but if you're having sex with him, then that makes my chances less." I thought about how black and white everything was to him.

"How can you even say stuff like that and think it's okay? Anyway, what Will and I do is none of your business, Alfie. All you need to know is that you and I aren't sleeping together."

Pouting his lips when I said it, Alfie looked sadly at me. "Any chance we can fix this, Lily?" He leaned back on the counter, his hips tilting in my direction.

Looking so sexy, standing there in his navy boxers, his toned body stretching and flexing as he rocked slightly. I really wanted to slide my arms around his waist and press my face to his chest.

Instead, I shook my head lamely. "Alfie, all I know is since I've met you, apart from the nights we spent together, I have never felt so fucking miserable in my life. So that's a resounding no. I used to be upbeat, an eternal optimist. But those nights with you, and then you pretending I don't exist around other people, changed all that for me. I've never felt so insignificant in my life."

Alfie looked hurt. His eyes pierced mine, then searched my face. "I told you the reason for that," he said softly, wandering over to rest a hand on my waist, despite my request for him not to touch me.

"Could you be miserable because we're not together, Lily?" His voice sounded seductive again and my breath hitched.

I dug deep and found the strength to argue back. "Alfie… we were never together. We had this weird-fucking-arrangement, that's all." I took a step backwards from him.

Stepping back as well, I leaned on the counter again. He waved a hand up and away from his body. "Okay, have it your way. Go, but know this, I never meant to hurt you."

Swallowing audibly, his eyes softened. "I want you. You *know* I want you. I just can't love you. I really, *really* like you though, Lily. I'd like to spend time with you. We could have some amazing times together."

Exhaling heavily, Alfie looked seriously at me, and I wished I didn't love him. "Can you at least think about what we talked about today? Will you text me? Promise me you'll text me… I still want to know how you are. If I can't have you physically, I'd like to be your friend."

I gave him a small smile, even though I wasn't feeling confident about his suggestion, but I was still in his home and wanted to appear as amicable for now. "Sure, I'll think about it." Even as I said it, I wasn't sure I'd ever be in a place where I felt able to be just friends with Alfie.

Turning, I headed for his front door and was on the other side of it walking toward my car, before he said anything else. The last thing I wanted was Alfie coming after me.

Inserting my key in the ignition, I started the car and drove slowly out of the driveway. In my rearview mirror I saw Alfie standing by the window, his head down, rubbing the back of his neck.

Steering the car in the right direction, I glanced back again at the window. He looked up with a sad expression on his face. Alfie placed his palm over his breastbone and began to rub it. I kind of wished that his action was because his heart ached because I was leaving, but I knew better than that.

Everything I felt about him, made me feel raw, so I tried to block him out on the way home. When I got into the safety of my bedroom, I threw myself onto my bed, facedown, and sobbed my heart out again.

My body ached for him. Everything about him was perfect to me, except his lack of commitment. He was bad for me. I fell asleep for about fifteen minutes and woke with my cell buzzing.

Will: B there in fifteen.

Shit. I'd overslept. I practically threw myself in the shower, pulled on some blue cargo pants and a cream t-shirt and was lacing my sandals up when Saffy walked in. "Will's waiting for you, honey." She smiled. "I didn't get much sleep. I went to Will's place, to wait for him getting back from his meeting last night," she said smiling ruefully.

I felt guilty but covered it up by trying to change

the subject and threw a cushion at her. "You are both like rabbits!" I'd been part of Will's meeting, and hoped my feelings of guilt didn't show. They didn't appear to as she winked back at me.

CHAPTER 28

PUTTING IT OUT THERE

Out of breath when I got into Will's car, I panted, "Hey," I said a little breathless. Will had obviously had a good night, and was grinning when he saw me. "Hi beautiful, how are you this morning?"

Managing a half smile. "Okay." Will was pulling out of the condo parking lot and stole a glance at me after pulling out onto the road.

"Are you sure?"

Looking again, his eyes narrowed, before focusing again on the road. "Okay, what's the deal, because you were fine when I left you last night." Will knew me well now, I couldn't fool him. I sighed and inhaled sharply before controlling my voice.

"I had a very interesting conversation with someone I was involved with last night, it's made me… I don't know, confused, I suppose." Will reached over and took my hand.

"Max?" I shook my head. "From home…in

London?" he asked again.

I felt bad. I hadn't been honest with Will. I needed to come clean with him about Alfie. "No Will, about Alfie… there's more to it than I've been letting on."

Will let go of my hand, and he gripped the steering wheel, his head snapped around to look at me. "Alfie? There is? What do you mean, I don't understand? He ignores you for the most part."

I told Will about meeting Alfie on campus and about my no-strings-sex with him. I stopped short of using the title 'fuck buddy'.

Sitting quietly, his mouth pursed in a tight line, he looked ahead at the road. Stealing glances at me, every now and then he mulled over what I had told him.

"Are you serious, Lily? This isn't one of your practical jokes?" I shook my head and had no idea what was running through his mind. Probably that he didn't know me at all.

"I'm not proud of it, Will." I would have to accept it if Will didn't trust me at all now, but I couldn't go on letting him defend me about Alfie. I'd been fooling him when he was angry with Alfie for ignoring me.

Dark and Angry eyes looked back at me. "Did the bastard play you, Lily? Did he force into having sex with you?"

"No, Will, nothing like that. I was more than willing."

I saw Will swallow hard when I admitted that. "We've been over for a while, since Max, but he doesn't want it to be finished. The crazy thing is, he doesn't want any commitment either." I was worried about Will's reaction now. "I was doing great, but now he's started coming around more and he's kind of in my face playing mind games with me."

My eyes filled with tears, and I looked up, blinking fast, as I struggled to keep them from falling. I was so tired of crying. I could tell he was processing what I had said and knew he'd have questions for me.

"So… this conversation last night, it happened in Mandy's kitchen I take it? Where did that go?" He looked disbelievingly at me. "Did you go home with him?" he asked softly.

"He was waiting for me outside. I didn't plan it. He said he only wanted to talk and persuaded me into giving him a ride home. I got upset and ended up staying at his house last night."

Will drove into the car lot on campus and switched his engine off.

He closed his eyes absorbing what I'd told him, and I waited to see how he was going to respond to my deceit.

"So you stayed the night?" I nodded.

"I didn't sleep with him though, if that's what you think. He slept on the couch. It was supposed to be a simple relationship, but it's turned out to be a really complicated one, and we're not even together."

"So… What? You want to talk about it with me now?" He seemed to be trying to contain his anger.

"I'm sorry I didn't tell you I knew him, but I wasn't proud of what happened. I could really use a friend right now, but I understand you're hurt that I lied to you."

Sniffing, I licked a tear that streaked over my

lips. "I told you because I don't want any secrets coming between us and our relationship. If talking about my love life, or the lack of it, does that I'll keep it to myself." I swallowed and waited for him to reply.

He chewed his lip, mulling over what I'd said and shrugged. "Why didn't you tell me?" I held his gaze, then lowered my eyes.

"I was ashamed, and although Saffy and Holly know I had a relationship with someone, they never knew who he was. So you are the only person who knows who it is, Will. I really want it to stay that way… and I don't want him to know you know."

His eyes went wide. "Really?" I shook my head. He squeezed my hand. "Guys like Alfie take what they want Lily. You should never have been with him. He would know exactly what it takes to charm you." I nodded to show Will I knew what he was saying.

"That's just it, I got that. It took me a little time, but I got there and broke it off… except he still wants me. This morning, I told him that I wouldn't go there again with him, and now he wants to be friends." Will moved my hair away from my face.

"Can you do that? Be friends with him? Maybe it would ease the tension for him, and he'd move on."

I considered what Will said. "I had that thought of that before too, so… maybe, I'll try."

"Meanwhile, talk about it, I'm here for you, and I'll be honest with you if that's what you need. Lily, your secret is safe with me." I felt relieved that someone could share this with me, and I knew that Will cared what happened to me.

"He… Alfie, asked me if we were sleeping together. He thinks that's part of the reason I'm not with him." Will looked wide eyed again, his jaw dropped open.

Giggling nervously at his shocked look, I exclaimed, "Hey, I'm not that bad!" But felt self-conscious at telling him this. "It's not the first time. Remember your exchange in the car lot on campus? Then in the kitchen at Mandy's there were comments too. This morning he asked if you were better than him."

Will's knuckles were white on the steering wheel as he growled, "fucking pervert." I giggled again, seeing the humor in Will's anger. "Why would he think we were having sex?" I bunched my brows thinking about that too.

"He said we played like we were in love."

Will raised an eyebrow and glared at me. "What did you tell him?"

I half smiled. "The truth Will, I told him what we have is better than sex." I then relayed Alfie's comments about Will and the sax, although I giggled a lot when I tried to tell him that part.

"Shit Lily." He chuckled heartily. His eyes went wide and sparkled with humor. I giggled embarrassed that I'd said anything. "How am I ever going to wrap my lips around my sax without thinking about that now?"

Scowling, he looked tormented. Will's thinking voice once again failed to stay in his head, and I blushed crimson. Will drew breath again. "He really thinks we are having sex? You think we give off a vibe or something?"

I shrugged. "What does that matter? We know we're not. Well, at least if we are, I'm just not feeling it with you, baby." I winked playfully, pretending to flirt.

He grinned, but his expression changed to serious. "Me neither... pity though," he said, chuckling, a mock seductive expression on his face. I swatted him on the arm and smiled warmly, he was funny.

The actual day at college went better than I expected. My midterm theory and performance exam results were great. I got a lift back from college with Neil, who was passing by my condo building.

Will and I didn't have any more discussions about Alfie, but our earlier conversation about him helped me put some perspective on the whole situation with him. I'd been thinking about how to deal with Alfie all day since and how Alfie thought I should try to be friends with him.

I definitely didn't want any more of the treatment I'd been getting from him lately. So I figured the best way to get over him would be to try hard to hang with him if I could and hope we got past this.

It would at least allow me some control over my feelings when we were in each other's company. I hoped by doing this that, maybe he'd move on to someone else when he realized we were definitely not acting on our lust anymore.

Being full of great ideas and impulses, I decided, rightly or wrongly, to put this to the test. I was going to try and get him out of my system once and for all. This was going to take some nerve on my part, but I felt confident that I could handle whatever happened.

I wandered into my bathroom with a plan formulating in my head. I quickly showered and changed into a soft flowing sleeveless blouse and some denim shorts. I grabbed my cell, took a deep breath, and punched out a text. I blew it out when I hit the send button.

> **Pink Lady: Can you really do just friends with me?**
>
> **SEXPERT: Sure. Want to get a drink?**

His reply was almost instantaneous. I hesitated, not sure if I wanted to put alcohol into the mix at this point. I didn't get the opportunity to reply before Alfie texted again.

> **SEXPERT: You have the advantage.**
>
> **Pink Lady: How so?**
>
> **SEXPERT: It's your call, I have popcorn and two new blue-rays, want to come to the movies?**

Could we really just hang and watch movies together?

> **Pink Lady: can you promise no sexual intent, or mind games?**
>
> **SEXPERT: X my heart, but we can flirt though? Agreed?**

Pink Lady: We may need boundaries around that, but I'll bite…for now. See you in thirty minutes.

By the time I'd driven over there I was nervous. I almost turned and bolted when I saw his house. I knocked, and Alfie opened the door. He was stripped bare except for a small towel. I backed away and the panic I was feeling must have registered on my face.

Alfie held the towel with one hand and put his other one out to stop me. "No, no, sorry, this wasn't planned Lily, I promise. I was painting when you texted me. I needed to clean up, you just came too quickly," he blurted out, grinned, and pulled his hand to his mouth with laughter.

"Shit! I just made a 'Freudian' slip too." He choked back a laugh before straightening his face and saying, "Sorry, I'm nervous. I'm not used to the just-being-friends thing yet." I tried to ignore the towel and took what he said at face value.

Alfie started to go upstairs and called back, "You want to set us up while I get dressed? The movies and popcorn are on the kitchen counter." Not sure what I was doing here, but now that I was, I went to pick up the movies. *Safe House*. I read the blurb on the back, and the other seemed like another action movie, so I figured this one was as good as the other.

He came back downstairs about five minutes later, shaking his hair, and I realized this was his version of brushing it. He padded barefooted into the kitchen, and I heard the fridge door open, then he rifled through his silverware drawer.

A few seconds later I heard a pop, and some

glasses clinking together, before he came back with a bottle of Pinot Noir and two glasses.

"Are you okay with red? I know it's quirky, but I like it from the fridge. You can leave it at room temperature to warm if you want." He gestured the bottle at me.

I held my hand up. "I'd better not. I have to drive back." He looked thoughtful.

"I shouldn't either then, eh?" I felt bad that I'd crashed his evening, and he was trying hard to be nice, so I relented a little.

"Okay, I'll have half a glass." I smiled shyly.

We sat awkwardly, shifting in our seats. I was having a hard time concentrating when he was in the same room. After about ten minutes of the movie he pressed pause and turned to face me.

His finger wagged between us. "Is this as awkward for you as it feels for me?" He stared at me seriously, but I wasn't sure whether it was a trick question.

"How do you mean?" I asked, thinking he was going to talk about us previously meeting to have sex.

"We're at opposite ends of the room, it feels so unnatural. Can we try something?" I was immediately guarded.

"Depends what that is Alfie," I replied honestly.

"You cuddle Will and Neil and you're not having sex with them, right?" I could see where this was heading.

"You want to cuddle me?" He grinned, and nodded. "Would that be okay?"

Furrowing my brows. "I thought you didn't do the emotional thing?"

Smiling softly, Alfie said, "This is about comfort, not emotions, Lily." As if it made perfect sense to him.

I sat staring at him for a few minutes. It felt like a bad idea to me. I seemed to be full of them since coming to the US. My mind wandered to the intimate times we had shared, and the fact that we sat here trying to act like those times had never happened.

We were trying to be friends. *How do we forget all the crazy, sensual, insane feelings that we evoked in each other? I had behaved shamelessly with him, completely uninhibited, when we were exploring each other and now we were this?*

The memories I had of him were painful, because I knew that I had tasted, felt, and pleasured his body, but he had never really felt what I had felt when he did it to me. It was physical pleasure to him. Nothing in my touch had reached his heart, the way his touch had reached mine.

Devastated, by that fact, and because I'd kind of failed him too. Alfie had been honest with me, but I hadn't been so honest with myself, because I had fallen in love with him. Worst still, I loved him, knowing full well that it was the last thing he wanted to happen.

Alfie cleared his throat, and I realized he was still waiting for my answer. My heart began to race. *Could I stand being near him? Would it weaken my resolve?* Sensing my conflict, he asked, "Do you want a safe word, Lily?"

I was puzzled, my brows furrowed. "What's that?" He gave me a sexy half smile.

"Your innocence is so adorable," he said shaking

his head at me. "If there is anything I do that you're not comfortable with, you can say it, and I'll know and promise to back off." This sounded like a must.

"Okay, yes." I nodded. Alfie waited, gazing at my face.

"What?" I asked, confused again.

He chuckled, heartily. "YOU pick the word, or a phrase, something we can remember." I couldn't think of anything at first, and then it came to me.

"Save me a space," I said in all seriousness.

He stifled a chuckle, his eyes sparkling with humor. "Is that the best you can come up with?" He struggled not to laugh, then gave in, laughing loudly, throwing his head back. "Too funny." He cackled, before rolling around on the couch holding his belly.

CHAPTER 29

SAFE

Realizing this was a rare thing, it was great to hear Alfie laugh, and God, it turned me on. He looked so fucking cute. I hadn't really heard him laugh too often, although he was funny and made me laugh.

I was failing to see the funny side of this though. He tried to calm down, looking at me staring back vacantly, before starting to laugh again. It was a few attempts before he got it under control.

"Say… say it again, I've forgotten." He was still chuckling intermittently, wiping a tear from his eye with the sleeve of his long sleeved t-shirt.

"Save me a space." I half giggled, because the sound of his giggling was too infectious. "What's so funny about that?" He tried harder to organize himself.

"Ahem," he said, clearing his throat. "Never heard that before…" He giggled again into his wine, before breathing out through his nose as another wave of humor hit him. His red wine splashed out of the glass and on to his leg.

Alfie instantly bent double and sucked it off, making slurping sound against his leg, and it was so fucking sexy. His action turned me on, making me feel too hot, wet, and totally focused on the raw sex appeal he had. "Okay," he said at last, "I'm sorry, but I've never heard that before."

Figuring maybe it was an English phrase, I tried to explain. "Well, it kind of means I'll be there in a few minutes, or I'll be with you in a minute… soon or something like that." I began laughing too.

"Well, shit! Lily, how the hell am I supposed to know what to do with it, if you can't even explain it?" We were both crying with laughter now.

Maybe you had to be there to see the funny side of it, but we were in hysterics. I stuck to my guns, and this was now the phrase I'd use if lines were becoming blurred between us.

The laughter had broken the ice for us anyway, and we seemed much more comfortable in each other's company.

Alfie turned the lamp out at the back of the sofa, complaining it was reflecting off the television, blocking his visual of Ryan Reynolds. The room was really dark now, except for the glow from the screen.

Throwing my leg over the arm of the chair, I tried to lie down more comfortably. It wasn't the biggest chair, and I only managed a few minutes in that position before needing to move again.

Alfie glanced over, and then patted the couch near him. "Come here, honey. It's more comfortable on the couch. I won't touch you if you don't want me to."

Moving onto the couch, I scooted up in the

opposite direction from where he was sitting, tucking my legs under me. He chuckled lightly, and looked back at the movie. "It's okay, Lily. Really, I won't touch you inappropriately," he reassured me, without taking his eyes off of the television.

Beginning to relax, I had to admit it was more comfortable. We ate popcorn, and Alfie laughed at me when my legs began running, during an action scene. I began climbing up the arm of the couch as the storyline got more exciting and hid my eyes.

At one point, I kicked out with fright, and he caught my bare leg, settling it over his knee. His arm rested on it in a casual way. I left it there because he didn't stroke it or anything, and I didn't want to make a big deal of moving it.

The movie ended and I realized how much I'd slouched into the couch. It was too comfortable. Alfie turned to face me. "Are you staying for the other one?"

I was so glad when he asked me this and wasn't making any assumptions about me being there with him. I didn't know whether I should though.

"What time is it?" I said, stretching. I noticed Alfie's eyes fall to my midriff, and realized my blouse had ridden up, so I quickly pulled it back into place.

Alfie sprung up. "Just going to get some nibbles, I'll be right back, it's only just before nine," he said. "Can you stay?" I was unsure as to whether I should, and when I hesitated he added, "Please? I hate watching movies alone. I can't share the good parts if no one is here." I could relate to that, so I agreed to stay.

The second movie had a darker, scarier plot to it.
I wasn't that keen on some of it and hid my face in
my hands. I buried my head in the back of the couch
at one point. Alfie laughed softly at my reactions.

"Come here, let me hold you, it'll help you
relax." *Really?* I shook my head. "Why did we bother
with the safe word if you're not going to need it?" He
smirked.

Breathing out slowly and moved nervously
beside him, my knees tucked up near his leg, and his
arm enveloped me, his hand rested on my belly.

Feeling nervous, I bit my thumb nail, and he
shrugged himself down a bit to make himself more
comfortable. He paid no attention to me, until he took
my thumb out of my mouth and laced his fingers with
me to stop me from biting it.

After a few minutes, I'd convinced myself that
this was as innocent as with Will, and I kind of
melded into his side. I was aware of his breathing and
heartbeat, both were steady. He was right, it was
comforting.

When I woke up, Alfie was stroking my hair. The
television shone a blank blue screen indicating that
the movie had ended. I began to move away, and
Alfie held me at his side with his strong arm running
the length of me. "Shush, it's okay, you fell asleep, no
rush," he whispered. I lay back, and kind of drifted
asleep again.

Hours later, I woke again; still lying on the
couch, with a soft throw over me. Alfie was nowhere
in sight. I crept around, but the house was still and in
darkness, except for a light upstairs.

Picking my way upstairs, when I stood on the

second from the top stair, it creaked. I'd heard it before, but only remembered after I stood on it this time. Alfie's room door was ajar, and he was lying naked, chest down on top of his bed, his head facing the door.

Looking devastatingly handsome lying there, Alfie's strong, muscular back made him look like something I would have expected to see flicking through a men's fitness magazine.

Staring longingly at the complex man I had fallen in love with, I wanted to cry. He looked so peaceful and carefree lying there, and I wondered how it was possible that he could look even more stunning as he slept.

Resisting the urge to lie down beside him, I swallowed hard. Alfie had kept his word. I was pleased that I meant enough for him to respect my feelings, even if he had nothing other than sexual feelings of his own around our relationship.

Sneaking out of his house, I slipped behind the wheel of my car. It was after one in the morning. I drove home and don't really remember getting into bed, I was bone tired.

Feeling a little better about Alfie, he could be in my life– even if it wasn't the 'hearts and flowers romantic relationship' I wanted. I was more confident about trying to do the 'friends without the benefits' thing after that evening.

Trying to be platonic friends wasn't going to be easy with him though. *Would I be able to suppress my feelings for him?* I knew it wasn't going to be easy, but I really wanted to try.

I'd enjoyed just spending time with him. He was

funny and charming, and seemed to enjoy just hanging with me.

The alarm buzzed loudly. The display flashed that it was 6:30am; I groaned and rolled over, stretched out my bones. I remembered my time with Alfie last night and felt happier about the pending day. I willed myself to slide out from under the sheets and get into the shower.

Soap cascaded down my body, and warm rivulets of water ran over my skin. I was meeting Will this morning and knew I had a couple of bridges to build with him over my deception around Alfie.

Driving into the car lot on campus, I still felt good about last night, when I saw Alfie talking to Will. They seemed deep in conversation, and I saw him pat Will's back. Will was nodding, then he seemed to lean in, and I saw Alfie's expression looked a little tense.

Will saw me, and his smile seemed a little forced. I wondered if they were talking about me. Alfie waved at me, then stopped Will by the touching his arm, saying something to him.

Alfie came toward me alone. Will sat back on a bench waiting for me. He hesitated, then leaned in and kissed me lightly on the cheek. It gave me goose bumps, but I tried to ignore them. "Hey," he cooed. "You were so peaceful last night I thought it best to leave you sleeping."

Smiling warmly and giving me his full attention, he asked, "What time did you leave?"

I shrugged. "Late." I was smiling, but felt a little shy around him today. "I really enjoyed last night."

Luscious lips curled into a beautiful smile, and

my smile widened, mirroring his. "Yeah, it was really nice. I liked it, thank you," I echoed his sentiment.

Alfie looked pleased with my answer. "You want to hang with my band tonight? We're playing in Orlando."

I hadn't actually heard his band play. "Can Will and Saffy come as well?" Alfie's brows tightened, before his face relaxed. "Yeah, why not, we're going down in a minivan. It'll be a late night though."

We agreed to arrange times later, and I turned to see Will begin to stand and walk toward me. "I'll catch you later, Alfie; Will's a little neglected this morning by the looks of things."

Walking over to Will, I could see he didn't look good at all. "What's going on for you?" Will hugged himself then gestured a shrug. I rubbed his shoulder. "That bad, huh?"

Something was badly wrong with Will he was almost in tears and hugged him tightly. "I don't think you're ready to say what you are thinking Will."

He nodded. "Yeah, Lily, you get me don't you?"

Guiding us into the canteen, I wandered over to the counter, coming back with two large lattes and some donuts. "Love sickness antidepressants." I commented, smiling. I was trying to lift his mood. Will couldn't really raise a smile, but seemed to appreciate my efforts.

"Come on, we have a booth booked, but we only have three hours today." We took our refreshments with us, and I was concerned about how Will's problem would affect our work.

Saffy was so important to me, but Will had become such a big part of my life since my arrival at college. "Listen Will Saffy is over there." I put one hand to one side of me and gestured between us with the other hand. "We're here. We have to compartmentalize her for the sake of our work. We'll deal with what's going on when you are ready to talk."

Will nodded. "Thanks honey," he said quietly. The session went terribly. I was having difficulty feeling the music with him today.

Will was shrouded in misery and wasn't connected. Neither of us could anticipate changes in the way we usually could. After two hours I decided enough was enough. "Right, you're coming with me." I got our stuff together. "Come on!"

Will dragged himself slowly behind me. He didn't protest or argue, it was as if he needed to be told what to do. We reached my car. "Get in," I said. Will got in the car, and I drove out of the college. "Don't you want to know where we're going?" Will looked at me.

"Seems like you're the boss of me today," he muttered, giving me a rueful smile.

"Are you ready to talk now Will?" He sighed heavily, and when he spoke his voice was shaky.

"I'm struggling," he said, stating the obvious to me.

"I can see that." I squeezed his hand, and pulled over, into a beach park. I parked the car and turned to face him. "Get out." Will looked over at me.

"Here?" I nodded.

"Being on the beach worked for my outpouring, it's your turn today." The beautiful white sandy beach was deserted.

We were both in shorts and t-shirts, so we sat on the sand near the shoreline. "Okay Will, shoot!" Will played with the sand, not looking up.

"It's so fucking difficult Lily."

"Obviously, or you wouldn't look like shit and not be able to eat a donut." I smiled, lacing the fingers of his hand in mine.

"If I say it, it changes everything. For me– for us– for Saffy." I panicked thinking I was somehow involved in his angst.

"Right, firstly, I feel secure enough to be honest with you Will. No matter what it is, we'll weather it. I can't speak for Saffy, but I'll support you if I can, but it is difficult to know to what extent until I know what it is."

I held Will's hand, taking it from the sand and placed it over my heart. He laced and unlaced his fingers through mine absentmindedly, then squeezed them.

"You know the other day when you said that I knew the feeling you had about being hurt? Well, you were right. I was doing well, just beginning to heal with Saffy and your friendship. You are two very special people in my life." I smiled, touched by his words, and squeezed his fingers back.

"My girl, Leanne, split with me because I chose to come to college. She wanted me to get a regular job and get married. It took me two extra years to save the money to be here. My dad worked too hard to give me everything he had. I wouldn't take all that he had to do it, so I worked my way here, Lily." I listened to him talk about his life and realized that outside of college, we hadn't talked much about life pre-college.

"Then my uncle died and left his house to me. Leanne wanted to move in and get married. She was pressuring me. My dad wanted me to sell it to pay for college. He believes in me and wants me to be happy."

He shrugged. "I couldn't sell the house because I couldn't part with it. My uncle was special to me, and he built that house." My heart surged with affection for Will; he was a good person, with a strong sense of right and wrong, good values and beliefs, and love for the people he cared about.

I felt he wasn't getting to the point, digressing from the main issue that was affecting him. "So Will, tell me what it is that's hurting you so much." He swallowed.

"I care about Saffy, Lily." I waited but he couldn't.

"But?" I prompted. Will's internal struggle showed on his face, he sighed and blew his breath out.

"Leanne says she's pregnant." I hugged him. I felt so bad for him. "This changes everything, Lily. I can't stay at college. I need to work to support her and my child."

Feeling angry for him, this was so unfair. I could help him if it came down to money. I was wealthy enough, but I needed to know more.

"No Will, you are not giving up, not when you've come this far." Will's expression looked dejected.

"It's pointless Lily. She's going to have to move in with me here, and I'll need to work. I feel bad you're going have difficulty finding someone to collaborate with this late into the year."

CHAPTER 30

GREAT ACTING

Rubbing Will's arm to comfort him, unsure of what to say to comfort him. "So how far along is she?" He twisted his mouth.

"About twelve weeks," he said. "So it was around the same time you came to college?" Will mulled this over.

"Yeah."

"Okay Will, let's look at this objectively. This girl wanted you to stay home, yes? She wanted to get married, yes? She didn't get that, and now she's pregnant? When did you last sleep with her?"

Will said, "She's about twelve weeks I think."

"I didn't ask you that, I asked when you last slept with her."

Shaking my head, cloud see he was taking everything the girl said at face value. "Listen Will, you need to find that out. Where is she?" Will rubbed his chest like he was embarrassed.

"She lives about thirty minutes from here."

Standing up, I dusted the sand off of my legs and shorts. "Get up. We're going to see her." Will looked terrified about this and looked at me disbelievingly when he realized I was serious.

"Are you fucking serious, Lily? We can't just rock up there." I scowled at Will's lack of self-preservation.

"I'm as serious as a heart attack, get in the car," I said authoritatively. "We're going to find out if you are going to be a daddy or not. You're not just rolling over without proof, Will. You said it yourself, she wanted to get married." His eyes widened.

"You think she's playing me?" Will's eyes widened, surprised that I could think that. "I'm not knocking on the door saying 'prove it'. I owe her that much," he said shaking his head.

"Well, my plan will be ready by the time we get there, and when I set eyes on her, I'll decide if I believe her or not. I'm usually a shrewd judge of character. It doesn't usually let me down…well, with women anyway," I huffed. "I'm especially relying on it today. Oh, and Will, for this event's credibility, you *are* fucking me." Will's eyes widened.

"Don't make me even more nervous, Lily." He managed a weak smile.

"Just take my lead. We'll get through this, okay?" He shrugged and raised his hands. "What do you have to lose?" I smiled at him, he shrugged. "That's my boy!" I slapped his thigh.

Leanne opened the door, and Will stood facing her. "Will! I knew you wouldn't let me down. Come inside." She threw her arms around his neck.

Will mumbled, "I have someone else with me you need to meet, Leanne." I stepped forward into her view.

"Hi Leanne, I've heard so much about you, my name is Lily, Will's girlfriend." Leanne's face was horror-stricken.

Trying to sound sincere, I said, "So…Will and I were a little shocked to hear your news, but you know, this isn't the sixties, it happens, right?" I smiled sweetly and shrugged at her, before I leaned forward and took her hand in mine. I placed my other hand over it as if to comfort her.

"So honey, we're all adults, and we're going to work together to make sure that Will's baby doesn't want for anything." I patted her hand. Leanne was so stunned she showed no reaction at all.

My thoughts were that, if she was indeed pregnant with Will's baby, she would be incensed that he'd brought someone else with him to see her, since she was having his baby.

Leanne's non-reaction told me she was either lying, not pregnant, or it wasn't his. I smiled at her saying, "Do you have some sonogram pictures of it, yet?" Then I spun in Will's direction. "Have you seen the pictures yet, Will?"

Will was trying his best not to wig out at my performance, which actually added authenticity to our 'scene' as he looked mortified and awkward at the same time.

Leanne looked at Will. "I thought you would do the right thing, Will," she said quietly.

Smiling slowly, I asked, "For whom, Leanne? Will is a good man, of course he'll accept his responsibilities, and I'll help of course."

I smiled again. "It isn't as if I'm short of money, but firstly, we're going to need to know when you are due. Any idea what the medical bills are? They can be sent to you, Will, and you'll want to speak with her obstetrician too," I said, still assessing Leanne's reaction.

Pretended to brush something off Will's shirt, I commented, "As soon as we have the paternity tests back, I'll have my family lawyers draw up a child support plan for your baby, Will. How many weeks are you by the way, what's your due date?" I turned to speak with Will. "We'll need that paperwork too."

Walking over to Will, I put my hand up inside Will's t-shirt, like it was an act of affection. Will shivered and grinned at me. I didn't expect what came next. Will's hand cupped my chin and he kissed me hard. It wasn't a lingering kiss, though, but Will had an instant erection. I tried to hide my snicker when I saw him readjust his pants.

Our act was working, I could see through Leanne. She hadn't become emotional or angry or displayed any emotions that I would expect from someone who was having her ex-boyfriend's baby, and who was scared to be out there on her own with the responsibility. Leanne wanted Will. She had wanted to control him, and this was her way of doing it.

"Will, can I speak with you alone?" Leanne said quietly. Will's eyes flicked to mine with a *WTF* look, but I felt confident that he could continue with our act on his own. "I'll be in the car. Nice to meet you Leanne, no doubt we'll be seeing a lot of each other in the future." I smiled sweetly and went to sit in the car.

Will came out of the house about ten minutes later, grinning. He glided into the seat in one smooth action. "Drive." I took off down the street and as we rounded the corner, he said. "Can you stop the car for a minute?"

Pulling over, I turned to see the delight and relief Will's eyes. "You need to excuse me for what I am about to do." I frowned, puzzled at what he meant to do. Will took my head in his hands and kissed me passionately. I hesitated for a second, and found myself kissing him back.

My head was swimming. Will broke away and stared at me. "That's for giving me my life back." I was flushed and more than a little breathless.

"Anything else I can do for you?" I asked, raising an eyebrow. We both started laughing. Will stamped his feet on the floor of the car with excitement, mimicking me from the last time we were excited. He was relieved after this close call.

Apparently, Leanne had told Will that she was only nine weeks pregnant, and it wasn't his. It was his friend's baby. Will was hurt his friend had made a play for her as soon as they had broken up but was glad to be out of the situation.

We had forced Leanne to be honest by pretending that, although Will would meet his responsibilities, they would be to his child, not to her. Our performance had encouraged Leanne to come clean. I could see the relief on Will's face and felt so happy that he had confided in me.

There was still the awkward subject of the two

kisses in half an hour to deal with, both instigated by
Will. I had to admit I was turned on a little with the
unexpectedness of it.

I took Will back to college to collect his car. "We
need to talk." He looked embarrassed.

"Yeah, I thought about my bad attitude toward
you all the way home." He looked sadly at me.

"What do you mean, your bad attitude, Will?" I
glanced at him and he lowered his gaze.

"I have to say I was a little curious, since you
told me that stuff about Alfie." I didn't know what to
say to Will at that, so I sighed.

"Look Will… you're emotional right now, hell I
am too with Alfie. It makes us do crazy things. I'm
not pissed that you kissed me, actually, I think I
kissed you back." I giggled. "We were caught up in a
moment. We both love Saffy though, and you need to
get back on track with that." Will just nodded.

Once we'd cleared the air, I mentioned Alfie's
offer to watch his band. "Sorry honey, I'd have loved
to do that with you, but Saffy has an event this
evening at her campus, and I kind of promised to
support her with that." I smiled.

"It's fine, I will probably skip this time, and we'll
do something next time he asks."

Driving away, I felt good that Will's future was
secure again, but he'd kissed me twice, and we'd just
have to get past that with time.

Nearing the exit to join the main road from the
campus, I noticed Alfie, his arms around the petite
blonde that had been watching him on campus the
day he ignored me.

Their arms were wrapped around his waist in

return, his face was bent close to hers, and they seemed wrapped up in each other, talking intimately.

Instantly, I felt my heart ache as it dawned on me, he could already be in an emotional relationship, maybe one that didn't fully satisfy his sexual needs, hence needing someone like me.

The subsequent drive home was painful. I sat numb, tears streaming down my face again. I felt stupid. I saw more than one driver do a double take and figured my face had gone its usual blotchy mess.

Extremely sad and more than a little angry at myself, for allowing myself to get tangled up with him again. *The mixed messages he sent out were incredible, no emotions, but comfort?* I was so confused by all these strange concepts he seemed to have.

On reflection, no matter how many times I had seen Alfie with women, I'd never seen him fully embrace any girl like he was holding her. Yet, with her, they seemed so natural. There was an air of contentment about the way he held her. I didn't reach my apartment before my cell buzzed.

SEXPERT: all set for tonight?

I sat staring at it. *Was I? How could he do this to her, to me?*

> **Pink Lady: Actually, I've changed my mind, I'm tired, early night, have fun.**
>
> **SEXPERT: Where are you?**

Pink Lady: In bed.

SEXPERT: my favorite place for you, can't you nap and I'll pick you up?

Pink Lady: What do you want from me???

SEXPERT: a friend.

I stared at the screen. To be fair, he had been fine since our truce. *Why should it matter to me that he's with someone if I was a friend?* My true feelings for him were anything but that of a friend. I didn't answer him. Instead, I rolled over and fell asleep, exhausted from crying

"Lily, honey… *Lily!*" Saffy was shaking me awake. I was disorientated because it was still daylight, but I was in bed. Then I remembered I was napping.

I cracked my eye open, and she smiled at me. "Alfie's here Lily, he said he's taking you to see his band." I sat bolt upright.

"He's here?" She nodded.

"Yup, thing is, I need to leave soon. Will's picking me up. I have an event on my campus this evening."

I smiled weakly. "Yeah, Will told me about it this morning."

Saffy huffed. "So, you need to get a wiggle on and make yourself decent. I need to leave in about fifteen."

The last thing I wanted was a scene with Alfie in

front of Saffy, so I went into the bathroom and took the quickest shower ever. It was too hot for jeans, so I put on a cute little skater dress. It was deep red with black edging. I accessorized this with some bangles and a couple of cloth bands on my wrists, then put on some ballet pump type shoes for comfort.

Alfie may not deal with emotions, but my stomach was in crisis. I had butterflies, the adrenaline in my veins pumping so fast I could hear it deafening me. A swooshing noise was in my ear, so loud it prevented me from eavesdropping on the conversation he and Saffy were having only feet away.

My smile hid my feelings, as I tried to enter the living room as breezily as I could. Saffy turned and smiled. "There you are. Okay guys have fun. See you tomorrow, Lily." She kissed my cheek and whispered, "You're a knockout in that dress." She winked at me and was out the door.

Following her to the door, I closed it behind her, when Alfie spoke. "Oh God, Lily, you look stunningly beautiful in that dress." Turning, I could see the pleasure I was giving him on his face.

My aching heart cracked again, that he desired me, but not enough to commit to anything. Alfie he looked such a bad-boy, and very sexy in his skinny jeans, white t-shirt, and brown leather jacket. I always struggled to look at his face without wanting to kiss it. I think I stared too long, and he moved beside me. "Are you ready?"

No, I'm never going to be ready to be just friends with you. "Sure," I squeaked out, sounding less convincing than the smile I was giving him.

Gathering up a wrap, even though it was Florida, because the air conditioning in some places was set so low, it made me feel uncomfortably cold. As we were leaving he tried to place a hand on the bottom of my back, but I kind of scooted to the side so it didn't linger there.

I thought I saw the beginnings of a smile in his eyes, but I let it pass when his body language seemed normal. As we walked to his car, I wanted to ask him about that woman on campus, but I had no clue how to start that conversation, and I didn't trust that I'd be able to carry on with the evening if his explanation wasn't what I wanted to hear.

My mouth was dry, suddenly nervous to be sitting next to him, my hands betraying my feelings as I kept picking at the hem of my dress. "Did you have a good nap?" He turned to look briefly at me smiling.

"Yeah, I think so." I was struggling to engage with him, dwelling on my earlier visual of him with his little blond woman. She was cute too, which made me feel even worse. I wasn't sure who I felt worse for, her or me.

Breaking the silence, Alfie said, "Is this how all our evenings are going to start?" I glanced at him, but he was looking straight ahead at the road.

"Sorry?" I offered puzzled. He flicked his eyes to me, giving me a half smile.

"You, not talking, being shy?"

I felt annoyed with him, but I tried hard to contain this. "I'm not sure what you want from me Alfie."

Suddenly his head snapped round quickly this time. "Didn't we do all this before? Friendship Lily,

331

isn't that what you wanted, too?" He looked back at the road. I tried to make it okay between us, but my feelings were becoming more of a barrier every day. I wanted to be with him in every way, yet it seemed that I'd have to choose one or another. I could either have sex with no feelings, or friendship with sexual frustration.

"Sorry, I just don't fully understand why we're doing this, it feels a bit weird." He did something I hadn't expected at that moment, he took my hand in reassurance.

"Lily, 'friends with no benefits', your call remember? If you change your mind, you only have to say, and we'll stop."

CHAPTER 31

PLAYING WITH ME

As we pulled up alongside our ride to Orlando, I was reassessing Alfie. "Why did you ask me to come with you tonight?" Not answering, he took the key from the ignition and got out. Walking to my side of the car, he opened my door for me.

"I wanted you to come and hear us. It'll be good for you. Now, enough of the soul searching, let's go let our hair down."

He led me to the minivan. This had been converted for them to travel around in. Some of the seats had been taken out. Others were set like two booths with tables in the middle.

The extra space held their guitars and bags. There were four other guys sitting there – one tuning a guitar, one reading a tablet, and two in conversation at the back.

"Guys…Lily, Lily…guys," he said, like that told all of us what we needed to know about each other.

He motioned at me to sit in the free seats with a table. "Beer or wine?" he asked, reaching into a large cooler and plucking out a wet beer bottle, sliding the excess water off with his hand, while he waited for my reply.

Feeling self-conscious, I blushed as all the guys' attention seemed to be focused on me. I was the only female, and if I was being totally honest, I felt a little exposed. "Wine please."

Alfie wasn't looking at me, but when he turned around, he produced an oversized plastic tumbler, which was almost three-quarters full, and sat facing me. "Jeez, Alfie, are you trying to get me drunk?"

He grinned wickedly. "Only enough to get into your panties." He smirked, and the other guys laughed out loud. I blushed, and felt that Alfie's remark wasn't said entirely in jest.

One of the guys sitting in the back walked past us, and the others were still staring at me. He pulled a beer from the cooler and came back, stopping beside me.

"Drew, pleased to meet you, Lily. Is that a London accent?" Drew was charming and almost as hot looking as Alfie. He was taller than Alfie, but just as muscularly toned, with a strong angular jaw and fabulous gray eyes. His hair was dark brown in color and mussed in just the right way.

He seemed a pretty laid-back guy, and as he spoke, I couldn't help but notice his perfect white teeth framed by a luscious mouth. When I looked closely at all the guys, they were collectively a great looking band.

We chatted for a few minutes, and I warmed to him. He was really easy to talk to. I was aware that

Alfie was studying us, his beer bottle almost stuck to his lips, but not really drinking it, and his eyes had narrowed. I wondered what he was thinking at that moment. He cleared his throat and clunked his beer bottle noisily on the table.

"Okay Drew, enough. Get your own girl." I blushed, and Drew quickly disappeared to the back again. I looked awkwardly at Alfie.

"Were we making you jealous, Alfie?" He held my gaze and smirked, but it didn't quite change the annoyance in his eyes, before he moved away and kicked his boots off.

Noticing me watching him, he offered, "Just making myself more comfortable, it's a couple of hours to Orlando, maybe we can get to know each other a little better." I blushed crimson, thinking this was an inference to his intimate knowledge of me already, or another of his games.

My eyes flicked nervously at the other guys, one of whom continued to watch me. Alfie's eyes widened, realizing what I thought and smirked. He leaned into my ear, and whispered, "Sorry, honey, I didn't mean anything by it. I meant life for you before Florida." He was smirking now. "You're too cute… though, I like the way your mind works." He winked at me.

I began to relax and told him about my life, the past few years of it anyway; my dad being a helicopter pilot, my mom a pediatrician, some stuff about my close family, and that I was an only child. Then some of the things I'd done before college, mainly the work in India and England with kids before coming to Florida.

The look on his face was one of admiration. "Dang, you've done some profound stuff in your short life already. So now it's your music? I heard you sing a little. Your voice is sweet, but there's a bit of grit in it, unique sounding. Would you sing with me sometime?"

I couldn't see why he would possibly want to sing with me. His voice was incredibly sexy from what I'd heard during our limited time on the lawn. "I'm not bullshitting you, Lily.

"I want to try some stuff I've been working on with you." I should have been flattered, but I was suspicious that this could be another one of his attempts to string me along.

"I wouldn't feel comfortable singing with you Alfie." His eyes went wide.

"Sure you would, once you were comfortable with the arrangement." I felt a little peeved that he dismissed my opinion so freely. He had no interest in finding out what my concerns were about us collaborating.

"Okay, your turn," I said as cheerily as possible. I wanted to try to get him to open up to me, and I also wanted to try to get to the bottom of his relationship with the girl on campus. She intrigued me too much. *What was it about her that had him so wrapped up in her?*

As soon as I began to probe about his life, he ran his hand through his hair. "Just a minute, refill," he said, shaking his empty beer bottle at me. He got up and made his way to the cooler. When he returned, he squeezed in alongside me.

Alfie's closeness gave me butterflies in my

stomach as his hip brushed alongside mine when he settled himself. My chest rose and fell quicker as my heart sped up. He bit his bottom lip, his tongue flicking out slowly moistening it, as his eyes briefly glanced over my mouth. I tried consciously not to swallow when he did this.

Lifting his arm, he leaned away from me, to make room between us. He slid his arm along the back of me without making contact. The anticipation that he could drop his arm around me at any moment made me feel really excited and uncomfortable at the same time.

When his eyes met mine, he held my gaze. My body tensed and I looked away, before crossing my legs in an effort to make some space between us. "What do you want to know? My life has been in Florida…born and raised here. I've always been here, apart from the occasional vacation. That might change though in the New Year, there's a hint we may open for a small tour in Europe."

Turning back, he focused on his beer. There was no eye contact after that. "There isn't anything else to say." He shrugged and picked at the label on his bottle, before taking a swig out of the bottle and setting it down. His eyes darted over to where his bandmates were.

I was conscious that he was possibly hiding something. It was probably the part about the girl, so I pressed on with my questions. "What about your family, girlfriend?"

Alfie sighed. "My sister and an aunt." His answer gave me nothing to work with.

There was still no mentioned the girl. "No one

else?" He shook his head, his eyes instantly showing a fleeting hint of pain.

"You need a refill?" he said, sliding off the bench and back to the cooler again. I knew he was being evasive with me and trying to close the conversation down.

Watched him stand with his back to me, I saw him pouring another glass of wine, before leaning into the cooler, pulling out another beer. After refilling my wine glass, he leaned forward and spoke to one of his bandmates. His conversation was inaudible over the acoustic guitar that one of them was strumming.

Alfie's brow was creased as he turned, and I saw what I felt was a forced smile as he came back handing me the wine. "I really can't drink that, Alfie. I'll be drunk!" I shook my head and put my hand up to refuse the glass. He pursed his lips and a slow grin appeared.

"That's the idea."

I was worried that if I did drink it, my defenses against him would be non- existent. He set the wine down in front of me. "Better get that, before it spills." He chuckled, letting the tumbler go, making me grab and steady it.

Stretching across me to open an air conditioning vent, his foot accidently brushed across my leg; the back of his arm, dragging lightly across my breast as he sat back. "Sorry, that wasn't intentional." He looked apologetically at me.

The accidental contact sparked feelings in me, even this minimal contact made me crave his touch. My body immediately reacted, wanting more. The guy that Alfie was speaking to before came over and sat down opposite him. They discussed the set order for the gig. Alfie was off the hook about his personal life just like that.

Wondering briefly, if the guy was conspiring to helping him to avoid resuming our previous conversation, I checked myself as being slightly paranoid at that thought. As they became engrossed in technical conversation, I was able to observe Alfie without him noticing.

His strong jawline was relaxed, his lips occasionally curling into a beautifully perfect smile that was as sexy as all hell. *Damn it.* There was no doubt about it, he's absolutely stunning, and I found myself staring at his mouth, his spoken words not registering at all.

My eyes scanned his flawless, close shaven skin, and fell back to his beautiful full lips and when he smiled again, that cute dimple seemed to wink at me from his cheek.

Alfie's sharp hazel eyes were like mood stones. He had a definite black ring circling each pupil making them piercing to look at. They changed color all the time.

Right now, they were hazel, more brown than green. However, when he looked at me intensely, they were more often than not green. They made me melt, especially when he smiled, but even more so when they were lusting. When I finished the checking-his-face-out phase, my attention tuned to his voice as he spoke.

His voice had rich dulcet tones. Listening to him speak softly made me feel calm. He definitely has a seductive and addictive voice.

Every now and again a little chuckle would escape his throat, reminding me of the times he did that when he was playfully nuzzling my neck. The effect he had on me was insane. He was turning me on, and he wasn't even communicating with me.

I realized that I'd been sipping the wine as I was having my 'Alfie feast', and when I looked at my glass it was almost gone. I shouldn't have drunk all that wine, but I was nervous. I now felt lightheaded and woozy just sitting quietly.

My eyes drooped closed, and I slid down in the seat. I could still hear him talking, alongside the lull of the engine of the bus. My head kept rolling to the side, and I felt myself moving as Alfie shifted me into position closer to him, leaning my head onto him.

He thought I was asleep, so I used this to my advantage and snuggled into his side. He sighed. "She's fucking wrecking me, dude." he murmured quietly to the guy across from him.

Hearing the guy leave the table, Alfie slipped down in the seat a little more, beside me. I had to consciously tell myself not to tense, because I was supposed to be asleep. He inhaled, smelling my hair and sighed again. His arm nestled down the side of me, and he drew me closer to him. I heard his heartbeat become stronger and a little faster at the close contact.

His reaction told me he wasn't exactly without feelings for me, and I hoped that it wasn't purely arousal. As his palm rested along my hip, he put slight pressure on it again, keeping me in place.

I felt a feather light kiss on my temple, his breath

on my cheek as he inhaled sharply, before controlling his exhale. The scent of him, his body wash, and the faint smell of leather on his skin from his jacket made me feel like I wanted to stay there forever.

He inhaled deeply again, before his breathing became a little heavier and ragged when he exhaled. Alfie tensed, but didn't move. He just stilled, swallowing hard, and eventually relaxed again.

Drew nudged both of us as we arrived at the 'Firestone Live' venue in Orlando. I stretched a little, opening one eye to peek up at him. "Do all English girls sleep as much as you?" he whispered, smiling slowly at me.

The urge to put my lips on his was so strong I had to restrain myself. "Nope, just me, I think. But the wine didn't help." I smiled sleepily, stretching a little again and groaned. He groaned in response and swept his index finger down my nose. He pushed me away from him and got up, looking as if he was fighting his urge for me too.

"Okay, Dan, our driver, is going to look after you, honey. I need to get with my band. You'll be okay in the wings with him. We can hang out, and watch the others when we're done." Smiling, I gave him a small wave.

"Go do your thing, rock star!"

Alfie grinned sexily at me, and kissed my forehead. I think he meant to hug me briefly, but he lingered a tad longer than was comfortable before turning to run after the others.

The fact that he lingered showed me that he was still struggling to keep our relationship platonic as well.

Dan wasn't a conversationalist, he just said, "Come with me." However, he did take care of me, making sure that I had a backstage pass, protected me from over enthusiastic fans hanging around by the stage door, and showed me where to go to watch Alfie's band perform.

His bandmates seemed like regular guys, unaffected by the adoration they received when they performed. I had a new found respect for him. Alfie didn't boast, and I hadn't seen him behave outlandishly given his popularity.

From my vantage point, I looked out and was stunned at how massive the audience was. All I could see was a multi-colored sea of people, thousands of them, stretching far into the distance. Their heads swayed as they moved around. There was a general buzz of conversation with the occasional loud laugh or cheer as the fans got in the mood for the bands.

The lights lowered and the emcee's voice boomed out introducing the hot new band, 'Crakt Soundzz', and I realized I knew nothing about them and hadn't even asked their name.

The tension of the crowd added to the atmosphere. There was a lot of whistling, and they seemed to heave and swell forward together, erupting in a roar of anticipation as the lighting in the auditorium went black.

CHAPTER 32

GETTING STRONGER

Alfie was just a few feet away from me in the darkness. I couldn't see him, but I felt his presence. I instinctively knew he was there, and I held my breath. The crowd fell silent… waiting.

I heard the drumsticks ticking, and knew the drummer was counting them in and suddenly, vibrations from the bass pulsed and the sound of the guitars reverberated loudly. The same vibrations rumbled across the floor and ran from my toes up and throughout my body, as the noise boomed loudly from the huge amplifiers to the side of me.

Simultaneously, Alfie screamed out, "Hello Orlando! We're so gonna rock the fucking roof off tonight." The crowd screamed and roared again, their noise swelling louder in appreciation. High pitched whistles and catcalls followed in unison, as the band's music blared from the massive speakers along the stage.

Alfie had so much energy, bouncing around playing the intro to their first song, and when he began to sing, the females in the crowd went wild with excitement.

The cacophony of the crowd was deafening between each song, but when they played and sang, the audience was right there with them. The lighting on stage was blinding and heat radiated down on the guys as they performed.

My feet continued to buzz under me with the vibrations of the bass' rumble, and the music continued to boom. The relentless heat of the lights on stage made all of the guys glisten with sweat, and they were half naked in no time.

I certainly wasn't one to complain, especially having a ringside seat to watch these guys. Alfie sang a mixture of fast-paced heavy rock and slower ballads. I was completely transfixed when he sang. His voice was just so incredible. Even though I was hearing them for the first time, I could tell instantly that Crakt Soundzz had something very special, and they would definitely be going places.

Alfie sang one particular ballad, and the music was slow and haunting. He stood completely still, hugging the mic. His fingers flexed and re-gripped it every now and again. His eyes were closed as he lost himself in the words of the song. It was as if he were singing it to one person.

Breaking eye contact a couple of times, I looked away, because it felt like I was intruding on intimate words to someone, especially when his face looked pained during some of the verses.

Complicated little riffs Drew played

accompanying the song it were pure inspiration and made the song all the more haunting. Near the end of the song, Alfie's eyes opened, and his head tilted to the side in my direction.

They were sad and dull eyes, deliberately seeking me out as I stood the wings. His gaze locked into mine as he sang the words, "If I can't let myself love you, I need to let you go."

Biting my lip in concentration as I listened, he broke the stare as he finished the line, his eyes flicking away toward the direction of the crowd before closing them again.

The crowd went berserk with emotion when he was done, and the band launched straight into a song about a guy fucking a girl to the beat of a rock song. I felt pretty sad after that, and if I hadn't known better, it was a clear message to me to get the fuck away from him.

It frustrated me that Alfie couldn't make a commitment to anyone, and I wondered if, like me, he was blocking himself from relationships because he had a bigger plan. I had stopped myself from getting involved with anyone back home, because I didn't want to leave someone behind. If I had fallen for someone, I might not have come here.

Seeing how he and his band played tonight made me think there might be something in that. I wonder if he has an inkling of how big his band might become and doesn't want the complication of leaving someone behind. *If that's the problem, what about the blond girl?*

There was no doubt about it though, these guys were mega-talented, natural rock stars, and their performance was flawless. I couldn't believe that I knew this incredibly sexy and amazingly talented man personally.

Impressed, not just by just his looks, but his talent and charisma too, the crowd went wild. Alfie was grinning and every now and then would wink and point at a female in the crowd. I couldn't help but feel kind of hurt by that, but I knew that was just his stage persona.

He was also drawing new fans by introducing them to his music. Alfie didn't owe me anything. Technically, listening to his pitch was perfect and the band's music had substance. They would definitely be going places, especially with a front man like him.

Every number they played had a catchy hook, and the crowd seemed to know some of their stuff. It was contagious. This made me think they were more renowned than I'd thought.

Suddenly, I felt that my music was very rudimentary in comparison to his genius. To call Alfie a musician wouldn't define him, although, that was what he was striving for. He's much more than a musician. Very much an artiste, performing with originality of thought and his acting skills were as adept as his musical ability.

When they came off stage, Alfie was buzzing; bouncing up and down on his toes with excitement. Someone threw him a towel and he wrapped it around his neck. He was drenched in sweat after giving the crowd everything he had out there. Grabbing my hand tightly, he smiled and said, "Let's go." Smirking, he began pulling me down a long dark corridor and eventually, into an area with lots of people milling around.

There were some couches, big mirrors, a makeup chair with a dressing table in the corner, and a large buffet and drinks on a table that ran the length of the room. There were two young girls in black and white uniforms keeping it looking tidy and replenishing stuff.

Alfie turned to me, holding both my hands. "So… did you have a good time?" I nodded.

"You were all fabulous." He smirked and looked bashful for a second.

"High praise indeed," he teased. "I'm gonna have a couple of beers here with the band first, then we can go out front and watch the main band. Is that okay with you?"

Feeling relaxed, I agreed. "Sure, take your time, I'm fine." I walked over and sat on one of the couches feeling a little awkward. Some guy came over and sat on the arm of the couch next to me.

"Well hi, there, sweet cheeks," he cooed.

The guy looked like he needed a good bath. His hair looked lank and greasy and his teeth were yellow. He flicked his hand through his hair, and the only thing I could concentrate on was his nicotine-stained fingers. He began to check me out, while scratching his crotch. He was gross.

When he'd finished checking me out, he smiled at me tucking his long hair behind his ear. It didn't improve his look. "How's it going?"

Thinking he was just being friendly, if a little lacking in his self- awareness and that he must be involved with Alfie and his band, I indulged him. "Yeah, great thanks, they were great, weren't they?" I gestured with my head at Alfie's band.

He licked his lips, and twisted his mouth. "Yeah, they're okay, for a warm-up. You want to come with me and meet the guys from Phoebe's Fix?" I felt a little star-struck. I knew who they were, but I didn't really know the band, since their music hadn't made it into the mainstream over the pond in the UK yet.

I'd heard a lot of their stuff on the radio since coming to the US, but they could be sitting next to me, and I'd have no clue they were there. I was flattered he wanted to do this for me, but said I'd told Alfie I would wait here.

Alfie's arm slipped around me, and suddenly he was kissing me hard on the lips. "Hey Lily darlin' quick, there's someone I want you to meet." Alfie addressed the guy, "Oh, sorry, man, Lily meet Harry, Harry... my girl Lily."

Incensed at what Alfie had just done, I was about to protest, but he pulled me away sharply, trailing me through some people. He stood me back against a wall in the corner of the room holding my hands in front of him. "What the..."

"Shush," he said softly. He bent his head. "You were almost fucked by a rock star honey." Seeing my startled gaze, he smirked. "Harry's the bass player in Phoebe's Fix. He's a crude bastard too. He fucks a girl, and offers her to others as his sloppy seconds."

I couldn't help myself as I said, "That's rich coming from you." He stared at me.

"What's that supposed to mean?" I looked incredulously at him.

"Are you fucking kidding me? Tell me if I'm wrong, but isn't being fucked by a rock star when they take what they want without any emotion or consideration for the other person's feelings?" I spat back at him under my breath.

Looking stunned at me, Alfie asked, "Is that what you think? It wasn't like that and you know it. We…" He gestured his finger between us. "We used each other, Lily. You knew what it was, and you begged me for it, I heard you." My mouth dropped open to protest, but he snickered and began laughing at me.

I glanced over at Harry, his eyes still staring at us. "He's still there," I whispered, cringing as I looked past Alfie's shoulder. Alfie was angry now and hissed at me.

"He probably thinks he can take you anyway, maybe I should just leave you to it."

"No," I said urgently, but with a pleading look. He raised an eyebrow and slowly began stroking my hair tenderly, his eyes locked on mine. It was hard to imagine that we were in the middle of an argument. We were arguing, but his touch felt so tender and intimate, and maybe it looked that way to anyone observing us.

Paralyzed by his touch, my head was telling me to push him away. My body was screaming for more, much more. It felt too right to stop. Alfie laced my fingers in his and sensually lifted them, to lean on the wall above my head, his forehead on mine.

Making my hips jut forward a little, Alfie was turning me on, the way he held me against the wall in that way. He moved one hand after taking both in the other. I tried so hard to resist his touch, his gaze intensely holding mine.

Smoldering eyes stared intensely at me,

unspoken emotion arcing between us, and it was probably the most erotic experience I'd ever had. I almost begged to have him again. Alfie pushed my knees apart with one knee, lining our bodies up together, and settled his hips against mine.

He was standing with his legs closed between my legs. He was erect, pressing solidly through the layers of material we were both wearing. His body was flush with mine. He hitched my leg on his hip, his bulge jutting further between my legs. It felt like a delicious punishment, and no doubt about it, he was turned on too.

Without warning his eyes dropped to my lips and I became weaker and weaker as he openly seduced me. Alfie licked his lips and pressed his hips harder into me. A moan escaped in a soft breathy sound and I promptly berated myself for making it.

Smiling at me, a soft chuckle escaped from him as he placed his face into my neck. I exhaled and groaned, "God." I'd been holding my breath again without realizing it. Alfie licked my neck and lightly nibbling my earlobe. It sent shivers and a rash of goose bumps over me. I moaned again and closed my eyes.

Alfie knew exactly how to seduce me. His hand trailed down my back, cupping my ass, as he pulled me even closer to him. As if he'd read my mind, he groaned, "God, Lily...I want you so much."

My panties were drenched with moist, silky, wet arousal, and my body was becoming so responsive, humming at his touch. My willpower was quickly evaporating.

I looked over, and Harry was nowhere to be seen.

I didn't tell Alfie this, and my eyes fell to his lips. He noticed and ran his tongue between them, wetting them and making me even wetter in my core, if that was possible. He leaned back to look at me, the lust clear in his eyes.

Leaning forward again, he placed his lips on the side of my mouth, and exhaled raggedly again. Alfie's head moved just a fraction, and he placed his lips on mine applying pressure, but with his lips still closed.

"Save me a space," I murmured, and found the strength to push him back before I surrendered completely.

Alfie moved away instantly, his breath was uneven. "Sorry." He looked sheepish, his hands up in a surrendering motion. He was fighting to slow his body down, breathing through his nostrils and the sound was much more labored than I've heard it before, even in the wildest throes of passion.

One of the guys from the band, I still hadn't got his name, Les or Des or something, shouted out to Alfie, in his rough New York accent, penetrating our trance-like state as we stared at each other.

"Jesus, Alfie, just fuck her already. The tension is killing me." I was mortified that his band had been watching me. Alfie turned and scowled, "Shut the fuck up and have some respect, dude." Then looked at me and seemed genuinely apologetic.

Tears welled in me. I just had to get out of there. I ran, not knowing where to. I had no clue where I was, but I knew I didn't want to be around these people. "Lily, wait!" I was a fool to think we could be friends. It would probably always be like this. My

351

distress confused me, but I somehow made it outside.

There were a couple of security guys and a roadie hanging around the doorway. I saw Dan, the bus driver, and was about to speak to him when Alfie softly said, "It's, okay, I've got her… I've got you." He had his hands out, and Dan backed off and walked away.

Alfie turned me to face him, and I was sobbing uncontrollably now. He engulfed me in a bear hug. I couldn't breathe, he was suffocating me with this hot and cold treatment, suffocating my love for him and using it to torment me.

This situation was all wrong. I could never be 'just friends' with him. Overwhelming feelings of love and the reality of this engulfed me. I couldn't settle for less than the whole deal with him. I was here in his arms, and I had to resist him.

I would have to hide my true feelings for him, he'd used them already. He was comforting me, rubbing my back, telling me, "shush." I let him because I needed something at that moment.

When I had calmed myself, I summoned up the energy to push him away from me. "I'm staying here tonight. I don't want to travel back with you. I just need a cab to take me to a hotel."

He put his hand out for me to take it. "Come here babe." I was incensed.

"I am not your babe, Alfie, stop it… I'm not your anything remember?" He actually looked tortured by my outburst.

"Come on Lily, I'm sorry, don't be ridiculous…" I was furious.

"Ridiculous? You and your perverted 'mind

fuck' treatment is what's ridiculous. I don't want to be around you, ever! I hate you. You play with me like I'm nothing. Leave me alone, don't fucking touch me again, don't call me, don't come near me. I can't stand this anymore. I don't want anything from you!" He looked stunned by my outburst.

I turned to a roadie who was standing watching me. "Please help me. I want him to stay away from me," I said pointing at Alfie. He stepped forward, and Alfie's jaw clenched.

"I got this buddy, she's always this dramatic when she's been drinking," he quipped.

My jaw dropped in disbelief, and I gave the roadie a pleading look. He leaned toward Alfie. "All the same dude, the girl's upset, and I would rather you gave her some space. I'll make sure she finds a place to stay, and you can take it up with her tomorrow."

Alfie was no match for the guy physically, so although he continued to try to sweet talk me, the guy wouldn't allow him to make eye contact with me. "Dude, you're done, back off," he said, ushering me away after another minute. The roadie continued to scowl in Alfie's direction until he walked away, running his hand through his hair.

Joel, the roadie helping me, was great. He didn't ask me any questions, but took me to a safe area of Orlando and checked me into a decent hotel. He even sorted out my car rental for me before leaving. We swapped cell numbers, and I agreed to call him if I needed him, should Alfie reappear.

CHAPTER 33

IT IS WHAT IT IS

Standing in the hotel room shower, I sobbed my heart out. Maybe being in the USA wasn't right for me. Since I'd arrived I've had relationship problems with almost everyone I've met. I considered whether it was a culture clash or my perception of people, or maybe my naivety or my poor willpower.

My nose was so blocked from all my tears, combined with the humidity, made it difficult to breathe. I felt I was suffocating, and I realized I was having a panic attack. I wished for the first time that my parents had been firmer with me and that I'd stayed in the UK.

Crawling into bed, my eyes were stinging, and I fell asleep too tired to think. When I awoke, my cell was ringing. Squinting at the Caller ID, I tried to focus in the dark. SEXPERT ID flashed so I let it ring out. A minute later there was a beep, telling me he'd left a message. That pattern continued for the next hour. I switched off my phone and sobbed again. *Why couldn't this guy just leave me alone? Does he do this to his other girls? Why does he live alone? Where is his family?*

Alfie had been relentless that week in his pursuit of me, yet there was the girl on campus. *Where was she while all of that was happening?*

Waking a little after nine the next morning, I had a pounding headache. There was no way I was going to make it to college that was for sure. I switched on my cell to call Will and explain. As soon as my cell fired up, I saw seventeen missed calls. Saffy three times, Will five, Alfie eight – five times last night, and three this morning – and one from Joel.

I rang Joel first figuring he'd be the quickest to deal with. I thanked him for all of his help and invited him and his wife to come visit with us after winter break. I rang Will next. "Where the hell are you, Lily? We've been out of our minds with worry here." His voice sounded really concerned.

Feeling horrible I hadn't let them know and I felt bad that I'd worried them, I lied that my cell battery had died, and that I'd stayed the night in Miami as it had been a late night. "Did you sleep with him?" I was taken aback by Will's directness.

"No Will, I didn't." He exhaled as if he had been holding his breath. "Good girl."

Cringing, I thought of the possibility of Will running into Alfie on campus and finding out what really happened. Saffy was with Will as he was dropping her off at her college campus. I was relieved that I didn't have to lie twice. Alfie, I didn't want to deal with at all. I deleted all his missed calls.

My voicemail envelope was flashing. I didn't want to check it, but felt I should, just in case my parents had called. Message #1, Alfie's voice— delete. I deleted the next six from him also. Message #8 was a little different, he sounded almost melancholic. "I won't let you walk away without us talking this out."

Feeling especially angry about that message, I called his number. I don't even think it rang before he answered. "Oh, thank God," he said. "I was worried sick." I smarted at that.

"Really, Alfie? That would imply you cared. Won't let me walk away from what?" My heart was already broken by his treatment of me. I snickered.

"Why were you worried? We're nothing, and anyway, I thought you didn't do emotions." He exhaled into his cell.

"This isn't the time for glib remarks," he said dryly. "Where are you?" I shook my head.

"Oh, no you don't, you don't get to be in the same room as me again, do you hear me? I don't want you. I don't want anything to do with you. Why won't you leave me alone? What the hell is wrong with you?"

His voice interrupted, "Meet me. We'll talk, I promise." My heart was thumping in my chest, my head bursting with anger.

"Are you out of your freaking mind? I'm not meeting you, I'm not… I'm just not… anything to you anymore. Correction, I was never anything to you." Alfie sighed heavily.

"That's not true," he snapped back at me. I tried to sound calm.

"Last night, on the bus, you had the opportunity to let me in. You avoided me."

Alfie was silent, and then he let out a long sigh. "You want to know about me? Meet me, I'll tell you anything you want to know." I huffed, tired of this carousel we always seemed to be on.

"Why? Why should I meet you? What does it matter now anyway? I'm walking away, Alfie. You've made me a mess, and I can't allow you any more of my time. You're not good for me."

"Wait!" he shouted, sensing that I was completely serious. "I'm begging you, meet me." His voice sounded desperate. I'd never heard any real emotion in his voice before except when he sang.

I don't know why, but I said, "You have one hour of my time, and only because I'm curious, fuck it up and you don't exist to me, got it?" Sighing again, but this time it sounded like relief.

"Okay, where are you?" I shrugged, even though he couldn't see me.

"I don't know, but my car will be here in a few minutes, give me a zip code and I'll meet you… somewhere public, Alfie."

So an hour later, I was sitting observing him from my rental car, before I went over to him. Alfie didn't look up when I drove into the restaurant car lot, but he didn't know it was me in the rental. Sitting rubbing his thighs, rocking back and forth, Alfie cut a lonely figure. Tilting his head, Alfie looked as if he were deep in thought, before dropping it again, and shaking it.

Whatever he was thinking, it was troubling him. *How could someone that looked that good make me feel this bad?* I had to get past how he looked and what I felt for him and remember why I was here.

Smiling weakly at me, he stood slowly as I walked toward him. When I reached him, he almost put his hand on my waist as he greeted me. I threw him a look, and he dropped it to his side. "Thanks for agreeing to meet me, Lily," he said his voice sounded soft and tired.

Alfie gestured to an outside table at the restaurant. The waitress brought coffee, and I set the alarm on my cell and placed it in front of me, "You have an hour Alfie. Say what you want to say." My tone was abrupt, and I was determined this time.

"You want to know about me? Okay, I'm twenty-four years old. I live in my family home… alone. My parents are dead, my mom when I was eighteen, my dad a couple of years ago, one from cancer the other drunk himself to death because he lost her… my mother. My sister won't come home to see me because she can't bring herself to come to the house that my parents died in. I can't leave it for the same reason."

I sat in silence, listening to him. For someone so young, he'd taken a huge hit emotionally, no wonder he was shut down. "There is stuff that I can't talk about. Or that I'm not ready to talk about. I really like you Lily, but trust me, I can't and won't get into a relationship." He gave me a half smile.

"So you think the way to deal with your grief is to fuck up someone else's mind?" He looked pensively at me. "How many 'fuck buddies' have you had Alfie?" He shifted in his seat.

"Honestly?" I cringed, when he said that

expecting at least double digits.

He looked as if he was counting then sighed. "One, you." A tear rolled down his cheek, he exhaled heavily and looked down at his hands. I digested what he was saying. "And, the other women?"

"They're… they don't count." I smirked at his dismissive tone.

"Me? What about me?" His eyes softened.

"When I touch you Lily, my head goes into meltdown. I just want to feel pleasure, which isn't the same feeling as love. I told you I wasn't capable of a hearts and flowers relationship." A silent pause passed between us. I just didn't know what to say, nothing I could say would make either one of us feel any better.

"I don't want to lose you." It was almost inaudible, and my eyes snapped up to his.

"Lose me? We're nothing to each other Alfie. You can't lose what you don't have." His speech faltered.

"I know… but still…" He struggled with himself, trying to figure out exactly what he meant. His hand ran through his hair again.

"Let me ask you something, I don't expect a reply, and if you walk away, I'll let you, because it's the best thing for you, but just let me say it." I waited as his gaze fixed on mine. Reaching over, he took my hand. I stiffened, and his eyes looked pleadingly at me not to fight this, so I let him continue to hold it in his.

"I didn't want last night to go like that. I'm really sorry, baby." My eyes shot up at him.

"I'm not your baby." He gave me a half smile,

and bit the inside of his cheek.

"I know, sorry." He looked a little embarrassed at his term of endearment.

Pleading with him, I asked, "Why don't you just leave me alone, you can't say you don't know you're hurting me?" He bit his lip, and cradled my hand between both of his. I was tired, I couldn't fight him and it was comforting to have him touch me, even though I'd pay for it later.

"I can't… I can't explain it, but I can't leave you alone." He lifted my hand and brushed his lips across the back of it. It was an intimate, affectionate gesture, but at the same time he knew he was crushing my heart.

A tear rolled down my face. He brushed it away with his thumb, leaving his hand caressing my cheek. "I don't want to use you Lily, I don't want to cause you pain. I want to spend time with you, I like you. I love being inside you, touching you, holding you. I wish I could love you, but I can't."

My heart cracked open at his honesty. I wanted to run away and never have to face him again. I sniffed. "Why, Alfie? If you can't love me then you need to let me be." He looked pale, his eyes sad.

"I can't do love… offer you that. I told you no hearts and flowers."

Angry and tired of hearing the same thing every time, I said, "So you keep telling me are so unfair. Please don't do this to me, I can't stand it." Alfie smoothed his hand over his t-shirt, rubbing his chest.

"Maybe if we spent more time together, you wouldn't feel this way.Maybe my emotions wouldn't be such a focus for you, if we were friends." A single tear fell onto my t-shirt.

"Alfie we were never just friends, friends don't hurt each other. Do you think I'm your fucking plaything, Alfie?" A sob escaped my throat. "How about this? You leave me alone. Maybe meet someone that can do all the things for me you can't Alfie, have you thought about that?" I picked at the napkin on the table.

"You as much as told two guys last night that I was your girl, I'm yours to any man that pays attention to me, but I'm not yours Alfie, just as much as you're not mine. All this hot sexual tension then the cold- shower behavior is screwing with my head."

Looking angry, he retorted, "If you were honest with yourself Lily, you'd agree that when I'm near you, it gives you pleasure too. I'm not wrong about the way you look at me."

Alfie shook his head at me, staring into my eyes. "You wanted me during those few moments. I could have had you every fucking time. I didn't take advantage of that." Alfie struggled to express himself.

"I can't help the endless sexual tension there is around us. I suppose it's because you gave me the best sex ever, but you feel it as well."

"That's just it!" I spat. "I don't want to do that. Well, maybe I do sometimes, just for fun," I said confused. He gave me a half smile and latched onto that last statement by widening his eyes in interest at me.

"If you are talking about your needs, mine count too, I'm not like you, Alfie. I need love as well as sex." I stared at his beautiful, sad face and whispered, "I deserve the man I'm with to love me, to make love

361

to me. I've had that now, so I know the difference. I know that I couldn't live without that for the rest of my life." He held my gaze and nodded slowly, letting go of my hand, and gave me a resigned smile.

The alarm went off on my cell. I switched it off and stood up. "How are you getting back?"

Alfie hugged himself.

"Don't worry about me. I'll get back." I couldn't leave him standing in the middle of Orlando, when I was going back anyway. "Come on, I'll give you a ride, but you're not to touch me."

Giving me a small grin, he shook his head and crossed his heart with his finger, commenting, "I promise, most definitely not."

I drove back, with music as our safe topic of conversation, and Alfie slept some of the way. He had been up all night looking for me, and I had been asleep. I know it shouldn't have, but it kind of made me feel better that he was worried enough not to sleep, but I did feel a little guilty about that all the same.

Alfie had said he couldn't give me up. I didn't know he'd had me, I didn't feel like I'd had him in any way, except the biblical sense that's for sure.

My heart squeezed to think of how fabulous we could have been together in all ways, but he just didn't want me enough. So…I wasn't enough for him. What I did know, was that our sexual chemistry made me vulnerable, Alfie himself had admitted that he was powerless to stop himself.

If I wasn't careful, I could also end up in a strange relationship that relied solely on sex. I knew by then, I didn't want that. However, my body craved his touch, and I needed to take control to prevent anything from happening between us again.

It wouldn't be a case of it may happen again. I, like he, knew it was a matter of when.

We arrived at his house, and he stretched out. "Sorry I was such bad company." He gave me a sad smile. I was glad he'd slept most the way. It saved yet another conversation full of angst. He got out of the car and walked around to my open window. He was holding my gaze, looking serious, a longing in his eyes.

"You're not going to speak to me again, are you?" I shrugged. I wasn't sure, but the thought of not speaking to him again made me miss him already. Whatever happened, I still loved him, even if he didn't know it. I put the car into gear and drove away.

CHAPTER 34

WILL'S CURIOSITY

Six weeks after Miami, it was Mandy's birthday. Neil surprised her by inviting everyone to a beach party for her. There was a campfire, and he'd got some battery powered rope lighting and decorated around the party site with it.

Neil made the beach scene look romantic for her with Tiki torches. He had some portable barbeques and coolers full of beer and wine. He even paid a freshman from another course to cook the food.

"Stop it Will." I swatted his hand away from ruffling my hair. We were all giggling at Will's antics around the campfire. The drinking game we were playing was fun, guessing the song from a random line, all of us singing the song when someone identified it.

I was surprised at how great a singer Will was. "You need to play and sing, Will. Don't hide that amazing voice of yours." His voice made the hair on the back of my neck stand on end.

Smiling slowly, Will cocked his head. "You think I'm a good singer?" I grabbed his hand, and hugged it to my chest.

"Honestly, I could listen to you sing all day, you have a very seductive voice." He narrowed his eyes and pouted at the word seductive, pretended to act that out.

Will's smile widened as he grabbed me by my t-shirt, pulling me in for a hug. "You're amazing Lily. You always make me feel so much better about myself." I glanced up at him.

"What's not to feel better about, you're an incredible person Will," I said patting my palm against his chest. He shook his head in disbelief.

He had just sung "*I Don't Want to Miss a Thing*" by Aerosmith. Even though it was a cheesy song, he sounded ridiculously seductive and sexy with this a cappella version of the song.

Saffy liked that she wasn't the center of his universe at that moment, and was clearly annoyed about it. Will had mingled amongst the other students, spending time getting to know them. The more he enjoyed himself, the less Saffy did. She became more and more irritated by him.

Eventually, she tried to call time on his drinking. "Enough Will, don't drink any more, you've had more than enough for tonight." Will was becoming increasingly annoyed with her.

Will's head snapped around, scanning to see if anyone had heard her before challenging her. "What is wrong with you? Why can't I have a good time with my friends? Who are you, my mother?" he

365

hissed quietly.

Saffy huffed at him and sat back down, but began to look more enraged as the minutes passed. She stood up. "Okay, we're done here Will, let's go home." She began moving toward the gate area, expecting Will to follow her.

Standing up, Will swigged back the last of his beer and threw his empty beer bottle in the cardboard box with the other empties. The loud clinking sound drew the attention of some of the others sitting near the fire. Tucking his fingers into his front jeans pockets, he swayed a little.

When he spoke, he had a slight slur. "Maybe *you're* done. Maybe I'm not. If you don't want to stay, don't let me keep you from your bed." Sweeping his arm dramatically toward the car lot Will indicated she was free to go if she wanted to.

Looking around her, she could see everyone was staring at her. She turned her attention to me. "Lily, can you help me get him to leave." I was not about to get in the middle of those two.

"Saffy, maybe if you leave him a few more minutes he'll come to that decision on his own." I didn't want to push it because I felt that this could only get worse for both of them.

Saffy's neck jutted back in disbelief and she twisted her lips at me, throwing her hand up in a 'stop' gesture. "Okay, fine, I'm going home, are you coming at least?" I didn't want her to fall out with me, but I didn't want to leave either. I was having fun.

"Saffy, please… I need to catch up with a few people yet, and I think someone should make sure that Will's okay."

Throwing both hands up in surrender, Saffy said, "Whatever! I'm going home. You two do what you like." She glanced over at Will, who was paying no attention to us, and had begun to sing with a group of students. They were all hugging and trying to out sing each other.

Another hour after Saffy left people began to leave. Lewis, one of the other students, offered us a ride home. He hadn't been drinking because he was taking some antibiotics following surgery. I didn't ask what his surgery was for; I was just pleased that he could give us a ride home.

Toying with the idea of taking Will back to our place, because he wasn't in a fit state to leave home alone, I decided against it. I didn't want to see a full-blown argument erupt in our condo, between Will and Saffy that I couldn't get away from.

I asked Lewis to help take Will into his house. He sat in the back of the car and asked several times where Saffy had gone to. He couldn't remember their conversations and seemed to be having difficulty taking any information on. Lewis and I struggled to keep Will upright.

"Are you fondling my junk?" he asked, giving me a drunken lopsided smile as I searched in his pocket for his keys. Lewis was worse than me, he'd pinked up with embarrassment, and I saw this in the porch light.

We both giggled at Will's comment though. "No Will, we're just helping you inside." We half walked, half dragged Will as far as his couch then planted him firmly on his side.

Will was now lying in a self-induced coma from the sheer amount of alcohol he'd consumed. He was a funny drunk, singing and dancing, as well as quick-witted and hysterical when he was trying to play the drinking games.

I asked Lewis to stay for a few minutes while I took off Will's shoes and socks, organizing him more on the couch, then I put a light sheet over him as it was still hot. I got a glass of water and tried to give it to him, but he was mostly unresponsive.

Lewis left, and I sent a text to Saffy. I didn't want her to get the wrong idea. I explained that another student had come back with me and helped Will onto the couch. I told her that I was staying the night because he was so drunk, and someone needed to be there to check on him. I also apologized for staying, but said that I was sure that she'd want Will to be okay too.

Not knowing what I wanted more, to sleep or a shower, I felt I needed both, but I knew I'd sleep better if I wasn't so hot, so the shower won. It felt strange showering in Will's bathroom, but I was doing the right thing. There was no way he could have been left on his own.

When I was clean and relaxed, I climbed into his bed and fell asleep quickly, too exhausted and drunk to think about anything.

Alfie had come over to see me, and we'd slipped into bed together, his mouth was on mine, his tongue running the length of my lips, my heart fluttered as his hands raked sensually across my belly, his big palm pushing lightly on my stomach as he settled his head between my thighs.

His warm, wet, tongue did that first flutter- tickle that was too light, but exquisite and I moved my sensitive flesh nearer trying to gain a greater contact from him. He groaned. "Mmm…fucking incredible you taste even sweeter than ever." The voice sounded lower.

Firm hands slipped under my ass to tilt my pelvis to allow his tongue greater access to me. The voice broke into my dream, and it was Will that was actually between my legs, his tongue lapping against my sensitive flesh. I'd been dreaming, but this part I was definitely awake for. This wasn't a dream, it was a waking nightmare.

Jumping back, I pulled my legs away, clamping them together, when remembering where I was. "Will what the fuck are you doing?" I hissed. My heart was racing, my mind numb. It was dark in the room, but I could hear his voice.

He jumped, pulling himself up and his silhouette pushed back onto his knees in the dark. "Lily, oh God, is that you?" Will's voice was almost a shriek. I grabbed the sheet and tried to wrap it around myself. From the resistance I was meeting, I guessed he was doing the same.

We both spent about a minute scrambling around on the bed, the weight of us on the mattress made us bounce around as we both moved aimlessly while freaking out. I'd been having an erotic dream and woke to Will doing those things to me.

Accidently, we made contact with each other again in the dark. "I don't fucking believe you did that, Will. What the hell were you thinking?"

A hurried whisper came back at me. "I'm so

sorry Lily, I had no idea it was you."

I heard Will swallow hard and take a in a deep breath, followed by his familiar low tone. "I didn't know you were here. I just woke up horny and climbed into bed." He sounded guilty.

"Yeah, that much was evident," I snapped at him.

"Can you turn the nightstand lamp on?" he asked.

"Fuck no, I'm naked you're not seeing me like this," I hissed, trying to pull the sheet up again. Will started to chuckle.

"Sorry, I can't…I'm sorry, but I just had my tongue inside your pussy Lily, we're a little late for any more embarrassment. Turn the fucking light on."

I shook my head with my eyes tightly closed, but it was dark, and he couldn't see me. I failed to see the humorous side of the situation, Saffy would kill me. "Well?" he prompted me again. I gulped and there wasn't nearly enough saliva in my mouth for a proper swallow.

"No."

Will started laughing, it sounded like a snicker at first, and then it erupted into a long belly laugh. "Damn, I didn't try to make it happen, it just did. It was accidental."

"Yeah, Will, tell that to the judge," I sneered wryly.

"You're just ticked because I've tasted you, and you're left wondering about me." My mouth fell open in the dark, I was glad he couldn't see my reaction.

"Will, Stop it!" I hissed, swiping blindly at him in the dark and missing, but as my hand fell down, I accidently knocked his erect cock. "Arghh."

This only made Will's laughter grow even

louder. I was mortified. I covered my eyes with my hand, even although he couldn't see me. He tried hard to calm himself. "Sorry, honey, it isn't something I planned. So either I find the funny side of this or I fuck you, because either way, I'm screwed."

I could just tell he was smirking in the dark. I didn't have to see him to know that. He started laughing again. "Or not screwed… sorry poor choice of words there."

Rolling around on the bed and I thought Will must have been stuffing the sheet or something in his mouth because his laughter became muffled. My heart was racing a mile a minute. I had no words, and I guess he had his own thing going on, and for me– I couldn't think.

It may have been unintentional, but hell this was a very intimate thing that was happening to me. Worse than that, I'd been enjoying it until I knew it wasn't a dream, and it was Will between my legs. None of this was funny to me. At some point he'd stopped laughing and had asked me something. "Lily?" I felt the sheet being pulled.

"Leave it," I hissed.

"I'm just freeing it, so that you can wrap yourself in it, okay?" I relaxed my grip and felt the sheet slide over my body until it was gone. There was a dip in the mattress near the edge of the bed, and it rose again.

"Come here, stand up." I climbed off the bed, and stood next to him. "Put your arms up." I did, and I felt myself being enveloped by the sheet, his hand brushed around the back of my shoulders, making me shudder.

"Good to know that I have some effect on you at least," he said when he felt that.

"Please Will…" He pulled me toward his chest once the sheet was in place. My cheek was resting on his slightly hairy chest. He smelled of beer, body wash, sea, and bonfire.

He kissed the top of my head. "I'm so sorry Lily," he muttered, and quickly added, "Although… you're hot. I can't be sorry I know what you taste like now. How can I be sorry about that? "

Pulling away from him, Will tugged me back into him again. I tensed and tried to move away. "No. I won't let you feel awkward about my mistake. It was a genuine accident, not something I'd planned. Fantasized about… hell yeah, but I didn't plan it."

Pushing me back to arm's length, I knew he was trying to look at me. I could see an outline of him, but not his features in the dark. "Can you honestly say you haven't been curious about me?"He snickered.

"The hours we've spent together? The hugs, the little touches all the flirting? The kisses, you haven't wondered how I'd feel?" I didn't answer him. I had, but there was no way I was going to admit it to him. He took a sharp intake of breath and blew it out of his nose. It blew gently over my hot forehead.

"Right, we're going to make this as awkward or as natural as it gets." Will pushed me back and flicked on the ceiling light. "Here I am. Ta-da."

Will gestured at himself, like he had in my apartment the day we went to the beach, except this time there were no shorts, and he was standing there naked.

He was still erect, and although he'd been

drinking, he looked amazingly sexy with his messed up hair and his shadowy stubble that was appearing. His full lips were placed together, his lips curved slightly in a smile.

Turning, he gave me a panoramic view of himself, and he had a great ass. "This is me, I'm naked. I was born like this, in my birthday-suit. Well, maybe except for the hair and the chubbie." He grinned.

"Come on Lily, your turn." I glared, still feeling freaked out and still way more sober than Will.

"I'm not taking this sheet off," I hissed.

Will smirked. "Well, I know it's not cuz you're hiding a cock there. My face was down there, remember," he joked. I was shocked at his brazen approach to this. Clutching the sheet tightly in my hands, I closed my eyes briefly.

Will's fingers closed over my hands, and began pulling them away. "Let it drop Lily, I'm not ever going to do anything you don't want to happen." I wasn't ashamed of my body, so I let him peel the sheet away, keeping my eyes closed.

I heard his breath hitch when he freed me of it. We stood in silence, which was broken by me several moments later. "Will?" I heard him swallow and his breathing sounded ragged.

"Yeah?" he husked.

"What do I do now?" Will blew a long slow breath out.

Will's voice was a little shaky. "That's your call. Don't put me in charge of what happens next, my cock has had a thousand ideas about how this plays out." I felt he was trying too hard to sound light hearted but I could hear his voice drop to a husk, and I knew I was in trouble.

I had no willpower with this sex stuff; it was all new to me. Opening my eyes, I saw Will was giving me his full attention, with his cock resting heavily in his hand. Stroking it, but he stopped when he saw me watching him. It twitched when he looked at me, looking at him. I licked my lips; my mouth was so dry.

"Do you have any water?" My voice sounded like it was in the distance. Reaching down to the floor, he produced a half drunk bottle of water. The plastic bottle was wet on the outside from the condensation of being brought from the cold fridge to the heat of the room.

"I snagged this from the fridge before coming to bed," he offered by way of an explanation. I opened the bottle and drew some liquid in, a little escaped and a drop splashed onto my breast.

Before either of us could think about it, Will had reacted and his index finger brushed it off of my breast, causing me to feel breathless at his touch.

CHAPTER 35

MOMENT OF WEAKNESS

Shivering at his sudden touch, my nipples pebbling as goose bumps radiated over my body. My eyes darted to Will and locked into his serious, sensual stare. His eyes twinkled in the light and his pupils almost engulfed the gray of his eyes. I could tell Will liked what he saw.

Lowering my eyes, I hadn't wanted him to see that I, too, was curious about him, and worse still, feeling like I'd stooped to a new low. Standing naked in a room with my best friend's boyfriend, and even with that knowledge, my feelings weren't being swayed by what we were doing.

Will lifted his hand and crooked his middle finger under my chin, raising my eyes again to meet his. He smiled at me, and I could tell he was waiting to see what my response was. He wanted me to take responsibility for this.

I couldn't do that, if anything was going to

happen, it needed to be Will's choice. I wasn't the one in the relationship.

"Can I kiss you?" His eyes searched mine, and I pinched my lips as if to hide them in my face. I stared at him, and he stroked his hands down my hair, then flicked it back over my shoulders to leave my breasts totally exposed.

Will wet his lips as his finger stroked up my cheek and traced around my chin. He raised my face up again. I kept telling myself not to do this. His head came forward and he pressed his closed mouth on mine. His lips felt plump and moist, but it was a tender kiss, not exploratory.

His other hand stroked the length of my arm, but his touch was tentative; he wasn't sure.

I was glad for that, it showed me that he was considering the implications of this before making any definitive moves on me. Will was letting me think about it.

"Do you have any wine?" I asked, my voice sounding flat. I felt I needed a drink and to give myself some time. I wanted to stall him and get myself out of this before I did something I'd regret.

He stepped back. "Sure, I'll be right back." He disappeared, and I could hear glasses clinking and the pop of a bottle cork, then he reappeared at the bedroom door.

"I had this bottle of champagne that we were given at the gig we did last week." He sat on the bed, the mattress dipping as he did this. I stood in front of him. He wasn't concerned by his nakedness or mine. I was more than a little shy that he kept looking at me.

Trailing the back of his finger down my arm, he

commented, "Your skin is so damned soft. I have never felt skin like it. I've wanted to tell you that so many times when I've stroked your arm, but thought you might think I was freaky, or had a fetish, or was coming on to you." He smiled cheekily.

"And now you are," I said quietly.

"Fuck, you're so fucking beautiful, and fuck... I don't want to be weird around you because of this Lily. Tell me if this is going to change us and I'll leave the house right now." I raised my eyebrow.

"Would you?"

Passing me the half full glass of champagne, I put my mouth to the rim of the flute and felt some of the bubbles disperse on my face before the dry taste invaded my mouth. Will shifted himself up the bed to lean against his headboard, pulling a pillow and tossing it behind him to support his head. He watched me over the glass.

Staring at him, I asked, "What are we doing Will?" He put his glass down, and crawled down the bed to me. I was now perched on the edge like a frightened kitten, ready to scoot out of the door. He cupped his hands over my shoulders; his touch made me shiver.

"See," he said, "I haven't touched you anywhere remotely erogenous yet and you're shivering."

"I don't think you can say that when your tongue..." I didn't finish what I was saying and Will was grinning at me.

"Sorry," he said. I sipped my drink again, looking at him as he shifted himself alongside me, his back to the edge of the bed and his legs curled to the side.

"I'm going to do something to either change this up or get us at it. If you say stop, we go back to doing what we've always done, and this never happened. Okay?" He came around in front of me. "Lily, I'm going to have to kiss you for this."

Will gave me little time to think, I couldn't. He pulled me onto my feet and grabbed my hair from the nape. The thumb of one hand stroked down my throat and across my collarbone, as his tongue pierced through my lips and explored my mouth.

His hand fell from my hair and traced down to the small of my back, and back up my ribs, to cup my breast. I shuddered under his touch. It was one of the most sensual kisses ever, full of feeling.

There was a pool of moist wet liquid that actually left my slit and found its way onto my leg. I moaned loudly, and he stepped away from me.

I felt like I'd lost an arm when he separated from me, as I waited for what was next, and he did something that completely shocked me, but was so fucking hot at the same time. The tension between us was now so high we couldn't have stopped even if we wanted to.

Taking his cock in his hand, he rubbed his thumb over his glans, smearing it in pre cum. Will traced it along my lips before pushing his thumb into my mouth. "Suck it, Lily… taste me." I parted my lips and his thumb slid across my tongue. "You know how I taste now."

Staring longingly at me, Will asked, "Are you curious how it feels? Do you want to feel me? Taking my hand palm up in his palm, he cupped my palm over his shaft; closing his hand around mine, and wrapped my fingers around his length.

Hitching his breath, Will held my hand in his. He began to stroke himself using my hand guided by his. It was so arousing, to watch him pleasure himself using me. "I want to taste you again, Lily. Do you want to taste more of me?" I didn't answer, but he dropped to his knees, lifting one of my legs, the mattress dipped slightly as he balanced my foot on it.

Gliding his fingertips my legs, he swallowed audibly, "Your legs are still splendid without the fuck-me heels." He smiled, his fingers finding my sensitive flesh, which was moist and warm. Will groaned and growled, as he drew his fingers down it, slipping one inside me as he struggled to control his breathing. "Fuck."

Kneeling down in front of me, caused his cock to come out of my hand, and he lifted my leg from the bed and placed it over his shoulder. Stroking his nose down my entrance, he buried his face deep between my legs.

Will's moist, tensed tongue swirled around my moist heat, arousing me further, taunting my nub, and teasing at my entrance. He sucked my juices and buried his tongue deep inside me."Mmm."

Making loud sucking noises, he groaned again, "God, so fucking delicious." His eyes stared up at me as I stared back at him. My eyes rolled at the pleasure he gave me, and I felt myself tighten inside.

My legs started shaking, and I buckled as I came. "I got you," he whispered. His tongue was replaced by two fingers as his other hand supported my weight.

Pushing me back on the bed, he replaced his fingers with his tongue again. I came hard again. "Oh,

God." Will commented as he licked and sucked at my clitoris, devouring me.

I tried to crawl backwards on the bed, away from him, but he clenched my thighs, locking them in his strong arms and dragged me back into place. He pulled away and smiled, stroking my belly, and I shuddered again.

"Ah, not finished yet?" he cooed. He stood, and I grasped his large stiff cock in my hand. I returned the act on him and withdrew him so that he came on my breasts. He smiled, and I smiled back, but felt bad at the same time, knowing that we were both going to regret this.

Will lay us on the bed, and we were quiet for a few minutes until he broke the silence. "You're feeling pretty shitty now, aren't you?" Silent tears ran down my face, and I realized that apart from when I came, I had not voiced my feelings at all during sex with him.

"Don't beat yourself up Lily. Saffy and I are done, so you didn't do anything wrong." I held my breath at what Will said, then exhaled heavily.

"Didn't do anything wrong, Will? Jesus, even this is a new low for me." Will sat up sharply folding his arms across his chest.

"Thanks," he mumbled. *Shit!* "I didn't mean it like that Will. I meant another major screw up on my part. I was the sober one. Your judgement is impaired because of the alcohol. I don't have that excuse."

"Oh, no you don't. You were the one that woke up with my head between your legs." He smirked. "Lily, I still made the move after I knew it was you."

He turned to face me. "You can't take the blame

for that." I hid my face in my hands.

"I should have told you to stop, I didn't." He lay back flat on his bed, stretched out and unashamed. "Well, I had a great time, so I'm not sorry."

Sighing, he sounded annoyed. "If Saffy hadn't acted all heavy tonight she'd be here and not you. I'm done with her now. I can't take any more of her shit. I had pretty much made my mind up when she stormed off earlier." I stared at him, not saying anything. *What could I say?*

CHAPTER 36

BEAUTIFUL GOODBYES

"Lily, I won't ever tell her we did this if that's what's worrying you." I felt ashamed.

"It isn't that she may find out, it's the fact that I did that to her." Will sighed.

"You didn't do anything. I'm not with her, and I'm not going back on that, Lily."

Jumping out of bed, I pulled on my jeans. "Where are you going? It's fucking two thirty in the morning." I continued clipping my bra at the back.

"No Will, this is wrong, this isn't good for us at all, and Saffy deserves better."

"It looks like she was right not to trust us." Will snorted and turned the nightstand light on. "Are we going to be okay? I'll speak to her tomorrow." I swiveled around on the balls of my feet.

"You mean can we still work together? Sure."

Pointing at the bed, I wagged my finger between us. "This isn't going to be repeated under any circumstances. I must be out of my mind to have been with you in that way."

Will looked hurt, but I couldn't comfort him. What we did was wrong, and I had to make sure that it didn't happen again. He meant too much to me. Calling a cab, I agreed to speak to him when I had a little more time to absorb what had happened between us.

"You're taking Saffy to the end-of-year party next week. You're not dumping her before that," I spat at him. "You can at least let her have a good time at Christmas."

Sitting in the cab on the way home, I was so angry at how weak I was, and angry with Will as well. We should have had more restraint. It made me think about my relationship with my closest and oldest friend, Jack, back in the UK.

Elle used to tell Jack and me, "Get a room, already," because of our flirty relationship. We've been friends since we were four years old and still remain as tight as ever.

The thought of that kind of thing happening with him would rock our relationship to the core. I had seen Will as someone who would be in my life a long time, but now, I wasn't sure that we hadn't blown our special connection. I guessed only time would tell.

Avoiding Saffy before college, I continued in that vein for most of that week. Will and I argued constantly both in college, and also about who was responsible for what happened. Saffy was determined that we get ready for the party at Will's place, when party night arrived, and if I hadn't gone it would have seemed most strange.

I had no choice but to give in to her, no matter how awkward it would be to have all three of us together where the 'crime' had taken place.

Every time she was nice to me, I wanted to burst into tears and tell her what happened.

Grabbing the tequila shots Will offered, I needed alcohol to numb the guilty feelings that threatened to consume me to such an extent that a confession was likely. I was a little tipsy by the time we left for the party.

Holly, Brett, Mandy, and Neil came over, and we had prearranged a passenger van with driver to take us so that we could really let our hair down.

It made me feel worse that everyone was in couples, so when a couple of Neil's friends came to sit with us at our table, I felt much less self-conscious about not having a partner. The way I had behaved I didn't deserve a relationship anyway.

Neil's friend, Nick, was a great guy though. We had met a few times previously. He leaned over the table smiling at me. "Has anyone told you how gorgeous you are tonight?" I blushed, they had, but I shook my head. It was nice to know that I was still attractive, even if inside I was an emotionally demolished slut.

Nick tugged on my arm, his voice lost in the loud music. "Dance with me?" His head gestured toward the dance floor. I was about to say no, but found myself nodding instead. I really didn't know what the hell my body was going to do from one minute to the next these days.

The place was buzzing, there was a great atmosphere. Being a music school a lot of us agreed to do a couple of songs each. There was a resident DJ too, so the mix of live music and popular dance tunes kept the entertainment fresh.

Nick led me onto the dance floor. There were a lot of people here already. A couple of them actually looked as if their party had started long before the official one. He was a fantastic dancer, and I noticed a few other women watching us together. I tried to relax and made myself a promise there and then to try to enjoy the night and forget about all the complex dramas in my life.

Will came over and shouted above the noise of the bass heavy music. "We're next up Lily, ten minutes." I nodded and grabbed Nick's waist, pulling him in close to me. He looked surprised, but smiled, bending to hear what I was saying. "I have to get ready, we're playing when this is done." He nodded and walked back to the bar with me.

I changed from my pumps into my stiletto ankle boots, with my short emerald fitted dress. I felt so much more confident in them. Neil commented, "Jesus, Lily you were sexy before the heels, now you're gonna have every man in the room's tongue hanging out."

Smiling, I blushed at Neil's comment, but I really didn't need any references about attracting men, or their tongues right now. Will chuckled, widening his big gray eyes. "Yeah, Lily's legs grow even longer in fuck-me heels." He smirked. Saffy scowled, batting his arm and told him not to make rude comments about me, and I felt bad again.

Walking toward the stage, Will leaned in, commenting under his breath, "I can't help it, they turn me on, legs in heels like that, scream for fingers to wander up them. "He grinned and I scowled, not wanting to offer him any encouragement.

"Don't do that, Will." After I said it, I realized that things would be different between us now.

We breezed through our number, and Will hugged me afterwards, spinning me around when he saw that Saffy was safely over on the other side of the bar with her back turned.

"Stop flirting!" I commented, annoyed he still was so tactile.

"Come, dance with me." He started pulling me toward the dance floor. I looked at over at Saffy and Will slung his arm around my shoulder, bending forward. "You know Lily we've got to move forward, it happened. I'm not sorry," he reminded me.

I didn't want to be the person he used to prove a point to my best friend though. It was fortunate that the DJ had put on an upbeat number, and not one that required any tactile behavior or Saffy may have had a coronary, and so might I have.

Nick was lining up shots when we joined the others. We all had three each. I protested saying I'd be too drunk to finish the evening if I swallowed them, but everyone clapped and goaded me until I found myself throwing the first one back. It burned, and I cringed. My tongue was hanging out once I'd swallowed it, and I spluttered and coughed as some went down my windpipe.

Everyone drunk all of theirs really quickly, leaving the focus on me again as I still had two left. "Come on Lily. Down, Down. Down," they chanted. I pinched my nose, forgetting about the salt altogether and threw another one back into my throat. It tasted marginally better than the last one.

My third shot was handed to me before I'd had time to recover. "Just do it." Will's eyes glinted at me humorously. I hesitated, then lifted the tequila to my lips. My throat was numb by that time, because I didn't really notice anything sting when I drunk it. I felt warm and happy as the alcohol hit my brain and put me into 'fuzzy motion.'

This was right up there with slow motion, but less coordinated. I became really tipsy though, I'd had two shots already and a white wine spritzer. Not to mention the vodka and cranberry when we'd arrived.

My face had a warm fuzzy feel about it, and I didn't feel nearly as inhibited as I had at the beginning of the night. Nick grabbed my hand, "Dance time." He began dragging me to the dance floor again.

The music had taken a more sexy tone, or maybe it was the drink. I'm not sure which, but Nick's dancing seemed much more suggestive toward me. I felt a tap on my shoulder.

"Hey," he cooed. "Dance, Lily?" Alfie's incredibly sexy smile was right there, at eye level. Turning his attention to Nick, Alfie asked, "Do you mind, dude?"

Nick was about to protest, but I put my hand on his arm. "It's fine." I smiled sweetly at him, half drunk, and looked back at Alfie who was as sexy looking as ever. "I would love to dance with Alfie." Nick looked annoyed, but headed toward the bar.

The music changed to a slower song, and Alfie tentatively gestured to me for permission to put his hands on my waist. I shrugged, and he slid his arms around my waist. I moved closer to him and put my arms around his neck.

We were slow dancing after all, and I'd had more to drink than I should have had. My breath still hitched when his arms slid around me, and he flashed a sexy smile at me when he noticed.

Sensual hooded eyes ticked over me. Alfie bent forward, his cheek supporting the side of my head as his head leaned against mine. *I've missed him.* I closed my eyes. He smelled familiar, of fresh body wash and… him. I'd forgotten how good he felt and smelled, and the tension I felt with him melted away.

Leaning my forehead on his shoulder, I inhaled and closed my eyes. My stomach fluttered, and I was shaking slightly with our closeness and his touch. My heart raced, and my mouth was dry. I licked my lips a few times, but thought I might be dehydrated from the alcohol.

We began moving slowly, and after a minute he leaned back to look at me, giving me his incredible smile that made me weak and broke my heart all over again. He brought his face back closer to my ear, whispering huskily, "Lily, you take my breath away. You're so beautiful tonight."

Speechless, I wanted to cry at his compliment, struggling with the hurt inside of me. His arms tightened around my body, his hands gliding lower to the base of my back, drawing me closer to him, so that we were connected from our heads to below our hips.

"Your hands feel good." I had said what I was thinking. It was stupid.

He smiled slowly, murmuring, "That's because they like feeling you." He leaned back to catch my gaze when he said it, then kissed the top of my head. Previously, his touch had left me paralyzed, but not this time. I was being just as tactile as he was.

My hands ran up his back, one came around to his chest, my fingers running up the length of him and tangling in his hair. He groaned loudly, "God." His heartbeat quickened at my touch, I heard it when my I laid my head against his chest and felt it under my hand.

Alfie sighed. "I've missed you being in my arms," he said softly. I tilted my head to look up at him and he smiled, his little dimple slightly breaking my heart again for the second time that night. His eyes had the green hue tonight, depicting his lust for me. I wanted him to look at me tonight and see someone who's confident and carefree. Even though I didn't feel like that around him.

Spinning me around, he stood close behind me, his hands moved down lightly onto my hips. Splaying his fingers of his strong hand wide, he saddling into me, nuzzled his face into my neck and kissed it lightly.

Circling his hips into mine, I leaned back against his chest, my arms reached up around his neck again, and basked in the feel of him against me. I could feel how turned on he was. My control was dissolving, and I wanted him so badly. He bent to kiss my temple, and then moved his lips to my ear. "Remember your safe words."

My body hummed as did his, and he was telling me how to tell him to back off, that I could stop this if

I wanted to. I didn't. "I don't need them tonight," I murmured, and moaned loudly when he hit a soft spot on my neck.

The way he looked, his scent, touch, and voice hypnotized me. I wanted to taste him as well. That night, I just wanted to feel him inside me again. Maybe to blur the memory of what happened with Will, or maybe just because…

Aflie leaned back, to make eye contact again. "I'm not going to use you, Lily. I just want to feel you near me," he growled. I smiled seductively.

"Pity…" I told him shamelessly. "Wouldn't you rather have a private party with me, or are you happy to stand here and dry hump me on the dance floor?"

Lusty eyes flashed with pleasure and his eye lids drooped seductively at my words and he grinned wickedly. "You're hot when you talk dirty," he murmured humorously kissing my neck. It sent a sensational current running between it and my clitoris and a rash of goose bumps cascading over my skin.

"Restroom and we need to get out of here," I said patting his chest and heading for the restrooms. Alfie grabbed my arm roughly.

"Don't fucking dick with me, Lily." I raised my eyebrow.

"I'm not…dicking." I smirked and turned on my heel.

Will was suddenly beside me, grabbing my arm as I reached the restroom door. He swung me around pulling me slightly close into him. He walked me back toward the wall.

"What the fuck are you doing, Lily? You were a mess because of him." I patted Will's chest.

"Not what the fuck am I doing Will, but whom?"
I giggled, still a bit tipsy.

Will's face was angry. "You want to go have
sex? Is that all? Can't you pick another guy in the
room?" I twisted my mouth.

"Who…you? Is that jealousy Will?" I sneered.

He crossed his arms over his chest. "You think I
want to fuck you, Lily?" I jutted my chin at him.

"You wouldn't if I offered?" He looked
exacerbated with me.

"I'm looking out for you." I held his cheek.

"I'm fine. I picked him this time." Will threw his
hands up in surrender.

"Fine! Go, fuck, have fun, don't bitch about it on
the way to the airport tomorrow is all." He walked
away waving a hand behind him.

Alfie was waiting at the cloakroom when I got
there. "I thought you'd changed your mind." I raised
an eyebrow.

"I want some mindless sex, and you're good," I
said it rather too loudly.

He didn't look as happy with that statement as
I'd expected. "I don't want you to be my fuck buddy,
I want to spend time with you, but I do want you
sexually too." I nodded.

"You want to fuck me, I want to fuck you, we're
buddies, so …fuck buddy, let's go."

Alfie looked pensive again. "You're sure about
this?" he said as we got into the cab.

"Are you? Why do you keep asking me?" I was
thinking about the girl, maybe he was having a pang
of guilt about having sex with me and seeing her.

He laced his fingers with mine. "Never been

more sure about what I want to do with you, but I don't want to hurt you." I smiled.

"You won't," I lied. "I'm looking forward to it." We arrived at his place, and Alfie took me inside. This time it felt different. He didn't dive on me as soon as we arrived.

"Drink?" he enquired, walking to the fridge.

"I think I've had enough for tonight." I had sobered up a bit and wanted to make sure that I could stay in control.

He looked seriously at me. "Is that why you're here, because you're drunk?

CHAPTER 37

DISTANT VERSES DISTANCE

Frowning at Alfie as we stood in his kitchen, I said, "I'm not here because I've been drinking, or maybe I am? I get horny when I drink, but I know what I'm doing." He continued to sip his wine and stare at me. "What are you thinking?" I murmured. He smiled and exhaled giving a soft laugh.

"You really don't want me to verbalize that for you." Alfie shook his head, winking playfully at me. I wanted to reach out and touch his beautiful lips.

"Maybe I do," I provoked.

Draining his wine glass, he walked over to me and set it down on the counter with a soft clink. Walked behind me, he whispered seductively in my ear, "I'd rather show you. Can I touch you now?"

Turning my head, I looked behind me, meeting his gaze that was really more of a lusty stare.

"We're already here. I don't have to answer that," I said deadpan.

Placing his hands on my ribs, he turned me around, then slid them down and around to my ass, and I shuddered. He pressed my front into the counter and pulled my hips back firmly grinding his erection hard against it. Pressing face close to the side of mine, I could feel him breathing down my neck and heard him inhale sharply as a hand moved to run up between my legs.

His thumb stopped just short of my sensitive flesh that was flowing with juices. Breath ragged, hands trembling, Alfie buried his face in my neck with soft kisses and inhaled deeply. "Fuck."

Tracing his tongue up my neck to my jawline, I shivered and moaned, "Oh, God." He smiled into my neck, before turning me to face him.

Alfie's mouth crashed on to mine, his tongue exploring deep into my mouth. I didn't get time to anticipate him kissing me, or the sudden, hungry, wet, hot tongue invading mine. He made me groan with pleasure.

Moaning loudly, I cried, "Oh, Alfie," eliciting a guttural growl from him, as he pressed me against, his lean body by gripping my ass cheeks and pulling me closer.

Alfie kicked my feet apart to get closer, putting his hands under my arms. He slid me up his hard body and lifted me onto the counter. His hands skimmed my inner thighs again, making my dress ride up, and he tugged the hem from under me pulling it up over my head. He dropped it to the floor, his eyes locked into mine.

Pushing my legs apart, he tugged my panties aside. Hot breath became a cool breeze as he blew on my clit, before fluttering his tongue lightly. I murmured, "Alfie, the window." We were in full view of the picture window near the door.

"I don't care who looks, I need to taste you. I can't stop." Sucking my folds into his mouth in exquisite pulses, he sent currents shooting off in all directions and an overflow of juice pooling between my legs. I gasped with the sensation of it.

"Oh. God." I slightly shook, and inhaled sharply.

Alfie pulled my panties off and slid his hand there, circling the moistness around my cleft before inserting a finger. Growling again, he swirled his finger inside of me, searching for my sweet spot and then put his head back to suck on my clitoris at the same time.

"So fucking sweet…" he muttered shakily when he came up for air. What he was doing was sensational.

"Oh.God. Uh, huh… Yeah… don't stop!" I moaned loudly, leaning back on my elbows, watching him.

Alfie broke free and grinned up at me. "If I'm going to pleasure you, could you at least try to remember my name," he muttered humorously.

He splayed my legs wider. "I should just take you here… now, you're so ready for me, I've waited too long." He growled watching my intimate pinkness, spreading his fingers and running his fingers around my slit lightly.

I tried to move and he pushed me back. "*No!* You've made me wait too long for this, stay where you are! I want to take my time," he commanded.

Licking and sucking again, I could feel myself

swelling with want under his expert touch, my juices running out of my core and down my seam to my butt and onto the granite counter.

Alfie continued to suckle and tease, and I felt myself chasing my climax, my body arching into him. Beginning to lick me faster, he flicked my clitoris until I shook and screamed.

I came so hard that I thought something inside would snap. "Oh sweet Jesus…yes…oh fuck… no… stop. No Alfie, please…" He was chuckling while he tormented me.

"You. Want. Me. To .Stop?" He lapped at me with each word, sending me almost insane with pleasure. With each word I jerked as another current pulsed and stretched out my climax.

Scooping me off the counter and into his arms, my ass was soaking wet. I wrapped my legs around him as he headed for the stairs. "I need you in my bed… *now!*" I moaned.

"Why the bedroom?" I panted.

Kissing me as he walked, I could taste myself on him. He broke the kiss, "Nightstand drawer."

Gasping into his neck. I giggled. "That has got to be the weirdest thing anyone has ever said, given the circumstances." Peppered my face with kisses, he smiled playfully as he spoke. "When. I. Get, Started. I. Wont. Stop… condoms." He said kissing me again. My face lit up in recognition of his explanation.

Laying me on the bed, he shucked his jeans to the floor, his action was seamless. I smiled, remembering his explanation of how to get into those. He crawled up the bed and motioned for me to come to him. As I scooted up, he lifted my leg over him, so that I was straddling him.

Alfie unhooked my bra, and it almost hurt when he pulled it free. He chucked it across the room, and it landed on his television on the wall. "Oh. My. God. Lily," he moaned, his hands trailed over me.

"You feel so good. I've fucking craved you, so badly." His hands trembled as he held my breasts. "You're so fucking beautiful, so perfect." He shook his head as if he couldn't believe he was touching me.

Alfie leaned into me, rolled his tongue around my nipple, and it instantly reacted by stiffening. He pulled it between his lips, then let it go sharply, and took it in his mouth, suckling hard. I moaned, throwing my head back. "Sweet, Jesus."

Feeling his length was beneath me, stretched out along my entrance, so I rocked on him, coating his hard, silky cock. Alfie rolled a condom on and placed me back on him, his fingers now teasing my slit. "So fucking sexy, so silky… so wet… so tight," he murmured. I smiled.

"Yeah, it kind of does that down there when I'm being teased and fondled."

He chuckled into my neck, and rolled me back over him, spreading my ass cheeks. He lifted me and rubbed around my entrance, testing me again. He brought his fingers up and sucked on them. "Mmm." He smiled and it was so hot.

Alfie eyes widened with excitement as he slid his thick tip along my moistness, lifting me slightly and lowering me onto him, his mouth claiming mine with his tongue probing at the same slow tantalizing speed.

"My Lily," he hissed. I stiffened when I heard that; I wasn't his, but in the heat of the moment he'd put that out there anyway. He grabbed my ass, rolling me on him as I rocked him, adding pressure to my nub.

The rolling rhythm was completely synchronized. I stretched and rubbed his cock, making it lengthen and harden more inside me. He growled. He pulled out long and thrust back deep, but so slowly.

Sticking his thumb in my mouth, I sucked it, causing another moan to escape from him. His eyes closed just for a second before he took it out, and rubbed it on my clitoris with just the right amount of pressure, in just the right way.

Becoming lost, my body was completely aroused by him and teetering near the edge. He sensed it and wouldn't let me come. Removed his thumb he sucked it, getting pleasure from my taste. We were both so turned on. His mouth found mine again, his kiss was almost brutal this time, urgent. "God, I need this...I needed you."

Suddenly he pinned me on my back, crawled down between my legs, and his tongue flicked and licked my clitoris again, and his fingers, first one then two, penetrated me, rubbing my soft spot. "Oh. God. Yes. Just like that…"I moaned loudly.

"I fucking love the sounds you make, and when you tell me what you want." He looked so crazy with lust. When he groaned into my slit, the vibrations sent shivers through me. They made me come so intensely, I thought I was going to die. He held me there on the mattress, climaxing over and over, as I screamed his name.

As I recovered, he flipped me over, grabbed my

hips, and pulled me up onto my knees. He entered me in one long glide all the way in to his root. He gasped and made a low groaning noise, "Oh, God… fuck."

I was trying to recover from how fast he'd penetrated me, when he slapped my right ass cheek, then massaged it in a circular motion with his fingers, and continued to thrust in and out of me. It turned me on, I never expected it would.

Grabbing my hips, his fingers dug in as he held me so tightly. He thrust harder. He grabbed my hair from behind, twirling it in his hand, before spanking my ass a couple of more times.

The whole experience was exciting and debasing at the same time. "You're… so… fucking… amazing… I can't live without this," he moaned into my back.

The way he rode me, although slightly rough, wasn't raw lust, it felt more like a need. He came quickly, his hot seed filling the condom inside me, his pulsing cock still throbbing as he held on tightly.

Pulling himself out slowly, he laid himself back on the bed, and I slumped onto my side facing him. "Sorry, I got desperate, it's been a while." He looked embarrassed. I squeezed his arm to make him feel better. I started to push myself off the bed, but he pulled me down beside him again.

"Can you stay?" I smiled.

"I wasn't leaving. I was going to give you some time to…"

He interrupted, "I want to hold you, is that okay?"

Choked by his request, I was suddenly hurt by his request. This was also very different from my other experiences with him. Alfie was normally sated and unconscious when I'd left him. Tears sprung to my eyes. "I need to pee." I pulled myself away before he could see me, and quickly headed for his bathroom, blinking back tears.

Sitting on the toilet seat with my head in my hands I scolded myself. *Stupid, Lily.* Alfie still wanted to take what he needed without thinking of my feelings.

What had just happened only made me feel worse, and even more in love with him. I had wanted to be with him, not to have sex, but because I needed to feel close to him and because I was leaving. We were together, but for completely different reasons.

Washing between my legs, I prepared to leave and went back to his room. Alfie was lying on one elbow, patting beside him. "I've been waiting." He looked so relaxed and perfect on his bed. I gave him a slow smile, but knew I had to go.

"I just want to go home now Alfie. I'm tired." I began putting my clothes on.

"Sleep with me, here." He gave me a half smile, a pleading look in his eyes. I felt for him, but remained resolute. He seemed to want more and more from me emotionally, but never gave anything I needed in return.

"I can't stay. I wasn't going to stay this late." He scrunched his brows at me.

"What's the hurry?" I shrugged. "I don't want to stay Alfie, there's stuff I have to do tomorrow."

Will was asked not to mention that I was leaving for the UK to anyone, only he and my housemates knew.

~ * ~

I hadn't wanted Alfie to know and for him to pull some last minute stunt to confuse me further. I'd had sex with him again, showing my weakness around him. I needed to walk away now. I wanted him to feel the loss of me, bad as that was.

Perhaps he would realize what I meant to him, if anything, or learn to leave me alone. After persuading him that I really did have to go, I called a cab and sat downstairs. He didn't come down to wait with me, I guessed he had fell asleep. The cab arrived, and I let myself out quietly, the door clicking softly behind me.

As we reached the junction, a passing car pulled onto his driveway. The blond girl from campus got out. Her head turned toward my cab, and I was sure she had seen me.

She seemed to let herself into his house. My heart sunk, as my tears flowed. I knew I wasn't his, and he didn't really care, but seeing her like that was like a punch to my heart.

Crying most of the night, by the time I got up at seven am, my throat hurt; I was exhausted and emotionally numb. Will came to take me to the airport as I was just finishing dressing. I had pulled on my comfortable 'flying jeans' and a blue fitted t-shirt, and carried a blue sweater for the plane.

"Damn, you look rough, Lily, hard night?" Will blushed after he said this, and I gave him a watery smile.

"Can we not talk about it?"

Hugging me, he kissed the top of my head. "All set?" I nodded yes. He'd taken Saffy back to his place, and I was pleased about that, because I didn't need anything else to think about.

We travelled to the airport in silence. Will had sensed that I was fragile. He turned to me when he parked, a grave look on his face. "You are coming back aren't you, Lily?" I shrugged.

"I need to work things out in my head Will." He looked sadly at me and took my hand.

"I didn't want you to be with him, but not because of me, Lily. He fucks with your mind." I shrugged and shook my head.

"I know nothing about him, Will. He didn't let me in at all. I think he's seeing someone else. I've seen him around campus with a blond girl; they look close. Last night, when I was leaving in a cab, she arrived and let herself into his house." Will squeezed my hand.

"Bastard."

"How about you? Ever get to the bottom of Saffy's insecurities?" I tried to change the subject.

"Nope, she won't speak to me about it." I bunched my brows again.

"I've screwed up so badly, Will, with you, Alfie, Saffy, Max; my life has become one huge cluster fuck, and I don't know what to do." I smirked.

"I think I need to come back, even if just to find out why these people we love are so fucked up." He hugged me.

"I love you, Lily. In a non- sexual… wouldn't dare want to fuck you … friend kind of way." He chuckled. I hugged him hard.

"I love you too. I'm so going to miss you."

I was about to switch off my cell, when a text

beeped.

**SEXPERT: I need to see you.
There is something you need to
know.**

No shit… really? I turned the screen to Will, who read it and twisted his lips. "Prick."

Pink Lady: Save me a space.

Switching my cell off, I threw it in my carry-on bag. Whatever Alfie had to say could wait. He had been given plenty of opportunities to talk to me, and I had gone a term without knowing whatever he wanted to say. A few weeks more wouldn't hurt… well not that much.

If you enjoyed **Enough Isn't Everything** the first book about Lily and Alfie's journey, make sure to look out for book two of the '*Everything Trilogy*'

Everything She Needs (Book #2)

This will be released on Kindle in late January 2014. If you would like to subscribe to be notified when this is released register your interest by clicking the link below.

SUBSCRIBE
Check out the latest releases on
http://www.klshandwick.com

Social media links.

https://www.facebook.com/KLShandwickAuthor
https://twitter.com/KLShandwick
http://www.pinterest.com/kshandwick/
http://www.goodreads.com/author/show/7581125.K_L_Shandwick
http://www.amazon.com/K.L.-Shandwick/e/B00LPVIRUS/ref=ntt_dp_epwbk_0

Made in the USA
Columbia, SC
16 April 2017